The Seeing Garden

"This well-written and captivating novel about social manners and stifling expectations imposed on women shines a light on a piece of California history that has been overlooked. A delight for the senses with Moyer's artistic descriptions of gardens and mansions, *The Seeing Garden* is a page-turner of a story that is sure to inspire today's women who seek creativity and love."
—Ann Weisgarber, author of *The Glovemaker*

"Fans of historical fiction, romance, and intelligent women will relish *The Seeing Garden*. At its core, Ginny Kubitz Moyer's debut novel is a passionate story of yearning and discovery, transporting readers back to early twentieth-century Northern California with vivid descriptions and colorful characters that will enchant readers everywhere!"
—Kristen Harnisch, author of The Vintner's Daughter series

"Like a flower that takes root in a garden, pushing its stem through gritty soil and unfolding its glory toward the sun, so does heroine Catherine Ogden. In *The Seeing Garden*, Moyer's story reminds us that the beauty of life can only be found when our eyes see the clear truths of our inner desires."
—Janis Robinson Daly, author of *The Unlocked Path*

"At what price freedom? In this finely tuned period novel, Ginny Kubitz Moyer quietly ramps up tension until its inevitable breaking point, opening the door for protagonist Catherine Ogden to make a pivotal choice: conforming to familial and societal pressures or following her heart. Laced with rich detail and historical accuracy, *The Seeing Garden* will satisfy readers of early twentieth-century historical fiction. A great book club read!"
—Ashley E. Sweeney, author of *Eliza Waite*

THE
SEEING
GARDEN

The

SEEING
GARDEN

A Novel

GINNY KUBITZ MOYER

SHE WRITES PRESS

Published 2023
Printed in the United States of America
Print ISBN: 978-1-64742-426-8
E-ISBN: 978-1-64742-427-5
Library of Congress Control Number: 2022918233

For information, address:
She Writes Press
1569 Solano Ave #546
Berkeley, CA 94707

Book Design by Stacey Aaronson

She Writes Press is a division of SparkPoint Studio, LLC.

For my mother, Linda, and my grandmothers, Alice and Ruth

Thank you for showing me what a garden can do.

PROLOGUE

Gloucester, Massachusetts
1899

On a sunny Tuesday three weeks after Catherine Ogden's father died, she and her mother left their apartment and walked five long blocks to the church of Our Lady of Good Voyage. The sounds of streetcars and seagulls faded as they entered the dark hush of the building, Catherine's small hand held tightly in Anne's. It was an hour after morning Mass, and the church was empty except for a few visitors who had come for silent prayer. A young man with the dusty clothes of a mason entered a middle pew, pausing to genuflect and cross himself. A woman in a wide feather-trimmed hat stood at the shrine to St. Jude, her lips moving in silent prayer, her hands resting on her abdomen.

The Ogdens rarely went to church, so being in the large, echoing space was a novelty to Catherine. She gazed for a long time at the statue of St. Patrick with his ornate gold-and-green robes, such a contrast to the nearly naked Jesus on the cross behind the altar. Her nose prickled with the smell of leftover incense; she heard the clink of a coin in the poor box and the muted boom of a kneeler lowered somewhere behind her.

But her favorite spot was the bank of candles at the foot of the Mary statue. As Anne knelt in the very last pew, forehead resting against her clasped hands, Catherine twisted her braid around her finger and studied the flames. Each one had its own personality; some were quiet and steady, some trembled and then righted themselves, others moved wildly around as if desperate to escape the wick. At eight years old, Catherine knew fire wasn't alive—her father had told her so just a month before he died—but deep down, she was not entirely convinced.

Her mother touched her shoulder. "It's time to go."

Together they walked down the aisle into the vestibule. There, by the front door, Anne stopped. Her face was wet with tears, and Catherine felt a pang of guilt. She'd been so dazzled by the candlelight that she had temporarily forgotten her father's sickness, her mother's grief, and the drawn expression on her face as she counted and recounted the coins in the tea tin.

"Mama?"

Anne turned to her daughter and embraced her tightly. "Always remember," she said through her tears, and Catherine had to strain to hear over the noise of the church door as an elderly woman opened and closed it behind her.

"Always remember," her mother said, "that anything you do can be forgiven."

PART

ONE

ONE

New York City
1910

On the lush green lawn knelt a young mother, smiling and serene, beside her baby son. The mother wore a rust-colored dress and a halo. The child had a halo, too, and stood on his tiptoes in a way no real baby could possibly do. The mother's left arm circled her son lightly in a gesture that promised freedom as well as shelter. *Madonna of the Springtime*, said the small plaque on the gilded frame.

Catherine was gazing at the painting when her aunt Abigail suddenly appeared at her side.

"I've just heard from Mrs. Anson," she said in a low voice, "that William Brandt is coming to town. From California. He will be at the Crosbys' ball next week."

It took a moment for Catherine to register the words. She'd been standing as close to the painting as she could without attracting the attention of the other museumgoers, totally absorbed in her study of color and line. "I'm sorry," she said to her aunt. "I didn't hear. Who will be there?"

"William Brandt."

Catherine smiled politely and turned back to the painting. Her aunt gave a barely audible sigh of exasperation, as she did every time Catherine showed a lack of interest in things other nineteen-year-old girls found important.

"It's good we learned this when we did," her aunt said, buttoning her coat. "I will telephone Madame Rainier and see if she can make you a new gown."

"I thought I was going to wear the pink one."

"That was before we knew who would be there," said Abigail firmly. "Come. You can look at the paintings another day."

After eleven years in her aunt's house, Catherine knew it was pointless to resist. But she followed her with deliberate slowness, looking back over her shoulder until the last possible moment, taking the image of the sunlit field with her into the drizzly February streets.

William Brandt was a name needing no explanation to Catherine or anyone else in New York society. The thirty-year-old heir of a California railroad magnate, he had taken his father's considerable fortune and increased it through shrewd investments and real estate sales. Among eligible bachelors, he was notable not only for the immensity of his wealth but also for the novelty of coming from a place few Easterners had ever seen: the San Francisco Peninsula, the long arm of land stretching south of the city between the bay and the ocean. He lived there on a country estate called Oakview, built by his father and said to be the prettiest one west of the Mississippi. It was rumored William had spent a small fortune enhancing what was already there, filling the home with artwork and making it the envy of the Peninsula elite. Though most New York matrons had a dim view of the West—all society was found in the East, as far as they were concerned—his prominence made them willing to rethink their old prejudices. After all, California was merely a few days' travel by train, and he owned a private railroad car whose luxury they could only imagine.

And so for the next week, Madame Rainier was awake for twenty hours at a time, snapping at her assistants and moving irritably through bolts of colored silk as she created the gowns that had suddenly, for New York's debutantes and their mothers, become very urgently needed.

%

After days of rain, Central Park was thronged with city dwellers eager for fresh air. As Catherine and her friend Lavinia Boscat strolled past the leafless trees, they had to step carefully out of the way of nursemaids pushing prams and children rolling wooden hoops. Undaunted by the crowds, they walked arm in arm, even though at five foot eight Catherine was nearly a head taller than her friend. "The goddess and the pixie," Lavinia's older brother had once christened them.

"Mama has been utterly undone by this news about William Brandt," Lavinia said in a low voice. She glanced at her mother and her mother's friend Mrs. Van Hare, who walked several feet ahead of the girls, intent on their own conversation. "An opportunity missed, she calls it. I actually heard her tell Father, 'What a shame Lavinia just got engaged!'"

"Aunt Abigail is the same," Catherine said, "but I don't have a ring to protect me." She took a deep breath, savoring the fragrance of a world washed clean by the rain. "How would you paint this smell?"

Lavinia, accustomed to such questions, obligingly took a deep breath. "Light green, with a hint of gray. Like that gown Edith had last season, remember?" She pulled off her left glove and polished her new diamond ring on her coat. "But you're the artist. I defer to you."

"I'm a pretty hopeless one," Catherine said. "Yesterday I

spent an hour sketching that bust of Apollo on the library mantel. When Mrs. Webb saw it, she said, 'Oh, what a lovely portrait of your aunt!'"

"Oh, dear." Lavinia didn't even try to stifle her laugh. "What did you say?"

"I thanked her, of course. I couldn't see a polite way to correct her. And if I had, it would only have exposed my lack of talent." She grinned at her friend. "I do have some pride, you know."

"Pride and manners before honesty," said Lavinia with mock gravity. "That's how it goes. That's the code of the debutantes."

"It's the code of everyone, I think." Catherine unintentionally clipped a pebble with her foot, and it bounced down the path. It was so satisfying to watch its trajectory that she kicked a second one, secure in the knowledge her aunt was not there to see it. "It has to be that way, I suppose. But sometimes . . ." Her parents' faces came to mind. "Well, sometimes, don't you wish it were different?"

"Perhaps it is different out West," said Lavinia mischievously. "Perhaps Mr. William Brandt is a refreshingly, charmingly honest man and you'll fall madly in love." She held up her left hand and admired her diamond as it caught the light. "And then I could visit you in California! We could eat oranges and lie in the sun."

"And fight grizzly bears," said Catherine, "and look for gold."

"I'm sure Mr. B. has plenty of that already."

"Probably." Catherine raised her eyes to the sky, which was bright blue with a few fat clouds adding texture. "Look how lovely that is. 'I wandered lonely as a cloud.' Remember reading that at the Academy?"

Lavinia grinned. "I take it back. You can't move to California. Who would point out the beauties of nature to me?"

"Beauties of nature, my eye." Catherine elbowed her friend. "All you care about is the beauty of your new ring."

Lavinia laughed unabashedly. "Right you are, dear friend of my youth." She took another fond glance at her diamond before putting her glove back on. "But truly, don't you want to fall in love someday? I do recommend it."

"Of course I do," Catherine said. "But it's like the beginning of *Pride and Prejudice*, isn't it? A rich man comes to town, and suddenly everyone is in a dither. We shouldn't even talk about love until we actually know William Brandt."

"Like you know George, perhaps?"

Catherine flashed her a quick, conspiratorial smile. George Langley, a young cousin of Lavinia's mother, had recently arrived in New York from Pittsburgh. Catherine had instinctively liked his dark-gold hair and wide grin and had been delighted to discover that he was a poet—he'd even had a few poems published in a magazine—who was just as likely to marvel over the clouds as she was. Their conversation shifted easily from lighthearted banter to more serious topics, a dynamic she found both comfortable and exciting. "I'll say this, Vinia," she admitted. "I like George very, very much indeed."

Lavinia made a *tut-tut* sound. "Don't say it too loudly. Remember that William Brandt is obscenely rich and you're divinely beautiful. It's a match made in heaven."

"Another girl might catch his eye," Catherine said.

Lavinia raised an eyebrow. "With you in the room?"

TWO

*C*atherine was twelve years old when she first realized she was pretty. Awareness had dawned when her uncle's friends began to look at her in a new way: surprised, intent, and somehow guilty. The face in the mirror was similar to her mother's, but where Anne's had been angular and arresting, with prominent cheekbones, Catherine's features were softer, tempered by the influence of her father. She had dark-blue eyes and almost-black hair, a combination found often in the tenements of Five Points but rarely in the townhomes of Fifth Avenue. Her complexion was nearly perfect, broken only by the constellation of three small freckles along her left jawbone, making a small triangle. She liked them, privately seeing them as a silent reminder that good things come in threes: her parents and herself, for example. Her resting expression was one of serenity, like a Madonna or a statue, but when she smiled her face came alive, showing the warm blood underneath the marble.

Yet beneath her poised exterior was a vein of restlessness, even dissatisfaction. She found herself growing weary of men who approached her with admiring eyes and predictable flattery. Since adolescence, her beauty had also inhibited her friendships with other girls, many of whom seemed unable to see her as anything but a rival or who interpreted her natural reserve as aloofness so they could have a reason other than jealousy to dislike her.

Lavinia was a notable exception. Frank and spontaneous while Catherine was pensive and deliberate, she was also as physically different from her friend as it was possible to be. From the start, their friendship had been encouraged by both Catherine's aunt and Lavinia's mother, who shared the tacit awareness that any man who was drawn to Lavinia's high blond spirits would never be tempted by Catherine's tall dark grace. The girls were confidantes, freer with each other than with anyone else.

That was why Catherine had received the news of her friend's engagement with two very different emotions. Clarence Perry and Lavinia were utterly in love; it was impossible not to be delighted for them. At the same time, Catherine felt an unmistakable wave of sadness. There was a stark difference between the lives of a single woman and a married one, and though she and Lavinia would always be friends, she knew their relationship would soon change in ways they could neither predict nor prevent. The park stroll on that February afternoon, chatting comfortably out of earshot of their chaperones, was more precious than such a walk had ever been before.

$\wp$

An hour later, in the large brownstone on Madison Avenue, she barely had time to take off her hat and coat before her aunt appeared on the stairs.

"You are late," Abigail said severely. She disliked Catherine's walks in the park, even chaperoned; young ladies of her own generation had limited their park outings to carriage rides.

"Only five minutes, Aunt. I'm sorry." She hurried into the music room, which, like the rest of the house, had heavy curtains protecting the carpets from the sunlight. After closing the door, she immediately went to the drapes and pushed them aside, as Mr. Perrin, her music teacher, rose from the piano bench where he had been arranging the sheet music.

"By all means, Miss Ogden," he said, "please let in the light."

Each lesson began the same way, with the forbidden opening of the curtains. In the sudden sunlight, Mr. Perrin's fringe of white hair glowed like a halo, but his smile was impish. She smiled back, their weekly ritual like a secret handshake.

"No one can play piano in a funeral parlor," he said with satisfaction. "Shall we begin?"

She sat down and played some scales, then began a piece by Chopin. Though not a naturally gifted musician, she enjoyed playing, for she had discovered that it offered her a rare opportunity to express emotion. She could pour her most intimate feelings into a piece by Beethoven, and no one would wonder about it.

"You have made progress," Mr. Perrin said when she was done. He helped her navigate a particularly difficult passage, and she played it again as he nodded in time.

She was under no illusions about what the piano lessons were for: to make her an irresistible partner to a prominent man, the wealthier the better. Since the age of twelve, she had been aware that only a brilliant match would ever be sanctioned by her aunt or her cousin Henry, who was ten years her senior (her uncle stayed out of all such conversation). This was true for all girls of her class, of course, yet Catherine suspected she felt the obligation more keenly than most. *Oliver Twist*, which she had wept over as a child, had been a vivid reminder of how lucky she was to have a home with her aunt and uncle. Although her aunt had never been particularly warm, for the past eleven years she had provided Catherine with a life few orphans could imagine. An advantageous marriage, one which would propel the Ogdens to even greater social prominence, was how Catherine was expected to repay her.

It was a depressingly unromantic prospect, but Catherine remained hopeful. Lavinia's engagement was proof that even within the small circle of acceptable men, it was possible to find true love. That's what I want, Catherine thought resolutely. To make my family happy and to make myself happy, too.

But what if she could not do both?

George's wide smile flashed into her thoughts. She liked him very much and might even be starting to love him, but although he came from an excellent family, she suspected he was not the kind of match her aunt and cousin expected her to make. In her distraction, she missed a note and had to replay it.

There was a rebellious streak inside her that she had learned to hide from her aunt and cousin, but at the piano she was free from all constraint. As she played, familiar longings rose to the surface, and she acknowledged them squarely and without fear. What she truly desired was not marriage but a life of challenge and meaning. Music lessons and drawing helped blunt her hunger, but they could not entirely satisfy it.

She remembered her father sitting at his easel, absorbed in his painting, and she longed to have a life like his, one where she created something of value to herself and others. But what was that something, and how could she ever find it? She often dreamed of walking out the front door, bag in hand, and traveling to a faraway place where she could discover what she was capable of beyond polite conversation and a graceful waltz.

It was only a dream, of course, impossible to make a reality. But as the piece slowed to an end, she was keenly aware that without the opportunity to see more and do more, she would never be entirely at peace.

She played the final chord, and it hung in the air for a moment before fading to nothing. Mr. Perrin exhaled in appreciation. "Excellent," he said, "excellent. You feel that piece, I think."

Then he looked startled and bowed slightly to someone beyond her shoulder, and she knew her aunt had entered the room.
Mr. Perrin immediately walked over to the drapes and closed
them guiltily while Catherine watched the sunlight vanish from
the keys.

THREE

*T*hree days before the ball, Catherine stood before the mirror in her aunt's bedroom while Madame Rainier arranged the folds of the new gown around her feet. Her aunt sat on the bed with her spaniel, Hawthorne, on her lap, stroking his long ears.

"What do you think?" she asked.

"I love the color," said Catherine. It was blue silk, veering somewhere between sapphire and slate, a shade that highlighted Catherine's eyes and hair while contrasting beautifully with her skin. While the Ogden family was sandy-haired in every generation, Catherine resembled her mother, with vivid coloring that could make even New York's most admired blondes fade into the wallpaper.

"It's much better than the pink dress," said Abigail approvingly. "Any girl can wear pink."

Catherine angled herself for a better view of the artful drape of the skirt. She typically showed only mild interest in her wardrobe, which appeared to irritate her aunt, but this dress compelled her gaze. She had seen the color before, but she could not remember where. It was elusive, the memory fluttering just out of reach.

"You will be the prettiest girl there," said Madame Rainier from the floor, where she was putting in the hem. The sincerity of her voice was evident even through the pins she held in her mouth.

"Thank you." In the mirror Catherine regarded herself, a tall, graceful figure in blue, the blue of a cloisonné box or a night of stars. And suddenly it came to her: the image of her own mother standing before a mirror in the boarding house in Gloucester, holding a scarf in the exact same color. Anne had wound it around her neck, then spontaneously draped it over her head like a veil. Her father had laughed admiringly.

"It's a blue bride! No, a princess from the Arabian nights!"

Catherine had tugged on the fringed end and cried, "Mama, let me try! Let me!"

"Come here, then," her mother said. Catherine stood squarely before the glass in her dress with a jam stain on the skirt while her mother draped the scarf around her shoulders. It pooled to the ground and Catherine processed slowly around the room, head held high, like a small empress.

"Just like your mother," her father said. "Blue is your color, too."

※

It had been an entirely different life, those eight years spent with her parents in Gloucester. Their apartment near the shore had a tiny kitchen and a big room for her parents' bed, the table and chairs, and her father's easel. Catherine's small gabled room was more of a closet, but it had a window and was large enough to hold a cot and bureau. Her father had gotten permission from Mrs. Groat, the landlady, to paint the walls of Catherine's room, and he covered them with marigolds, roses, lilacs, forget-me-nots, tulips, and flowers of every color. "Why not make them all bloom at the same time?" he had said, putting a dab of yellow in the center of a daisy.

She loved the garden. It filled her with delight to run her

fingers over the walls and trace the layers that made each distinct flower. On sunlit mornings she could even see the individual brushstrokes, and she'd lie in bed and hold an imaginary paintbrush and pretend to paint them herself.

Nearly every day, her family went for a stroll along the beach. They moved slowly; her father had a slight limp from a childhood accident, but he told her it was a blessing as it kept him from rushing and made him walk at exactly the right speed to notice things to paint. Her mother, almost the same height as her husband, always walked with her arm in his. They often murmured together, saying things Catherine couldn't hear over the waves and didn't need to hear; she was confident in their love for her and thus was happy to give them their private moments. She was more interested in running on the sand, turning cartwheels, chasing the birds, and tasting the salty spray on her lips.

Her father earned a small living selling his seascapes and garden pictures. Her mother was his assistant, his champion, and helped Mrs. Groat with housework and baking for a reduction in rent. At times, she sat for portraits, and Catherine always marveled to see how still her mother could be, wearing her best shirtwaist or the blue scarf while forehead, cheeks, nose, and lips slowly took form on her father's canvas. It seemed like hours.

"How do you sit for so long?" she asked her once.

"I think back over my life," said her mother. "I think of people I love. I remember beautiful things I've seen."

"Are there so many beautiful things?"

"You would be surprised how many, when you really think about it."

Catherine knew very little about the rest of the family. She knew her father had been born in New York in a big house, and his father and older brother had been something called "lawyers."

"Why don't we live in New York?" she asked one day as he sat at his easel.

"I met your mother. And I realized I could become an artist, like I always wanted to be." He saw her perched on the chair, her small face intent, and leaned over to kiss her forehead. "When I wonder what your mother looked like as a child, I only need to look at you," he said, settling back in his seat and picking up the brush. "Thou art thy mother's glass, and she in thee / Calls back the lovely April of her prime."

"That doesn't make any sense, Papa."

"It does if you're Shakespeare," he said. "It means you are your mother's mirror. You look just like her."

"Why don't we ever see your family?"

"They didn't want me to marry your mother and become an artist."

"Why not?"

There was a pause. "Not everyone values art," he said finally. "Some people value money more. They would rather have a big house and fine clothes to impress people with."

"Don't they need art for their big houses?"

He laughed. "You are so much wiser than they are." She waited while he added a few brushstrokes to the canvas. "I had to choose their way of living or my way of living, Cathy. I couldn't have both."

Catherine was silent; a world where family was a barrier to happiness was a world she could not imagine. Her father saw her face, put down his brush, and turned toward her.

"Sometimes, Cathy," he said gently, "life gives you a choice between two things. And all the different parts of you, good and bad, get caught up in making that choice. You have to decide whether you will choose from the best that is in you or the worst that is in you."

She looked back at him, her face stern, as it always was when she was confused. He smiled and kissed her again.

"Maybe it's like Shakespeare," he said as he returned to his painting. "You won't understand it until you're older."

❧

The next day she tried her mother. "Why didn't Papa's family want him to marry you?"

They were in Mrs. Groat's kitchen downstairs, where Anne was making bread. Catherine sat perched on a stool, watching her and enjoying the warmth of the kitchen with its huge stove, red gingham curtains, and the tabby cat asleep in the corner.

Her mother worked the dough, turning it over. "They didn't like how I met your father," she said slowly.

"What do you mean?"

Anne straightened, stretched her back, and sighed. She looked at Catherine pensively. "I think you should know more than your father has told you." A fly buzzed past, and she swatted it away. "I was a model for your father. He used to paint me."

"He still does paint you."

"No, not like that." Her eyes met her daughter's: clear blue looking at clear blue, Catherine's full of innocent curiosity. Anne smiled gently. "I mean, yes, it was just like that," she said. "But to your father's family, Papa should not have been painting at all. He should have been studying the law and going to balls and courting a girl from the same class."

"Aren't you from the same class?"

Her mother laughed. "No."

"So they never saw him again?"

"He had to choose between them and me."

"And he chose you." Catherine felt a surge of pride on her mother's behalf.

"Yes." She gazed out the window at the gray sky; for a moment, she seemed to be somewhere else.

"Aren't you happy he did?"

"Of course, silly." Anne turned to Catherine, cupping her cheek in her hand. "But in a perfect world, you know, we would not have to make such a choice." She curled her daughter's hair ribbon around her finger. "Always undone, these ribbons of yours."

"I like them that way," Catherine said.

Her mother's eyes crinkled at the corners as she smiled, but then she became serious. "There may come a time when he needs his family," she said, letting the ribbon fall. "He doesn't see that, but I do."

"But they don't want him."

Anne turned back to the bread and began to knead it. "No," she said evenly. "It's me they don't want."

FOUR

*T*he afternoon of the ball, Catherine was reading *The Winter's Tale* in the library when the door opened. In pattered the aged Hawthorne, wheezing heavily, and behind him Catherine's cousin Henry.

"Catherine," he said pleasantly. "I thought you'd want to rest before tonight."

"There's nothing more restful than reading," she said.

Hawthorne curled up on the hearth as Henry settled his stoutish frame into the wing chair. He was twenty-nine and had light hair, a wide forehead, and a briskly courteous, attentive manner. When she had first come to live in New York, he was just starting at Princeton and had little to do with her; it wasn't until she was twelve that he began to notice her, draw her into conversation, and encourage her study of piano. At the time, she had been grateful for the attention, though they had nothing in common beyond the bond of family. He had recently married Ethel Mills, the daughter of one his father's law partners, a compact brunette with a perfect nose and a palpable coolness toward Catherine. They were living temporarily in the house on Madison Avenue while their own home was undergoing renovations.

"What are you reading? Shakespeare again?"

"*The Winter's Tale*," she said. "I've never read it before."

"It's not one of our books, is it?" he asked, holding out his hand. Though not a reader himself, Henry respected his family's possessions and was quick to recognize anything that did not belong. "May I?"

She hesitated briefly, then gave it to him. He studied the cover as if admiring the gold stamping of the title, lingering a moment too long for the interest to be genuine, then opened the book. His square fingers rifled through the first few pages, then paused, creasing the paper. She waited.

He looked up. "From George. George Langley?"

"Yes."

He frowned at the inscription, written in dark ink across the title page. "Why did he give you this?"

"Because neither of us has ever read it. He bought one for himself and gave me one."

"Did you write in his copy?"

"No." And what if I had? she thought.

He sat back in the armchair, eyes on her, the book lying open across his thighs. She hated to see it there and wanted to ask for it but did not. There was silence, broken only by the ticking of the clock and the sound of Hawthorne biting underneath his leg.

"I don't believe George is an acquaintance you should encourage," he said finally.

"Why not?"

"You could do much better. He is charming and pleasant, I grant you, but has no head for success. He tried a career in law and failed."

"Law isn't everything."

Henry gave an indulgent smile. "I know it's every girl's dream to have a poet say beautiful things to her. But sonnets don't pay the bills."

"George is hardly a pauper," she said. "It's not as if he lives on the streets."

"No, but you might find yourself living in some uninspiring flat with faded drapes. It would be very different from the life you know."

But it would be no different from the life I used to know, she thought. Her eyes must have said it even if her lips did not, for Henry was suddenly alert, regarding her keenly. She wondered what her cousin would say if she spoke freely of her childhood in the gabled attic rooms, the life she reviewed regularly in her memory so as not to lose it altogether. In the silence, Hawthorne sneezed, a pathetic little sound.

Then Henry smiled and handed her the book. "I am not forbidding you to speak to George," he said. "I only ask you to be sensible."

"I intend to be."

He nodded approvingly. She had a sudden glimpse of him in court, knowing just what to say, just how to present himself for maximum impact. "And I want you to be aware that there are men who are poised to give you more opportunities than you have ever had before. More opportunities to see the world, to meet fascinating and accomplished people. You have always wanted that, I think," he said, and she was surprised he would know it. For all his solid geniality, there was a shrewdness to Henry.

"I will think about what you've said," she told him. It was a response she knew would end the conversation; it had the added advantage of being neither a lie nor a promise.

"Good," he said warmly. "And Ethel and I look forward to seeing you tonight. I'm sure you will be beautiful in the new dress that Mother bought for you."

The last five words were unnecessary, but she knew why he had said them. They were a reminder of the debt she owed and of the expectation she would act accordingly.

⁊⊙

The debt began a month after Catherine's father had died. Over the winter he had developed a cough, and though Anne exhorted him to stay in bed, he continued the daily strolls along the beach, swaddled in his old coat. Anne's face grew pinched with worry. Catherine believed her father when he said the cough was nothing, even though it kept her awake on the other side of the wall.

When they finally called in a doctor, he listened to Arthur's chest and then looked up grimly. "Is there somewhere your daughter can go for the next few minutes?" he asked Anne.

"Catherine," said Anne, "go downstairs and see Mrs. Groat."

Catherine went to the big kitchen, petted the tabby cat, and sorted through the scraps of fabric the landlady was saving for a quilt. "We can make one together," said Mrs. Groat, who was even kinder than usual that day. When they heard the doctor leave, Catherine rose to go upstairs, but Mrs. Groat stopped her.

"Let your mother have a moment to rest, dear," she said. "Here. I've found a few more scraps."

When Anne finally came down, her eyes were red, and Mrs. Groat passed her a cup of tea. "We will hope for the best," she said, clasping her hand.

But the best did not happen, and two weeks later, Arthur died. He left a stricken wife and daughter, a stack of paintings, and the wish that his family in New York would not be told of his death.

Paying for the burial plot took most of the small savings they had left. Anne sold whatever paintings she could. She spent hours in the downstairs kitchen, cooking for Mrs. Groat as much as possible, but Mrs. Groat's son owned the house and while his mother would have let them work to earn their keep, her son showed no inclination to charity. And Anne, with no other option, found a job as a live-in housemaid in Boston and wrote a letter she had never wanted to write.

Five weeks after Arthur's death, Aunt Abigail and Uncle Oliver came to Gloucester. Catherine had never seen them before and was disposed to dislike them, but Anne held her sobbing daughter the night before their arrival and tried her best to be soothing.

"It won't be forever, I promise," she said. "I can't take you to my new job. They are being so kind, really, taking you in. And as soon as I can afford a place for the two of us, I'll send for you."

"But they don't like you," Catherine said.

Anne wiped the tears from her daughter's face. "They don't really know me," she said slowly. "I think if they did, they might like me." She kissed Catherine's hair, then reached into her pocket and drew out a black rosary. "Here," she said, pressing it into her daughter's palm. "This is yours now. When you are lonely, take it out and hold it."

Catherine gazed at the beads, momentarily diverted from her grief. The rosary had always fascinated her. On the rare times they had gone to Mass, Catherine had seen women holding them, fingers moving from bead to bead while their lips moved silently, as if in private worlds of their own. "It's meant for praying," Anne had said, but she never explained how, and Catherine had never seen her mother use it. But the beads were solid and comforting, as if holding them were a prayer in itself.

"But you won't have it anymore," she said.

"I will know that you have it," said her mother, "and that will make me happy." She watched Catherine as she fingered the beads. "But it's our secret, Cathy. Don't let your aunt and uncle see it."

Her aunt Abigail had light-brown hair, a regal, prominent nose, and a fine dress. Her uncle Oliver had sandy hair, like her father, but was bulky while her father had been rail thin. Catherine had never known any rich people before; her parents' friends were people like Charlie and Daisy, fellow artists who went barefoot on the sand and sometimes in the house. Catherine doubted her aunt went barefoot even in her bath.

They were brief and businesslike, and Catherine had never seen her mother so subdued. "You must promise me this," whispered Anne as she embraced her daughter at the door. "Promise that you will try to like them."

"I promise," said Catherine. She held on to her mother so tightly that her uncle had to clear his throat.

"Come along, little miss," he said awkwardly. "We will be late for our train."

Her aunt finally took Catherine's arm and peeled it gently but firmly away from Anne's neck.

Catherine watched her mother until the cab turned the corner. The graceful dark figure who was the center of her life became smaller and smaller, and the tears in Catherine's eyes blurred her vision until her mother looked like a spot of watercolor on a canvas.

﹩

The home on Madison Avenue was unlike anything Catherine had ever seen. It was four stories high, with stained glass panels, its own library, and maids in black dresses and white aprons who moved noiselessly around the carpeted floors. She was given a room with a huge walnut bed and wallpaper of ugly, indeterminate flowers on a maroon background, a stark contrast to the colorful garden her father had painted in her old room. She could not bear to think of Mrs. Groat's son painting it over and preferred to think the flowers would stay there forever.

The calico dresses her mother had made were taken before Catherine knew they were going and replaced with clothes that were stiff and heavy. A governess was hired, an unsmiling woman named Miss Foster, for whom Catherine felt an instinctive dislike. She met her aunt and uncle's friends, who greeted her with flickers of compassion and lifted eyebrows when she said or did something she should not. Though she was a cooperative child, she did not know she couldn't walk around the house in her stockings or keep her hair ribbons deliberately untied. One bright spot was Hawthorne, her aunt's spaniel puppy, when Catherine was permitted to play with him. Mostly, though, she lived for evenings, when she was alone in her room and could gaze out the window (she kept the curtains open, a fact that Orla, the housemaid, was happy to conceal) and see the streetlamps like comforting lighthouses against the dark. And she wondered how long it would be before her mother came to get her, and she hoped it would be soon.

But every time she asked, her aunt would look disapproving. "We've had no word from your mother," she would say, in a tone that prevented further questions.

Finally, Catherine asked for paper and an envelope and wrote a letter herself, which was mostly a sketch of the view of the street from her window. She gave it to her aunt to mail and began counting the days until she could expect a reply.

But a week later she and Miss Foster returned home from the park to find her letter sitting on the sideboard, unopened. "Addressee Unknown," someone had written on the front. "What does that mean?" she asked Miss Foster.

"It means that your mother is not living there anymore."

"But where is she living?"

"How would I possibly know that, Catherine?" Miss Foster regarded her frostily. "Stand up straight."

An hour later, Catherine found her aunt doing needlework in the morning room. Without preamble, she handed her the letter and the envelope.

"Greet me politely, Catherine," said her aunt. "Don't just thrust something in my lap."

"Good afternoon, Aunt," said Catherine. "This is the letter I sent my mother."

Abigail put down her needlepoint. She took the envelope in her hands and regarded it for a moment, then looked at her niece. Catherine saw in her eyes an unusual softness and a hint of pity.

"She must have a new address," said Catherine. "What is it?"

Her aunt put the letter down on the end table. "I don't know," she said quietly. "The letters I've written have come back, too."

℘

Three weeks later, on a blazing, warm day that made Catherine long to go to the beach, Orla knocked on the door and told Miss Foster that Catherine's presence was requested in the library. Glad to have a reprieve from her penmanship lesson, Catherine straightened her dress and hurried down the flight of stairs.

She found not just her aunt but her uncle, who stood beside his wife as she sat in the carved walnut chair. Her aunt's hands were clasped tightly in her lap.

"Catherine," she said. "We have received a letter from your mother. She has written to ask that you stay with us."

The joy that had just begun to surge in Catherine's chest was stilled. "For how long?"

Her aunt and uncle glanced at each other, and in their gaze, Catherine saw the answer they did not want to say. "Forever?" she asked. Her aunt nodded stiffly. "But why?"

There was another pause. "We can give you more than she can," said Abigail finally. "You can have a life here that you could not have with her."

"But I can have things with her that I cannot have here," said Catherine. The words came out involuntarily; she could not stop them any more than she could stop the rising tears. Her aunt's face twitched with emotion, but it was her uncle Oliver who came forward and rested a tentative but gentle hand on Catherine's head.

"A mother does not do this lightly," he said. "We must trust that she has a good reason."

The kindness of his gesture unleashed Catherine's sobs. They shook her small frame, and she did not even try to hold them back.

"You can write to her," said Oliver helplessly. He pressed a handkerchief into her hand, but she did not use it, clinging to it as she wept.

"There's no return address, Oliver," said her aunt in a voice of quiet reprimand.

Two days later, Catherine was going up the stairs when she heard her aunt and her best friend, Mrs. Hadley, talking in the library. "So you're to have your niece as a permanent ward, I hear," said Mrs. Hadley.

"Yes," said Abigail. Catherine, just out of view of the open door, stopped on the stairs and held her breath. "It was a short letter, said very little. Just that she was leaving Catherine to us."

"It's surprising she wouldn't give a reason," said Mrs. Hadley. "But the Irish do things differently, I suppose." There was the clink of a teacup settling in a saucer. "Perhaps the woman is dying."

Catherine stared at the molding of the doorframe as her heart beat in her ears.

"It's very possible," said her aunt. "That was my first reaction, too."

"You said she was a bohemian, didn't you?" Mrs. Hadley said the noun as if it were a word she was not accustomed to using. "Perhaps she wanted the freedom of not having a child anymore."

"No, I don't think so," said Abigail slowly. "I did not know the woman at all, of course. But I think it's far more likely that she is dying."

⁊

The following week was a terrible one. Catherine slipped into numbness, silent and still, hardly responsive to those who tried to speak to her. "You are so ungrateful," Miss Foster said. "Here you are with this fine house to live in. You could be in an orphanage, like I was. And yet nothing seems to move you."

Miss Foster was wrong; Catherine was moved, but by things she did not want to share with her governess. After the first wave of grief had passed, she began to notice things she had never seen before. She noticed the pattern of leaves making shade on the sidewalk, like moving lace, and she sat and watched as the clock ticked the afternoon by. The next day she noticed the steam from the teapot curl upward like something alive, sinuous and beautiful. Her father would have remarked upon it, she thought, but because she could not share those things with Miss Foster, they remained locked inside. At night she clutched the rosary, held it to her cheek, and cried into the beads.

Weeks passed, and the leaves in the park turned brilliant red and orange. One day after seeing a funeral procession on the street, Catherine asked her aunt where her mother was buried. Abigail drew herself up even taller, which Catherine was coming to recognize as her aunt's way of mastering unpleasant emotion.

"We have received no news at all," she said. She added, quietly but firmly, "Forget the past, Catherine. We will not speak of it anymore. This is your life now."

That night, lying in bed and clutching the rosary, Catherine willed herself to see her mother's face. She could do it if she closed her eyes and concentrated. She could hold in her mind an image of her, her black hair, the laughter and love in her blue eyes. Her aunt had told her to forget, but she would not.

A memory came to mind: her mother sitting for the portrait, saying she used the time to think of all the people she loved. I can do that, too, thought Catherine. Her mother and father came first, of course; then she thought of Mrs. Groat, Charlie and Daisy, and the friends who used to go with them to the free concerts in the park. And she thought of the man who delivered the ice and always waved at her, and the old man who sat on the bench in Gloucester with his dachshund. The dog would wag its entire body when Catherine came over, and the man would always say, "Ah now, you've made him smile with his whole self, you have." It was comforting to think of those people, even though she would never see them again.

She reviewed her list every night, and gradually she began to add people from her life in New York, too. There was Orla with her freckles and broad smile, and there was the old woman in the park who fed pigeons and spoke to them lovingly; Catherine had wanted to talk to her, but Miss Foster pulled her away before she could. She added her uncle, too, because although she saw him rarely, he always greeted her kindly. Miss Foster never made the list. Neither did her aunt, and although Catherine felt a slight pang of guilt at the omission, she was determined that in this nightly review, one no one else knew about, she would be completely truthful with herself.

After a few nights, it occurred to her that the rosary could become a part of her ritual. The idea felt as powerful as if she had discovered fire. She pictured one face for each bead, and though there were not enough for all the beads on the string, she somehow was sure she was using the rosary exactly as she was meant to. Soon she realized she could use the beads to count not just people but everything she liked, things both large and small. She began to think back over her day and name everything that had made her happy: the smell of the air after the rain, the yellow roses on the library table, the laughter of the maids that sometimes floated up the stairs, the way Hawthorne lifted his paw to get her attention. When she first started, she filled three sections of the rosary, which seemed like a great victory. Later she challenged herself to think of more and more, and some days she was able to circle the whole string. Sometimes she drifted off with the beads still in her hand, a gentle transition into sleep.

As the years passed, she kept up the nightly habit, and it never failed to ground her. New York society accepted her as an orphan; she learned to follow its rules so completely that, in time, few of her acquaintances remembered she had ever lived anywhere else. But the rosary remained, a secret link to her lost mother, a touchstone reminding her of who she truly was and what she truly loved. In a world of stiff clothing, careful conversation, and little room for error, with the beads in her hand she always felt alive.

FIVE

*T*he night of the ball, Catherine sensed more than the usual excitement. As the guests arrived at the Crosbys' palatial residence on Fifth Avenue, the men resplendent in evening dress and the ladies glittering in satin and jewels, there was a palpable sense of anticipation as they waited for the great man to appear. At the sight of Catherine in the blue dress, George Langley gave her a grin of open admiration from across the crowded foyer. His reaction lightened her heart, but she felt a weight of expectation that made the evening less comfortable than such gatherings usually were. As she chatted with Lavinia, she saw Henry look her over and then whisper something to his mother, who immediately came over to Catherine and discreetly adjusted her necklace.

But when William Brandt arrived, she had to admit he was more attractive than she had expected. He was quite a bit taller than she was, with shoulders broad enough to give an immediate impression of solid presence, a man who even without his fame would not pass unnoticed in a social gathering. His hair was dark and satiny in the light; his eyes were also dark, and his face was square and clean-shaven and he had a strong chin with a slight cleft. People fluttered about him, but in his fine evening clothes, he gave the impression of controlled calmness, of a man who could decide where and when to direct his attention.

It wasn't long before Catherine found it directed at her. As

Mrs. Crosby introduced him to the Ogdens, he greeted each family member politely, but his gaze returned to Catherine and stayed. In the small talk that followed, she was conscious of her aunt and cousin watching William's reactions keenly, which made her perversely determined not to fawn. George's admiring grin had also fanned the spark of her rebellion, so when William commented on how fine the weather was, looking directly at Catherine as he said it, she merely smiled politely and said, "Yes, indeed," and looked off into the crowd.

At dinner, however, he was seated to her left. To Catherine's right was Doctor Winthrop, and after exchanging some polite words, the doctor was asked a question by the woman across the table. In the ensuing pause, Catherine turned toward William. He was looking at her and, she knew, had been doing so for some time.

"And how has your visit been, Mr. Brandt?"

"Very pleasant, Miss Ogden," he said. "Every time I come east, I enjoy myself. Tonight most of all."

There was a pause as they were served. When she glanced up, he was still watching her and, unlike most men, did not glance away when she caught him doing so. She felt both a prickle of defensiveness and a sensation that she recognized as a most banal feeling of being flattered. His eyes were very dark brown, so dark it was not clear where the pupils began.

"What do you like to do with your leisure time, Miss Ogden?"

"The same things girls do in California, I suppose. Read, play the piano, visit the park and galleries."

"Do you enjoy these things, or do you do them just because they're expected?"

"I do enjoy them. I'm very fond of the piano. And there's nothing more enjoyable than a walk in the park, especially in springtime."

"I agree." He took a sip of wine. "Do you go to the park for the trees, the flowers, the people?"

"Everything, really. My father used to say that an afternoon in Central Park was enough to fill your thoughts for a month, if you have your eyes open."

"He sounds like a poet. Or an artist."

She arranged her napkin, uncertain as to what he may have heard about her past. "He had the soul of both, I believe."

"And you have inherited his soul."

"I like to think so, yes."

He took another sip. His hands were large, the nails impeccably maintained. "I assume your beauty was inherited from your mother."

The expected response to such a compliment was to blush demurely, but the predictability of his words made her mutinous. She raised her head and looked at him squarely. "My mother was the most beautiful woman I've ever seen," she said. "But what I remember most is her kindness and generosity."

William did not seem surprised by the directness of her gaze. "I suspect," he said, "that as we become better acquainted, I will find that you've inherited all of her attractive traits."

Catherine glanced across the table at George, who was seated several places down. He was looking warily at her dinner companion, and she could not catch his eye. She turned back to William. "Would you say that kindness and generosity are as important as beauty?"

"I'm a great admirer of beauty. Everyone is, if they're honest." He nodded his head to indicate the chandeliers, the gowns, and the elaborate floral arrangements. "And yet I can't deny the importance of kindness and generosity in women."

"But not in men?"

He smiled. "Women are naturally suited for kindness," he

said. "Wise men know they can't compete, so they put their energies elsewhere."

⁓

In the ballroom ringed with potted palms, she found herself the center of a knot of girls unable to hide their interest in her dinner companion.

"What's he like? He's so much more handsome than I thought."

"Did he tell you all about California?"

"You were so lucky to sit next to him. My mother would have died of happiness if that had been me."

She gave half answers, scanning the ballroom. George would surely come find her for a dance; she thought she glimpsed his blond head over by the door.

The group of girls suddenly parted, and her aunt appeared, William Brandt at her side.

"Here she is," Abigail said brightly. William nodded to all the girls, but his eyes were on Catherine.

"Miss Ogden," he said, "may I interest you in some refreshment?"

She said yes automatically, but as he steered her toward the tables, hand on her elbow, she wished she had thought to make some excuse. The blond figure she'd seen was now lost in the crowd.

"I also hope," he told her, handing her a glass, "that I may have the pleasure of a dance with you tonight."

She held out her dance card. He opened it and smiled. "No one yet. You see why I came to you right away."

"Have you ever read *The Winter's Tale*?" she asked abruptly.

He glanced up, lifting an eyebrow. "No," he said. "My knowledge of Shakespeare does not extend that far." She waited for him to ask why she had inquired and was conscious of a slight disappointment when he did not.

"I'd be honored to have the first dance with you, Miss Ogden," he said, taking up the pencil. "And the last."

⁊⊙

Her card was soon filled. George was the last to claim a dance, signing his name for a polka, and the way he scanned the names made her long to give him reassurance. There was no mistaking the strong signature scrawled twice on her card.

"Someone likes to make the first and the last impression, I see," he said without smiling.

"But he has never read *The Winter's Tale*," she said archly.

George's eyes widened. "You asked him that?"

"I did."

He threw back his head and laughed. The sound of it warmed her; nothing between them had changed.

"At least I have one advantage over the millionaire," he said. "He has a fortune, but I boldly wrestle with iambic pentameter."

"My kingdom for a sonnet," she quipped, and she was heartened by his answering grin.

The musicians took their seats and within moments, William was by her side. He nodded politely to George, whom she realized he had not yet met.

"Mr. William Brandt, this is Mr. George Langley," she said. After a moment she added, "We were just discussing poetry. Mr. Langley is a poet, you see."

"Indeed," said William. His gaze rested neutrally on George, who straightened to his full height.

"Yes, I am. Do you read much poetry, Mr. Brandt?"

"Not much."

"That's a shame," said George, almost aggressively. "There's some excellent work coming out of California." He thrust his hands in his pockets. "'A Wine of Wizardry,' for example. Astonishing poem by George Sterling. You've heard of him, perhaps?"

"I've met him," said William calmly. "A singular fellow. He spends much of his time on the Monterey Peninsula, I believe."

Catherine glanced at George, whose face was like stone. "And you share his name," she added quickly. "That seems auspicious." She opened her mouth to say more, but the musicians began to tune their instruments and William, with a perfunctory nod to George, held out his arm. She had no choice but to take it, feeling at once resentful and confused as they crossed the floor.

But William was a competent dancer, more graceful than she had expected. His arm under her hand felt muscular and not unpleasant, and he did not hold her too closely, which she appreciated. They waltzed for a few measures in silence before he spoke.

"You mentioned Shakespeare, Miss Ogden. Is he your favorite author?"

"One of them. He's always a pleasure to read. But I also enjoy discovering new authors."

"How do you choose what to read?"

"I take the recommendations of friends, mostly," she said. Then she added daringly, "Mr. Langley, in particular." She half expected him to react to that, but he did not speak, nor did he break his step. As they whirled about the room, she saw her aunt watching her, and suddenly the closeness of William's gaze, inches from her face, was too much. "I'm feeling dizzy," she said abruptly. "I'd like to get some air."

"Of course."

He held her elbow solicitously as he escorted her off the floor and out of the ballroom. The nearby library was dimly lit and empty of others; he led her to its open window, and she took a deep breath, grateful for the cool air but keenly aware that she had merely traded one undesirable situation for another. He walked back to the door and directed a passing maid to bring her water, then returned to her side.

"I'm sorry," she said. "I'm spoiling the waltz for you."

"My interest was in my partner," he said, "not in the waltz."

There was a pause while a car drove by, the sound of its motor trailing down the street. No one else came into the room.

Catherine had a sudden sense of being confined, a butterfly in a net. Behind her was a ballroom of other men, George included, who would not dare approach her as long as William was there. She wondered if this was how it happened: the man with the most money and status made a choice, and everyone else ceded the field. She willed someone to come challenge his right to her attention, yet they remained alone in the library, the music muted and far away.

He handed her a glass of water, his eyes following her appreciatively as she drank. She thought, not for the first time, that it was incorrect to say a woman's beauty gave her power. In the dress so carefully chosen to attract and impress, she felt that she had no power at all, that she was being propelled inexorably down a path she did not wish to take.

"There are so many lovely girls here," she said, almost desperately.

"Indeed there are." She expected him to add, "But I am with the prettiest," or something else predictably flattering, but he did not. She had the uncanny sense that he was reading her mind.

"How are you feeling now?" he asked as she put down the glass.

"Better, thank you."

The music of the waltz drew to an end. "I believe you have someone waiting for your next dance," he said. "Let's not disappoint him."

She took his arm and moved back into the close air of the ballroom and the scrutiny of the crowd. Red-haired Harold Overton came up to them, smiling tentatively, to claim her for the next dance.

"Until the final waltz," said William, letting her go with a smile.

॰

It was half an hour before she saw George again, for the designated polka. They attempted to discuss *The Winter's Tale*, but the tempo of the dance made it difficult to converse in depth. At one point he missed a step and nearly collided with a nearby couple. "I'm all thumbs tonight," he said irritably. "In my feet."

"It doesn't matter," she said.

"Yes, it does," he said shortly, and he did not speak again. Though she understood the reason for his mood, she felt an undeniable frustration with him. It was one of their few opportunities to talk, and he was silent and sullen, like a child.

He left before the final dance, which was another waltz. It was a relief, in a way, for she did not have to worry about his feelings at seeing her in William's arms once again. Much to her surprise, the waltz was almost enjoyable. Her previous partner had been stiff and awkward, and his hold had been too confining; William's arms were solid but correct, circling her lightly, making it easy to follow in spite of her weariness. Her eyes rested on his broad left shoulder as she recalled something a dancing teacher had once said: "The man makes the frame, and the girl is the painting." Does that make me a Botticelli or a Da Vinci? she thought, smiling suddenly at the absurdity of the metaphor.

She looked up to find William's eyes on her. She considered telling him why she had smiled but chose not to.

"You've danced every dance, Miss Ogden," he said after a moment. "You must be tired."

"Not very. It's been a lovely evening."

"It has indeed," he said.

At such proximity to him she could not help admiring the regularity of his features and the strong line of his jaw. He is quite handsome, she found herself thinking, a thought that felt stunningly disloyal. In her confusion she stumbled slightly, but his arms, which were holding her more tightly than she had realized, kept her in place.

⁊੦

"Well," said her uncle Oliver, "I'm glad to be home again." He exhaled comfortably and settled into the drawing room wing chair, closing his eyes.

"I thought it was a very pleasant evening," said Ethel. She paused in the removal of her gloves and wrinkled her nose. "Mother, have the maids been forgetting to change the water for the flowers?"

Catherine's aunt peered into the nearest vase, then pulled back with a grimace. "Apparently so. I don't know what to do with these girls. The maids in my mother's time would never have let that go."

"You should hire Swedish girls," said Ethel. "They work hard and don't complain. These Irish girls are too headstrong."

"Perhaps," said Abigail shortly.

"William Brandt certainly seemed to enjoy dancing with

you, Catherine," Henry observed. He wore the genial but alert look she recognized as the preamble to a longer conversation. She was too tired to respond, so she merely smiled.

"And you seemed to find his company very agreeable," he said. It was less a statement than a question, one that required a response.

Wishing to be alone, she rose to her feet. Three pairs of eyes regarded her: Henry's shrewd, her aunt's attentive, and Ethel's with their usual coolness. Her uncle's eyes were still closed. She knew the easiest way to end the conversation, to be free to go to her room and hold her rosary beads until she fell asleep.

"Yes," she said simply. "I did."

SIX

atherine saw more of William in the following days. This happened at the expense of her weekly piano lesson and a luncheon at Lavinia's home, both of which were canceled by Abigail in favor of events that she knew William would attend. Catherine suspected that the second cancellation was also motivated by her aunt's desire to keep her away from George, so when she saw him two days later at tea at the Pieters mansion, she felt a subversive joy; there were some situations even her aunt could not control. Her happiness was short-lived, though, for it was William who approached her first, inviting her to have a seat on the divan while George watched them from across the room.

"You take sugar, I believe," said William, passing her the silver bowl. He had taken tea with her only once before, in a large group of people, and she was surprised he had noticed.

As she sipped her tea, she saw that Henry had joined George near the large fireplace. Her cousin's face was serious, and he talked at length. George leaned against the mantel, hardly speaking; twice he glanced in Catherine's direction. She longed to hear what they were saying, so it was a relief when William was drawn away by Mrs. Van Hare. She put down her teacup and started toward the fireplace, but she had barely moved three feet before old Mrs. Pieters greeted her warmly.

"I hear you are learning to play Beethoven," Mrs. Pieters said. "So brave of you, my dear. He nearly defeated me when I was your age." She was a frank, amusing lady, and Catherine had always enjoyed her company, but at the moment she wished her miles away. Over the woman's gray head she saw Henry still speaking, as grave as if he were presenting a case in court, while George's face grew more and more sober.

With great force of will, Catherine smiled and affirmed Mrs. Pieters's opinions about the sprightliness of Mozart and the intricacies of playing Chopin. When she looked away a moment later, George was no longer near the fireplace. Turning, she saw him going quietly out the door.

She gave a hurried excuse to Mrs. Pieters and swiftly left the parlor, coming upon him as he stood in the foyer. He was putting on his coat. "George."

"I'm sorry, Catherine," he said. "I . . . that is, I have to return to Pittsburgh."

Her heart sank. "Why?"

"Just things," he said evasively. "Something has come up. I should be there."

There was the sudden sound of conversation as someone opened the parlor door. It closed again and a maid walked past them, a tea tray in her hands. Catherine felt the urgency of the moment; her aunt and cousin were sure to notice her absence.

"I wish you could stay," she said, abandoning all attempt at propriety. "I would rather talk to you than anyone. I hope you see that."

He laughed a quick, bitter laugh. "I do. I see that so clearly. And I wish I had half your spirit." He touched her cheek, something he'd never done before. She looked at him, her eyes full of naked longing, and he took his hand away and reached for his hat.

"Let's call ourselves star-crossed lovers," he said finally. "It sounds so much better than what we really are—a brave and beautiful girl and a wretched excuse for a man." He gave her one last smile, the rumpled grin with a cynical twist she hadn't seen before, then opened the door and was gone.

*

In the days that followed, William seemed to be everywhere Catherine went. On Sunday morning, he even joined the Ogdens in their pew at St. Thomas Episcopal Church, later offering her his arm for the weekly promenade down Fifth Avenue. As at the ball, others left them alone, seemingly accepting the inevitability of them as a couple. Catherine did not. It was true that George's abrupt goodbye had shaken her; she felt not just the pang of loss but also a sharp disappointment in him, one that she knew was deserved. Still, the memories of their banter and shared laughter made it impossible to think ill of him for long. Deep inside, she harbored the hope that a letter would arrive from Pittsburgh, alternately witty and apologetic, reviving their acquaintance. With William, then, she resolved to be polite but cool.

But she could not help being intrigued by his life in California. She learned that he, too, had lost both parents; his mother had died when he was twenty, his father five years later. He told her about his home on the Peninsula, and though he lacked George's facility of description, she was able to picture the ridge of high tree-covered hills running from north to south. On the eastern side was his estate, settled in a small valley, while on the other side was the ocean.

He told her about San Francisco, proudly rebuilt after the earthquake, which he had felt at Oakview. She wondered aloud if an earthquake felt like riding in a carriage, and he said no, it was more like standing on a platform being pulled abruptly from side to side. "Did it frighten you?" she asked.

"No," he said.

"What does frighten you?" She had not expected to ask so blunt a question, but once it came into her mind, she could not ignore it.

He smiled. "Nothing."

She knew he could not be telling the truth. Everyone was afraid of something.

"Let me ask you the same question," he said unexpectedly. His dark eyes held hers. "What frightens you, Miss Ogden?"

A life without freedom, she thought immediately. A life without the chance to live. It surprised her how quickly she knew the answer, even though she had never been asked the question before.

But she, too, merely smiled. "Nothing," she said.

§

On a walk in the park, he told her about the robust social life in California. San Francisco had a symphony orchestra and grand theaters and splendid houses, and the Peninsula had a few large towns and many country estates, including his own. A few miles to the south was Stanford University, with red-tiled roofs and sandstone buildings. His descriptions fleshed out pictures she had once seen in a magazine. It sounded so different from the East, more colorful and alive.

And he described the house built by his father. It had ten bedrooms, a ballroom, and a library of many volumes, along with acres of garden, stables, and a garage.

"I'm always adding to the art collection," he told her. "I keep a close eye on the auction catalogs."

"What kind of art do you like?"

"Whatever is beautiful and most desirable." Desirable to

whom, he did not say. "I don't want anything unless it's the only one of its kind."

He told her of an English landscape he'd just purchased the week before. The bidding had come down to himself and just one other collector, but he had won, and the piece was now being crated to be shipped home. From his description of the process, she understood how he had become the successful man he was.

"I enjoy the challenge of getting what is not easily won." He studied the sky as if he could possess even its blue brilliance; then he smiled at her. "But once I have it, I never take it for granted."

❧

"So," said Lavinia the next day over tea, "do you like him?"

Catherine twisted her locket on its chain as she considered the question. William was certainly intelligent, well traveled, and interesting to talk to. But though their conversations never lagged, they lacked the easy comfort of her talks with George. At times, too, something in his manner gave her an instinctive desire to be contrary; she would catch him looking at her with leisurely confidence in his dark eyes, which made her want to lift her chin and turn away. At the same time, she had to admit that it was pleasing to be pursued by such a handsome man. It bothered her that she had those two feelings simultaneously, for they seemed to validate the worst stereotypes of women as fickle creatures.

If he had been a boor or a rogue, it would have been easy to dismiss him. But he was unfailingly courteous, and his description of his home piqued her interest. She was sure that a man who appreciated art as much as he did must have depth of character.

"I think I do," she said finally. "But . . ."

Lavinia looked sympathetic. "George."

"Yes."

Lavinia sighed. "I understand. George is nothing if not en-dearing." She turned her ring around on her finger and paused, as if choosing her words with deliberation. "But he isn't a fighter, you know."

"Does he have to be?"

Lavinia gave her a pointed look. "You know your aunt and your cousin."

Catherine dropped a sugar cube into her cup, remembering the day at the Pieters home. She knew Henry had been the cata-lyst for George's departure, but it was painful to acknowledge that her suitor would be discouraged so easily.

"I know you, Catherine," said Lavinia. "There are some things you see so clearly. A cloud in the sky, a painting, that sort of thing. But sometimes you miss what really matters." She put down her teacup. "George is witty and charming, but he folds like an umbrella when anyone challenges him. There's a lot to be said for a man who won't give up at the first sign of trouble." She reached over and took Catherine's hand. "Maybe that's William, and maybe it's someone you haven't met yet. But you deserve a man who will fight for you."

Catherine squeezed her friend's hand gratefully before letting it go. Stirring her tea, she watched the sugar cube dissolve. She had the sudden, cynical thought that life was about encounters, encounters in which one party always overpowered the other. The hot tea was stronger than the sugar; her cousin's social am-bitions were stronger than George's affection.

How nice it must be to have an encounter—or a relation-ship—where the strength was evenly matched. Was that the dynamic she had with William? The prickle of confrontation she felt with him at times . . . was she seeing it as a problem when it was actually a sign that they were equals, that she could hold her own? And was that not a good thing in a marriage?

She sipped her tea, wondering.

SEVEN

*T*he following morning, Catherine suggested an afternoon trip to the Metropolitan Museum of Art. Henry
and Ethel accompanied them as chaperones, though once inside
they left William and Catherine alone. "We'll go at our own
pace, shall we?" Henry said, drawing his wife away. "I'd like to
show Ethel something in the other room."

Before the visit was over, Catherine took William to see
Madonna of the Springtime. They stood in front of it silently, and
she resolved not to speak first. He doesn't know it, she thought,
but this is a test.

"It's a lovely work," he said at last.

"What do you like about it?"

He studied it again. "The beauty of the mother's face. The
whole scene is simple, but that's what makes it powerful. I like
the line of dark trees in the background, too. It would be very
different without that contrast."

She was more impressed with his answer than she had expected to be, which broke down her reserve. "When I see this, I
try to imagine being the artist. I wish I could paint like this."

"Have you ever been painted?" he asked.

"My portrait?"

"Yes."

"No," she said. Then she recalled her father unrolling a

painting of herself as a toddler, with a red ribbon in her hair and her beloved stuffed dog held against her chest. "You wouldn't sit still," he'd said with a smile, "so I had to do this from memory."

"No," she said again.

"That's a pity." William's gaze was dark and direct. "A portrait of you would rival this Madonna."

The compliment gave her a perverse desire to be contrary. "I would much rather be the one doing the painting," she said. "It must be so gratifying."

"But every artist needs a subject. I should think most women would be honored to inspire a work of art like this."

She thought of her mother sitting perfectly still in the Gloucester apartment. "But it's the artist we remember now, isn't it? Who knows the name of the woman who sat for this picture? All we know is what she looks like."

"But people have admired her for centuries. What drew you to this picture in the first place? The woman and her beauty."

"No," she said, realizing the truth as she said it aloud. "What really drew me is the relationship. The way she's holding the child." She indicated the baby held lightly in the curve of his mother's arm. "Any woman would be beautiful making such a gesture." She looked up at him, wondering if he would disagree.

He met her gaze. "Perhaps you are right," he said evenly.

Henry materialized, glancing at his watch. "It's nearly four o'clock. Shall we move on?"

William smiled and offered her his arm. The conversation still echoed in her mind as they moved toward the exit. She had not ceded any ground, and she was glad of that; but neither, she realized, had William.

The next day, Catherine had just sat down at the piano when the door opened, and her aunt and uncle entered the music room. It was unusual to see her uncle at home in the morning; she glanced up in surprise.

"We've had an invitation, all of us," her aunt said without preamble. "Mr. Brandt has invited us to his home. In California."

"California?"

Her aunt nodded. Catherine had never seen her so visibly excited. "He's offered to take us in his private railroad car. Your uncle can't go, he has to be in the office these next few weeks, but Mr. Brandt has invited Henry and Ethel, as well."

"I see." Catherine's mind raced. "When would we go?"

"The end of next week." Catherine opened her mouth, and her aunt continued, anticipating her question. "We'd stay no more than three weeks at the most. We know you want to be back well before Lavinia's wedding in May. He was very agreeable to that."

"Would you like to accept?" asked her uncle.

Abigail made a dismissive gesture with her hand. "Of course she would. It's a great compliment, this invitation."

"Would you like to accept, Catherine?" her uncle said again, and Catherine was surprised. He usually deferred to his wife in such matters.

She put her fingers on the piano keys, tracing them noiselessly. To go would mean tacitly accepting William's interest. But it would mean seeing a land of ocean and redwoods, fog and earthquakes. It meant change and discovery, a chance to satisfy that keen, restless hunger to explore horizons beyond New York.

And this isn't a marriage proposal, she told herself. He is inviting me to visit his home, that's all. If a proposal does come while I am in California—the mere name of the state gave her a thrill—I will decide then what I want to say.

"Yes," she said suddenly, turning back to her aunt and uncle. "Yes. I would like to go."

Abigail exhaled. "Excellent," she said, giving Catherine a rare smile of unmitigated approval. "Excellent. I knew you would." She quickly rang the bell for the maid. "I'll see if Madame Rainier is free this afternoon. You'll need a new dinner dress, perhaps some new shirtwaists as well." She turned to her husband. "Oliver, telephone Mr. Brandt and let him know that we accept. And of course, tell Henry and Ethel, too." She was animated and efficient, in her element.

Catherine played a scale, loud and quick, repeating the last note for joyful emphasis. There was a heady feeling of power in making a choice that would shape her future. She had no idea what that future would be, but it was exhilarating simply to know that her life would, absolutely and irrevocably, change.

EIGHT

*M*arch in California felt like May in New York: sun-drenched, warm, and languorous.

"This isn't unusual weather for this time of year," said William, but Catherine marveled that anyone could grow accustomed to it. As she sat back against the cushions of William's black Pierce-Arrow, driven by a uniformed chauffeur whom William addressed as Anderson, she closed her eyes and let the balmy air whisper past her face. Then she opened her eyes again, eager not to miss anything on the last leg of the journey to Oakview.

William, who was sitting next to the driver, looked over his shoulder and smiled. "It's quite different from the East, isn't it?"

"Very much so."

The differences between William's life and her own had become clear the moment they boarded the train in New York. William's private railroad car was luxurious, with mahogany and velvet interiors, gliding along the track like a house on wheels. The landscapes they passed were an ever-changing tapestry of hills, farms, and plains that stretched in all directions under a sky larger than any Catherine had seen in New York. She would have liked to spend the entire trip gazing out the window, letting the sights fill her eyes and set her dreams spinning.

All the same, she was glad to reach the journey's end. It had been confining to be in such constant proximity to her family and

William, with no chance to escape into a piano sonata or down the paths of a park. She had brought several books along—including a novel by Gertrude Atherton, to give her a preview of California life—and they gave her the occasional respite from the demands of conversation. The black rosary had come along, too, tucked carefully into a pocket of her luggage, but with so little privacy there had been no chance to use it.

Sitting in the first of William's two automobiles, though, she felt as excited as a child. The cars caravanned slowly down a road through hills lush with the green of early spring. Taller hills to the west were covered with trees and looked much like a stage set, each layer a different shade of dark green in the afternoon sun.

"What are those mountains called?" she asked.

"They're part of the Santa Cruz mountain range," William said.

"Santa Cruz," she repeated, trying out the feel of the words.

"Many places in California have Spanish names," said William. "It used to be a territory of Mexico, as you know." He indicated a fork in the road ahead of them. "We'll turn here."

As the car changed direction, the layered hills were no longer to their side but directly before them, spread out in a panorama. Catherine caught her breath at the sight. "What is behind those mountains?"

"The coast," said William.

Another turn, and the car proceeded down a wide dirt road. There were trees on either side and grass that was bright green in the sunlight.

"You can see the roof of the house in the distance there," said William, and sure enough multiple chimneys were just discernible through the trees.

"Have you any near neighbors?" asked Abigail.

"Not near, exactly," said William. "There are some estates a few miles away. San Mateo, the closest large city, has some very fine homes. But we're rather removed in the valley here."

The auto turned onto a driveway, long and lined with oaks, many with moss hanging from their branches. Horses grazed behind a fence, long tails swishing with the unhurried ease of being at home. They passed over a bridge spanning a small creek; then the road bent to the left and they came to a large open gate.

Moments later, the house came into view. It was large and graceful, made of mellow light stone, with two wings extending forward on either side. In size and shape, it resembled an English country house, but discreet wrought-iron balconies along the second-story windows gave it an Italian air. A wisteria vine, not yet in bloom, hung with heavy grace over the square columned portico of the entrance.

On either side of the house were the large oaks that gave the estate its name. They were nearly as tall as the house, reaching almost to the tiny third-story windows. The entire view was breathtaking, a perfectly harmonious blend of architecture and nature.

"It's beautiful," said Catherine when she could find her voice.

The road became a gravel drive, which took them up to the front door. In the curve of the drive was a fountain, topped by a modest marble nymph in Grecian dress. In low urns around the fountain were the prettiest hyacinths Catherine had ever seen, white alternating with violet and lavender-blue, dense and abundant.

"Those flowers!" she exclaimed.

William smiled at her delight. "They make quite a show, every spring."

The two cars stopped at the front door, at which stood a butler in a black suit. He appeared to be in his early sixties, with thick gray hair and bushy eyebrows. He came down to greet them as the chauffeurs opened the doors and helped out the passengers.

"Good afternoon, Hayes," said William.

"Good afternoon, sir," said the butler. "And welcome home."

"This is Mrs. Ogden and Miss Ogden," said William, indicating Abigail and Catherine. "And Mr. Ogden and Mrs. Ogden." Catherine had to stifle a grin; remembering the guests' names would be easier than usual for the staff. But no one else was smiling. Her aunt looked up at the wisteria vine, Ethel was discreetly trying to peer into the open door of the house, and Henry had his habitual air of pleasant authority. Hayes, apparently a consummate professional, bowed slightly, his face conveying nothing but the most correct level of greeting.

"Welcome to Oakview," he said.

The house was cool, hushed, and light. Through the marble-floored entrance hall they entered a double door into a large, high-ceilinged reception room. The walls were covered in gray-blue linen while French windows at the far end gave a glimpse of a terrace framed by an elegant balustrade. Flowers stood in vases on every surface. There were toile-covered sofas and gilt chairs, and an ornate fireplace displayed a gleaming clock on its mantel. The drapes were open.

"Would you like a tour now, or would you prefer to rest first?" William asked as two maids helped them off with their coats and hats.

"Now would be lovely," said Ethel immediately.

It was a home unlike any Catherine had ever seen, not just in the fineness of its furnishings but in the open, airy feel of every room. The dining room walls were paneled in white and light green, with silver candle sconces gracing the long table. There was a music room with tall windows and a piano facing a large mirror, which made the room feel even more spacious.

Her uncle would love the library, Catherine was sure, with its floor-to-ceiling bookshelves, massive fireplace, and a female portrait that looked very much like a Romney. William had a separate study, an unmistakably masculine room with wood paneling and red leather chairs. There was a ballroom with gleaming parquet floors and crystal chandeliers, and on the other side of the house was a covered porch, where wicker furniture was arranged for a view over the lawn to the wooded hills beyond. A small breakfast room was decorated in white and blue, with Dutch tiles around the fireplace and paintings of floral bouquets on the walls. The entire home was a testament to luxury and taste, classically elegant with enough modern touches to make it comfortable. This is a house, thought Catherine as she gazed up at the high ceiling, that lets you breathe.

The room she was given on the second floor, up a gracefully curved staircase, was papered with a pattern of forget-me-nots. A four-poster bed faced a marble fireplace, and white curtains billowed lightly in the breeze. Because it was a corner room, it had windows on two sides, and she looked eagerly out of each one. From one window, she saw the balustrade below, then what seemed a mile of lawn and the hills beyond. From the other side, she saw a garden house, brick walls and pathways, more oak trees, and lush, colorful flower beds.

"And this room has its own bathroom," said Ethel, opening a door on tiled elegance, with a large claw-footed tub. "Look," she said to her mother-in-law, but Abigail was watching her niece.

"Do you like it?" she asked.

"I do," said Catherine, leaning out of the window, her face radiant. "I absolutely love it."

NINE

"*I* don't have any particular plans in mind for tomorrow," William said at dinner. "I thought you might like to rest here before we go on any excursions." He helped himself to filet of sole, offered on a silver platter by the impassive Hayes. "But before you go home, we will visit the redwoods, San Francisco, the coast, and anything else you wish to see."

"That all sounds delightful," said Abigail. "I'm sure the estate will keep us busy tomorrow."

Sitting across from her aunt in a new gown of green velvet, Catherine silently agreed. The dining room was beautiful in the light of the crystal chandelier, which illuminated the white lilies massed in a low bowl in the center of the table.

"If you ride, you can see even more of the estate," said William. "Jackson, the groom, can find you the best horse from the stables. There are plenty of trails leading up into the hills."

"How large are the gardens?" asked Catherine.

"Sixteen acres. There is a rose garden, a reflecting pool, and an orchard. You could spend the whole day wandering the paths."

"Then that's what I shall do tomorrow," said Catherine, her eyes alight.

William smiled. "I hope they don't disappoint," he said, in a tone indicating he was confident they would not.

By the time they finished breakfast in the blue-and-white room, the morning clouds had scrolled back to reveal a bright springtime sky. Ethel had not yet appeared—"She had a hard time falling asleep, poor girl, so much excitement," Henry said as he accepted a cup of coffee from Hayes—so William, Catherine, and her aunt set out together onto the terrace, down the short flight of steps and into what Catherine could only think of as paradise.

"My mother called the garden her second house," William said as he led the way along the paths. "It was designed to have separate rooms."

There were ivy-cloaked walls dividing the various sections of the garden, with arched doorways that opened onto colorful vistas of lawn and flower bed. A garden house made of brick, with tall windows on four sides, sat on the other side of a croquet lawn. Potted magnolias reached their graceful arms along the inside walls, and a large cage in the corner held two white doves. Catherine leaned in to look at them and they fluttered in mild alarm, then settled down and ignored her.

"What are their names?" she asked.

"I don't know that they have names," William said. "The gardening staff looks after them."

On the other side of the garden house, down a few steps, was a rectangular reflecting pool bordered with cypress trees at either end. "It reminds me of Italy," said Abigail.

"Especially in summer, when the sun is bright," said William. "You'll find that the garden has a new look with each season." The subtext to his comment was evident to Catherine: this would not be the Ogdens' only visit to Oakview.

They passed beds of red tulips and eventually went through another arched doorway, where an oak tree stood in in the middle of a lawn, a small bench at its base.

"It's so huge!" Catherine exclaimed.

"The largest tree on the property," said William. "Three hundred years old, they say."

Heedless of the damp grass, Catherine crossed to the base of the tree, marveling at the huge branches reaching out in all directions. They extended up and then down in striking, sinuous lines, showing bits of sky in the spaces between. Her father would have loved this tree, she thought. It was living poetry; it had both structure and grace.

William had come up behind her. "We're at the center point of the garden. The landscape architect designed the grounds so this tree would be at the heart of it all."

"It's the prettiest thing on the estate," she said, captivated. She tilted her head, following the branches, searching for the highest point.

"It was the prettiest," he said in an intimate voice, obviously calculated so Catherine's aunt could not hear. "Until yesterday."

The compliment broke her reverie and demanded a response. She looked at him standing a few feet away, hands in the pockets of his fine linen suit, eyes on her. To be pinned in his leisurely, unapologetic gaze made her feel both flustered and flattered, which in turn made her feel annoyed.

"Shall we continue on?" she asked, turning in the direction of her aunt.

He gave the barest hint of a smile, as if her reaction amused him, and stepped back to let her go first.

❧

Catherine woke early the next morning, so early that when she slipped out of bed and padded to the window, she could see the rose of daybreak in the sky. For a moment she leaned on the sill, smiling into the dawn; then on a sudden impulse she quickly dressed and went downstairs.

No one saw her but a maid opening the reception-room drapes and the butler, who asked if she required anything. If he was surprised at seeing her up so early, with her hair tied back in a braid, his face did not reveal it.

Down the terrace she went, skirting the dew-wet grass. Yesterday they had played croquet on this lawn, which had been alive with voices and the thwack of mallets on balls. But now it was empty and still, a world just waking up, beautiful in its freshness. She thought of Eden, then almost laughed at her own triteness. But it did feel like a paradise, untouched by trouble.

Her unhurried steps took her to the huge oak she'd admired the day before. In the early dawn, it was even more impressive, its leafless branches making fascinating patterns in the sky. She loved how they curved up and then down and then out, restless and graceful, like reaching arms. Something so beautiful should have a name, but the only name that came to mind was the Tree of the Knowledge of Good and Evil. Eden again; she couldn't get away from it. But if Paradise had looked like this, no wonder Adam and Eve had cried upon leaving it.

As in Central Park, she kept her eyes open, absorbing the beauty around her—well-tended gravel walkways, ivy hugging the walls, and lush flower beds, each one bright with massed blooms of a single color. In the rose garden she spied small buds, delicate and green, among the reddish foliage.

Basking in the new sunlight, she imagined herself living at Oakview. Every morning she could stroll through the gardens, choosing flowers to arrange in the dining room. She could take tea in the garden house, play piano in the music room, and read by the fire in the bedroom on a cold night (she was sure there must be some cold nights, even in California). It was an appealing thought.

But then she imagined the door to the bedroom opening and William entering, confident in his right to be there. And she stopped walking, pausing irresolutely by a boxwood hedge.

Catherine wasn't ignorant of the details of married life. This was no credit to her aunt, whose conversation on the subject of sex had been limited to the vague warning that no man would marry a girl who was no longer pure. It was at finishing school that Catherine and Lavinia had been told the mechanics of the act by a young maid, pretty and talkative, who was later dismissed from the school for pregnancy. Catherine's initial surprise and disgust had given way, over time, to curiosity; after all, she decided, if the act were truly repugnant, no wife would ever wish to do it. Surely literature and life proved that women must find some enjoyment in it.

And she could not deny that she found William attractive. His arm as they walked was solid and appealing, and sometimes his physical nearness made her pulse quicken in a way that was new to her. But her interactions with him often had that odd undercurrent of challenge, a dynamic that was undeniably invigorating, if not entirely comfortable. Lavinia would have said she was finally learning to be flirtatious, but she didn't think it was that. Her instinctive resistance came not from a desire to increase his interest, but from something deeper, some need to draw a boundary around herself. But to protect herself from what? She didn't know.

She began to walk again, entering the orchard and an avenue of pear trees whose just-blossoming branches filtered the early sunlight. Her father would have loved to sketch them. She imagined her parents walking with her, her father with his slight limp, her mother with her hair braided low on her neck and her ready laugh. If only you were here to help me decide, she thought as she walked along. If only you were still here to guide me.

She was so lost in her thoughts that as she rounded a corner of the path she almost tripped over a wheelbarrow whose handles extended beyond a nearby flower bed. She felt the impact just below her knees and halted, bent over in shock and pain.

A man emerged from the foliage, holding a branch in one hand and pruning shears in the other. "Are you hurt?" He quickly dropped the branch and shears at his feet and held out a hand to steady her.

"I'm fine," she gasped, instinctively taking hold of his outstretched arm. The pain was not great; it was the shock that had winded her.

"I'm sorry. I shouldn't have left the wheelbarrow near the path like that," he said. "I'm not used to people being out so early."

"It's quite all right. I'm not used to being out so early myself." She straightened and let go of his arm, giving a brief smile of thanks, wanting to dispel any hint of blame. "But the garden is beautiful at this time of day."

Assured that she was fine, he smiled, too. He appeared to be in his midtwenties and was a few inches taller than she, with wavy brown hair and olive skin. Something about his face had surprised her from the first, and she realized now it was the color of his eyes, light blue in a face where she would have expected brown.

"It is," he said. "This is the best time in the garden, next to dusk." He bent down and moved the wheelbarrow off the path.

"Why?"

If he was surprised by her interest, he gave no sign of it. "In the morning, it's a new start," he said. "Anything can happen."

"And dusk?"

"What's happened has happened," he said. "You can remember it, which is like living it again."

She thought of her nightly rosary ritual, of moments of kindness and beauty counted on the beads. "Yes. That's true."

"I'm sorry again for the wheelbarrow. I hope you don't get a bruise."

"I'm sure I won't," she said, though she knew she would. He had a red scarf knotted around his neck, a splash of color against the brown of his corduroy coat. She wanted to prolong the conversation but did not know what else to say.

"What is your name?" she asked awkwardly.

"Thomas O'Shea."

"Well," she said. "Thank you, Thomas. For the beautiful garden, I mean." She gestured about her.

"You're welcome," he said, picking up his shears. He stood there holding them, politely waiting to see if she needed anything else before returning to his work. After a moment, she nodded goodbye and walked briskly down the path toward the house.

TEN

Every day that followed brought new sights and discoveries. In William's two gleaming cars, the Ogdens took the winding road out to the coast. They visited a place called Coyote Point on the edge of the bay, a small beach bordered by eucalyptus trees with strips of bark falling off their trunks. A drizzly evening was spent with several of William's friends and neighbors, who came to Oakview for a dinner party and cards. They toured San Francisco, where Catherine was astonished by the streets climbing up and down the hills, so steep it seemed the autos must rush headlong into the bay. At the end of the day, they took a late dinner at William's spacious apartment on the top floor of the St. Francis Hotel on Union Square. "I find it easier to stay in town sometimes," he said, "relating to business." It was after nine when they left the city for Oakview, following the road under a sky that showed off a dazzling array of stars.

When Catherine held her rosary beads at night, her mind was full of beautiful things: the huge oak, which she continued to think of as the Tree of Knowledge; the wooded hills, covered with trees in varying shades of green and brown, looking as if she could run her hands over them like velvet; the evocative blare of foghorns in the bay as they drove through San Francisco streets; the airy beauty of the house, with its drapes drawn back as if the sunlight were a welcome guest; and the gleaming piano in the music room, which she played after dinner to admiring applause.

Even her family seemed different. Removed from their normal stage to a larger one, they had diminished in stature in a way she would not have expected. Though William was an accommodating host, deferring to their wishes, the grandeur of his home gave him an even greater air of authority than he had displayed in New York. He was a man of influence, a message reinforced every time his wealth became obvious in a new way, such as the fleet of musicians brought in to entertain for merely an hour at the dinner party.

As the days passed, Catherine thought about the differences between the East and the West. Life in New York City seemed narrower, squeezed between tall brownstones and the demands of a close and exacting society, but in California there was space and room. Her soul seemed to expand, as if it had been corseted and could at last be its true size. She was grateful to William for bringing her to a place so inviting and beautiful.

But although there was much that she liked about him and although she knew her family was expecting that she would one day become Mrs. William Brandt, the thought of marriage still caused a little jolt of resistance deep within her, like a small backward tug on a line. It was not something she could explain, but it was there. So she pushed it out of mind, focusing her gaze on what was in front of her—house, garden, hills—instead of a vague, still-unasked question waiting beyond the horizon.

9○

One afternoon they met William's friends Peter and Vivian Powell, who came for luncheon from their own estate north of Oakview. Vivian was a few years older than Catherine and many years younger than her husband, who was gray-haired, red-faced, and corpulent. Watching him in conversation with William,

Catherine realized that in spite of their physical differences, they were fundamentally similar men, accustomed to wealth and wearing it easily.

Vivian, like her name, was vivid and quick. In her presence, Catherine was reminded of Lavinia's frank, energetic manner. She had deep-red hair and dark brown eyes, a striking combination; her face, though not beautiful, was mobile and compelling. All the same, there was an appraising look to her that was not like Lavinia, giving the impression that she was measuring you and making an amused internal accounting. Catherine could see that Ethel disliked her intensely, but Ethel liked few people, so her coolness did little to affect Catherine's opinion of her new acquaintance.

As the others finished luncheon in the garden house, Vivian and Catherine took a leisurely stroll along the paths. Having another woman for company made Catherine recall her walks with Lavinia, and she felt a sudden pang at being so far away from her friend.

"Penny for your thoughts," said Vivian unexpectedly.

"I was just thinking of my best friend back home. She's getting married in May."

"Is she? Poor girl." It was the kind of comment Vivian made often, her tone breezy and offhand.

"She's quite happy with her fiancé," Catherine said loyally. "They're an excellent match."

"Well, that's something." Vivian paused by a branch of flowering dogwood and ran her fingers along its length, then snapped off the end. "How pretty is this?" She tucked the bloom behind one ear. "William certainly knows how to make his garden grow."

"Have you known him long?"

"Nearly all my life," said Vivian. "His father and my father—

and my husband, come to that—were all in business together."

"And you live not far from here?"

"A few miles. An estate called Madrone Hill. We'll have you all up there, if you like."

"That would be lovely," said Catherine politely.

Vivian smiled as if the correctness of the response amused her. "It won't be," she said. "It's a gloomy pile, actually. The first wife had a strange passion for stained glass and carved wood. You expect to hear monks singing a dirge the moment you open the door."

Catherine laughed. "My aunt's home in New York feels like that." She looked off toward the house, its roofline visible beyond the oaks. "This house is so different. Everything is so beautiful and light."

"It certainly is," said Vivian. "William has always wanted the very best. In everything."

There was a barely perceptible shift in her tone, a grace note of bitterness. Before Catherine could wonder at it too deeply, they were passing the archway into the rose garden, where Thomas stood several flower beds away, turning the soil. Vivian stopped and nudged Catherine. "Who is that?"

"One of the gardeners." He wore the same red scarf he'd worn the morning of their conversation, but the corduroy coat was gone, and his brown shirt was open at the neck. "His name is Thomas, I believe."

"I haven't seen him in a long time," said Vivian. She continued to watch Thomas as he bent and straightened over the spade, unaware of their presence. "What a beautiful man," she added, in a tone very unlike her usual breezy one.

"Shall we go back?" Catherine asked awkwardly.

Vivian turned to her, smiling the appraising smile. "I've shocked you, haven't I. But there's no harm in pointing out the obvious." After another look at Thomas, she took Catherine's arm and they walked back the way they had come. The sound of his spade echoed in the warm air.

"It's been a lovely stroll, my dear," said Vivian, when they drew close to the garden house. "I hope I haven't said anything to make you think of Californians as uncouth or savage."

"Not at all. It's a nice change, meeting people who aren't from the East."

"No doubt," said Vivian. They were close enough now to see Ethel through the open door of the garden house, irritably waving away a fly that had dared to enter her orbit. "I'm just sorry your cousin's wife didn't join us," she said archly. "It's not fair that you get all the fun of her company."

Catherine laughed out loud, causing a small bird on the path in front of them to startle and take flight.

ELEVEN

*T*he next morning, a steady rain made outdoor activities impossible. After writing a letter to Lavinia, Catherine wandered along the main hallway, studying the now-familiar framed paintings on the walls. She lingered over her favorite, a Dutch still life of glistening fruit piled high on a table, an orange peel hanging over the edge of the plate like a question mark.

At the far end of the hall, just outside William's study, was one that was easy to overlook due to its placement in a small alcove. It was an oil painting of the Grand Canal in Venice, and she stood before it, enchanted. On the gray-blue water, lit with sunlight, small standing men steered numerous gondolas while ornate houses rose almost vertically from the canal. The precision of the painting was exquisite. Catherine could practically hear the lapping of the water on the sides of the quays, could almost feel the rocking of the waves. She moved closer, standing inches away from the canvas.

"Do you like it?" said William, and she turned in surprise.

"It's beautiful. I feel as though I'm part of the scene."

"I did, too, when I first saw it."

"Did you buy it in Venice?"

"No, in New York, at an auction. It's a Canaletto."

"I love it," she said. "It's so detailed and full of life." She smiled at him more broadly than she usually did, and he smiled in turn and moved closer.

"See here." He indicated the foreground of the canvas,

touching the small of her back as he did so. "These two men in the gondola." One figure was pointing toward the water and the other was bending to follow his gaze. "They seem to be having an important conversation."

"Perhaps something fell in the water. A hat, maybe? They could be talking about how to retrieve it."

"We'll never know, will we," said William. The whimsical turn of the conversation pleased Catherine, and she felt closer to him than she ever had before. His hand still rested on the small of her back, and she had no desire for him to move it away.

"And see here," she said. One gondola had a square canopy, and in the dim depths was a figure, somehow recognizably female. Her face was tiny, barely the size of a pea, but her expression was clearly fixed on the viewer, the only figure in the whole painting who was looking directly out of the canvas. "She's staring right at us. I wonder what she's thinking."

"I must admit, I've never thought about that before," said William. The pressure on her back increased slightly. "Having you here is an education." He looked at her mouth, and she had the sudden thought that he was going to kiss her in broad daylight, in the hall where anyone could see. The idea excited her as much as it terrified her.

"I've always seen paintings like this in museums," she said, turning away to hide her confusion, "and wondered how it would feel to paint them. I used to wish I could touch the canvas, like the artist did."

"So do it," William said.

She looked up at him swiftly.

"Do it. It's my painting. No one will eject you from the premises."

Tentatively, she reached out a hand. She touched the gondola with the woman inside, lightly, with the tip of her finger. It was smoother than she expected, only the barest hint of texture. She had an image of Canaletto, in a light-filled studio in Venice, carefully painting the face peering out mysteriously from the shadows. She felt a thrill that was hard to describe.

"This is why I collect art," said William, his voice close to her ear. "It's far different to own something than it is just to admire it."

Then Ethel came into the hall, folding down the flap of an envelope to post, and William moved decorously away. But every time Catherine looked at the painting, she recalled both the pressure of his hand on her back and the smoothness of the woman's face under her finger.

૭૦

A new houseguest arrived by train the next day, from Southern California. Lloyd Dixon was an old friend of William's. ("We shared many a caper during our college days," he said, giving his host a good-natured slap on the shoulder.) He had a lean, graceful build and a slightly receding hairline that somehow made him more attractive, not less. While William had an air of calm and imperturbable control, Lloyd had a warm, lighthearted manner that put the others instantly at ease.

Like his friend, Lloyd was the son and heir of a railroad man. He was having a new home built in Pasadena, and his offhand descriptions indicated a house nearly as grand as Oakview, but Catherine was more impressed by his liveliness and good humor. She was clearly not alone in finding him a welcome addition to the house party; in his presence, Ethel became animated and even playful, a side of her that Catherine had never seen before.

Upon meeting Catherine, Lloyd had taken her hand in both of his. "It's a great pleasure to meet you," he said. "I've heard wonderful things about you, and now I see that every single one of them was absolutely true." It was said with such sincerity and such an earnest smile that the words, though they may have been trite coming from someone else, felt like a great compliment.

Lloyd was engaged to be married the following year, to a young debutante from San Diego. "Hazel is a grand girl," he said as they sat on the porch. "Pretty, bright, graceful, and entirely too good for me. Her father agreed to the engagement on the condition that she take a tour of Europe first and then come back and marry me."

"It must be difficult to be so far away," said Abigail.

"It is, Mrs. Ogden. Our letters cross the Atlantic with great regularity. I believe her parents are hoping she'll be swept off her feet by some more deserving chap, but, happily, there's no sign of that." He settled back comfortably in the wicker chair and drained the last of his lemonade.

"What would a more deserving chap be like?" asked Catherine. It was hard to imagine any parent not warming to a man so wealthy and likable.

Lloyd bowed his head in recognition of the compliment. "Your disbelief is greatly flattering, Miss Ogden." He held his glass out to Hayes for a refill. "A man with a title, perhaps. The Prince of Wales. The Marquis of Evrémonde. The King of Hearts. But she is a constant young woman, bless her." He raised his glass and smiled at Catherine, then included Ethel and Abigail in the toast. "To constant women. Where would we be without them?"

"To constant women," they all responded—even Abigail— and drank.

TWELVE

illiam's only sibling was a sister named Harriet, who lived with her husband and son in San Diego. "You'll have a chance to meet her soon," he had told the Ogdens shortly after their arrival. "I've invited her for a visit while you're here." She was the daughter of his father's first wife, who had died when Harriet was four. By doing the math, Catherine figured Harriet was fifteen years older than her half brother, old enough to be more a mother than a sister.

She arrived at Oakview two days after Lloyd, accompanied by her ladies' maid. There was a definite echo of William in her face; like him, she had a strong jaw and slight cleft in her chin, but she was much shorter and had a rounded figure artfully contained by corsets underneath a beautifully made traveling suit. She greeted her brother with an affectionate kiss and pat on the cheek.

"A good journey?" he asked.

"Very pleasant," she said. "I do enjoy the green hills this time of year."

William made the introductions, and when it was Catherine's turn, she saw Harriet's eyes light up approvingly.

"How lovely you are, my dear," she said warmly. "It's such a pleasure to meet you."

Lloyd, who had unfolded his lean figure from the club chair, came in for a kiss. "Harriet," he said. "It's been too long, hasn't it? But you haven't changed a whit."

"Lloyd," she said, delighted. "How wonderful to see you again. I hear you're engaged to that darling girl. Will she be coming, too?"

"I wish she could," said Lloyd. "She's off with the mater and pater, doing a tour of the Continent."

"Well, now is the time, when you're young." She sat down on the divan, smoothing her light-brown hair with a ringed hand. "My husband and son are doing the tour, too. Howard is interested in music, you see, so they're spending a few months in Vienna. So kind of William to invite me here, or I'd be all alone."

"Vienna is not a place you enjoy, then," said Abigail.

Harriet shook her head. "Oh, it's very pretty, but they eat such strange foods there, sausages and things. And even the best hotels are not as comfortable as home. The older I get, the happier I am staying with what is familiar." She looked around the reception room, content and relaxed, taking in the drapes, fireplace, and floral arrangements. "The place is more beautiful than ever, William."

William's gaze moved to Catherine, sitting in her green dress by a tall vase of lilies. "I do my best," he said.

ॐ

Just after two the following afternoon, Catherine paused at the window on the staircase landing. She gazed out at the front courtyard with its fountain and hyacinth urns, then at the oak trees lining the drive as it curved away and disappeared into the distance.

Her aunt and the other houseguests had gone to see the redwood forests, but a headache had kept Catherine behind. William, upon hearing she was unwell, had immediately offered to stay back with her. Although her aunt had clearly been displeased—they would be unchaperoned in the house—William had assured her that he would be in the study, catching up on business correspondence. "I will have the housekeeper check in on her," he said, and Abigail had yielded. Catherine would never have thought her aunt capable of backing down. Once again, it seemed, California was challenging the assumptions she'd always held to be true.

Mrs. Callahan, a solicitous woman with graying dark hair, came to Catherine's room bearing hot tea and a cold compress. After an hour, Catherine felt much better. The porcelain clock on her bedroom mantel showed it would likely be hours before the others arrived home. She felt a sudden restlessness and desire to explore the house alone.

Once downstairs, she lingered for a moment in the hallway. The study door was open a crack, and she heard William's voice saying something about property and eviction, the pauses indicating he was on the telephone. She continued down the hall, passing a maid who was dusting the picture frames.

At the far end of the hall, she came upon the double doors leading to the kitchen. Her first instinct was to turn around, but she had a vivid memory of the cozy kitchen in Gloucester with its gingham curtains, the sleepy tabby cat, and the easy flow of conversation as her mother and Mrs. Groat made bread or jam. On a whim, she crossed swiftly to the doors and pushed them open. If anyone asked, she could say that she was looking for Mrs. Callahan.

The doors swung noiselessly onto the first of several rooms. It was light and bright, with a deep sink and high windows facing the back courtyard. It was empty, but there were voices coming from an adjoining room. After a moment's hesitation, she crossed to the doorway.

In the second room, a young, dark-haired maid stood at a

table kneading bread and speaking to Thomas, the gardener. He was sitting across from her and leaning back in the chair, his hands resting behind his head. A half-empty mug of tea sat on the table in front of him. He and the maid were speaking easily and comfortably in a language Catherine did not know, one that bubbled and flowed and made her think of a fountain in the sun.

It was a moment before they became aware of her presence. At the sight of her, Thomas instantly rose to his feet. The maid stopped kneading, her dimpled smile turning to wariness.

"Please, don't stop," Catherine said. "I'm sorry to interrupt you."

"May I help you?" asked Thomas.

"I . . . ," she said, then paused. She felt unsure of what to say, realizing that she wanted to stay with them and listen to them speak in the language she didn't even know. The young maid was looking at her with a sort of defensiveness, as if already on her guard. She was very pretty, Catherine noticed, with dark eyes framed by arched eyebrows.

"What language were you speaking?" she asked.

"Spanish," Thomas said. "This is Graciela, Miss Ogden," and Catherine smiled at the girl, who, after a moment, smiled back, though still wary.

"I've never heard it before," she said. "It's beautiful."

Graciela's eyes widened in surprise. Thomas smiled, a brief and polite smile.

"Thank you for saying so," he said quietly. Something in his tone made her uncomfortable; she had not intended to imply that the language needed her approval.

There was a pause, and Catherine realized they were waiting for her to speak. "I was looking for Mrs. Callahan."

"She's in the kitchen garden," said Thomas. "Shall I fetch her for you?"

"That's not necessary. I'll go myself." Graciela had started to knead the bread again, and the sight of it made Catherine feel another wave of nostalgia. It occurred to her that if her mother were alive and in this house, she would feel more at home in the kitchen than anywhere else.

"I'll take you there," Thomas said. "The kitchen garden isn't easy to find."

"Thank you." Catherine turned to go back the way she had come and was stopped by Thomas's voice saying, "I'll meet you outside the front door, Miss Ogden."

She was confused for a moment, then understood; a gardener in work clothes would use the kitchen exit out to the back courtyard, not go through the house.

"Oh," she said. "Then I'll go out this way, too."

She waited as he pushed the chair under the table and said to Graciela, "Thank you for the tea. And the conversation."

The maid smiled at him, with a brief flash of dimples. "You're welcome. Come back tomorrow for more."

The door closed gently behind Catherine and Thomas as they entered the graveled courtyard. The sun was as warm as it had appeared to be from the upstairs landing. Her aunt would have insisted on a hat or a parasol.

Thomas led her through the courtyard door into the garden, its lawn dipping down and running in perfect lushness to the garden house. They took the path that led past the reflecting pool with its tall cypresses, walking in silence, the chatter of the birds distinctly audible over the light crunch of their footsteps on the gravel.

Catherine found it strange to have a man other than William at her side. She realized that over the past weeks, she had learned to define herself in relation to him and his solid presence. Walking next to Thomas felt markedly different; there was a looseness and ease to him, as if strolling through the garden was his natural state. She stood back as he opened a gate for her, and she noticed his forearms, visible because of his rolled sleeves, the hair on them golden in the sun.

"How do you know Spanish?" she asked.

"My mother's family is Mexican. I grew up speaking both Spanish and English."

"And your father?"

"He's Irish," he said. "Was," he added quickly.

"Was?"

"He died a few weeks ago."

"I'm so sorry." The memory of her own crippling grief eleven years earlier made her want to say more than those inadequate words, so after a moment she added, "That must be so hard for you and your mother."

"My mother died when I was seventeen," he said. "But yes, it is difficult."

They came upon a bed of new tulips, the orange flowers vivid on their green stalks, and she stopped and Thomas stopped, too. She gently touched the nearest flower, thinking of her father's painted garden. There had been orange tulips there, as well as purple, yellow, and red. He'd even tucked in a blue one, saying it was a shortcoming in nature that there were no blue tulips, so why not invent one?

"I lost my parents, too," she said. "When I was eight years old."

Thomas looked directly at her, for the first time on the walk. "Then it was worse for you than for me," he said after a moment. "I had my parents longer than you did."

The tulips swayed in the light breeze, as if offering assent. "My father was an artist," she found herself saying. "He painted a garden on my wall. It had tulips and roses and all kinds of flowers. The garden here reminds me of him." She had an image of her father smiling at her over his shoulder and telling her to choose the color of the next flower. She saw his sandy hair extending beyond his frayed collar, his long fingers holding the brush, the forward tilt of his body as he made a bare wall come alive for his little girl. For a moment she glanced away, surprised to be blinking back tears.

When she looked back, Thomas was still watching her. His blue gaze was steady and different than it had been in the kitchen. Some instinct deep within her made her want to turn toward him, as a flower turns toward the light.

But instead, she took a step back and smiled, a brisk and dismissive smile. "You have done a beautiful job here," she said in the tone her aunt would use.

It worked, her sudden retreat into rank, for he looked away. "My father planted it," he said. "I'm just maintaining it." He lifted his hand to indicate the way down the path, and they walked in silence until they came upon the wall to the kitchen garden. Through its arched doorway, she could see Mrs. Callahan, a long basket on her arm. At the sight of Catherine and Thomas, she put the basket down and started toward them.

"And we've found her," Thomas said. "Good afternoon, Miss Ogden." He left the way he had come, leaving Catherine to invent some urgent reason to speak to the housekeeper.

THIRTEEN

*T*he following evening, Catherine sat at the vanity table while her aunt's maid deftly arranged her hair in a pompadour. A knock at the door pulled her out of her reverie; it was Abigail, dressed for dinner in a gray chiffon dress with silver beading.

"You're still not ready? Henry and Ethel have already gone downstairs."

"I'll be dressed soon."

Abigail walked around the room, pausing at the windows. "These are beautiful views," she said. "He gave you the nicest room, I believe."

"It is lovely."

The maid put the last pin in Catherine's hair, then reached for her green gown. "Mary," said Abigail, "return in ten minutes and finish then."

"Yes, ma'am," said Mary.

Catherine waited until the door closed. "What is it, Aunt?"

"Come here." She indicated the armchair by the window. "I want to talk to you."

Catherine sat down. Her aunt settled into the chair opposite, hands folded in her lap.

"How do you feel about William?" she asked.

Catherine reached for the drapes, playing with the fabric. "He's an excellent host."

"And?"

"And he has impeccable taste," Catherine said. "His home is beautiful."

"It could be yours one day."

"Yes. I know."

Her aunt got up and walked toward the vanity table, then turned back. "I think you should know that before we left New York, he asked your uncle for your hand in marriage. You should expect a proposal before we return home."

Catherine continued to pleat the fabric of the drapes. "Stop that," said her aunt sharply. She was more tense than Catherine had ever seen her before. "When he asks you, what will you say?"

"I don't know yet, Aunt," Catherine said slowly. "I can't help feeling that something is missing that should be there."

"What is missing? He's handsome and charming. He is well respected and successful."

"I know."

"Then what is it?"

A feeling of safety, Catherine thought. She was not sure exactly what that meant, but with him some part of her was always on her guard.

"I'm not sure I can put it into words," she said.

"Then it's not worth considering," said her aunt firmly. "Make your decision based on all the advantages of this match. You can certainly put those into words." She regarded her niece expectantly.

"I'm not sure I love him," Catherine said after a moment.

Abigail looked satisfied, and Catherine realized this particular argument was the one she had anticipated.

"You must understand, Catherine," she said in a gentler tone, "that those of us who are married have valuable insight into this subject." She sat down again. "Love doesn't always come on at once, like it does in novels. It's something that grows. It's building a life together, having children together, that leads to love. Real, enduring love, not false love."

Catherine stared at the flowers on the carpet, thinking of her parents. She had always assumed theirs had been a fairy-tale kind of love, as strong at the start as it was in the end, but was she wrong? Had it actually deepened and grown as the years passed? There was no one on earth who could tell her, a fact that made her suddenly depressed.

"And you should know," said her aunt, "that there is a great deal of freedom that comes with being a wife. You would be the lady of the house, this beautiful house. You would have a husband who is besotted with you and would let you run it as you wish." She adjusted the bracelet on her left wrist. "I remember it well, those first few days of marriage," she continued in a different tone, "when I realized I no longer had to answer to my mother's whims. I could hardly believe my good fortune."

Catherine regarded her in surprise; her aunt had never revealed anything so personal before. At her niece's expression, Abigail stood up. "So," she said, in a tone of finality, "I hope you will consider what I've said."

"I will, Aunt."

"Good. If you accept his proposal, you can be sure that love will come." She indicated the window. "And isn't this a beautiful place for it to grow?"

Catherine looked out to the sweep of the lawn, the hills, the huge tree sitting in majesty in the center of the walled garden. In the evening light, the shadows were lengthening, and the fresh, sweet smell of the garden was discernible through the open window. "It is. I've never seen a prettier one."

Her aunt smiled. "I believe you already have your answer," she said, and she opened the door for the maid.

Dinner was even more enjoyable than usual. William had invited Peter and Vivian and the Westons, a friendly couple from Menlo Park, and conversation was easy and engaging. Catherine exclaimed over the vases of lilies and daffodils on the dining room table, breathtaking in their abundance. "Those are from the garden," William said. "Mrs. Callahan likes to arrange them."

In his eyes was the same attentive confidence she had seen many times before. Her aunt was surely right that a proposal would be forthcoming, and on such an agreeable evening, she felt her usual resistance slipping away. Or perhaps that was due to the wine; it was a German wine, sweet and delicious, and it softened the edges of everything, making her somehow both more relaxed and more daring.

After dinner, the men had their cigars while the women chatted by the fireplace; then they all gathered in the music room and she played. It was becoming a habit, this post-dinner performance. She loved the feel of the smooth keys under her fingers and the warm light of the music room, creating an atmosphere in which the melodies seemed more evocative than usual. As she played, it occurred to her that she was feeling almost like the lady of the house, not a visitor. It was not an unpleasant realization.

Once the goodbyes had been said and the guests had left, Abigail yawned discreetly and Henry and Ethel rose to go upstairs. William took Catherine's hand in both of his, pressing it gently before letting it go. Lloyd gave a genial good night while pouring himself another brandy.

"It's too fine a night for me to sleep just yet," he said. "And it's also morning in Paris, where my beloved is no doubt starting her day. I'll stay awake a while and imagine her with me. Perhaps

I'll even write a letter, if my host can lend me some writing paper and stamps?"

"Far be it from me to inhibit a romance," William said. "Take whatever you want."

Lloyd grinned. "You're a good friend, William," he said.

℘

Once upstairs, Catherine moved restlessly around the room. Perhaps it was the wine, but she had no desire to sleep, sending the maid away when she came to help her undress. The air through the open window was sweet and beckoned her outside. Drawing a shawl over her evening dress, she went down the stairs, passed through the hall and reception room, and slipped quietly onto the terrace.

She heard the whisper of wind in the leaves and vines and the faint sounds of the gramophone from William's study. There was enough light to see by, so she made her way down the steps onto the croquet lawn. The white hyacinths glowed; the other flowers seemed colorless. She walked slowly among the paths, barely thinking, savoring the solitude and the dark freshness of the earth.

It was as she drew near the garden house that she first heard it, a noise that did not come from the wind in the trees. It sounded vaguely like an animal, and she paused irresolutely for a moment before continuing. As she came within a few feet of the garden house, she heard the noise again. It was followed by murmurings and the sound of a female voice, high and excited, and then a deeper, insistent voice saying something in response.

Her cheeks flamed and she stopped, half-hidden by the edge of a large camellia bush. She knew immediately that she was hearing something intimate and entirely beyond her scope of experience. It came from the corner of the garden house, from the hidden space made by the open door and the wall.

And then there was no sound at all but the rustling of cloth, and then a sudden loud exhalation of male breath, and she wanted to turn and run away. But before she could, the door creaked back and she saw the shadowy figures of Lloyd and Graciela, the kitchen maid. He was bent over her, and they were kissing in a way she had never seen two people kiss before, her arms running over his back. His own hands were busy fumbling with her skirts, lifting them up in front.

Swiftly she turned and half ran back over the gravel path, trying to move without a sound, her heart pounding.

FOURTEEN

*W*hen Catherine went down for breakfast the next morning, William was the only one at the table. "Did you have a pleasant sleep?" he asked, rising from his chair as Hayes pulled out a seat for her.

"Yes, thank you." She had in fact lain awake for hours, staring at the patch of moonlight in her room and trying to block out the vision of the two shadowy figures by the garden house door. Her first instinct, once she had returned to her room, was to share what she had seen, but whom would she tell? More to the point, what would be gained by doing so? She had no desire to expose the relationship between Lloyd and the maid; all she wanted was to reduce her own shock that so likable a man could betray his fiancée with such apparent ease. His engaging manners, which had helped make the visit so pleasant, now felt false and tainted.

"Would you like to drive down to Stanford today?" William asked, handing her the toast rack. "You said you wanted to see it before you leave on Thursday."

"I did," she said, "That is, I do. Thank you."

He smiled as if he found her absentmindedness endearing. She had a momentary flash of insight into how it would feel to be married to him, eating together in the breakfast room. Would William ever be unfaithful? She studied him covertly as he bent his head over the toast he was buttering with his customary deliberate movements.

He suddenly looked up and caught her watching him. She was embarrassed at the turn her thoughts had taken, and at her blush he smiled again, his eyes lit by a quick flicker of desire. For a moment there was silence. Lloyd would fill this pause with easy banter, she realized, and yet William did not. He never spoke just for the sake of talking or to charm those around him. In many ways, she mused, he was as different from Lloyd as a man could be. The contrast filled her with something like relief, and she looked down to arrange the napkin on her lap, glad that Hayes offered a distraction by pouring the coffee.

She had just taken a sip when the door swung open and Ethel entered laughing, followed by Lloyd, who was obviously finishing an anecdote. "So you see," he said, "I realized that I'd never win Hazel's heart through poetry, so I decided to try dancing instead. And I believe it was a certain waltz on Coronado Island that made her accept my proposal. Or perhaps she was simply too exhausted from whirling about the floor to tender a refusal."

He greeted William and Catherine warmly, but she found it hard to look at him. It was difficult to reconcile the affable morning-Lloyd with the one she had seen and heard the night before.

"I wish we were staying longer and you could teach Henry to dance," said Ethel, taking the seat Hayes held out for her. "He waltzes like a bear."

"And he could surely teach me a great deal about being a lawyer," Lloyd said diplomatically, unfolding his napkin. "Your husband is obviously a most effective orator. It's a talent I lack, sadly. My path in life would be so much smoother if I had the skill of speaking persuasively." He reached for the toast, offering some to Ethel before taking his own.

"Don't believe him, Ethel," said William as he put down his coffee cup. "My friend here has always been very good at getting exactly what he wants." It was so close to what Catherine had been thinking that she felt as if William had read her mind. He was looking at Lloyd, amusement in his eyes.

"And perhaps it's time to change the subject," Lloyd said genially, helping himself to a liberal spoonful of jam.

⁊ↄ

At ten thirty that night, Catherine sat alone by the open bedroom window. The evening was cool, and she wrapped her dressing gown more closely around her, but she made no move to shut out the night air. The fragrance of the California countryside, earthy and fresh, was a scent she would miss when she left. That was the first bead on her rosary as she reviewed the day—the clean, living smell of the present moment.

She admired the stars spread out against the dark canvas of the sky, and her fingers moved to the next bead. In New York one could forget the stars even existed, but here they asserted their presence quietly each night. She had even seen a shooting star, something she'd read about but had never before witnessed.

Her fingers continued to move over the beads as she reviewed the impressions of the day. Stanford University had been fascinating, with its Romanesque buildings and red tile roofs, its campus landscaped with palms and pungent eucalyptus trees. Even more intriguing were the numerous young women holding books under their arms and talking with the men. Seeing them, Catherine had felt a stab of envy. College had never been an option for her; when she turned eighteen and had raised it as a possibility, her aunt had looked surprised. "You have no need to prepare for a career," she'd said.

"I know," Catherine had responded, "but I'd love to learn more. About art, and books, and the world."

Abigail had resumed her needlepoint. "We have a library here, and art museums just a few blocks away." It was a tone Catherine knew well, one indicating there was no need for further discussion.

Sitting with the rosary in her hand, she paused at the memory of the young women with their books. She would never be a college student; she had accepted that. What, then, would satisfy the ache in her to do more, to know more?

In two days, she would be getting back on the train for New York. She would return to the narrow house on Madison Avenue, to her old room with the maroon wallpaper, to a life of surreptitiously opening the drapes while she played piano and closing them when she was done. She would return to see Lavinia married and moving on. She would return to a life that could not sustain the little seeds of discovery that California had dropped into the deepest part of her soul.

But she could return to New York knowing she would come back again to Oakview. The choice was hers. All it would take was one word, three letters long, the answer to a question she knew was soon to come. Marriage to William would make her family happy, that was certain; could she trust that it would make her happy, as well?

Angling herself, she looked at the Tree of Knowledge. From her high perch, she could see its gray crown, ghostly but solid. She thought of the branches reaching up then out, frozen in attitudes of longing.

She wound the string of beads tightly around her hand and, closing her eyes, willed herself to decide.

FIFTEEN

*B*efore dinner the next evening, having told her aunt where she was going, Catherine walked out to the giant oak. She sat down on the marble bench which, in spite of the sun that had shone all day, felt cool through the layers of her green evening dress.

She had her answer. Now she awaited the question that would make it final.

It did not take long. Fifteen minutes later she heard footsteps on the gravel path, and William appeared, the white shirtfront of his evening suit aggressively stark in the dusk. He greeted her and sat down beside her on the bench. Although she moved to make space for him, he took more room than she had expected, and they sat close together, their legs touching. It was a kind of contact they had never shared before, and she felt her pulse quicken at the feel of his thigh against hers. She fixed her attention on the view before her, trying to slow down the rapid beat of her heart.

"It's a beautiful evening," he said finally.

"It is."

"You seem to like it here. This house and garden. California."

"I do. Very much."

The slight breeze rustled the branches above them, and she drew her silk shawl a bit more closely around her shoulders.

"Catherine."

She faced him. He took her hands and as he did so the shawl

slipped from her shoulders, and he picked it up and draped it again slowly. His covering of her body felt almost as intimate as uncovering it would be, yet he gave no hint of being flustered. She wondered if anything would ever make him lose the calm command with which he did everything.

"I know you are aware of my feelings for you," he said. "From the first moment we met, I knew I would never meet another woman like you. I love you, your grace, and your beauty. I would be honored beyond words to have you as my wife."

He reached into his coat pocket, took out a small box, and opened it. The ring was a large and beautiful sapphire, set with diamonds on a gold band. He held it before her, waiting for her to speak.

In his eyes she saw confidence, desire, but no fear. He knew she would say yes; he had probably known it longer than she had. And if she still felt a tinge of doubt, it was only a tiny flicker, one she could extinguish by reminding herself of what would be gained by the marriage: new advantages for her family, yes, but also a new life for herself in a place she had come to love. "Base your decision on the things you can put into words," her aunt had said.

But first, she had to be completely honest.

"I am very honored, William," she said. "But I respect you too much not to tell you something."

The look in his eyes changed perceptibly, the easy confidence shifting to steel. She had the feeling she was saying it all wrong, and the next words came out in a rush. "I would be honored to accept you, but I don't love you. Yet."

He smiled, and the hard look disappeared, so quickly she almost doubted she had even seen it. "Your honesty does you credit. Most girls would never have admitted that." He took her left hand, brushing the ring finger with his thumb. "I'm not worried. Am I right in believing that you respect me and like me?"

"Yes," she said truthfully.

"Then I'm content," he said. "I have faith that love will come in time."

There was nothing more to do but say the words she had decided to say. "Then, yes, William, I will marry you."

He drew her to him and kissed her. She had never been kissed before, and at first she was distracted by the novelty and the import of the moment; then it passed and she became conscious of the pleasing warmth of his mouth. After the kiss he drew back and looked at her, assessing her reaction before leaning in and kissing her again, this time with more intensity. She was not expecting it and stiffened slightly, and he let her go with a smile. "All in good time," he said softly.

He slipped the ring on her finger, and a single bird sang in the distance as she held her hand up to the last of the light. She thought suddenly of Jane Eyre and Rochester and their proposal in the garden, the summer evening giving way to wind and thunder. But the air at Oakview smelled just as sweet as it had before, and the breeze was gentle in the branches above as they got up and walked down the path to the house. "This will be your garden, and your house," he said, and she smiled up at him and said, "That will be lovely."

Later that evening, after the joyful congratulations from the company and the spontaneous embrace from her aunt and the rare smile from Hayes and the bottles of champagne ordered from the cellar by William, she climbed into bed and gazed at the moonlight shining on the floor. She found the rosary under her pillow and started to review the moments of her day, but she could not move beyond the proposal on the bench in the twilight. "I don't love you," she had told William, and he had smiled and said not to worry. He meant to marry her anyhow, in spite of that.

It shows his generosity and understanding, said a voice inside her. *You should be comforted that he did not mind.*

No, said another voice. *You should be concerned that he did not mind.*

She held the first bead tightly in her fingers, staring at the moonlight and listening to the brush of leaves outside her window, until at last she fell asleep.

PART
TWO

SIXTEEN

"All this," Lavinia said, making a sweeping gesture toward the table spread with wedding gifts. "Can you believe all this has arrived in just the last week?" She made a slow circuit around the table, its surface covered with silver teapots, plated serving utensils, gleaming china, and a framed oil painting of a bouquet of roses. "I'll be writing thank-you notes for the rest of the year."

"You and Clarence have everything you need," Catherine said. She fanned herself with the notebook she was holding; it was a stifling day in the city.

Lavinia grinned. "Including," she said, "this little fellow." She pointed to a small statuette of a gargoyle sitting on his haunches, his wings folded and his mouth open. "Courtesy of my great-aunt Beatrice, the one who lives in France. I think she's making a statement about my marriage."

Catherine laughed. "Does she mean it as a warning?"

"It wouldn't surprise me," Lavinia said. "She's the one who married that English viscount and then left him, went off to live in Paris. They said there was another man involved. Old family scandal, don't you know. My grandmother did her best to bury it, but I finally heard the whole story last week."

The door opened and Clarence entered, a newspaper tucked under his arm. He greeted both girls, then went quickly to Lavinia and kissed her cheek. "Hello, future Mrs. Perry," he said.

"Hello, future Mr. Lavinia," she countered, pulling him down for a kiss on the lips. "Come take a look at the spoils."

"Good God," he said, lifting the gargoyle. "When did this arrive?"

"Just today. It's from Great-Aunt Beatrice."

"Well, it's better than another chafing dish." Clarence viewed the statuette from every angle. "Ugly little fellow, isn't he?"

"Be kind," said Lavinia. "We can't all be as handsome as you."

Clarence put down the gargoyle, regarded the laden table, and shook his head slightly. "This is really happening, isn't it." He put his arms around Lavinia while Catherine moved discreetly away, pretending to make an entry in the notebook. "All this china, when the only thing I want is you," he said, resting his chin on Lavinia's head.

Catherine lifted up a vase and then set it down, distracted. It seemed unreal that within three months' time, she'd be cataloging gifts of her own. The wedding had been set for September 3, which William had assured them was the nicest time of year on the Peninsula. "There's golden sunlight, hardly any fog," he said. "It's even more pleasant than summer."

At first, Abigail had strenuously objected to the idea of having the wedding at Oakview. "All of our friends and family are in the East," she had insisted, and Catherine knew she was thinking not just of them but of the entire network of New York elite. This wedding would be the event of the year; Abigail wanted as large an audience as possible.

William, however, had assured them he was prepared to welcome everyone who mattered to the Ogdens. "The Peninsula Hotel caters to society," he said, "and will be reserved in its entirety for all guests from out of town." He made the offhand remark that pictures of the wedding and reception would be in papers all over the country, and Catherine sensed her aunt making the mental calculation that the splendor of Oakview, even if seen only in black-and-white newsprint, would be a more impressive backdrop than anything in New York. And with Henry's vocal enthusiasm for William's plan, her aunt was convinced.

"Thanks for helping with this pirate's treasure, Catherine," said Clarence, recalling her to the present. "And if you took that gargoyle home with you, you'd be doing us a favor."

Catherine laughed. "It's hard to picture him at Oakview."

"Have fun at your club." Lavinia straightened her fiancé's tie with a proprietary gesture. "See you tomorrow."

He grinned. "Don't talk about me too much while I'm gone."

"You? Never."

Clarence gave Lavinia one more kiss on the lips, smiled a little bashfully at Catherine, and left.

"Just think," Catherine said after the door had closed. "This time next week, you'll be married."

Lavinia sighed, her face simultaneously blissful and impish. "And it's about time, too." She fanned herself. "My goodness, it's hot. Let's hope that changes, or I'll be the first melting bride New York has ever seen." Moving along the table, she trailed her hand lightly over the gifts, then paused by the gargoyle. "Poor Aunt Beatrice. I wonder if she started out as happy as I am, before it all went wrong."

"Surely not," said Catherine. "Her husband must have done something terrible to drive her away like that."

"I could ask Mother," Lavinia said. "It's funny; she never used to tell me anything. Being engaged changes so much. It's like they suddenly trust you with things they would never have told you before." She looked at the clock on the mantelpiece. "Are you hungry? Maybe we can have an early lunch."

Catherine put down the notebook. "Sounds wonderful."

"Good." Lavinia smiled daringly. "And while we eat, I'll tell you all the details of the Stanford White murder trial. Mother actually told me the whole story yesterday."

"She did?" Catherine was incredulous. Four years earlier, the murder, involving one of New York's prominent architects and the husband of a beautiful chorus girl, had been a scandal that rocked the city, but the precise details had been strenuously kept from the two curious girls.

"It was far more sordid than we suspected, believe me," said Lavinia. "Just another thing Mother now trusts me to know."

§

When Catherine returned to the brownstone on Madison Avenue, she overheard voices raised in disagreement in the dining room. That was unusual; her aunt believed in keeping all conflict below the surface. Catherine handed her hat and coat to Minnie, one of the maids, her eyebrows lifted in a question.

"I don't know what it's about, miss," said Minnie, "only that they've been talking that way for the last half hour. They haven't let any of us in to clear the lunch dishes."

Catherine opened the door to the dining room. Her uncle sat in his usual place at the end of the table, her aunt to his right. Henry, hands in pockets, was pacing the length of the room. At her entrance he stopped and whirled to face her. "Catherine," he said, as if unsure whether her presence was welcome.

"Is something wrong?"

Abigail looked up at Oliver, who in turn looked at Henry. He pulled out a chair and Catherine sat down, waiting.

Her uncle spoke first. "I've received a letter from Mr. Brandt, with a rather unexpected request. He would like you to come to Oakview for the summer. After Lavinia's wedding. You would leave here in two weeks' time and stay there until your own wedding."

This was a surprise. Catherine looked swiftly at her aunt, whose chin was tilted in resistance.

"It's unheard of," she said. "You can't live in the same house as your fiancé."

"Mother," said Henry, "we've been over this."

"No," said her aunt. "I may be old-fashioned, Henry, and hopelessly behind the times. But there is such a thing as propriety."

"She would not be there alone." Henry's voice had an audible tinge of exasperation. "William's sister would be there to chaperone; he made that very clear. A mature woman, with a child of her own. There's nothing scandalous about it. And he invited us to come as well, don't forget."

"But we can't," said Abigail, "so it's irrelevant, isn't it?"

"You can't?" asked Catherine.

"Your uncle and Henry can't leave the office for that long," said her aunt. "And I've committed to hosting the summer charity concert in Newport. You know that. Ethel, naturally, wouldn't think of going without Henry."

Catherine nodded, trying to appear regretful, but her mind was racing. A summer at Oakview meant long sunny days in the garden, twilight on the lawn, roses in bloom. It was an intoxicating prospect.

"Mr. Brandt," said her uncle, "would like you to become familiar with California society as soon as possible. As his wife you will be involved in many local events. The sooner you can start that, the better."

"And of course, he misses your company," said Henry. He smiled. "I couldn't keep myself away from Ethel when we were engaged."

Catherine played with a napkin on the table, pleating it and staring at the folds but seeing instead the Tree of Knowledge, the walled gardens, and the green of the hills.

"You're acting as if this is a perfectly normal request." Her aunt's tone added more heat to the stifling room. Henry opened his mouth to speak, but she silenced him with a gesture. "Under the same roof as her fiancé. I don't understand how you can possibly be so cavalier about this."

"Cavalier?" Henry gripped the back of a chair with both hands. "Give us some credit, Mother. They will be chaperoned. And surely you trust Catherine to know how to behave. Have some trust in her morals and in your own influence. You have taught her well."

Abigail turned to her niece then looked swiftly away, but in that one unguarded moment Catherine understood. Her aunt was thinking not of the world of Madison Avenue but of the gabled apartment in Gloucester, of the brother-in-law who defied society and married beneath him, of the wife who raised her daughter to go barefoot and speak her own thoughts. In California, away from her own influence, what would happen?

Surprisingly, it made her feel a sudden sympathy for her aunt.

"Aunt Abigail," she said, "I would like to go. William is right. If my life will be lived there, it might as well begin as soon as possible. And I know what kind of behavior is proper. I won't forget that."

It was silent in the room, so silent she heard the strains of a hurdy-gurdy man playing "Sidewalks of New York" on the street outside. A yellow petal fell from one of the roses in the centerpiece, landing noiselessly on the tablecloth.

After a moment, Henry went to his mother and put his hand lightly on her shoulder. "You see?"

Abigail turned to her husband. "What do you say, Oliver?" she asked, and Catherine could tell from her tone that she was wavering.

Oliver smiled gently and put his hand over his wife's. "I believe Catherine is right," he said. "I think she is ready to go."

For a moment, no one moved or spoke. They all looked at Abigail, sitting tall in her lavender high-collared dress, the gray hair around her temples noticeably damp with the heat.

"Very well," she said. Her chin was up, her jaw resolute. "Very well. She may go. But I will tell everyone here that Mr. Brandt will be living in his San Francisco apartment all summer, not at Oakview." She rose from the chair. "And I hope you will do the same."

Catherine nodded, willing her expression to remain grave. Only with great effort did she keep her delight hidden until Henry and her aunt, the latter in regal disapproval, had disappeared through the door. Then she turned to her uncle, her face radiant. He smiled, too, in affection and relief.

"I'm glad she finally gave in," he said, taking out his handkerchief and wiping his face. "I would not have liked to say no to Mr. Brandt."

SEVENTEEN

*T*he days passed in a blur. Abigail scheduled appointments for the wedding dress, which would be made in New York then sent to Oakview, where final fittings would be done by a society seamstress recommended by Harriet. There was the buying of the trousseau, an assortment of stockings and underclothes finer than any Catherine had ever had. The long pink negligee trimmed with lace was the kind of garment only a married woman would possess; it was a sign of her impending rite of passage.

Catherine packed her clothes, books, and knickknacks. It was a much easier process than she had expected. Looking about the bedroom in which she had spent eleven years, she realized how much of it was actually the property of her aunt and uncle. It was exciting to think that at Oakview, she would have the opportunity to create a life that was more fully her own.

One afternoon as she carefully crated her books, she stopped and picked up the black rosary. She cupped it in the palm of her hand, the beads clicking lightly against one another.

She had stopped doing her bedtime ritual the day she had left Oakview. Though it had been an essential part of her childhood, it seemed somehow at odds with her new identity as an engaged woman. *I will hardly be able to do it once I'm married,* she had told herself, heat rising to her face at the thought of sharing a bed with William, *so I might as well stop now.* And with the whirl of shopping, packing, and assisting with preparations for Lavinia's wedding, most nights she had been too distracted to miss it.

But she still felt a visceral loyalty to the rosary itself. As a stricken child, it had helped her see what was still good in a world that had caved in on her. She thought of the moment when her mother had pressed the beads into her hand. "When you are lonely," her mother had said, "take it out and hold it."

Catherine crossed the room to her jewelry box and tucked the rosary inside. She had no intention of restarting the old ritual, but the rosary itself—that tangible, precious link to her past— was something she would keep forever.

⁊○

Fortunately for Lavinia and Clarence, the heat wave ended. The day of the wedding was perfect, May at its most radiant.

Lavinia, for once, was almost grave as she processed up the aisle in her white dress and veil. Only Catherine caught the wink she gave Clarence as they took their places in front of the minister. Clarence flashed her a quick grin, and as they stood side by side the excitement between them was nearly palpable. They would be happy together; there was no doubt of that.

As the ceremony went on, Catherine's thoughts drifted into the future. What would it be like, the day of her own wedding? Sometimes her engagement still felt more like a dream than a reality. This was not William's fault, for he was attentive even at a distance. He regularly sent her flowers, and the week before she had received from him a beautifully illustrated edition of *Ramona*, which she had once mentioned she had never read. Still, it was difficult to feel close to him when he was on the other side of the country. It was good that she was going to California for the summer, she thought. There would be time for her and William to grow into a couple before the wedding and also—she looked up just as Lavinia and Clarence moved eagerly together for the kiss—time for her to fall in love.

⁊○

As Catherine had expected, George Langley was among the many guests. She was keenly aware of his presence throughout the morning, but it was not until the end of the reception that he came up to her. "Catherine," he said guardedly. "You are looking lovely."

"Thank you. It's good to see you."

He twirled the stem of his glass between his fingers. "I hear you are engaged to William Brandt," he said. "Congratulations. You must be very happy."

The words were absolutely correct, but his tone irked her. There was an implied judgment in his voice, as if her alliance to the richest man available proved her to be a different woman than he had believed. But George had been aware of her feelings for him and had been too weak to fight for her. William, by contrast, had done everything he could to win her hand.

"Thank you," she said, lifting her chin. "I am very happy."

"Catherine." Mrs. Boscat suddenly broke upon them in a cloud of rose scent. "Lavinia would like to see you upstairs."

Catherine was grateful for an excuse to leave. "I hope you enjoy the rest of your stay," she said to George in the tone her aunt would have used. Having thus dismissed him, she hurried up the staircase.

Lavinia, in her bedroom, had changed into her pale-blue going-away suit. "Next stop, Philadelphia," she said joyfully. She and Clarence were going to Pennsylvania to visit his invalid grandmother before returning to New York and then sailing for England.

"I'm going to miss you so much," Catherine said, feeling a tightening in her throat. Lavinia, with the wedding ring on her finger and the new picture hat and the excited gleam in her eye, seemed like a different person.

"I'll miss you, too." Lavinia grabbed Catherine's hand and squeezed it. "I will write, I promise."

"And I'll save you the best room at Oakview when you come for the wedding."

"I'm counting on it," said Lavinia. "For goodness' sake, don't give it to Ethel." She turned back to the mirror, her eyes wide, as if seeing herself for the first time. "So this is what being married is like."

"Good, I hope."

Lavinia grinned. "Wonderful."

The two girls embraced tightly, and Catherine fumbled for a handkerchief. "Stop that," said Lavinia, "or you'll make me cry, too." She indicated the two of them in the mirror. "Look at us. You'd think I'm going to the guillotine or something."

Catherine laughed. "Not at all," she said; then she repeated the words Lavinia's mother had said the day before: "This isn't an end but a beginning." She was not sure she believed it, but the words were comforting.

"Right you are," said Lavinia, her face radiant. She picked up her gloves. "And Mrs. Perry is ready to begin."

EIGHTEEN

*C*atherine was glad she did not have long to wait before returning to California. New York was strange with Lavinia gone, and the final preparations for the trip made her feel as if she were in a limbo between two worlds. The feeling of unreality was heightened when she saw the newspaper article about Lavinia's wedding. Almost as large as the picture of the bride and groom was a photo of Catherine herself, next to one of William. "Date Set for Maid of Honor to Wed William Brandt," the caption read.

Henry was visibly pleased. "Another mention of your engagement. Even the king of England doesn't receive this much press."

"I'm not sure why people care so much," she said. It was a flattering photograph, but the publicity made her uncomfortable.

Henry folded the paper carefully. "Because you and William have everything that people want," he said with uncharacteristic bluntness. "Wealth and beauty. They can live through you."

⁋

Two nights before her departure, Catherine was passing her uncle's study when he opened the door. "Catherine," he said. "Can you spare a moment?"

"Of course, Uncle Oliver."

It felt odd to enter the study, a room in which she'd spent

very little time over the years. There were bookshelves, a large carved desk, two leather club chairs in front of a marble fireplace, and a side table with decanters and glasses.

"Have a seat, my dear," her uncle said, and she took one of the chairs. He sat in the other one, sinking into it easily, and she realized this room was the place where he felt most at home.

"As we get ready to say goodbye," he said, "I realize I've not been the most attentive uncle. So much of these past eleven years, I've passed you on to my wife. And she, I suppose, has passed you on to other people."

"Please, Uncle Oliver," said Catherine. "You've been so kind, taking me in and raising me."

He smiled with a furrowed brow, as if acknowledging her generosity but not letting it sway him from his own contrition. "All the same, as you are about to leave us, I feel . . ." He cleared his throat. She waited.

"There are some things I'd like you to know about your parents," he said finally, and her heart began to beat faster. "You've probably had questions, all these years, that you haven't been able to ask."

"Yes," she said, leaning forward.

"I have no idea what your parents told you about themselves. Do you know about how they met and why your father ended all contact with the family?"

"No. I know almost nothing."

He nodded. "I'll start at the beginning, then." He poured himself a small measure of brandy from the decanter by the table and then settled back into the chair.

"Your father was twelve years younger than I, a late-in-life surprise for my parents. And he was raised, as I was, with the expectation that he'd go into the family business. He studied the law, even though he obviously preferred art. He'd spend every spare moment sketching or painting. He was always happiest in front of a canvas."

Tears came to Catherine's eyes, and her uncle smiled affectionately. "You knew that much, of course."

"Yes."

"We assumed he'd have the life Father expected, that we all expected. The painting could be a hobby, but he'd become a partner for Ogden and Mills and marry the right kind of woman and have a summer house in Newport and all the rest. Your father never intended to live that kind of life. He actually had something like hatred for the legal profession. But our father, your grandfather, was a man you didn't challenge, so Arthur played along." Uncle Oliver glanced briefly at the portrait of his father above the fireplace: a man with sandy sideburns, a high forehead, and a piercing gaze. "Then he met your mother. And at that point, he stopped pretending."

Catherine's heart pounded in her ears. "How did he meet her?"

He looked at her with a smile that she could not read. "Your mother, as you no doubt know, was Irish," he said. "She came over as a child. From the time she was a young woman, she worked as a maid."

"Did she work here? In this house?"

Oliver shifted in his seat. "No," he said. "Before she ever met your father, she left service and became an artist's model." He cleared his throat. "You . . . are aware of what that means?"

A vague memory tugged at Catherine, a conversation with her mother in the kitchen at Mrs. Groat's house. "You mean that they painted her without . . ." She could not say the rest out loud to her uncle. He nodded.

"That's how your father met her, at the art school where she modeled. He fell in love. Head over heels, as they say."

Catherine was silent, processing the news. She knew she should be shocked to learn that her mother had let strangers paint her naked body, and yet other than an awkwardness in discussing such a thing with her uncle, she was not. A shared love of art was central to her understanding of her parents; the manner of their meeting was almost comforting, as if confirming that her memories of them were correct. She hungered for details that could help her understand the parents whom she had now spent more years living without than with.

Oliver misread her silence. "I don't want to give you the wrong impression of your mother, my dear," he said. "I know there are those who think that women who model are . . . well, not moral, or perhaps free with their attentions to men. Your father insisted it was not true of her. I was skeptical at first; of course a man in love would say that. And I assumed your mother was just telling your father what he wanted to hear because she wanted his money. But I was wrong. She loved your father as much as he loved her.

"Your grandfather found out about her and was livid. He tried to force your father to give up your mother, threatening disinheritance, but your father refused. Your mother did, too. It was the first time I met her; your father brought her home and we all stood here, in this very room. I expected her to be a loose and vulgar woman, but she was not. She had a strong sense of who she was, and money did not matter to her. Your father mattered to her." He paused for a moment, then said quietly and without self-pity, "I was actually a bit jealous of my brother. Not just because of her beauty but because she would fight so hard to be with the man she loved."

Catherine reached for her handkerchief. Her uncle smiled sympathetically. "I hope I'm doing the right thing in telling you this."

"You are," she said. "I know so little."

The clock on the mantel struck the half hour. It occurred to her that it was the first time she could remember hearing the clock in her uncle's study, and that it would probably be the last. She felt a pang at the time wasted, time she could have spent getting to know this surprisingly wistful man who had once been so close to her father. For eleven years she had followed her aunt's admonition not to speak of the past, never knowing her uncle would gladly have talked about it if she'd asked. Or perhaps he was only doing so now that she was marrying and moving away. "They treat you differently when you are engaged," Lavinia had said.

"Why did my father dislike the law so much?" she asked.

Her uncle grimaced slightly. "It's not a story that reflects well on my father, or on me. But before your father met your mother, we were representing a wealthy client. I won't go into the details, but our defense involved exposing some rather personal and humiliating facts about the man who was accusing him." He swirled the drink in his glass. "I didn't think we should share those things. They were not crimes, just intimate details no man would want trotted out for public view. But Father was ruthless, and so we used every weapon we had to discredit the plaintiff. We won the case, but the man whom we had humiliated was devastated and later shot himself. Your father was disgusted, said that if this was the law, he wanted no part of it."

Oliver looked again at the portrait of Rufus Ogden. "Father was an excellent lawyer," he said. "Sometimes that means sacrificing one's compassionate side. I'm afraid I was a bit of a disappointment to him in that regard." He put down the glass. "It's a shame he didn't live long enough to see Henry in the courtroom."

"Did you ever see my father again, after he left?"

"No," said Oliver. "I missed him very much, but I was comforted by the fact that he had a wife he loved, and who loved him. Your parents were poor, I know, but they lived life on their own terms. And I believe you would say that they were happy."

"They were." Catherine gazed into the fire, watching the flames, remembering the peace and harmony of that small apartment by the sea.

"Uncle Oliver," she said, "do you think we will ever find out what happened to my mother?"

He looked at her, his eyes gentle. "I did try," he said quietly. "I made inquiries a few months after you came to us, my dear. There was a woman found dead by the river in Boston, never identified. The coroner's description matched the description of your mother. She had already been buried by the time I made my inquiry." He gave a small shrug. "I have no proof it was her, of course. But even if it was not . . . well, Catherine, I believe you must accept what we have all understood to be true these last eleven years."

Her tears fell, and he got up and put his hand on her head, as he had when she was a child.

"I know how much she loved you," he said quietly. "The love she had for your father, she had for you. I hope you have always felt that love, even in your loss."

As she wiped her eyes, her uncle walked over to his desk. "I shouldn't keep you, as I know tomorrow is a busy day. But before you leave, there's something I've been saving for you." He opened a drawer, took out a paper, and brought it to Catherine. She unfolded it wordlessly.

It was a pencil sketch of her mother, from the waist up. Her bare back was to the artist, and her chin was angled over her left shoulder, her face tilted toward the viewer. Her hair was up, casually, many strands loose. There was a smile on her lips and a crinkle in the corner of her eye. It was the look Catherine had seen her mother give her father countless times, and seeing it again on paper was like unlocking a room full of memories that were all at once painful and sweet. She couldn't speak.

"I found this in one of your father's books. He left most of his things behind when he got married. He had probably done so many of her that he forgot this one was even here." Oliver smiled. "Which was lucky for you, I suppose."

A tear fell on the drawing and she wiped it away quickly. "Thank you for keeping it."

"You are very welcome," he said sincerely, and she was grateful she had at last seen this side of her uncle: a man who loved his younger brother, admired his brother's strong and spirited wife, and wished, on some quiet level he had never articulated to anyone else, that his own life had been lived differently.

He bent over and kissed her on the forehead. "I wish you great happiness," he said formally. She stood up and put her arms around him, her emotions too full to express in words.

"One more thing," he said as she prepared to leave. "Your fiancé. I've told him you are an orphan, but he knows little else about your parents. If he knew that your mother was a maid and a model, he might find it . . . objectionable."

She looked down at her mother's bare back, the curve of her shoulder. "I'll keep this to myself."

"That would be wise, I think," he said quietly.

As she walked to the door, she stopped. "Uncle Oliver," she said, facing him. "Do you remember which book you found this in?"

"I do indeed," he said. His smile was a hint that she would be pleased by the answer. "*The Sonnets of Shakespeare.*"

NINETEEN

The landscape took Catherine by surprise. "It's gold!" she exclaimed, craning her neck to look out of William's car. The lush green hills that had greeted her on her first visit to California were now covered with tawny grass waving lightly in the breeze.

"The hills always turn this color in summer," said William, who was sitting next to her in the back seat. "The rainy season is over now. Nothing to keep the grass green."

"When will it be green again?"

"February, maybe."

"It won't rain at all during the summer?"

"It never does."

Catherine stared at the slopes as they motored past, absorbing the change. The California in her memory had been green and pastoral, like an English landscape. These ochre hills with their gray-green oak trees presented an entirely different aspect. The aridity was somehow unsettling, though she had to concede that there was a certain beauty to the light-brown hills curving against the hard blue bowl of the sky. It was no longer gentle, but it was striking and compelled the eye.

William took her hand. "It's good to have you back."

She pulled her attention away from the landscape and smiled at him. "It's good to be back," she said self-consciously, aware of the chauffeur in the front seat.

"Harriet is so pleased you've come for the summer. She loves having people around. My visits to the city make Oakview rather dull for her, at times."

"Do you often go to the city?"

"My office is there, so I go in a few times a week. Occasionally I stay overnight for appointments." He looked at her with his dark, leisurely gaze. "But you will have plenty of ways to entertain yourself. Vivian is around this summer, and you'll get to know the other neighbors as well. It won't take long for you to become accustomed to life here."

"I suppose I should start with the hills," she said. "They're so different from how they were in the spring. I wasn't expecting it at all."

"You make it sound as though I proposed under false pretenses," William said. She could not tell from his tone whether he was joking, but she saw the hint of a smile in the corners of his mouth. She decided a light response was the right one.

"As long as the garden looks the same," she said playfully, "I shall not mind the hills."

⁊○

Her reunion with the garden had to wait. First there was the formal welcome from Hayes and the effusive welcome from Harriet, then a restorative lemonade on the porch overlooking the lawn, and finally the supervision of her things carried up to the same corner bedroom as before.

"We've put you in here again for the summer," said Harriet. "William is in our father's old suite, which connects with the rooms that were my mother's. You'll move there after the wedding, of course."

"Of course," said Catherine, turning quickly to smell the

roses in the vase by the bed. They were white with a hint of pink and divinely fragrant.

"Shall I iron this dress for dinner, miss?" asked the new ladies' maid, holding up the green gown. Her name was Agnes, and she was a rail-thin woman with a pleasant face and light-brown hair. Her efficiency was impressive; she had already unpacked half of Catherine's trunk and arranged her toilet articles on the vanity table. Harriet had hired her after, Catherine was informed, extensive vetting. ("Many maids think they want to work here, but then they find it is too remote after working in San Francisco.")

"Thank you, yes," said Catherine. "You are so quick."

Agnes gave a brief, professional smile. "I do my best, Miss Ogden," she said, picking up the gown and taking it out of the room.

"She's a very hard worker," said Harriet. "I often find that girls with brown hair are more serious in their purpose than the blondes, don't you?" She seemed not to expect a response to this observation, which was good as Catherine felt quite at a loss to give one. "I'm so happy you're here. Shall we play a game of cards before dinner, or would you like to rest?"

Catherine wavered between honesty and politeness, finally deciding on the former. "I would really love to see the garden," she said, then added, "Would you like to join me?"

"I'm not fond of walking in this heat. Perhaps you could tear William away from his correspondence."

"No, I hate to bother him," said Catherine. "I don't mind going alone."

❧

The garden had also changed. Gone were the daffodils, the tulips, the camellias, and the musky blue hyacinths, but Catherine found beautiful things in their place. There were large beds of blooming lavender around the reflecting pool; when Catherine rolled the stalks between her fingers, the tiny blossoms crumbled and released the clean, astringent scent of summer. Climbing on a trellis were red and pink and purple sweet peas, their delicately ruffled blossoms looking like tissue paper. A white waterfall of jasmine tumbled over the nearby wall. The lawns, unlike the hills, were still green; Catherine heard the swish of sprinklers in the distance.

The Tree of Knowledge was different now, less mysterious and more full. Small green leaves obscured the sculptural drama of the branches, and for a moment Catherine was disappointed. But when she stood underneath its canopy, resting her hand on the rough trunk, she could still catch a glimpse of the reaching branches that had captivated her weeks before.

This was her home now, and she was glad of it.

She sat down on the marble bench, remembering the night in March that had brought her back to Oakview. It seemed a lifetime ago, her acceptance of William's proposal and all the confusion preceding it. But the memory of that confusion was sharper than she had expected, like suddenly treading on a stone in her shoe. She got up abruptly from the bench and crossed the lawn. Perhaps she should have plucked William from his study and asked him to accompany her on the walk. I'll bring him out here tomorrow, she told herself. Sharing the garden, walking the beautiful paths together: surely that would make her feel closer to him.

Left to her own devices she would have continued her stroll, but the shadows had lengthened and she had to dress for dinner. The rose garden would have to wait. I'll go first thing in the morning, she thought, and she smiled up at the sky.

TWENTY

*W*illiam, she soon discovered, was more interested in making her familiar with the house than with the garden. "You need a full tour, basement to attic," he said after dinner as he changed records on the phonograph. "You won't have much to do to manage it. Mrs. Callahan handles all that. But I've asked her to show you around tomorrow morning."

"I'd planned to spend the morning sketching in the rose garden," Catherine said. "I'm so eager to see it in bloom."

"The roses won't go anywhere," he said. "You may spend as much time there as you wish, after the tour is done."

She thought of persisting, but the phonograph began to crackle and soon the opening bars of "Shine On, Harvest Moon" filled the room.

The tour began promptly after breakfast, in the dining room. Mrs. Callahan, clearly pleased to serve as Catherine's guide, led the way through the swinging doors into the kitchen. The gray-haired cook, Mrs. Dean, sat at a small table with a mug, intently reading a picture magazine. She sprang up when they entered, almost upsetting her tea. "I was just taking my morning break," she said.

"No need to apologize, Mrs. Dean," said the housekeeper. "Please carry on."

Catherine smiled as warmly as she could, realizing that to the staff, William's marriage meant a potentially major change in the running of the household. So much of a servant's happiness depended on her employer, as she knew from the surreptitious mutterings of the housemaids on Madison Avenue. The staff at Oakview was surely wondering what sort of a mistress she would be.

At another, larger table, two maids were busily polishing silver. "This is Sadie," the housekeeper said, indicating a girl with straw-blond hair, "and Graciela."

"Good morning," said Catherine.

Both girls nodded deferentially, Sadie surveying Catherine's lilac-colored dress with frank interest. Graciela looked swiftly back down at the polishing cloth, and Catherine was struck by how young she was. She pushed back the memory of the two figures joined by the door of the garden house.

They visited the baking room, the silver room, and the small office for Hayes. The servants' dining hall was a large, comfortable room with high windows overlooking the kitchen courtyard.

"How many staff are employed here?" Catherine asked.

"Twenty-three."

"So many?"

"An estate this size requires quite a lot of labor," said the housekeeper. "There is Mr. Hayes, myself, and Mrs. Dean, as well as two footmen, four housemaids, two kitchen maids, and one laundress. Mr. Brandt has a valet, John. There is a groom and stable boy, and we have one head gardener and four undergardeners. There is a groundskeeper, who fixes things that need fixing, and he has an assistant. There is also Anderson, the chauffeur. And, of course, now we have your ladies' maid and Mrs. Cartwright's ladies' maid." She smiled. "Perhaps I should have said twenty-five. It's always nice to have the new additions."

"How much time off do the staff receive?" Catherine asked.

"One afternoon a week, and a day every other week."

They went down into the basement, through the laundry room with its large basins, and into the wine cellar, where Hayes was silently inventorying the bottles. They climbed back up to the first floor, and Mrs. Callahan opened a door to reveal yet another staircase, tiled with a strip of brown carpet down the center. "We've a bit of a climb, now, Miss Ogden. I do apologize."

The two women ascended slowly, passing a maid on her way downstairs with an armful of linen. At the landing to the third floor, Catherine had to pause to catch her breath. "Please take your time," said the housekeeper kindly.

"If only there were an elevator," said Catherine.

"Mr. Brandt's mother did ask for one," the housekeeper said. "But old Mr. Brandt felt it would destroy the serenity of the house to have it moving up and down at all hours." She appeared to realize her words could be interpreted as criticism, for she quickly added, "I'm sure he was right. And it does keep us fit, climbing the stairs."

At the head of the stairs were two hallways, branching to either side. "The male staff sleeps on the left side of the stairwell," she said, "and the women here." She led Catherine down an uncarpeted hall lined with doors and opened one, revealing a gabled room with two white iron bedsteads, two bureaus, a washstand, and a small writing table and chair. "This is the room that Sadie and Graciela share. The kitchen maids you met downstairs. All the rooms look like this one."

On the wall opposite the door was a small window. Catherine moved toward it and looked down. From her high perch she saw the terrace at the back of the house and the lawn like a bright green sheet. It was not dissimilar to the view from her own room, but it felt much removed, as if she were seeing the beauty of the estate through some glass that altered the normal perspective of things.

But then she raised her eyes and gave an exclamation of surprise. The hills beyond the estate seemed different than they did from her own window . . . closer, more accessible, less of a barrier to the world beyond. "Those hills don't seem nearly as high as they do on the second floor," she said, as if it were a great discovery.

"No," said the housekeeper politely. "The compensation for climbing the stairs, perhaps."

Catherine turned back to the door, noting the colorful patchwork bedspreads and the braided rug. On top of one bureau sat a small milk glass vase of dried flowers and a framed photograph of a family of blond children, partially obscured by a Gibson Girl picture cut from a magazine. Arranged on the other bureau was a colorful image of the Virgin Mary, a worn rag doll, and a crudely painted china figurine of a shepherdess with a young gallant bending over her hand. Catherine looked away quickly, feeling as if she were trespassing on the private lives of the girls who lived there.

Her own mother would have slept in such a room. For a moment, she tried to picture her as a young girl, setting her own things on a bare bureau, gazing out a small window at a busy New York street far below.

What was it like to be a maid? Busy, surely, and exhausting, and dull. Her own life used to feel confined, but maids had far less opportunity than she'd ever had living in her aunt's house. With no education and very little time off, how could a girl ever escape from a life spent peeling potatoes and climbing three flights to an attic room? She wished she knew more about how her mother had found her way out of service and into the world of art.

Moving toward the door, she took a last look behind her, as if to reassure herself that the maids' quarters were comfortable ones. The room was relatively spacious, but it was plain and, she imagined, would receive very little sunlight. Then again, the maids were surely not in their rooms very much during the day.

"Do all the staff sleep on the third floor?" she asked.

"Nearly all," said Mrs. Callahan, closing the door behind them. "The head gardener has a cottage to himself, back beyond the kitchen garden. The groom and stable boy are in the stables, on the northern end of the estate. And the chauffeur has an apartment over the garage."

"How many people on the estate know how to drive?" she asked, as they moved down the hall.

"Anderson has taught a few of the other members of the staff. Five or six, I believe. And Mr. Brandt can drive, too, of course, though he rarely chooses to."

"Do you drive?"

"Goodness, no," said the housekeeper with a laugh.

Catherine ran her hand over the rail of the staircase, pausing before the descent. "I would rather like to learn someday," she said, the idea new and daring. "Do you think Anderson would teach me?"

"I'm sure he would," said Mrs. Callahan, surprised, "but that would be for Mr. Brandt to say." She smiled and indicated the stairs. "After you, Miss Ogden."

❧

As soon as the tour ended, Catherine returned to her room, collected a hat and her sketchbook and pencils, and made her way to the rose garden. It was a beautiful morning, the sky blue with only the barest wisps of cloud.

As she walked down the sun-warmed paths, she felt a click in her soul, as if something had settled into its proper place. It was astonishing to realize that Oakview felt more like home than the house and city in which she had spent eleven years of her life. A stone lay on the path in front of her and she kicked it and watched it scuttle ahead, then she ran and joyfully kicked it again. She felt free, buoyant, like that little girl who used to turn cartwheels on the beach.

Passing under the archway of the brick wall, she paused in delight before the rose garden. Where there had been reddish-green leaves in March, there were now blooms of red, white, pink, lavender, and yellow. She took a slow circuit around the beds, smelling the open flowers as she passed. Some were ruffled and layered, almost resembling peonies, while others were elegant with petals like porcelain. She found a white rose with edges of pink and identified it as the source of the blooms by her bed. "Thank you," she said to the bush, then felt silly, but there was no one to hear but the birds twittering in the ivy.

In the center of the garden stood a white sundial with semicircular benches at its base. Choosing one, she sat facing a bed of red roses. She opened her book and, with a sense of deep contentment, began to sketch.

After half an hour, she felt less buoyant. As in New York, she was confronted by her inability to capture what she saw in front of her. She frowned at the drawing, which looked less like a rose bush than a tangle of yarn, then folded the sketchbook and walked slowly to the far end of the garden. It was disappointing that she could not draw the roses as her father would have done.

Her wanderings took her through the kitchen garden, where a young gardener was busy weeding the rows, and into the orchard, past the pear and apple trees. It occurred to her that she had never gone to the farthest reach of the garden, through the doorway that stood at the southwest corner of the orchard, so she walked through it and found herself in another walled area.

It could not be called a garden yet, for it had no flowers. Gravel paths were laid out, framing five large, diamond-shaped planting areas. The diamonds were rich with fresh earth, dark and full of promise.

As she gazed at the empty flower beds, she thought of the paper in her sketchbook. To a gardener, this was a canvas; seeds and flowers were the paint. Someone would transform this into a beautiful space, alive with color and fragrance. What was it like, she wondered, to be that kind of artist?

She heard a sound behind her and turned. Thomas the gardener was just coming up the path through the orchard. Upon seeing her he nodded politely, taking off his cap. "Miss Ogden."

"Good morning," she said, her face and voice animated by the thoughts she'd just been having. "Are you planting this garden?"

He swept his dark hair back with one hand. Unlike William's, which was brilliantined and glowed like ebony, his was slightly wavy, with reddish highlights in the sun. "I'm hoping to," he said. "It used to be a place where we stored garden equipment, but they've built a new shed for that. My father had it designed and laid out like this. He died before it was completed."

She thought of their conversation by the tulips and flushed slightly, remembering the emotion she'd revealed and the look in his blue eyes. "I see. What will you put in them?"

"Dad kept his ideas in his head, unfortunately, not on paper." He surveyed the empty beds. "I suppose it's left to me, then."

Her face must have asked a question, for he said, "I'm not the gardener, not officially. I grew up helping my father, but I'm only here now on a break from my studies."

"What are you studying?"

"Medicine."

"Oh." She could not keep the surprise out of her voice and

was instantly ashamed, but he only smiled briefly as if her reaction were not unexpected.

"I came back here when my father was ill and offered to stay until they found a new gardener. It's what he would have wanted."

"You'll be moving on, then?"

He nodded, folding his arms across his chest. "At the end of the summer, I'll be going back to the city and my studies."

"I see." A bird trilled above them, and another responded in staccato chirps. "Medicine. What made you want to be a doctor?"

"That's a long answer," he said. "If I start now, I'll be keeping you from other things."

She looked up at the sky. The sun was at its peak. "I suppose I should start back to the house. I've lost track of time."

"That can happen, in a garden." He indicated the book under her arm. "Particularly for an artist."

She was suddenly embarrassed. "I try to sketch, but I'm not good at all. I can't draw like my father could."

"I can't design gardens like my father could," Thomas said. "He had a gift for it."

She knew she should return to the house, but the warmth of the sun on her face was too inviting to leave. "I was just thinking that these flower beds are like a canvas for a painter. Or a blank page for a writer."

"They are," he said. "There are many different ways to be an artist."

The bird chirped again, the same regular beat. A seed of an idea took root in her mind.

"I'm sorry," he said out of nowhere, and she turned to him. "I haven't yet congratulated you. On your engagement."

"Oh," she said, then added, "Thank you very much."

She waited for the usual follow-up of well-wishes, but he

only looked at her. His blue gaze was intent and, oddly, compassionate.

"Well," she said briskly, "I'm afraid I'm already late for lunch. Good day."

"Good day, Miss Ogden." And he moved toward the center flower bed, arms crossed, as she walked quickly toward the house.

⁂

"William," she said, as they strolled by the reflecting pool after lunch, "there's a new garden waiting to be planted. Back behind the orchard."

"I remember. The old gardener had some plans for it, I think. How does it look?"

"It's not planted yet," she said. "That is, the soil looks ready, but there's nothing in the ground."

"As long as it's finished before the wedding." He took her hand and lifted it to the sunlight. He regarded the sapphire with approval, and she thought about how strange it was to have someone else lift her hand as it were a part of his own body.

"I have an idea," she said, as he tucked her hand back in the crook of his arm. "I could help design the new garden."

He smiled down at her. "I had no idea landscaping was one of your talents."

"It isn't," she said. "That is, I've never had the chance to try. But I'd love to feel that some part of the garden was mine."

"It will all be yours, very soon."

"I know, but . . . well, I've always wanted to create something of my own. Like an artist would do." She realized it was the first time she had ever voiced that desire to him; she felt oddly nervous about his reaction.

"Of course you may, if you like." He stopped and bent to kiss her, ducking slightly to bypass the brim of her large hat. Pleasant as it was to be kissed by him, part of her still felt self-conscious, as if her aunt were watching censoriously.

"Do whatever you want with the garden," he said, as they strolled on. "I'll talk to Thomas, the head gardener. He'll be here for a few more months. Plenty of time to get it done."

"I shall," she said, looking up at him with eyes that were radiant with the promise of a project. William stopped walking and kissed her so hard that she had to draw back, smiling and gasping, to take a breath.

TWENTY-ONE

*C*atherine appreciated Oakview even more the following day, when she and William paid a visit to Madrone Hill, the estate owned by Peter and Vivian Powell. The house was a massive mansion of the mid-eighties, with somber wood paneling and dark stained glass that let in little of the light from the vast grounds outside.

"I know," Vivian said, as if reading Catherine's mind. "Isn't it hideous?"

Catherine strove to say something polite, but Vivian's knowing glance made her realize that dissembling was not only unnecessary but would actually be unwelcome. "It is, rather," she said, with an unfamiliar feeling of liberation.

"Here," said Vivian. "I'll show you the morning room. It's the first one I changed." She led the way through the reception hall, over a large bearskin rug with gaping jaws. "My husband doesn't like any animal you can't shoot," she said over her shoulder as Catherine scrambled to keep up with her brisk stride.

The morning room was a welcome contrast to the entrance hall, airy and bright, with gold accents and Japanese prints in blue and green. A maid was dusting the furniture, and at their arrival she prepared to leave, but Vivian waved at her to continue her work.

Catherine admired a porcelain vase as Vivian pulled aside a silk curtain. "At least there's a good view. Peter had this house built so high you can almost see over the hills."

Catherine moved to the window. The view was indeed beautiful, offering a vista of lawn and treetops and canyons far below.

"Peek into his study," said Vivian. "You'll see what this room looked like before we pried the paneling off the walls."

Through the adjoining door, Catherine saw a huge fireplace, dark walnut walls, and a massive desk with carved claw feet. A stag's head hung above the fireplace, its glassy eyes fixed on nothing. "The morning room is much nicer."

"I'm glad you agree." Vivian closed the door. "That stag's head is an abomination. How the first wife endured it, I have no idea." She took a cigarette from a case on the end table and lit it, offering one to Catherine, who declined. "That's right; you don't smoke."

"How long have you been married?" Catherine asked.

"Almost three years." Vivian took a long drag of her cigarette and blew the smoke toward the curtains, carefully away from her guest. She looked at the porcelain clock on the mantel. "We'd better go back. The gents will be waiting for tea."

They walked back through the hall and past an empty suit of armor standing at attention, its gauntlets holding a sword. "Is that a historical piece?" Catherine asked.

"Something like that. Peter picked it up in England," said Vivian without breaking her stride. "A man's home is his castle, and all that."

"It's very striking."

"That's one word for it. He thinks it gives him an air of ferocity, having these animal heads and weapons in the house." She paused by an end table to stub out the cigarette. "All men want to inspire fear, you know."

Catherine thought of Peter, his portly body, his face red and glistening with sweat. "Do they?"

"Absolutely," said Vivian, leading the way into the conservatory. "But some are more naturally suited for it than others." She stopped by the tea table where china and sandwiches were spread out on the lace cloth. "Where did they go?"

Peering through the windows, Catherine could just discern Peter and William standing by the marble balustrade. "On the terrace."

Vivian surveyed the tea table as if assessing its quality. "Now your fiancé," she said, carefully straightening a teacup on its saucer. "He's very well suited for it. He can be terrifying."

Catherine didn't know what to say. "Terrifying?" she asked after a moment, her tone deliberately light.

Vivian smiled. "I guess you haven't seen it yet," she said. "Maybe you never will, being you. But no woman wants a weak man, does she?" Her gaze was frank and appraising as she stood behind the tea table, and Catherine wondered how much of what she said was true and how much was meant for effect. With Vivian, it was not always easy to tell.

The door opened and the men entered. "Ready at last," Peter said genially. "What have you ladies been gossiping about?"

"You, of course," said Vivian. "What other topic of conversation is there?" But she was looking at William as she said it, not at her husband.

"I'm glad to see you have your priorities in order," William said smoothly, moving to Catherine's side and pulling out her chair.

༄

After breakfast the next morning, Catherine walked eagerly to the unfinished garden. She brought the two watercolors she'd done the evening before, absorbed and happy as she painted alone in her bedroom.

Thomas arrived right on time. "Good morning, Miss Ogden."

"Good morning," she said. She knew William had called Thomas into his study the previous day, informing him that she would take charge of designing the garden. This was the first time they had spoken since then.

He seemed guarded, standing with his hands in his pockets. She wondered if he saw her interest as an intrusion. It was not his garden, and he was surely accustomed to taking orders, but after eleven years with her aunt, Catherine understood how it felt to have no agency. Now that she was the lady of the house—in practice, if not yet in fact—she resolved to give directions graciously.

"Thank you for meeting me," she said. "I know about color, but I'm afraid I don't know anything about the practical side of gardening. I'll need your help to bring these ideas to life."

"I'm happy to help, Miss Ogden." His words were correct, but his tone was distant.

"Let me show you the two designs I've made." She handed him the watercolors. "I don't know which kinds of flowers would match, but I thought these colors would look nice together." For some reason she felt nervous about showing him.

He studied each design in turn. His hands holding the paper were large, the fingernails edged with dirt. There was a small ring on his fifth finger, a simple gold band. It seemed natural, like a part of his skin.

He turned to her, and his expression was softer than before. "You obviously love color," he said, and she blushed as if it were a compliment.

"I have my father to thank for that," she said.

He held out the first drawing, in which each of the five large beds was a solid color. "This design is in keeping with the rest of the garden. Mr. Brandt's mother always liked the beds to be planted with a single color." Then he held up the second sketch, in which each bed contained flowers of one color in the center and another around the edge: blue with yellow, red with purple, pink with white. "But the colors you've chosen here go very well together. Do you like one approach more than the other?"

"I don't know. I suppose the first one is more . . . traditional." He was silent, letting her think aloud. "But the second is more lively. More interesting, somehow."

"And there are the flower varieties to consider," he said. "You can start with color, but the height of the flowers will also have to be taken into account. And anything we plant now is temporary, of course. What blooms now won't bloom in the winter."

"This is more complex than I thought it would be."

"Every garden has to start somewhere," he said. "Often you can't even see the path until you've taken the first step."

She squinted at the beds, visualizing the different designs. She looked down at the sketches and then up again and finally back at Thomas, who was gauging her reaction. Her heart felt suddenly light, full of the promise of creation.

"I think I'm going to enjoy this," she said impulsively and was pleased to see him smile.

TWENTY-TWO

*A*s the days passed, Catherine continued to be delighted with her new life. It afforded more freedom than she had ever had in her aunt's house. When William was working, she could stay out in the garden for hours if she wished; likewise, she and Harriet could request the use of the car to drive them to the shops or on a pleasure trip through the hills.

Her acclimation to Peninsula society, which William had wished to make a priority, began right away. Invitations were extended and received, and the circle of her acquaintance expanded rapidly. The second week she was there, Anderson drove them to a dinner party at El Cerrito, a large Tudor-style estate in San Mateo. Catherine was captivated by the grounds of the estate, where palm trees and English hedges coexisted in surprising harmony. It was further proof that gardeners were artists, and that California was a canvas where any unique vision could be realized.

On a hot afternoon, they attended a garden party at Linden Towers, a huge white wedding-cake of a mansion. Its owner was James Flood, whose father had been born to Irish immigrant parents and had made his fortune from a silver mine. An Irish millionaire was a new concept to Catherine. She almost said as much to William on the way home but decided against it. Though she could not imagine him objecting to her Irish blood, she was wary of initiating a conversation that might lead to the disclosure of what she had just learned about her mother.

She need not have worried. William never asked questions

about her childhood and asked very few questions about her life in general. He seemed satisfied to share light conversation over meals and to have her play piano for him and take his arm at social gatherings. At times she wondered if he should be more curious about her past, but whenever the thought entered her mind, she pushed it away. It's a good sign, really, she told herself. It means he doesn't need much in order to love me.

On a bright Saturday they explored San Francisco, William identifying landmarks from the back seat of the Pierce-Arrow. She enjoyed gazing up at the buildings of Market Street, so unlike those of New York. Many pedestrians stared at the gleaming auto; their attention was the only part of the ride that she disliked.

Catherine was captivated by Chinatown and the sense of being in an entirely new country, one with painted balconies and signs written in Chinese characters and the smell of unfamiliar cooking in the air. When she asked William if they could leave the car and walk around the streets, he gave one of his rare refusals. "You can see just as well from here."

"But I'm sure there are fascinating things down those alleys," she said, pointing to one where linens were hanging like flags on clotheslines.

"Things that a young woman like you should not see."

She was intrigued. "What?"

"Opium dens, for one thing."

She looked back down another alley as they passed it. All she saw was a young girl with a toddler holding her hand. "And yet families live here. And it's broad daylight."

"You must listen to what I'm telling you," he said. "It's neither safe nor seemly for you to be walking down these streets."

She had no idea whether he was right, but the steel in his voice made the old contrariness come to the fore. "Well," she said, lifting her chin, "I'll just have to come when you aren't looking."

"In that case," he said, "I will always be looking." There was no lightness in his tone, and his eyes held hers until she turned away.

☙

Harriet, though she was willing to go on most excursions, proved to be a less satisfying companion than Catherine had hoped. Their conversation seemed destined to remain on a pleasant but superficial level. When Catherine asked about the grand tour on which Harriet had taken her son years earlier, eager to learn about life in London, Florence, and Munich, Harriet was more interested in describing the ocean liner on which they had traveled. ("Why they would make the upholstery blue, I have no idea. There is enough blue outside the window of a ship, isn't there?") She was unfailingly kind and warm, but a surrogate for Lavinia she was not.

Vivian, then, became Catherine's default companion. They played croquet at Oakview and tennis at Madrone Hill and spent a lively evening of cards with Peter and William. Though Catherine could not always discern how many of Vivian's offhand comments were truly meant, she came to value the quickness and bluntness of her new friend, such a change from the careful manners her aunt had always taught her were appropriate for a woman.

Their companionship had its confusing moments, though, such as the afternoon they went out to see the unplanted garden. Catherine had decided, after some reflection, on the two-color design. When she had told Thomas, his smile indicated he would have made the same choice. The next step, he said, would be selecting flowers to match the designs. Further work had been delayed by a constant stream of social engagements, but as Catherine stood in the sun and described the layout to Vivian, she felt a new impatience to begin.

"It will look nice, I'm sure," said Vivian. "Nothing wrong with mixing your colors." She flicked a ladybug off of her arm with a precise snap of her finger.

"Do you help with the garden at Madrone Hill?" Catherine asked.

"No. The house gives me enough to work on. And our gardener is a fearsome Scot who won't tolerate my interference. Very wise of him."

"I honestly don't know what I'm doing," said Catherine, "but it's nice to have a project. And the head gardener will do the actual work."

Together they strolled back through the rose garden in the still afternoon sunlight. Catherine stopped periodically to admire the blooms while Vivian whistled "A Bird in a Gilded Cage" and tapped her furled parasol against her leg. At the far end of the garden, Thomas was deadheading roses, and he nodded politely to both of them.

"Ah, yes," said Vivian to Catherine. "I remember him."

"Come and look at this one." Catherine directed her friend toward a double-colored bloom, light yellow with dark pink. "I think it's my favorite. The colors are so perfect together."

"Very nice," said Vivian.

Catherine bent to the nearest rose, inhaling its rich scent. She moved around the bush, admiring each bloom in turn.

A moment later she realized Vivian had moved away and was approaching Thomas, who straightened deferentially at her approach. "You are doing beautiful work here," she could hear Vivian say.

"Thank you," said Thomas.

"Perhaps," said Vivian, "when you're finished with this garden, you could come to Madrone Hill and help with mine?"

The words themselves were innocuous, but there was an

edge to Vivian's tone—pointed, even flirtatious—that made Catherine look swiftly up from the roses. There was a moment of uncomfortable silence; then Thomas spoke.

"The garden here will occupy all of my available time," he said evenly. "Excuse me."

He picked up the shears and walked toward the gate in the garden wall. He did not acknowledge Catherine as he strode past, and she felt an uncomfortable sting of guilt by association, a feeling that was made keener when Vivian came up to her and took her arm chummily.

"I had to try," she said, sounding almost apologetic. "Who wouldn't want to look at that man every day?"

The pleasure had gone out of the garden for Catherine. She silently led her friend back to the house.

✑

The next day Catherine received a letter from Lavinia. She took it eagerly into the music room and opened it.

Dearest friend,

You are surely reading this letter while basking in the California sun—lucky you! I'm writing it from a steamer chair on a ship in the middle of the big blue sea. Luckily, the waters are calm enough that my penmanship will be no more dreadful than usual.

I've a mere twenty minutes before I must dress for dinner, but I simply had to write and tell you how happy I am. Truly, madly, wildly happy. Marriage is so much more than I had ever imagined. Clarence is such a darling. I knew that already, but I see it even more clearly now that he's my husband. It's like having a best friend, but even better. (I know you well enough to know that you won't be offended by that statement!)

And you know how we used to wonder about the physical side of marriage? Well, I am happy to report that it is, in fact, divine. Surprising at first, yes, but a husband finds ways to make you enjoy it just as much as he does. I'm practically blushing writing that, and please don't ask me for details, but trust me that you have nothing to fear . . . and a great, great deal to enjoy. (Good thing Clarence isn't looking over my shoulder as I write this! I don't think men have any idea of how much women share with one another. If you still lived with your aunt, I'd tell you to burn this letter!)

I'll think of you as we go to country houses and look at the art. I'll try to remember everything you have said to me about what makes a painting Great. And if we get as far as the Lake District, I will think of Wordsworth and look for someone wandering lonely as a cloud. But lucky Lavinia . . . that lonely someone will not be me!

I am so happy, my dear—and so happy that YOU will soon be just as happy as I am.

With the warmest and sweetest love always,
Lavinia Perry (how strange and wonderful to write my new name!)

Catherine read the letter twice, folded it, and replaced it in the envelope. It was gratifying to hear that her friend was so happy, but as she sat on the piano bench and gazed out the window onto the terrace, she felt curiously subdued. When she caught a glimpse of herself in the mirror behind the piano, her expression was sober.

Turning to the keys, she began to play her favorite Chopin nocturne. The melody made her think of Mr. Perrin and his impish smile. How he'd love to give lessons in a room like this one, so airy and flooded with natural light. It was strange to recall how she used to sit at the piano in her aunt's house and dream of new horizons. She had them now, and she was happy, but Lavinia's letter had exposed an undeniable vein of discontent. She knew the reason for it. Although she loved Oakview, she did not yet love William.

But I will in time, she thought, striking a chord. Love is inevitable. Everything else is there: the respect, the shared interests, the attraction—

She felt a hand on her shoulder and looked up at the mirror. William was standing behind her.

"That's beautiful," he said as she stopped. "No, keep playing."

She had lost the thread of the melody and had to start the piece again from the beginning. He continued to stand behind her, his hand warm and solid on her shoulder, and as she played, she thought of Lavinia's letter and felt the heat of desire rise to her face. She would soon have the experiences Lavinia had written about, and she was more curious than ever.

But it was uncomfortable to have such thoughts in his presence. As her fingers moved over the keys, she was keenly conscious of him standing behind her. When she glanced up, he was there, too, in the mirror, watching her play. So she focused her gaze on the keyboard, the one place where he was not.

TWENTY-THREE

*W*hen Catherine and Thomas met the next morning in the garden, he had brought a pile of seed catalogs and gardening books. "You can look through these and find what you like," he said. "I'm happy to answer any questions."

She felt a new awkwardness being with him, remembering the overheard conversation with Vivian in the rose garden. "I'm grateful for your help," she said, hoping in some small way to convey an apology for the behavior of her friend. "I know you would probably rather be resuming your studies than spending the summer here." The moment she said it, she wished she had not; it sounded graceless.

Thomas shielded his eyes from the sun, looking off toward the hills. "It's a way to be close to my father. I'm afraid my motive is more selfish than anything, in that regard."

"No," she said, "I think that's a lovely reason." She turned the leaves of the catalogs, studying the brightly colored pictures. The choices were almost overwhelming.

As she paused at a drawing of red and purple verbena, her thoughts turned to memories of her father. The garden he had painted on her wall was a cheerful mix of flowers, all blooming together. It had been beautiful, glorious chaos; might it provide inspiration?

She closed the book impulsively.

"My father painted a garden when I was young," she said. "If I remember what the flowers were, can we find a way to put them here?"

"It depends on what they are. Some may bloom at different times or need different amounts of light or shade."

She closed her eyes, visualizing the wall, remembering its design and the feel of the paint under her fingers. "Marigolds. Poppies and daisies. I think he also put in forget-me-nots; I remember loving the name. And snapdragons: I loved that name, too. And roses and tulips." When she opened her eyes, Thomas was looking at her.

"We can work with that," he said after a moment. "Some of those flowers bloom in spring, some in summer. But we can match the colors, if not the actual varieties."

"Let's put more than two colors in each bed, then," she said. "Let's do a whole mix of them, as many as we can. It will be like my father's painting come to life." She felt a momentary qualm at making the plans more complex. "This won't create more work for you?"

"Not at all. It may take a little more time to track down the flowers, but the planting time won't change. We can use as many colors as you like."

She gazed at the beds. Freed from the limitations of her previous design, she imagined red, yellow, blue, purple, orange, and pink sharing the same space. It would look like a stained-glass window, with distinct sections of color making a harmonious and bright whole. That was the design she wanted: the exuberance of her father's vision, translated into real life in California soil.

"There's no such thing as a blue tulip, though, is there?" she asked.

"No. The closest you'll get is purple."

She smiled. "My father painted one for me. He always liked to dwell in possibility."

He smiled, too, his eyes crinkling at the corners. "So did mine."

⁊◦

"What was your father like?" she asked William the next afternoon. They had just finished lunch in the garden house and, at her suggestion, had set off to look at the roses.

"Successful," he said. "Single-minded. Able to make things happen."

"What things?"

"The railroad, of course. And buildings and business deals of various kinds."

She mused on that, twirling the handle of the parasol. "What did he teach you? About life and work?"

"This is a surprise. Why the sudden interest?"

"No particular reason, just curious." They passed the lavender bushes, their fragrant spears brushing against her skirt.

"My father taught me to have a goal and make it happen," he said. "Other people will have their reasons for stopping you, but there can only be one winner in each contest. That's the person you always want to be."

"Did your father ever lose, at anything?"

"One thing," William said after a pause. "He ran for the Senate but didn't win."

"Why not?"

"Because the other candidate received more votes." She could not tell whether he was joking or trying to evade the question.

"I should think he would win," she persisted. They walked

past the reflecting pool, where the hills and cypresses were reflected in the still water. "A man so successful seems like a natural fit for the Senate."

"Successful men often face opposition from others," said William. "There are always those who don't want progress, even if it actually benefits them. They focus on one small part of the process and complain. My father had to deal with many people like that."

"What did they complain about?"

"This and that. The Chinese workers, for one thing."

"Which Chinese workers?"

William frowned into the sun. "My father hired Chinese workers for the railroad. They had steady employment, but they wanted higher wages, so they went on a hunger strike and refused to work. After some of them grew sick and died, they came back to him begging to work. He hired them on again."

"At the same wages they were earning before?"

"No. Less."

She felt a frisson of disgust. "Why less?"

"They took a gamble and lost. They knew the risk."

She moved along slowly, looking ahead in the distance, and was silent.

"I can guess what you're thinking," he said, "but don't pity them. It was long ago. And you rely on the railroad. We all do. If my father had backed down, it might never have been built."

"It would have been built," she retorted, without thinking. "It simply would have cost more to do so. Your father would have made a smaller profit, that's all."

William stopped suddenly on the path and turned to face her. Looking at him, she realized she had gone too far. He is not used to criticism, she thought, recognizing something she had unconsciously sensed from the beginning of their acquaintance.

"You're living in the house that his profit built," William said. "This garden you love is here because of my father and his choices."

It was true. She could not deny it.

"I'm sorry," she said, trying to sound contrite. "I suppose I don't know enough about it to be critical."

William regarded her closely, as if trying to detect insincerity. She was reminded of Henry studying her across the library on Madison Avenue, the book from George open on his lap. So much of her life, she realized with sudden weariness, involved men measuring and appraising her. To avoid his gaze she looked at her skirt, pretending to remove a bit of dirt.

Her silence seemed to satisfy William. "Let's forget the whole thing," he said easily. He took her arm and threaded it through his own, and they resumed walking.

"Shall we go back to the house?" she asked after a moment. "It's hotter than it was before."

"There will be more shade if we go under the oaks," he said, leading her to the path that skirted the boundaries of the garden. They continued on in silence, their footsteps crunching on the gravel path.

"I have some news that I think you'll like," he said. "We're going to host a dinner party here, in two weeks."

"Oh. I didn't know. Will it be a large party?"

"Ten or twelve guests, nothing too big. Nathaniel Law will be in town. He used to be the governor, made his fortune in copper. He and his wife, Alma, will stay with us for the weekend."

"What are they like?"

"Connected. They know everything that happens in this state."

"Do you know them well?"

"We've met several times. He was a guest here perhaps six

years ago, before my father died. You and Harriet can entertain his wife."

At one time the prospect of meeting a California copper king would have been intriguing, but now her spirits sank at the thought of a weekend making small talk with people she did not know. She thought of the menus to be chosen, the staff to be supervised, the weight of expectation that came with entertaining important guests. William, she suspected, would want everything to be perfect.

"You won't have to plan alone," William said in an echo of her thoughts. "Harriet loves this sort of thing. See how she does it, so you'll know for the future."

They had reached the entrance to the rose garden. William stopped and set her in place right underneath the archway, then stepped back a few paces. The roses were behind her, a Persian carpet of color. He smiled at her. "You look like a painting."

She turned to go into the garden. "No, don't move," he said. "It reminds me that I should be getting a letter soon. I'm arranging an artist to paint your portrait."

"Out here?" she asked hopefully. If she had to spend hours sitting still, the garden was the place she'd like to do it.

"No," he said, "In the ballroom, I think."

He moved forward and bent his face to hers. Every time they kissed, she felt both the undeniable pleasure of his lips on hers and the odd sensation of being outside of herself, an observer of the act as much as a participant. Perhaps she would have to be married before she could fully relax into his kisses. Perhaps it was that way with all girls and their fiancés. But no, she realized as William moved away, it had not been so with Lavinia and Clarence.

At the central path leading to the sundial, they encountered Thomas, who was directing a young undergardener pushing a wheelbarrow. The boy stopped and took off his cap as they drew near, revealing a crop of red hair.

"Good afternoon, Miss Ogden," Thomas said. He nodded to William. "Mr. Brandt."

William inclined his head briefly. "The new garden is coming along, Thomas?"

"It's all planned," said Thomas. "The next step is purchasing the plants."

"Will it be done by the first?"

"The first of July?"

"Yes."

Thomas's eyebrows rose in surprise. "It's unlikely," he said. "It will take longer than that to collect the plants we want." He looked at Catherine. "If you would like it done by then, we would have to simplify the designs."

"It would be nice to have it done before the Laws come," said William to Catherine. "There's no interest in an empty flower bed."

"But surely," she said, thinking protectively of all the plans she'd made, "it would be better to go with the original designs? I've put so much thought into them. Or rather, we have," she said, turning to include Thomas.

For a moment no one spoke. There was a far-off drone of insects as the three of them stood on the path in the almost-palpable heat of the summer day. The young gardener, aware he was not part of the conversation, was inspecting the bloom of a white rose nearby.

At last William nodded. "Let's stay with the original plans then," he said, and it was only when Catherine exhaled that she realized she had been holding her breath. "As long as the garden is done by the wedding, Thomas."

"It will be," said Thomas.

"Good." William smiled at Catherine with an air of finished business. "Shall we go back? I think it's time for a cold drink."

She took his arm. After a few steps she glanced over her shoulder at Thomas, but he had already turned back to the roses.

TWENTY-FOUR

*H*arriet was delighted by the upcoming visit. "It will be just like old times," she said, "to have the Laws here. I remember the last time I saw Alma, maybe two years ago in Pasadena. She had the most glorious gown, gold satin, with an amethyst-and-diamond necklace. So original. A hard combination to make successful, but she did."

"What shall we do when they are here?" asked Catherine. "Will they want to see any of the local sights?"

"They may want to ride, perhaps," said Harriet. "I remember both of them being very keen on it. They are arriving on a Thursday?"

"Friday," said William, opening his newspaper. They were sitting on the covered porch, and he looked in the direction of the stables, far off in the distance. "I'll speak to Jackson. We'll make sure he has everything ready for a ride in the hills." He turned to Catherine. "We must have you learn to ride sometime."

"I have an idea," said Harriet, putting down her glass. "On Saturday, we can do an alfresco lunch. Out by the stables, in the clearing under the trees. Then those who wish to ride can do so."

William considered it for a moment, then nodded. "As long as it's done properly, tables and linens. I don't want a juvenile picnic with baskets."

"Of course it will be done properly," said Harriet, too pleased with the idea to be offended. She rose to her feet. "I'll talk to Mrs. Callahan immediately. The more time the staff has to prepare this, the better." She smiled at Catherine. "Would you like to come along?"

Caught between her bright gaze and William's expectant one regarding her over the edge of the newspaper, there was only one possible answer.

"Yes," Catherine said, putting down her glass and getting to her feet.

୨౦

The next morning William left for the city, with plans to spend the night at his apartment in the St. Francis Hotel. It was the third time he had done so in as many weeks. "I have an appointment this evening and one tomorrow morning," he told her, "so it's easier to stay. I'm sorry to abandon you again."

"It's all right," she said, thinking of the garden. "I'll find a way to entertain myself."

"You can telephone Vivian. Perhaps she and Peter are free for dinner. And you can practice that new piano piece. You'll want to play for the Laws next weekend, of course."

She waved goodbye from the front step as Anderson drove away. After the car had disappeared down the drive, she tilted her head and looked up into the sky. The early overcast had already rolled back beyond the hills, and the sky was brilliantly blue. She smiled and hurried back inside for her hat.

"You're off, dear?" asked Harriet, who was ascending the stairs as she came down. "Into the garden again? We just can't keep you out of it."

Catherine felt a small pang of guilt at being such a poor

companion. "I do love it. I don't know how I lived without a garden for so long."

"Well, it's a nice day for it. There may be a breeze later, though. There often is, this time of year."

"I'll come back in if I'm cold."

She had just gone down the terrace when she encountered Thomas. Instead of his usual gardening clothes, he wore a brown suit and green tie. The change was so unexpected that it took her a moment to recognize him.

"Good morning," she said.

"Miss Ogden. You will be happy to know that I'm making some progress on the garden today."

"Oh?"

"I'm taking one of the estate cars out to a nursery in Half Moon Bay. I'll be able to pick up some of the plants we need."

"That's wonderful," she said. "How many will you get?"

"Not all of them, by any means, but it's a start. There are other nurseries in Redwood City. I'll find a day to drive down there next week."

"Half Moon Bay. What a lovely name."

"It's a town on the coast, through the hills. Quite a nice drive." He paused, then said formally, "You are welcome to come, if you care to."

"Could I really?"

"Of course. Then you can pick out the plants yourself."

If William were there, she would have felt the need to ask if she could go. She was sure he would assent, though she could picture the slight lift of his eyebrows, wondering why she would wish to be involved in a task that he paid the staff to do. But she was beholden to no one on this crystalline June day, and the realization made her feel buoyant.

"I'd love to go. I'll get my coat."

Twenty minutes later, she hurried to the kitchen courtyard. Thomas was already there, being handed a small hamper by Graciela. The girl nodded at Catherine's approach but slipped noiselessly back into the house before Catherine could say anything.

"I asked about taking a lunch," Thomas said, lifting the basket into the car, "since we'll be a few hours. And I've brought along a blanket. We may even be able to eat on the beach, if there's time."

"There is," she said. "William will be in the city until tomorrow, and I've told Harriet where I'm going. I have nothing to hurry back for."

He gave his hand to help her into the Ford, a more serviceable auto than William's glamorous Pierce-Arrow. She tightened the veil that held on her hat, feeling a thrill of adventure at the unexpected direction her morning had taken.

"When did you learn to drive?" she asked as the auto moved away from the house.

"A few years ago," he said. "I wanted to help my father. He never quite trusted autos and didn't want to learn."

They drove under the canopy of oaks and over the creek, which made only a perfunctory summertime trickle.

"You spent your childhood at Oakview, didn't you?" she asked.

"Yes, my father came on staff here when I was two years old."

"So you grew up with William."

"In a manner of speaking," he said guardedly. "He's four years older. Our paths did not often cross."

What was he like when he was young? she wanted to ask, but Thomas's eyes were fixed on the road ahead, even though there were no autos in either direction.

"It must have been a lovely place to be a child," she said after a pause.

"It was. The garden was just being laid out then, but there were still so many paths to run down and places to explore. The cottage was the perfect size for the three of us."

"You don't have any siblings?"

"I had one sister, but she died the year before I was born."

"What was her name?"

He looked at her, as if surprised by her interest. "Marisol," he said as he turned back to the road.

"Marisol. I've never heard that name before."

"It's Spanish. My parents liked it because it had the words 'mar' and 'sol'—'sea' and 'sun.'"

"Sea and sun," she said. "I like that, too."

The car began to climb up the dirt road. It was unpaved, as were many of the roads around Oakview, and Thomas had to drop his speed. Catherine didn't mind, for the landscape was beautiful. There were oak trees and bay trees in abundance, and soon they found themselves by the deep blue waters of the Crystal Springs Reservoir, reflecting the wooded hills beyond.

"I'd love to learn Spanish sometime," she said. "It has such a musical sound."

"You said once that it was beautiful," he said. "I never thought about that, growing up. It was just a language I spoke. But I agree with you."

She was pleased at his comment, and that made her bold. "Teach me to say something," she said impulsively.

"What would you like to know?"

"How do you say 'please'"?

"*Por favor.*"

"*Por favor.*" She could not make her *r*'s sound the way his did, soft and rolling. "How do you say 'Thank you'?"

"*Gracias a Dios.*"

"*Gracias a Dios,*" she repeated.

"Actually, that's 'thanks to God.' My mother always said it that way. It's really just *gracias.*"

"*Gracias.* It sounds like Graciela," she said.

"Yes, I suppose so."

"You don't have a Spanish name, though," she observed.

"Actually, I do. Thomas was my father's name, but there's a Spanish version. Tomás. That's how my mother always said my name."

"Tomás," she said experimentally. "How nice to be named after your father."

"Were you named after anyone?"

She frowned as they turned and the sun came into her eyes. "I don't actually know." She tilted her hat down, blocking the light, and just at that moment there was a rustle in the under-brush and a doe and two spotted fawns suddenly bounded in front of the car. They were far enough in front of the auto that there was no danger of a collision, but Catherine still caught her breath in surprise. Their lithe brown-and-white bodies streaked across the road with a remarkable intentness of purpose. "They had good timing," she said.

"I worry about the deer sometimes," said Thomas. "So many autos on the road, where there only used to be wagons and the occasional stagecoach. And not everyone is a careful driver."

"But I suppose it's worth it to have the automobiles," she said. "That's what progress is all about." She heard in her words a slight echo of William's comments by the reflecting pool, and she shifted uncomfortably in the seat.

"I wouldn't want to stop progress," he said, "but I don't think we have to choose between that and humanity." Up ahead, the road was a ribbon through rolling hills on either side. "We go up and then down, into a valley. I'm sorry if it seems like we're crawling. This is a road one has to take slow."

"That's quite all right," she said. "I'm perfectly happy to take my time."

After a glimpse of the ocean from above and then the slow descent into the valley, they turned onto a smaller road where acres of flowers grew in the fields on either side. VIEIRA'S NURSERY read a sign by the road. William carefully maneuvered the car into a spot by a farmhouse, which stood in front of two large barns and several greenhouses.

At the sound of the car, a small man with a full head of gray hair came out of the barn. He saw Thomas and his face broke into a smile. "Thomas O'Shea!" he said, running to the car.

"Francis," said Thomas, getting out of the auto. "It's good to see you."

The two men embraced quickly, with vigorous pats on the back; then Thomas opened the car door for Catherine, offering a hand to help her out.

"Miss Ogden, this is Mr. Francis Vieira; Francis, this is Miss Ogden."

"Ah," said Francis, noticing her for the first time. Then he said it again, his voice going up and down the scale, investing it with significance. He looked from one to the other, his eyes alert and eager.

"She is engaged to Mr. Brandt," said Thomas swiftly.

Francis, who had been about to speak, suddenly closed his mouth. "I see," he said. He recovered and took Catherine's hand and bent over it, formally. "How nice to meet you, Miss . . . Ogden, is it?"

"Yes," she said, discomfited by his assumption about her and Thomas. "It's nice to meet you."

"Miss Ogden has an interest in design," said Thomas, "and she's here to help me pick the plants for a new garden."

"Well then," said Francis, "we are here to help." He put his hand on Thomas's shoulder, for which he had to reach quite far, and gripped it tightly, fraternally. "I have not seen you since your father's funeral," he said, his voice low. "He was a good man. He is in our prayers, Lucia and me."

"Thank you."

"And you are, too. Doctor O'Shea. How proud he was of you." He gave the shoulder a final squeeze, then pointed the way to the greenhouse. "In here, miss, you'll find the best flowers Half Moon Bay has to offer. And welcome."

❧

Before long, the back of the automobile was packed with multi-colored snapdragons, white marguerites, and bright-blue delphiniums. The other plants they'd chosen would be delivered later; Francis had them set aside in a special corner, with directions given to his son, Afonso. The language in which they had spoken was new and yet somehow familiar, though Catherine couldn't have said why. "Which language was that?" she asked Thomas as the car started toward the main road.

"It was Portuguese."

A memory flashed into Catherine's mind: the wharf at Gloucester, with its rough wooden boards and huge tables where men in overalls talked and sang as they cleaned towering piles of fish. She was standing with her mother, watching them work, fascinated by the speed of their movements. "They are talking in Portuguese," her mother had said, holding Catherine's hand. "Doesn't it sound pretty?"

Thomas's voice broke into her reverie. "We could take the

picnic basket to the beach," he said, "and eat there. It may be a little bit breezy, though. If you don't want to attempt it, we can find another place."

"I don't mind. I'd love to see the ocean. And the sun will be warm." *Sea and sun*, she thought to herself. In her mind she practiced the Spanish she had learned so far. *Marisol. Por favor. Gracias. Tomás.*

"As you like," he said, and he turned the car west.

TWENTY-FIVE

At the beach, Thomas spread the blanket on the sand. After Catherine was settled, he sat down, too, carefully taking a place near the edge.

Catherine had decided to leave her hat in the auto, and as they walked down to the sand she felt the breeze pulling wisps of hair out of her pompadour. Though their spot on the beach was sheltered by rocks, the wind had already done its damage. She thought of the sketch of her mother, her hair undone as she looked frankly over her shoulder. On her it had been beautiful; her father had clearly not considered it a flaw.

Thomas, who had put on a beige pullover sweater, reached for the hamper. He unpacked sandwiches, part of a leftover pie, a bottle of cold tea, and strawberries. "Graciela took good care of us."

"I should go by the kitchen and thank her," said Catherine.

"I think she'd be surprised by that," Thomas said, pouring the tea. "Most women don't give a lot of thought to their kitchen maids." He handed her the cup. "I hope you aren't offended by my frankness."

"Not at all." She sipped the tea and then cradled the cup in her hands, gazing at the water near the horizon. It was a perfect blue, like the scarf her mother used to have.

"My mother was a maid," she said suddenly.

Thomas looked up from the tea. "Was she?"

Catherine put down the cup, picked up some sand, and let it slide through her fingers. "She was Irish, too."

He smiled. "That doesn't surprise me. You have the look about you."

Catherine stretched out her legs, leaning back on her hands. She wiggled her toes, feeling somehow lighter. "It feels strange to talk about this," she said. "The people I knew in New York would find it shameful to be Irish. But here . . . well, even the former mayor of San Francisco is Irish. It's so much more free."

"For the Irish, maybe. But not for everyone." He divided the strawberries between two plates, setting them on the blanket.

She admired the color of the berries before taking one. "Who are the Irish here?"

"The Chinese. The Japanese. And the Mexicans, to some degree." Thomas closed the hamper. "It's ironic, really. The Mexicans owned all this land, not so long ago."

Catherine took a sandwich and gazed at the sea as she ate. Ships would have come over that horizon, bringing people to San Francisco from countries far away. Nearly everyone here came to California from someplace else, and yet the same was true of New York. The families in the mansions on Fifth Avenue had all come from Holland, England, or France. It was easy to forget that, given how firmly the families had become entrenched in their positions, creating the impression that they had always been there.

"So I'm curious," said Thomas. "How does the daughter of a maid end up in the same circles as William Brandt? Forgive me if that sounds rude."

"Not at all." His interest gave her a little flutter of pleasure; usually he was the one answering her questions. "My father came from a wealthy family, but he was more interested in art than in being a lawyer. My mother had been a maid before she met my father. When she met him, she was working as something else." She folded over the corner of the blanket, pondering what else to say. Caution vied with a desire to acknowledge the truth; his calm blue gaze, looking over the rim of his cup, helped tip the balance. "She was working as an artist's model," she said finally. "That's also something I'm not supposed to tell people. I'm not even supposed to know it about, either."

"I'll keep it to myself," he said.

"You aren't shocked?"

"I'd have no business becoming a doctor if I were shocked by the human body." He offered her more tea, and she held out her cup.

"My father's father disowned him for loving my mother," she said, "so they married and went to live in Massachusetts. We lived in an upstairs flat by the ocean. Papa worked as an artist, and Mama did cooking and housework. We didn't have much money, but we were happy." She sifted some sand with her fingers, remembering the family walks by the seaside. "And then my father died, and I went to live with my aunt and uncle. It was . . . an adjustment."

"I'm sure it was," he said quietly.

A seagull flapped by them; she threw a crust out to him, and he bent down and picked it up with a swift, practiced movement.

"So I feel strange, sometimes," she said. "For the past eleven years I've been living like my aunt and uncle. But before that, I lived a totally different sort of life. Most people don't know that. Or if they do, they want me to forget it."

"You must feel as though you belong to two different worlds."

"Yes, exactly." Something in his expression made her add, with dawning awareness, "You probably know how that feels."

"I do."

"Is it difficult? Being half Irish and half Mexican?"

"Not really." He seemed to regret his answer, for he added, quickly, "No."

"Not really?"

He grinned wryly, caught. "There are times when I'm on the receiving end of people's ignorance." A breeze ruffled his hair and he smoothed it back. "It happens."

"What do you do?"

"I think of my mother and how she never let anyone demean her. For someone who stood five foot one, she had a mighty presence. My father was the quiet type, but he loved her for her strength. They made a good pair."

"My parents did, too," she said, and she hugged her knees to her chin and gazed at the waves. In her mind's eye she saw her father and mother walking arm in arm along the shore, heads bent together while she frolicked among the birds and created garlands of seaweed. Her uncle's story had made her realize how deeply their devotion had run and how steadfast they must have been to defy not just her grandfather but the entire world he represented.

A conversation with her father, long forgotten, rose to the surface of her memory. "You have to decide whether you will choose from the best that is in you," he had once said, "or the worst." Love had directed his choices, and probably a good amount of courage, too. The young girl dancing by the waves had been ignorant of the magnitude of his decision, but now she could truly see and appreciate it. He had chosen to create a life he loved . . . a life that she had loved, too, and which was somehow feeling closer to her in California than it had in New York.

As she listened to the waves, other memories, long buried, drifted into her consciousness. "I remember," she said, then stopped.

"You remember what?" Thomas asked.

"I remember the first time I went to the seaside in New York. I hadn't been to the beach since leaving Gloucester, and I was so excited to be there." She hugged her knees more tightly, eyes on the horizon. "The first thing I did when I got to the sand was a cartwheel, just like I used to do. But my governess grabbed me and slapped my face. 'Well-bred girls don't do that in public,' she said. I was shocked because I had never been hit before. And I was surprised because I didn't think of myself as a well-bred girl." She took a deep breath of the salty air and let it out again. "But I realized that day that I had to become one." For a few moments there was nothing but the sound of the waves and the cries of the gulls.

Thomas was sitting as she was, his arms around his knees. "Then that governess was cruel but effective," he said at last. "Until today, I believed you were born with a silver spoon in your mouth."

She hesitated a moment before asking, "Does knowing the truth change your opinion of me?"

He looked at her, the sun shining on his hair like the gold leaf of a painting. "It does," he said quietly. "Perhaps that's a sign that I have prejudices of my own to overcome."

Another seagull flapped beside them, and this time Thomas threw a scrap of bread. Two other gulls landed nearby, and he took the next piece of crust and divided it. Catherine watched the line of his arm, easily discernible beneath the sweater, as he threw the bread. Then he turned back to her and she glanced away, feeling a blush rise to her face.

"We'd better go," he said. "Word will get out among the seagulls. And it's a long drive back."

She got up and began to gather the plates and cups, pouring the dregs of the tea onto the sand as he folded the blanket. She felt a sudden, sharp regret at the thought of leaving. If I were still doing my rosary, she thought, this time at the beach would be the first bead.

Thomas picked up the basket. "I'll go on ahead and put this in the auto. Stay here and enjoy the view a few minutes longer." He flashed a conspiratorial smile. "The perfect chance to do a cartwheel, if you want."

Catherine watched him go up the rise and through the dunes. When he was out of sight, she went slowly to the water's edge. She walked along the firm sand, gradually gaining speed, until finally in a burst she began to run. It felt unfamiliar and familiar all at once. For a few moments her hair blew in the wind, and her heart pounded, just as it had when she was a child. Then she stopped, breathless but exhilarated, and smiled at the sunlit sea before turning back toward the dunes.

TWENTY-SIX

*W*illiam, predictably, was surprised to hear of her excursion. "There's no need for you to do the actual work of making the garden," he said the next day. "That's what the staff is for."

"I know," she said. "But I wanted to go."

They were in his study, where the late-afternoon sun formed large patches of light on the carpet. She moved until she was standing in one of them, tilting her face to the warmth.

William was sorting through letters at his desk. "Well, Thomas is a decent driver. I'm sure he was able to handle the roads."

"He did. It was a lovely drive."

He opened a letter, read it, and said, "Good. It's all arranged."

"What is?"

"Your portrait." He handed her the letter, written on stationery engraved with *Hotel Del Monte, Monterey, California.* "I've arranged for Martin Madsen to come and paint you."

"Martin Madsen." She studied the signature, a confident, unreadable scrawl in blue ink. "I don't know the name."

"He did that portrait of Vera De Sabla that you saw at El Cerrito. He's the best portrait painter on this coast. In the country, even."

"Have you met him?"

"Not personally, no. But he'll come on the sixth and stay until the portrait is done."

She folded the letter, thinking of having an artist in the house. There would be canvas, tubes of oil paint, brushes of various sizes . . . things that were common in her childhood in Gloucester. Part of her welcomed the idea of the portrait, recognizing it as a link back to her father. But this time she would be her mother, sitting perfectly still, forced to spend hours indoors rather than in the garden.

"I thought you'd be happy about it," said William, and she quickly altered her expression.

"I am. Thank you for arranging it."

"I hope he'll be a good houseguest," said William, taking the letter back. "Artists can be temperamental. But I suppose he'll know who is paying him."

⁹₀

Later that night, Catherine opened the bedroom window facing west. Evening fog had crept over the hills, and the air was misty and cool. Leaning forward, she breathed deeply, savoring the feeling of communion with the still world outside.

After a few moments, she crossed to the bedside table and opened the drawer. She took out her father's sketch and unfolded it, gazing at her mother's face.

"I wish you could see California, Mama," she said aloud. "It's such a beautiful place." It felt strange to be talking to a picture, but at the same time it didn't. Her father had captured her mother's features so vividly that Catherine could almost imagine her there.

She sat on the bed in her nightgown, still holding the drawing. "An artist is coming to do my portrait. I'll be sitting for him

168 | GINNY KUBITZ MOYER

like you did for Papa." In the light of the bedside lamp, she saw the groove of the pencil line forming the curve of her mother's bare back, and she grinned. "Well, not *exactly* like you did for Papa." She flattened the paper gently. "I hate giving up the time in the garden, but it will be good to see a famous artist at work. Maybe I'll learn a thing or two."

The softness of the bed reminded her of how tired she was. She yawned loudly, in defiance of her aunt's admonition that a lady's yawns are always silent.

"Goodbye for now, Mama," she said, and she folded the drawing and put it back in the drawer. Then she turned out the light and fell into a deep, restful sleep.

ॐ

The next morning, Catherine found Thomas planting a marigold border against the brick wall by the Tree of Knowledge. The flowers were light orange, vivid and bright.

"They're so cheerful, aren't they?" She gently rubbed the ruffled head of the nearest bloom. The scent was pungent and oddly pleasing.

"Yes," he said briefly. He was pulling the last of the spent forget-me-nots out of the bed.

"We're going to put some of these in our garden, too, aren't we?"

"That's the plan, yes."

There was an abruptness and preoccupation in his manner, one at odds with the easy companionship of their trip to the beach. He barely looked up as he moved about the bed, tossing the old plants to one side.

"Is something wrong?" she finally asked.

He straightened and looked at her for a moment, as if uncertain how to answer. At last, he picked up the shovel. "Graciela is expecting a baby."

"Oh," she said. Then her cheeks reddened as she remembered the two figures entwined together by the garden house. "Oh."

He began to dig, turning the earth with brisk movements. "She's desperate and scared, so she confided in me. I told her she had to tell Mrs. Callahan. She can't hide it much longer."

Catherine paused before asking, "Who is the father?"

Thomas straightened and stuck the shovel in the earth, resting one foot on it. "It's no one on staff," he said at last.

"I think I know," she said quietly.

"You do?"

"Lloyd Dixon."

It was clear she had surprised him. She smoothed a fold in her skirt, embarrassed to be remembering the scene in his presence. "It was when I was here in the spring. I went for a walk one evening, late, after dark. And I . . . well, I saw the two of them by the garden house."

Thomas stood still, clasping the handle of the shovel. His expression was hard to read.

"What will she do?" she asked finally.

He went back to digging. "Leave in disgrace. Go live with her sister in San Jose. Have the baby."

"I could try to get Lloyd's address, if you like," she said. He stopped digging. "Perhaps he could make it right," she added.

"How? By marrying her?"

"Yes. Maybe."

Thomas stuck the shovel in the dirt and left it there. He pulled out the red kerchief and wiped his face and neck, then put it back in his pocket.

"It would be nice, wouldn't it," he said, with a heat she'd

never heard from him before, "for a man like him to take responsibility. But he won't."

"Maybe he would."

Thomas gave a short laugh. "A man with a fortune and a rich fiancée. He's going to marry a kitchen maid? Not a chance." He picked up a large stone and tossed it into the wheelbarrow with an abrupt clang.

She knew he was right. "Does she want to tell him?"

"No, because she knows what would happen. He'd deny it was his and she'd be even more humiliated. She doesn't even want to tell Mrs. Callahan who the father is."

"But perhaps he could send some money to support her."

"And admit responsibility? Never."

She bent to the wheelbarrow full of marigolds, touching the blooms helplessly. Their sharp smell was a distraction from his bitterness and from the thoughts moving swiftly through her mind.

"I'm sorry," he said at last in a gentler tone. "I don't mean to take my anger out on you. But I've seen this too many times, rich men taking whatever they want and leaving others to suffer."

She remembered his face weeks earlier, in the garden. He had congratulated her on her engagement, and there had been something like pity in his eyes. Was her own fiancé one of those men? While she had initially found a kind of parity in the fact that neither she nor William knew the details of each other's history, it now occurred to her that a wealthy man of thirty naturally had much more in his past than did a nineteen-year-old girl. It was a discomfiting thought, and she pushed it away.

"What can I do to help?" she asked.

"Nothing," he said. "If she's pregnant, she won't be allowed to keep working here. And I don't think she'd want to, anyhow." He picked up a clod of dirt. "It was hard at times even before this. Mrs. Callahan is kind, but not everyone here is so . . . broad-minded."

Catherine thought of their conversation at the beach, his allusion to the prejudice he'd encountered. She was suddenly ashamed never to have considered that Graciela could be facing such attitudes among the staff at Oakview. And though any girl could have fallen prey to Lloyd's many charms—even Ethel had been susceptible—those who disdained Graciela's race would not see it that way. They would take her pregnancy as confirmation of their beliefs. She stared at the empty flower bed, absorbing the injustice.

"I'm glad she has you to confide in," she said after a moment.

He shrugged. "It would be pretty poor of me not to help someone who needs it. Especially when she's like a sister to me." He resumed digging, and she watched him silently for a time before she turned back to the marigolds.

TWENTY-SEVEN

After dinner, Harriet excused herself to go finish a letter to her husband. At William's request, Catherine played a nocturne by Chopin. It was fortunate that she knew the piece well, for her mind was distracted.

"Very nice," said William when she finished. He was sitting in the wing chair, a tumbler of brandy in one hand. "You should play that one next weekend."

"Next weekend?"

"The dinner party. With the Laws."

"Yes, of course." She made a little movement as if to clear her head. "My mind was elsewhere."

"Where?"

She carefully closed the piano. "This and that. The letter I owe to Lavinia. My plans for the garden."

He smiled. "The wedding, too, I hope."

Catherine smiled brightly. "Yes, of course." The lie did not come easily off her lips, and she reopened the piano.

There was a knock at the door. "Come in," said William.

It was Hayes, his posture more deferential than usual. "I'm terribly sorry to bother you, sir, but something has come up."

"Yes?"

"Something with the staff."

William put the empty tumbler down. "What is it?"

Hayes looked at Catherine, his unease evident even with his

impeccable demeanor. "It's perhaps something I should tell you in private, sir."

"Nonsense. Miss Ogden will soon be running the household. There's nothing she can't hear."

Hayes's face tightened stoically. "Very good, sir," he said. "It's one of the maids. She is expecting a baby."

"I see," William said. He sighed and reached for a cigar from the wooden box on the table. "Which maid?"

"Graciela. She helps Mrs. Dean with the cooking."

William cut the end of the cigar. "Who is the father? One of the stable boys or gardeners, presumably."

"She won't say, sir, only that it's no one on staff."

There was the rasp of a match, and William lit the cigar. "Someone from town, then. Someone she meets on her afternoon off."

"I don't know, sir."

William got up and threw the match into the fireplace. "Well, it's fairly obvious, isn't it, Hayes? She'll have to be dismissed without pay. I wonder why you need to involve me."

"Only that we'll now be short a kitchen maid, sir, before the weekend's guests. Mrs. Callahan was asking if she could have Anderson drive her into town tomorrow morning to hire a replacement."

"Yes, Anderson may drive her." William paused in front of the mirror, straightening his bow tie. "If she can't find anyone to hire in time, borrow a maid from the Powells. We've helped them out in the past."

"Very good, sir. And I'm sorry to bother you and Miss Ogden."

William nodded. Hayes left, closing the door with a whisper.

Catherine, still sitting on the piano bench, watched her fiancé. He sat back down in the armchair, picked up a newspaper, and began to read.

She looked about the room with its thick carpet, its plaster ceiling medallions, its large windows with the heavy gold-threaded drapes. The clock ticked, a subtly domestic sound, and occasionally she heard the comforting crackle of the fire in the fireplace. All was warm elegance and ease while two floors up, in the uncarpeted wing of the house, Graciela was surely in the small gabled bedroom, packing her things and facing an uncertain future.

Catherine tried to imagine how she must have felt, walking into the hall at dinnertime with the entire staff knowing about the pregnancy. To be an unwed mother was the height of social disgrace, for girls of every class—that, at least, was democratic. But not every woman had to endure the shame while also facing prejudice against her race. Not every woman's experience was equal.

As Catherine watched the fire and remembered the conversation with Thomas, she realized he had never once condemned the maid for her pregnancy. Lloyd, not Graciela, had received the heat of his disdain. As he should, she thought, with rising disgust at the man she had initially found so likable.

"William," she said.

"Mm?"

"What will she do now?"

The paper rustled as he turned the page. "Have the baby, presumably."

"But how will she support herself?"

"That's not our concern," he said. "She should have thought of that before."

She watched as he read the paper, cigar in one hand, lifting it to his lips and sending a plume of quiet smoke into the soft glow of the room.

"I know who the father is," she said after a moment.

William looked up. "What?"

Her heart pounded. She was not sure why she had said it, but something inside her compelled her to continue. "I know who the man is. I saw them together."

William put down the paper, his eyes keen. "Who?"

"Lloyd. I saw him with her when he was here. Out by the garden house."

In his eyes she saw a quick involuntary flash of irritation, but no trace of surprise. He had known.

"Perhaps you did," he said. "But that doesn't mean he's the father."

"Of course it does," she said heatedly.

"No, it doesn't. A girl like that, who would give herself so easily to one man, would give herself to others. And there are multiple opportunities on an estate like this, and in town on her days off." He folded the paper. "And if you saw them talking, or even kissing each other, it doesn't mean that it went any further than that."

"It was more than kissing," she said, blushing both with embarrassment and anger.

Her words hung in the air, taking on significance in the silence. William regarded her intently, and she was suddenly conscious of her low neckline and bare arms. To hide her discomfiture, she walked to the sideboard and poured herself a glass of water.

"It's not your concern," he said finally. "She's leaving. And there is no reason for Lloyd to hear about this." He got up himself and poked the fire, creating a shower of sparks; then he faced her, his suit dark against the flame. "Don't you agree?"

She was silent.

"Don't you agree?"

She twisted the stem of the goblet in her fingers, still angry, not trusting herself to speak.

"If you don't have an answer, then I'll give you one," he said. "This topic is closed. There's no reason to speak of it again, to each other or to Lloyd."

The clock struck the hour. For the space of ten chimes, they stood on opposite sides of the room, regarding one another across the gilded furniture.

Then William closed the lid of the cigar box with a definitive snap. "It's quite late, isn't it?" he said pleasantly. "Don't you and Harriet have some plans to go shopping tomorrow?"

"Yes."

"Then I won't keep you from your sleep." He crossed the room and his gaze flickered briefly over her body before he kissed her goodnight. It was a deeper kiss than usual, even though she did nothing to encourage it.

∾

The next morning, Catherine woke at seven to the abrupt sound of the alarm clock. For a moment she lay in bed, surfacing slowly from sleep; then she remembered why she had set it and quickly swung her feet to the plush carpet. She put on an old shirtwaist and skirt, then briskly brushed her hair and tied it back with a bow. Picking up the cardigan she'd draped over the armchair the night before, she slipped out of the room.

She met no one on her way through the house. Carefully, she opened the heavy door that led to the covered porch and then hurried down the terrace steps. It would be a warm day; the cardigan would not be necessary later.

At the bottom of the terrace, she found the young red-haired gardener watering pots of zinnias. "Excuse me," she said. "Have you seen Thomas?"

"Thomas? Yes, Miss Ogden. He's just gone to the kitchen."

"Thank you," she said. Then she turned back to him. "I'm sorry, I don't know your name."

He smiled, showing a broad space between his teeth. "It's Gerald, Miss."

"Thank you, Gerald."

"You're welcome, Miss Ogden."

She walked quickly down the path, almost running in the direction Thomas would have taken. Rounding the corner of the ivied wall, she spotted him just passing the camellia bushes by the garden house. He heard the sound of her feet and turned, clearly surprised to see her. "Good morning," he said.

"Thomas." She stopped to catch her breath. "Is Graciela still here?"

"She's leaving at noon."

"Will you give her this?" She reached into the pocket of the cardigan and drew out an envelope.

He took it. "Yes, of course." His face asked the question, so she answered it.

"It's money," she said simply. "It's twenty dollars. My uncle gave it to me before I left New York. I want her to have it."

He said nothing. Close as she was, she saw a red patch on one area of his chin, as if he'd shaved in a hurry. "She doesn't have to know it's from me. I just want her to have it."

Thomas folded the envelope carefully, tucking it in the breast pocket of his coat. He cleared his throat. "I'll make sure she gets it," he said. "May I ask what . . . what prompted this?"

Catherine thrust her hands into the empty pockets of her sweater. "It feels like the right thing to do. And somehow—" She stopped, remembering the face that had looked at her out of the sketch last night. "Somehow, I think it's what my mother would have done."

For a moment they stood on the path, an arm's length apart.

A strand of hair had escaped her bow, and she pushed it away from her forehead, but before she could put her hand back in her pocket, he reached out to take it, pressing it briefly with both of his.

"Thank you," he said quietly.

He let her hand go, and she moved quickly down the path, back to the house. The sun was now flooding the lawn with light. Yes, indeed, she thought joyfully, it will be a beautiful day.

TWENTY-EIGHT

*T*he next day Catherine settled into a chair on the porch with stationery and a pencil. Using a book as a tabletop, she began to write.

Dear Mrs. Perry (!),

Hello from Oakview, where I received your letter with great excitement. It made me smile, dear friend, to read how happy you are. I'm glad that marriage—all parts of it!—has lived up to its promise. And it does not surprise me that Clarence is an attentive and generous husband. (But who could not be, to someone like you?)

Life out West is anything but dull. No grizzlies or earthquakes, but there are more social engagements than I ever anticipated. In spite of them, I am spending as much time as I can in the garden. I wish you could see it, Vinia! The color, the sunlight; it's heavenly. And best of all, I'm actually designing a new section of it. At last, I've found a kind of art that suits me. Isn't it wonderful? I'm helped in this by Thomas, the head gardener. He is patience incarnate and somehow understands even my wildest artistic notions. I am so fortunate that he is here.

She tapped her pencil against her teeth. On the lawn in front of her, the sprinklers swished. The arc of water looked like diamonds in the sunlight.

To be honest, Vinia, I'd spend all summer outside, if I could. But we are hosting the former governor of California and his wife here next weekend. Yes, these are the exalted circles in which I now move. You cannot imagine the discussions about menus, linens, etc. They make my head spin. I'm so grateful Harriet is here to take charge. She does so with great relish, thankfully.

She heard the clock striking inside, three chimes in the quiet reception room.

I will have to stop, brief as this is. We are planning a luncheon at the stables, and William wants me to go with him this afternoon to see where the table will be laid. He cares very much about the success of the weekend. So I will leave it here for now, dear friend, and send you my warmest California kisses across the globe. Give my fond love to Clarence, too, and thank him for taking such good care of you.

Until next time,
The future Mrs. Brandt

She put down the pencil, feeling odd. Lavinia was right. It was a strange thing to write one's new name.

"Harriet certainly enjoys entertaining, doesn't she?" Catherine said to William as they walked toward the stables.

"She always has."

"I'm not sure I do," she said frankly.

He looked at her. "No?"

"No. I admire those who do it well, but it's not something I take pleasure in."

"I'm surprised by that," he said. "Entertaining is a big part of being a wife."

"I can do it, if I must. But I don't enjoy it as much as I do other things."

"Such as?"

She thought for a moment, ordering her answers with care. "Playing the piano. Reading. Designing the garden."

"Those have limited value for a hostess," he said, "though piano is good, of course." He waved away a fly. "It's probably just lack of experience. You haven't had enough opportunities to entertain. We'll do what we can to change that."

It was not welcome news. "Will there be other house parties this summer?"

"Not this summer. But after the wedding, I want to make Oakview as it was when my mother was alive. A place where prominent people feel comfortable and at home."

"People like the Laws."

"Exactly."

"Why are they so important to you?" she asked abruptly.

They were nearly at the stables, the peak of the roof visible through the trees. She heard the whinny of a horse and the regular cadence of hooves. The sun seemed stronger than it had at the house.

"Because," said William, "they are connected to everyone who matters in this state. And they are not easily impressed."

"But they will be, after next weekend?"

His gaze, calm and appraising, moved from her eyes to her cheekbones to her lips and then back again. He smiled. "I believe they will."

⁊⊙

"What made you want to become a doctor?" Catherine asked Thomas the next afternoon. "You said once that it was a long story."

"It was because of my mother," said Thomas. He was setting potted flowers in the dirt of one of the beds, trying out their placement before planting. When he was done, he stood beside Catherine on the path and together they surveyed his handiwork. "Does this do justice to your design?"

"It does," she said. "Though I feel like an imposter, calling it a design. I'm just an amateur."

"Don't say that," he said. She surreptitiously studied his face: the blue eyes, the strong nose, the slight upturn at the corners of his mouth. "You had the ideas. I would never have thought of mixing all these colors."

"Oh dear. That must mean my designs are crazy."

"No. Original."

His smile felt different at close range than it did at their usual distance; she could even see the little lines made by the creases in the corners of his eyes. It occurred to her that William never smiled with his eyes, only with his mouth and, then, only barely.

"Well," she said, "I hope it will look as good as I imagine."

"If not, you can always try again next season. Nothing is permanent in a garden." He moved the wheelbarrow to the next bed, where he took out more plants.

"You won't be here, though."

"No, but there will be a new head gardener. They've begun to advertise for one."

Leaning her parasol against the edge of the wheelbarrow, Catherine carefully picked up a potted daisy and carried it over to the flower bed, setting it in the dirt. After studying it, she moved it a fraction to the left, satisfied to be doing a part of the work herself. "So, you were talking about your mother."

"She died when I was seventeen, of cancer." He picked up a snapdragon, its ruffled petals the color of a sunset sky. "She was sick for several months before she died, and when she did, I was devastated. And angry. Mostly angry." He set it down and turned to her for approval. "There?"

"That's perfect."

"It was too late for the doctors to operate. She died the day after my seventeenth birthday, here in the gardener's cottage, where I grew up." He nodded toward the brick house just beyond the orchard. "I took it hard. My mother had always been my champion. Not that my father wasn't, but it was different. Dad and I were very alike, you see, quiet and reserved. My mother was the one with spirit. She could pull us out of ourselves and make us laugh, make things exciting. And for a while when she died, nothing seemed right. Dad and I were like a pair of ghosts."

A hummingbird appeared, seemingly out of nowhere. It hovered just a few feet above them, and they both watched it. When it flew off, Thomas turned back to the wheelbarrow. "But it was her death that helped me see what my life would be."

"Was that the first time you thought of becoming a doctor?"

"No, I'd wanted to be one since I was a boy. I was always fascinated by how they would open that black bag and take out instruments and decide what was going on inside a person when they didn't even know it themselves. There was one time when I wanted to be a lawyer, but that didn't last."

"Why a lawyer?"

He gave a brief, wry smile. "I was sixteen and in love. She was the daughter of a judge. I thought a lawyer was a profession she'd respect." He righted a fallen snapdragon. "But she had no serious interest in me, and I finally realized that. Then my mother became sick, which showed me there was nothing more important than making another person well. Or trying to, at least." He stepped back, surveying the flower bed. "It's a long process and I had to start late, work and earn the tuition first. But I'm about halfway through now. They were very decent about me taking this time away when Dad was ill."

He took another snapdragon out of the barrow after first disentangling two stalks. She looked at his hands with the dirt around the nails and imagined them touching a feverish forehead or feeling for a broken bone. He would be a good doctor, she could tell. He had both patience and the desire to make things grow. Perhaps medicine was much like gardening.

"When did you stop being angry about your mother?" she asked.

"September 16, 1901."

The exactness of his answer surprised her. "What happened?"

He moved the wheelbarrow slightly, and she could see he was unaccustomed to telling the story.

"I had a dream one night," he said, indicating the Tree of Knowledge off in the distance. "I dreamed I was in the garden by the big oak there, and my mother came walking down the path toward me. 'You're alive!' I said. And she said, 'Yes, but just for today. I just need you to know that I'm all right.'

"I remember being upset in the dream because I wanted her

to stay longer. Her presence was so vivid; everything about her, the inflection in her voice and the combs she used to wear in her hair and the way she would reach up and move my hair out of my eyes. 'Why can't you stay?' I asked.

"She said, 'Because I belong there now. One day, you'll understand. But I just came back to tell you that I'm all right, and to tell that to your father.'

"I woke up and felt a mixture of joy and disappointment. I just wanted to stay in that dream with her. I kept turning it over in my memory, remembering how it felt to be in her presence again. But from that day on, I had a peace about it all. Not that I don't miss her, of course, but the anger is gone."

Catherine reached in her pocket for her handkerchief. "I didn't mean to make you cry," he said.

"It's a lovely story," she said, wiping her eyes. "But it does make me rather jealous. I wish I could have a dream like that about my mother."

"How did she die?" he asked.

"I don't know." He looked surprised, and she hastened to explain. "I was only going to live with my aunt and uncle for a short time, but then she wrote to say that I should stay with them. We think it's because she was dying. We never heard from her again." Saying it aloud, something she had almost never had occasion to do, made her hear the story in a new way. "My uncle made inquiries, and we think she died in Boston shortly after she wrote."

His gaze was sympathetic and steady. It emboldened her to think something she had never thought before.

"Perhaps," she said, "someday I can go to Boston. Maybe I can find out for certain what happened." The idea made her heart beat more quickly, with possibility or with fear, she did not know.

"I'm sure Mr. Brandt has the resources to look into it," said

Thomas, "if he wants to do so. If you want to do so," he corrected himself.

"I can talk to him next week, maybe. After the guests have gone." She smoothed the handkerchief with her fingers. "At least now I have a drawing of her. My uncle gave it to me before I came here."

"One of your father's drawings?"

She nodded. "I'm so happy to have it. I talk to her, ask her questions. I would give anything if she could speak back."

She looked up from the handkerchief to find his eyes on hers. Then his gaze moved to her cheek and stayed there.

"There's some dirt on your face," he said.

She quickly put her hand to her cheek. "Here?"

"A little farther up." He was looking intently at her cheekbone and, for a brief, almost exquisitely suspenseful moment, she wondered if he would reach out and touch her face, but of course he did not.

"Thank you," she said, wiping briskly with the handkerchief. "I suppose I'd better go back, anyhow." It would be so easy to linger in the garden and forget the time.

"We've made a start here. I'll get the other gardeners to help with the rest."

"Thank you."

He picked up her parasol and handed it to her. She was a few steps down the path when he spoke again.

"About your mother," he said, and she turned back. He was standing on the path, his arms crossed. "I suspect she does speak to you, in some way or another. I have a feeling that even death can't keep a mother from her children." He gave a shrug. "For what my opinion is worth, that is."

"Thank you," she said again. It is worth a great deal, she thought, but for some reason she did not want to say it out loud.

TWENTY-NINE

*I*t surprised Catherine to find that Nathaniel Law, who was well into his seventies, was an extremely attractive man. Watching him from across the reception room, she tried to pinpoint the reason for his appeal. He had an athletic figure, with only the slightest paunch. His hair was steely gray mixed with black, and he had a well-trimmed Prince of Wales beard, which gave him a look of urbane sophistication. But most of all, it was his charisma, the way he had of fastening his complete attention on the person who was speaking, as if nothing else mattered. And his every movement, even one as small as lighting a cigarette, was the briskly robust action of a much younger man.

Alma was as attractive as her husband, though in a different way. She had a statuesque, beautiful figure, and her hair was the kind of silver that still looks blond, giving her a more youthful look than most women in their late fifties. While Nathaniel was dynamic magnetism, she was coolness: correct, but utterly lacking in warmth. Catherine was grateful Harriet was there to lead the conversation as the three women, sitting by the French windows, made the requisite small talk.

"It's been quite a while since you were last at Oakview," said Harriet. "I believe my father was alive, was he not?"

"He was," said Alma. "We were here before the earthquake."

"I hope you find it just as beautiful as before," said Harriet warmly.

"I'm sure I shall."

"You live in Sacramento, I believe?" asked Catherine.

"Outside the city, yes." Alma held her empty glass out to the side and Hayes darted in to take it from her. "I've never liked big cities. I positively hated our years in San Francisco."

"The Laws have a large ranch," said Harriet to Catherine. "They breed horses there."

"We don't. I do," said Alma, with an emphasis on the pronouns. She glanced at her husband, who was deep in conversation with William. "Nathaniel likes to ride, but that's the extent of his interest."

Catherine scoured her memory for anything she knew about horse breeding but came up short. "It must be a fascinating hobby," she finally said.

"Oh, it's more than a hobby." Alma turned to look directly at Catherine. "It's my raison d'être. There is nothing more gratifying than the birth of a foal. And sometimes you attain perfection." She accepted the refilled glass from Hayes and took a sip.

In the pause, Catherine tried to think of the next place to direct the conversation. She wondered if Nathaniel and Alma had any children, but it seemed the wrong moment to ask.

"You will enjoy our plans for tomorrow," said Harriet, who, unlike Catherine, appeared to be perfectly at ease. "We thought we'd do lunch at the stables and go for a long ride in the hills."

"What an excellent idea," said Alma. She had become more animated ever since horses were mentioned. It was proof, thought Catherine, of her aunt's maxim that a good hostess remembers what her guests enjoy. Harriet was a natural.

"It should be a beautiful day for it," said Harriet. "Unfortunately, Catherine doesn't yet know how to ride."

"No?"

"No," said Catherine.

Alma looked at her with pity. "I can't imagine my life without riding," she said. "People always disappoint me. Horses rarely do."

❧

Catherine came down the staircase for dinner, trailing her hand on the polished banister. In the gilt-framed mirror on the landing, she saw the full effect of the new red dinner gown, one of the dresses hastily ordered from Madame Rainier before the return to Oakview. Agnes had been full of admiration as she helped Catherine fasten it, saying, "It's the most striking dress you've ever worn, Miss Ogden." And as her reflection came closer, Catherine saw that it was indeed a dress meant to command attention. She had never before worn red—the color was outside her aunt's conservative view of what was appropriate for unmarried girls—and for a brief, self-conscious moment she was tempted to change into something more familiar.

But William, crossing the hall at the foot of the stairs, had seen her. He stopped and watched her as she descended, and it was evident from the look in his eyes that he would not wish her to change. His admiration filled her with a rush of confidence. She deliberately slowed her steps, enjoying the headiness of feminine power and her ability to keep him waiting.

"It's a new dress," she said as she came down the last step.

"I know. I would have remembered if you'd worn it before." He took in all the details: the jeweled pin in her pompadour, the long white gloves, and the gold necklace with an inset ruby, which had been given to her on her eighteenth birthday. "Very nice." His eyes lit on her right wrist. "It's a shame you don't have a matching bracelet."

"I don't mind," she said. "It's easier to play piano without one."

He offered her his arm, and together they went out to the sunporch. Nathaniel stood alone in his evening clothes, drinking a sherry and gazing toward the hills. He turned to face them and, at the sight of Catherine, his expression of patrician benevolence gave way to something else, a look both avid and involuntary.

But it passed quickly, and he recovered his usual gallantry. "Miss Ogden. You are a vision."

"Please, call me Catherine."

He indicated a chair and she sat down. He did the same after first expertly flipping the tails of his suit.

She nodded toward the fog creeping over the hills. "Look at that. It will be cold tonight, I think." She had finally grown used to the switch from sun-drenched days to evening fog, sometimes accompanied by a keen breeze that drove one inside.

"It's a welcome change," Nathaniel said. "In Sacramento, the summers are unbearably hot. We'd give anything for some of that fog."

"It's always so dramatic, coming over the hills," she said. "Almost like another mountain range. It would be a beautiful painting."

"Speaking of paintings," William said, "this is a good time to show Nathaniel the art collection. If I know my sister, she won't be ready for another half hour at least."

"Nor will Alma," said Nathaniel. "And she's not interested in art, anyhow." He got up and offered his arm to Catherine. "Will you give me a tour?"

She looked at William, who nodded. "You two go ahead. I have something to do in my study."

Nathaniel told her to start with the painting she liked best, so she led him to the Van Dyck still life. "And what makes it your favorite?" he asked.

"How simple it is. Just plates and fruit, and yet it's worthy of a painting. Van Dyck must have studied these things so closely to see how beautiful they are."

As they moved along, he asked her questions about the artists and subjects of the paintings. She answered most of them, and even when she could not, she still felt clever and knowledgeable due to his intent gaze, the slight lean of his body toward her, and his charming manner.

There was no doubt he found her attractive, and yet his every word and move was entirely appropriate. She had a sudden insight that when it came to women other than his wife, he knew exactly how far to go and went no further.

They paused before the Canaletto. "Beautiful," he said. "Now this really feels like Venice, doesn't it?"

"I wouldn't know, I'm afraid. I've never been there."

"You haven't?"

"No."

Nathaniel gave a quick shake of his head. "And they think westerners are the savages." She laughed and he took her hand and squeezed it, as if pretending to be grateful she had not taken offense. "You have a sense of humor," he said. "That's good."

He held her hand just a fraction beyond what she was expecting, then let it go. Buoyed by the interaction and the power of the red dress, she felt a more potent kind of beautiful than she had ever felt before.

"So," he said, "William has come into his own, after all." He cast an approving eye at the paintings stretching back down the hallway. "I must say I'm impressed. He's a man to be reckoned with, it seems."

"He has been so looking forward to your visit," said Catherine.

"I don't wonder. He has a great deal to be proud of." He

turned back to her, and for a moment, the avid look came back into his eyes. "Lucky devil," he said softly.

He offered her his arm, and they went back down the hall, just in time to meet Alma coming down the stairs for dinner.

THIRTY

*T*hough Harriet had hoped for mild weather on the day of the picnic, by eleven o'clock it was undeniably hot. All the same, there was an air of excitement as the house party, joined by Vivian and Peter, gathered in the reception room to proceed to the stables. Catherine was the only woman not wearing a riding suit, and Peter was the only man not in jodhpurs.

William usually went to the stables early in the morning, so it was unusual for Catherine to see him in his riding clothes at midday. She looked at him as if seeing him for the first time: a tall, handsome man whose muscular physique was more evident in the close-cut jodhpurs and white shirt than in his usual attire. He was what the novelists would call a "fine figure of a man," she thought.

"Shall we walk or drive?" William asked. "The stables are about half a mile away."

"Walk, of course," said Alma immediately. Peter, who had opened his mouth to speak, quickly closed it.

"Vivian?" William asked.

"I say walk," she said. "It will sharpen our appetites."

"There will be a car taking a few of the items for our luncheon," said Harriet. "I could ask Anderson to take anyone who would prefer to ride." She said this delicately, directing it not at Peter but at the entire group.

"Not I," said Peter with obvious effort. "If my wife will walk, so will I."

Vivian, who stood before the mirror arranging the veil on her hat, ignored him entirely. She wore a riding costume of olive green trimmed with brown; with her dark red hair, she had the vivid brilliance of a forest in autumn.

"Let's be off, then," said Alma, leading the way out to the terrace.

The path to the stables branched off from the north side of the house, opposite from the gardens. It was graveled, which kept the dust from rising as they walked. Once they passed the edge of the fenced lawn, they were in an open field where the tawny grass smelled both subtle and sweet.

They walked in stages. Alma led the way with William, then came Nathaniel and Vivian and Harriet. Catherine slowed her gait to keep pace with Peter, who was more flushed than usual. He frequently used his handkerchief to wipe his face, and every time he took off his straw boater, she saw the red rim about his damp forehead.

"We are fortunate it's not humid, at least," she said. "As New York would be."

"It's hot enough, though," he wheezed, and she saw conversation was difficult for him, so she did not speak again.

There was so much to look at anyhow: the blue sky, the long dry grass the color of a tabby cat, the occasional oak standing in splendor in the field. Catherine remembered how surprised she'd been on her return to Oakview, seeing the golden hills for the first time. She marveled at how completely the summer palette had worked its way into her affection. It was different from the East, so different it had to be appreciated as something entirely separate and unique.

As they walked, she found herself watching William. He is a

very impressive man, she thought for the second time that morning. She was conscious of a sudden wash of warm feeling for him,
for the beautiful home he had made, the way he had invited her
into it, and the freedom his life had given to her own. And as she
watched him, she imagined him without the neat white shirt,
wondering what the muscles of his back looked like and how
they would feel underneath her hands. She felt warm in a way that
had nothing to do with the sun, and she stole a glance at Peter to
see if he had noticed. But he was running his finger inside his
collar with a look of stoic suffering, and she relaxed, knowing
her unladylike thoughts were safely hidden inside her mind.

&

Just beyond the immaculately kept stables was a clearing under
the oaks. Hayes was there with two of the footmen, standing by
a buffet table spread with silver dishes. The round table where
they were to eat was covered in a spotless tablecloth, laid out as
if for lunch in the dining room. The trees created a canopy,
which kept off the heat of the sun.

The lunch, which began with tomato aspic and ended with
orange cake, was excellent. Alma was more talkative than usual,
engaging William in an animated conversation about the Kentucky
Derby. At one point he glanced across the table at Catherine with
a look of satisfaction. *This visit is turning out well*, his eyes seemed
to say, and she smiled back, telegraphing her agreement.

When lunch was finished, they all walked to the stables,
where the groom and the stable boy led out the horses. Everyone
but Catherine and Peter chose one to ride.

"What is the trail like?" Catherine asked as they mounted.

"Narrow," said William, "but otherwise very good. Shady,
too, with lots of oaks and bays."

"Like a forest in a fairy tale," said Vivian, with a gleam in her eye. "The dark woods, where anything can happen." She seemed almost as eager to set off as Alma, who was moving her horse about restlessly.

"We won't be long," said Harriet to Catherine and Peter, patting the neck of her white mare. "We'll probably be back here in an hour."

"Speak for yourself," called Alma. "I may not return before sunset."

Catherine would not have thought it possible for William to appear any more imposing than he normally did, but seeing him on the back of the stallion, she realized she'd been wrong. Perhaps that was why so many emperors had their portraits painted on horseback; it gave a man an extra air of power.

And a woman, too, she realized, looking at Vivian. She had brought her horse near William's, and though the brown stallion was spirited, she handled him expertly, reining him in while simultaneously saying something to William that made him burst out laughing. It was a sound Catherine had never heard from him. Vivian, too, seemed to have undergone a change; she glowed with vigor and excitement, very different from her usually jaded demeanor.

"Look at my wife," Peter said approvingly. "She's like an Amazon princess on that horse." She rode off, giving him the barest backward wave as she and William followed the others into the distance.

"You don't ride?" Catherine asked Peter as the two of them returned to the clearing.

"Oh, I did when I was young," he said. "But not for many years now. I wouldn't do that to the horse."

Back at the table, he sank down into one of the chairs and crossed his hands over his stomach, sighing contentedly. The staff was clearing away the lunch things with silent efficiency, and Catherine sat down and looked up at the trees.

She recalled a French painting she had seen once, of an outside luncheon party. She had studied it for a long time in the museum, admiring the table with the remains of a meal, the half-full glasses of wine, the raffish diners relaxing easily against the chairs and each other as they savored the languor of a summer's day. Her afternoon was like that painting; it was even better, she realized, for here there was the spicy smell of the bay trees and the filtered warmth of the sun through the oaks, along with the insistent but somehow pleasant hum of the cicadas. She leaned back in her chair as far as her corset would allow and smiled up at the sky.

"I just love California," she said impulsively.

Peter opened his eyes. "What?"

"I just love California. I'm so happy I'm here."

"That's good," he said, stifling a yawn. "I hope you like Washington just as much."

"Pardon?"

"I hope you like Washington as much as you like it here." She looked at him blankly, and he lifted himself up in the chair to converse more easily. "When William goes into the Senate."

"The Senate?"

"He hasn't told you?" Peter seemed surprised by her ignorance. "That's his goal, you know, to become a senator. He's wanted that for years."

"No," she said slowly. "He didn't tell me."

"His father ran once and lost. I think William has always wanted to prove that a Brandt can win." He yawned, settling back in his seat. "He's planning to throw his hat in the ring at the next opportunity."

"I see."

He misinterpreted her tone. "Oh, I'm sure he'll win. He has more finesse than his father did. And you, my dear, are a great asset to him." He closed his eyes, hands crossed on his stomach.

The hum of the cicadas grew more insistent, restless, and louder than before. It mirrored Catherine's thoughts as she stared at a faraway bay tree, not seeing it, her heartbeat increasing in speed as the moments passed.

Abruptly she stood up, her chair scraping on the ground. At the sound, Peter opened his eyes.

"I'm going to walk back to the house," she said.

"Would you like me to accompany you?" he asked dutifully.

"No, thank you," she said. "I can find my way alone."

THIRTY-ONE

At five o'clock, Catherine opened the door to the billiards room. William was there alone in his evening clothes, cue in hand. He straightened and smiled. "You're down early. I hope you had a good rest."

"William," she said without preamble. "You never told me about running for the Senate."

She had obviously taken him by surprise. After a moment he set the cue on the table. "Where did you hear that?"

"Peter. I would have thought you would be the one to tell me something as important as that."

Her voice was charged with heat, and he raised a warning eyebrow, then walked past her to close the door.

"It's true," he said calmly. "I've considered it for a long time. But I hadn't decided exactly when."

"Peter said it would be at the first opportunity."

"Perhaps. We'll see."

She put a hand on her ribs to collect herself. He was looking down at her, outwardly as composed as always, but there was an alertness in his eyes that inflamed her own sense of battle.

"This affects everything," she said. "It means our lives are totally different."

"From what?"

"From what I expected." She gestured out the window. "We wouldn't be living here, at Oakview."

"Not all the time, no. We would be in the East a good part of the year."

"But you should have told me that. You should have told me last spring, when you proposed. You owed me that much."

He could do it so easily, pin her in his gaze and make it impossible for her to look away. It became so silent in the room that she could even hear a bird trilling outside the closed window.

"Are you saying it would have changed your answer?" he asked.

She did not know what to say. She looked up at him mutely, aware that she had somehow lost the moral advantage she'd had when the conversation began. He smiled as if the conflict were over.

"It was a surprise, I'm sure," he said. "But we'll discuss it later, when you've had time to get used to it. Let's focus on tonight and having a good time with our guests."

"Now I see why you wanted to impress the Laws. They can help your ambitions."

"Of course. That's the nature of politics, Catherine."

After a pause she added, "And I can help your ambitions, too."

At her tone, he glanced up swiftly. "You can," he said with quiet emphasis. "And I expect that you will."

The door opened and Nathaniel came into the billiards room. He stopped at the sight of Catherine and William together. "Oh, excuse me," he said with an urbane smile. "It seems I'm interrupting."

"Not at all," said William. He picked up his cue, then took down another one. "We've time to play before drinks. As long as Catherine doesn't mind?"

She managed a smile at Nathaniel and left, her heart still pounding in her ears.

૭૦

Two years earlier, on a morning in April, Lavinia had come to the house on Madison Avenue and gone up to Catherine's room and closed the door. "You should have heard Mama and Papa fight last night," she said, her eyes wide. "They could probably hear them in Brooklyn."

"What were they fighting about?"

Lavinia shrugged. "I couldn't make it all out, but Mama was furious that Papa was home late again. She was angry, so angry."

Catherine thought of the musical event the Boscats were hosting that evening. "Will they cancel the concert?"

"Not a chance."

At the concert, Mr. and Mrs. Boscat stood side by side and greeted their guests warmly and graciously. As they took their seats for the performance, Mr. Boscat put his hand on his wife's back, and she did not rebuff him. There was no hint of discord between them. They seemed perfectly happy and at ease with each other.

"Your parents must have reconciled," Catherine whispered to Lavinia.

"Not at all," said Lavinia. "Mama's still furious. But she would die before letting the world know there was anything wrong."

That evening at Oakview, Catherine understood. Her anger at William had not cooled by the time the guests arrived. It still beat along her veins, hot and steady. She had never been to Washington, but she knew the feeling of a city where every action was scrutinized, where a wife's misstep could materially damage her husband's career. It was not a life she wished for herself, and he had been wrong, so wrong, to conceal his ambitions. And yet she found that pride, instilled in her by the example of the women of New York, could temporarily be anger's equal.

She remained poised and welcoming as the other dinner guests arrived. She had met all of them before, and she knew how to strike the right balance between formality and familiarity, smiling graciously even though the sight of William leaning against the mantel and talking with Herbert and Marion Eaton made her anger flare up deep inside.

Perhaps I should have been an actress, she thought as Emmeline Platt, the wife of a local banker, asked her about wedding preparations. Catherine answered with appropriate excitement, and Emmeline smiled nostalgically.

"Oh, so thrilling," she said. "A wedding is such a happy time." She was an attractive woman in her late thirties with a complexion that glowed with rosy health. "My own wedding is a distant memory, four children ago, but oh, how I loved it."

"Are your children boys or girls?" Catherine asked.

"Two of each. They're sweet children, though they run positively wild in the summer. But the Peninsula is a wonderful place to raise a family. So much land, and so much nicer than the city."

Catherine's thoughts had been momentarily diverted from Washington, but now they raced back. She glanced at William as he lit a cigarette; his eyes briefly met hers, relaxed and confident, as he turned back to the Eatons. Clearly, he had no fear she would give any hint of the argument in the billiards room. He had full faith in her New York upbringing, in the importance of never revealing what you really thought if it posed the slightest risk of shaking you from your place on the social ladder.

And she, with her poise and smiles, was proving him right.

THIRTY-TWO

*W*hen they adjourned to the dining room, Louis Sumner was seated to Catherine's left. He was a prominent architect and writer with a narrow face and an artistically intense manner.

"You seem to be embracing life in California," he said to her pleasantly as they started on their consommé. The innocent comment caused a fresh flare of anger, but she answered him with a smile.

"I am, very much," she said.

"Have you had the chance to see many other parts of the state?"

"Not yet. I'm eager to do so."

"It's a place with so much variety," Louis said. "You go east to the Sierra Nevada and the mountains are astonishing, so tall and remote. Hours from that, there's the desert. Down along the coast, you have Monterey and Pacific Grove, with their beautiful beaches. You could travel all over this state and never be bored."

"That's certainly true," said John Platt, Emmeline's husband. He was round-faced and friendly, glowing with unforced kindness. "It would take a lifetime to see every part of California. You are wise to start so young, Miss Ogden."

"I've often wondered why it's called California," said Catherine. "What does the name mean?" She looked across the table to John and Marion Eaton, both of whom met her question with blank faces. Marion turned to her husband, whose own conversation with Nathaniel had finished, and asked, "Do you know, Herbert?"

"What?"

"Why it's called California?"

Herbert, a balding man with a large white moustache, shook his head. "I can't say I do," he said. "I don't think anyone knows anymore." Catherine sensed he was irritated by his own ignorance.

Louis put down his spoon. "Actually, the Spanish explorers gave it that name. There was a novel written in Spain in the sixteenth century. It featured an island named California."

"Really?" said Harriet. "I had no idea."

"And this island," Louis continued, "was inhabited only by women."

"Well," said Vivian. "Isn't that something."

"They were warriors," said Louis, "and had a Black queen named Calafia. If any man came onto their island, they gave him to their pet griffins to be devoured."

"Oh my," said Marion with a laugh.

"I rather like that," said Vivian. "Why shouldn't we women stick together?"

"And devour the men?" asked William, amused. "That seems excessive."

Vivian raised her chin and looked directly at him. In her dress of turquoise blue, she reminded Catherine of a peacock, bright and dazzling. "Not if you've done something to deserve it," she said, her voice like an arrow.

Her words and tone, so at odds with the easy conversation, added a charge to the air. In the uncomfortable silence that followed, Alma's gaze darted from Vivian to William, alert and amused. Catherine turned to her fiancé. His demeanor was imperturbable, but his eyes, fixed on Vivian, were dark with warning.

Just then the double doors swung open, and Hayes entered, carrying a large silver tray of roast lamb. Two footmen, bearing serving platters, followed behind.

"Ah," said Peter, who had seemed oblivious to the tension in the room, "that looks delicious."

"Speaking of devouring," said Nathaniel smoothly, "I can't recall when I've been more well-fed. My compliments to your cook."

With the arrival of the main course, the easy tone of the evening was restored. As conversation resumed, Catherine looked around the table. In the dim light, the party had a certain air of unreality, like watching actors in a play. Emmeline Platt lightly touched her napkin to her lips, Herbert leaned forward with intensity to underscore his point to John, and Harriet discreetly signaled to Hayes, who bent down for a whispered direction then disappeared into the kitchen. If this is a play, she thought, then I'm part of it myself. Catherine Ogden in the role of the happy ingenue, blissfully in love with her fiancé.

"Pride and manners before honesty," Lavinia had once said. "That's the code of the debutantes."

Catherine looked again at William as he sat at the head of the table, intently listening to Nathaniel. He was so solid and strong, like a man of marble. Earlier in the day, that strength had been appealing, the mere thought of it capable of making heat rise to her face. But earlier in the day, she had been unaware that he was deliberately withholding something she had every right to know.

Over dessert of pudding and fresh fruit from the greenhouse, the conversation turned to local news. "Our estate is part of a new city now," Herbert told Nathaniel and Alma. "Just weeks ago, we voted to break away from Burlingame. Hillsborough, the name is. It's a relief to have that done."

"Burlingame was getting too crowded, you see," said Marion. "So many little homes cropping up in the east side. We wanted to keep the dignity of the old estates."

"And they would have forced us to have sidewalks and streetlights," said Herbert. "Imagine, people walking by your home at all hours. The next thing you know, it will be like San Francisco."

"That's one of the effects of the earthquake," Louis explained to Catherine. "Many people have chosen to move out of the city and down the Peninsula."

"I can see why they would wish to go somewhere safer," she said.

"But my dear, nowhere is safe." Herbert had a pedantic air, which was more noticeable every time he addressed the women at the table. "You do understand that the ground could move at any moment, anywhere in this state."

"But there's no denying that one is safer on a country estate than in a crowded apartment building on Market Street," said Vivian. "That's just common sense."

"It is fascinating," said Harriet, "to think of how each region of the country has its own perils. We have earthquakes, but we don't have hurricanes or tornadoes. I can't decide which one I would rather face, can you?"

"Oh, not tornadoes," said Emmeline. "Not after reading *The Wizard of Oz*. Though my children think a flying house would be quite an adventure."

Herbert was not to be diverted. "At any rate," he said, raising his voice, "this influx of new residents is just one threat. Our generation has worked hard to make this a beautiful place to live. We must be vigilant about protecting it." His wife offered him a cluster of green grapes, and he irritably dismissed her.

"Perhaps," said Alma unexpectedly, "that's how those women warriors felt." In the dim light her eyes gleamed with mischief. "They merely wanted to protect their island from outsiders."

"Nonsense," said Herbert. "A society without men would crumble."

"Would it?" Vivian raised an eyebrow.

"Absolutely," said Herbert. "Men are a stabilizing influence."

"I certainly wouldn't want to live without them," Emmeline said as she delicately peeled a nectarine. "Women can be so catty, you know."

"Indeed," said Marion. "It pains me to admit it, but it's true."

"What was it your father used to say?" Nathaniel turned to William, who was refilling his wine glass. "A society without women is uncivilized, but a society without men would be savage?"

William laughed and passed him the decanter. "That sounds like my father. He had a memorable turn of phrase."

"And now women are angling for the vote," said Herbert. "You know the local suffragettes are starting to campaign again. Just the other day there were some on the steps of the library."

"Isn't it natural for women to want the vote?" Catherine asked.

Silence greeted her question, which was broken after a moment by Herbert. He looked across the table at her, his spoon paused in midair. "Why should we change the status quo, is the question," he said. "The mechanisms of society are functioning smoothly as they are. You don't fix something that isn't broken." He raised the spoon to his mouth, where it disappeared under his white whiskers.

Catherine waited for one of the other women to respond, but none of them did. "How easy it is for a man to say it isn't broken," she said, surprised by the energy in her own voice. "You are the ones who have the power." Out of the corner of her eye, she saw William look up at her swiftly, but she ignored him.

"My objection to women's suffrage," Herbert said, the pedantic tone once again creeping into his voice, "is that there are different spheres for men and women. Politics is a man's sphere. The home is a woman's. That's how it has always been. And it's that way because it works." He smiled benevolently, as if instructing her in a truth she could not be expected to know.

Emmeline nodded as she put down her water glass. "And you know, if women have the vote, it may cause discord in the home. Imagine a woman having different political views than her husband."

"I'm sure that happens already, in many homes," said Louis mildly.

"Absolutely," said Alma, flashing a glance at her husband as she reached for an orange.

"But it would be more problematic if women had the ability to vote," said Herbert. "If those differences were a reality, not just a theory."

Catherine's heartbeats were coming faster, but she had no desire to stop. "If any society should be called savage," she said, turning to William, "it's the one we currently have. A truly civilized society would grant the vote to all of its members."

"All of its members?" repeated Herbert before William could respond. "So you would have children vote? The deranged?"

"If you deny women the right to vote," Catherine said, "then

you are saying we're no different than children or the deranged."
She looked directly at him. "Is that what you believe?"

There was silence. Catherine caught a glimpse of Vivian
across the table, her eyes wide. Harriet leaned forward, about to
speak, but before she could, William had pushed back his chair
and stood up.

His voice was flint covered with politeness. "We won't solve
this tonight, will we." He nodded at Harriet. "Perhaps you ladies
would like to adjourn to the drawing room."

As the women sat with their coffee, Catherine's adrenaline subsided. Her last comment to Herbert had been like riding the
crest of a wave; then her pulse slowed and she regained equanimity. Harriet, always poised, steered the conversation into less
controversial channels, including the latest news from her son in
Europe and what was scheduled for the rest of the summer at
the country club. And apart from Vivian flashing Catherine a
look of ironic sympathy, no reference was made to the uncomfortable finish to the dinner. By the time the men joined them for
cards, Catherine only wanted the evening to end.

It did after eleven, with the leave-taking of their guests.
Herbert bowed over Catherine's hand and even smiled briefly as
he said his farewell. She politely returned his goodbye, and none
of the guests referred to what had taken place over dessert. It's
just like New York, she thought. You act as if nothing has happened, although in reality no one ever forgets.

Once the Laws and Harriet had gone upstairs, Catherine
turned to do the same. "Don't go," said William. He opened the
door of his study. "I want to talk to you."

The study was dark but for the light on William's massive

desk. The moon shone through the high windows, and she stood looking out at the terrace while William closed the door and switched on the electric lights.

"That," he said quietly, "was a ridiculous thing to say."

She almost asked what he was talking about, but she knew, and he knew that she knew, so she was silent as she turned to face him.

"You made a fool of yourself," he said, "and of me. Speaking that way to a guest."

She felt like a child again, scolded by Miss Foster or her aunt, but she was not a child and his tone revived her anger. "He was the one being ridiculous. His attitudes are almost medieval."

"He was our guest, which is all that matters. Surely your aunt raised you better than that."

"Do you agree with him?" she asked. "Are you also against women's suffrage?"

He swept the issue away with an impatient gesture. "I don't give a damn one way or another," he said. "If women want to vote, fine. But to insult a guest in that way—it's unpardonable. I can only wonder what the Laws thought."

"They didn't mind," she said, although she was not certain it was true.

"They were too polite to show their true feelings. As you should have been. And I mind. I need you to be a gracious hostess, not a . . . a harpy."

"You are forbidding me to have opinions," she said with heat.

"No," he said, his tone matching hers. "No, only to share them without thinking. If they're likely to cause conflict, keep them to yourself."

The mention of conflict made her recall something. "Vivian," she said suddenly. "What did she mean? That comment she made to you?"

He looked surprised, then angry. "Don't change the subject. Your behavior was beneath you, and you must promise not to repeat it."

"Very well," she said, to end the argument. "In the future I will keep my views on women's suffrage to myself. Good night." She moved to go, but he stepped in her path.

"I know what this is really about," he said. "You're angry at me, and this is how you're showing it."

He was right, at least in part, but she would not give him the satisfaction of saying so.

"It's late," she said, turning away. "I don't want to talk about this anymore."

"Don't go," he said. "I haven't finished."

She ignored him and moved toward the closed door. Before her hand could touch the knob, he had crossed to her and grabbed her wrist and jerked her toward him. Her shock at this was so great she could only stare him.

"You're hurting me," she said when she could speak. But he held her wrist just as tightly as before, and he was so close to her she felt the front of his evening shirt against her décolletage.

"We need to be very clear about this," he said in a low voice. "I will not let you, or anyone, undermine me. No matter how angry you happen to be."

She nodded, and he released her. She opened the door and walked down the hall to the staircase, her wrist throbbing and her eyelids stinging. At the far end of the hall, she saw a maid crossing into the kitchen with a tray and Hayes carefully moving a chair back into place. The next morning, all visible traces of the party would be gone.

॰

It had been years since she had cried into her pillow, and she felt like a child again, crying just as she had her first summer in New York. This time the tears were not of grief but of fear, confusion, and loneliness. She realized how isolated she was in the house. There was no one whom she could tell about William's anger and the shocking, viselike grip on her wrist.

She imagined her aunt being there, witnessing the whole evening. What would she think?

"You were terribly uncouth," her aunt would say. "A hostess never insults her guests in that way. I am surprised at you."

"But I was so angry about what he was saying," Catherine would respond. "And angry at William for not telling me his plans."

"It makes no difference," her aunt would say. "There are certain things you hide from others."

"But he grabbed my wrist and hurt me."

And here she could not imagine what her aunt would say in response. At times she heard her say, "You were not letting him speak. He was simply trying to get your attention."

And at other times she looked at Catherine with pity and concern. "Your uncle has never done that to me, and he never would."

Catherine tossed and turned, taking care to avoid her sore wrist. As she did so, fragments of the day kept flashing into her memory, like flickering pictures at the movie palace. William in his stark white riding shirt; the remains of the roast lamb on the silver tray; the light filtering through the oak leaves by the stables, in the still moments before Peter spoke; a tribe of women on horseback, united and ferocious; Vivian's wide eyes above the peacock blue of her gown.

"Your fiancé can be terrifying," she had once said.

She was right.

THIRTY-THREE

"Was it a nice party?" Agnes asked the next morning.

"It was," said Catherine, wondering if her maid knew anything about what had transpired. Hayes had been in the room during the uncomfortable finish to dessert, but surely he, so reserved and correct, would never gossip with the staff. "It was very nice." She had dressed herself that morning, for when she woke, she noticed a hint of greenish purple circling the fair skin of her wrist, and it was not something she wished the maid to see. Luckily, it was hidden by the long sleeves of her dress.

"I had a little too much wine, perhaps," added Catherine with forced levity. She had to offer some explanation for the hints of the sleepless night visible in her face.

"I'm sure it was a delicious dinner," said Agnes a shade wistfully as she expertly pinned Catherine's hair.

There was a knock on the door, and Agnes went to open it. Mrs. Callahan stood in the hallway, her expression kind and apologetic.

"Excuse me, Miss Ogden. Mr. Brandt asked me to give you a message. He would like to speak to you before breakfast, in the study."

"Thank you," Catherine said. There was a curl of apprehension in the pit of her stomach, but she tamped it down. "And thank you for all your help in planning last night. Everything was beautiful."

The housekeeper smiled. "I'm pleased it was such a success."

❧

Catherine had never before noticed how noiseless the halls of Oakview were. The thick carpet swallowed up her footsteps, and she was glad, for she had no desire to call attention to herself. As she passed the large window on the staircase, she caught a glimpse of the front drive, framed by vines, early sunlight on the water in the fountain. If only she could slip out to the garden, hide among the flowers, and not see anyone for the rest of the day.

William's study door was ajar, the only view a slice of carpet and leather club chair and window. Her wrist throbbed with the memory of the night before and she almost turned to leave, but after a moment she pushed open the door and went in.

He looked up from the paper he was reading. "Good morning."

She nodded, closing the door.

He came out from behind the desk and stood a few feet away. There was no sign on his face that he, like she, had spent a sleepless night, but she thought she saw evidence of careful rehearsal in his manner as he set down the paper and put his hands in his pockets. His eyes, at least, did not have the alarming expression of the night before.

"Neither one of us was at our best last night," he said. He watched her as he spoke, as if waiting for assent. She looked down, and he seemed to interpret it as agreement.

"I see now that I should have told you about the Senate," he said. "And I think you see now that you should not have expressed your anger in the way you did. I hope we can both put this behind us."

It was a poor apology, yet she felt a wave of relief. Had he greeted her with more anger or another hint of violence, she would have been forced to a crisis point that terrified her. Like all girls of her class, she had been taught how to become engaged but had received absolutely no guidance on the way to become unengaged. It had been impossible to imagine how she, alone and unsupported, would begin to undo a union that had been reported in newspapers on both coasts. But now I won't need to, she thought gratefully, closing her ears to the small voice inside that called her a coward.

"I hope so," she said. "I would like to put this behind us."

"Good," he said, and he smiled. It was wider than his smiles usually were, with a flicker of something that could have been relief. "And we won't abandon Oakview, even when I'm in the Senate. We can divide our time between there and here. That will make you happy, I think."

"It will. Thank you."

"Before we go to breakfast," he said, "I have something to give you." He moved back to his desk and opened a drawer, taking out a jewelry box.

It was a wide bracelet, rows of diamonds bordered with rubies. She had never seen anything so opulent, and, for a moment, she was speechless.

"You needed something to wear with your red dress," said William. "Now you have it."

"That didn't take long."

"You should know me by now. I'm not one to hesitate." He took the bracelet out of the box, and, after a moment, she held out her right wrist. If the gesture made him recall his behavior of the night before, he gave no hint of it. He fastened the bracelet around her lace sleeve and then held her by her fingertips, admiring it.

"Perfect," he said. "It could have been made just for you."

The close-fitting bracelet made her aware of the tenderness of her wrist, but she just looked up at him and smiled. "Thank you. It's very beautiful." And when he bent to kiss her, she closed her eyes. It's in the past, she thought. I will move forward and forget about what happened last night.

But the bracelet will always remind you, said the same inconvenient voice inside her head.

॰

The Laws had one more day before leaving, and it passed without incident. Catherine, wanting to erase all memory of the dinner party debacle, tried to be an exemplary hostess. At breakfast, she had the odd sensation of being outside of herself, watching a smiling, dark-haired woman skillfully direct the conversation into channels pleasing to her guests, even drawing Alma into a lighthearted debate about the merits of coffee versus tea. Nathaniel regarded her with the same admiration he had shown the night of the red dress, and William leaned back in his chair with his habitual air of relaxed confidence.

But when Nathaniel asked to see the new garden, she demurred. "Oh, it's barely started. There's really nothing to see." She was surprised at how visceral her response was, how little she wanted to share it with the Laws.

"But you indulged our love of riding," Nathaniel said gallantly. "This is our chance to return the favor. And you can describe how it will look when it's all finished."

"Let's go see it," said William. "You'll be impressed by Catherine's vision."

Half an hour later, the two couples were standing in the new garden. The snapdragons and the white marguerites were the only flowers that had been planted, but Catherine briefly described which colors would fill in the remaining spaces. "It will look much nicer in a few weeks. Or I hope it will. I'm new at this."

"Catherine has an artistic eye, as you see," said William.

"She does indeed," said Nathaniel admiringly.

Thomas appeared through the archway, pushing a wheelbarrow of flowers. He took off his cap at the sight of Catherine and Alma. "Good morning," he said.

Catherine returned his greeting. The men nodded, and Alma, who had not worn a hat, put her hand to her forehead to shade the sun as she studied him.

"Shall we go back?" Catherine asked. "Harriet is waiting for us."

As the two couples walked back through the orchard, Alma turned to Catherine. "Your gardener," she said. "What is his parentage?"

"Pardon?"

"His parentage. His race." Nathaniel, walking by her side, gave an audible sigh.

"Oh," said Catherine. "He is half-Mexican and half-Irish. I believe."

"Hmm." Alma looked back down the path. "I would have guessed Italian. Striking, at any rate."

"What is it about women?" said Nathaniel to the sky. He gestured to William in mock appeal. "Why are they always so fascinated by half-breeds?"

Catherine flinched at the word. William noticed. "Are you all right?" he asked.

"Yes," she said automatically. "It was just a bee. It's gone now." Sometime in the last week, she had apparently learned how to lie without thinking.

THIRTY-FOUR

*T*he Laws left for Sacramento late the next morning, Harriet waving a fond goodbye as they motored off. Catherine was relieved to see them go. Left to her own devices, she would have spent the morning working in the garden, but she and Vivian had been invited to a ladies' tennis luncheon in Woodside, and her own plans had to wait. "Let's motor down together," Vivian had said. "Strength in numbers, you know."

As the Powells' car approached the house, Catherine was surprised to see Vivian herself behind the wheel. "I'm giving the chauffeur the day off," she said as Hayes helped Catherine into the seat.

"I didn't know you could drive."

"Oh, I'm full of surprises," said Vivian. "I can also dress myself and fasten my own shoes."

The car puttered away through the oaks. It was a hot day; the air was thick and there seemed to be wavering lines in the distance.

"Tennis will be difficult in this sun," Catherine said.

"The court is in the shade. And the tennis is just a pretext, really. Most of the time we'll be gossiping about women who aren't there." Vivian tilted her hat against the sun. "They're all itching to talk about Lillian Sims."

"Why?"

"Her husband is keeping a woman on the side. She's acting

like she doesn't know, but of course she does. He's been staying overnight in the city. That's always the first clue." She sounded the horn and a few crows on the road flapped away with ragged cries.

Catherine thought of William's recent nights at the St. Francis Hotel. For a moment, she hovered between two options: either let herself consider their potential significance or shut her mind to it altogether. How strange to realize she could actually decide whether or not to acknowledge the possibility that her fiancé might be unfaithful. It was stranger still to find she was automatically choosing, with a sort of numb detachment, not to do so.

"So you had a good visit with the Laws," said Vivian.

Catherine was wary. "We did. They're very pleasant company."

"Nathaniel, maybe. Alma's an ice queen. But put her on a horse, and she'll thaw." After a pause, she asked in a casual tone, "Was William happy with the weekend?"

"Yes," said Catherine carefully. "On the whole, he was very pleased."

Vivian laughed. "On the whole," she repeated. She turned to Catherine, her eyes keen. "With the exception of Saturday night."

Since Vivian was not looking at the road, Catherine did. It was empty in either direction. "It's fine. We've put that behind us."

"Good," said Vivian.

There was silence for a few moments. Catherine focused on the dusty road, the brown hills, the hard blue sky.

"Let me give you a little advice," said Vivian, "friend to friend." Her expression, for once, was almost grave. "If there's one thing William can't stand, it's being made to look ridiculous."

"I believe all men dislike that," said Catherine stiffly.

Vivian shrugged. "Just a tip. Do with it what you will."

Another car was entering the road, driven by a man swathed in a gray coat, his face obscured by goggles. Vivian raised a hand in greeting as they passed, and he did a visible double take at seeing her behind the wheel.

"Look at that," Vivian said. "Some men are still surprised to see a woman drive." She glanced at Catherine mischievously. "What are the chances that was Herbert Eaton?"

Catherine smiled with effort. Woodside was not very far away, but the drive already seemed endless.

 ℘

The next morning, William left for the city at eight thirty. By eight forty-five, Catherine was in the new garden, where Thomas was planting delphiniums in the center of one of the beds. "I just love that deep blue," she said. "It's always been a favorite color of mine."

"Mine too. And it's surprisingly rare in a garden."

"Which other flowers are blue?"

"Some hydrangeas. Morning glories. And forget-me-nots, of course."

"I've always loved that name," she said. "Forget-me-not. I wonder who named them."

"Someone who didn't want to be forgotten, apparently." He straightened, stretching his back. "I suppose that's all of us, if you think about it."

"Probably so." Catherine turned to the wheelbarrow of sweet williams, tiny plants started from seed in the greenhouses. When Thomas had told her the name, she'd had to bite back an uncharacteristically cynical response; it was an adjective she'd never apply to her fiancé. But they were lovely flowers, with gently crimped edges and a deep red color.

"May I help you plant these?" she asked.

Thomas looked up from the soil; then his gaze moved to her pristine white skirt. Please don't mention my dress, she thought.

"Of course," he said. "I may be able to find you some gloves."

"I don't mind going without them." Her hands could be washed, and she hungered to make contact with the dirt.

"Let me give you this, at least," he said, taking his corduroy coat from the handles of the wheelbarrow and laying it on the soil. "You can kneel here."

Kneeling in the dirt beside her, he showed her how to make a small hole in the ground with the trowel, then how to tease the flower gently out of the tray and put it in, tamping down the dirt. "You make a little well around it, for the water to collect," he said. His hands were tan and large, the small ring on his little finger glinting in the sun. He was so close she could smell his skin. Then he handed her the trowel and got up. "Your turn."

She hadn't had her hands in the dirt for years, since she was a child in the park in Gloucester. As she dug, she remembered herself at five years old, burying rocks one day to grow a rock garden. "Oh, Cathy," her mother had laughed, "that's not what a rock garden is. Rocks don't grow."

Catherine's crestfallen gaze had caused her mother to stop laughing. She lifted one eyebrow as she always did when she had an idea. "But let's make them into a garden of our own."

Together they had unearthed the small stones and collected more and arranged them into the shape of two daisies, with long stems and radiating petals and leaves. When they had finished, Anne stood up, put her arm around her daughter, and smiled at their creation.

"I wish I could take it home," said Catherine.

"It's better here," her mother said. "It's a little surprise for someone else to find now."

Catherine smiled at the memory. She looked at the starlike red blossom, dwarfed by the sea of dirt around it. It was such a small thing, but it would grow. She breathed deeply, savoring the fragrance of the dark soil. It smelled like beginnings.

"So what do you want to be remembered for?" asked Thomas.

"I'm sorry?"

"Forget-me-nots." He was in the nearby flower bed, planting another delphinium. "What do you want to be remembered for?"

She pondered the question as she dug another hole. "I don't know," she said at last. "I don't have the talent to be remembered as a great artist or writer or anything like that. I wish I did, sometimes." She gently teased a plant out of the tray. "It must be so gratifying to be someone like Shakespeare, to have people read your plays hundreds of years later."

"I wonder if he had any idea that would happen."

Catherine set the flower carefully in place. "I wonder that, too. About all famous artists and writers. But I suppose they can't see the future any more than we can. Just the past and the present."

"Especially the present," said Thomas. "Maybe artists see that more clearly than the rest of us do."

Catherine looked up from the flower bed. "You're right," she said. "That's how they do it. How they create things that last." She sat back on her heels, delighted by the epiphany. "Artists see things the rest of us miss, even the little things. And they paint them or write about them, and that helps us see our own lives more clearly."

Thomas nodded as he reached for the spade. "Perhaps in the end, life is all about seeing. Seeing and recognizing."

The rosary flashed into her mind's eye: the jet-black beads, the litany of experiences and impressions she reviewed each night. That had been a kind of seeing, one that she had chosen not to continue. Would anything in her life be different if she had?

She felt uncomfortable in a way she did not want to explore and reached for another plant. "How is it coming along?" Thomas asked.

"Fine," she said. "It's nice being so close to the earth."

"Gloves do make it easier. I believe there are still some that my mother had, if you'd like to use them next time."

They worked in companionable silence as the remaining clouds scrolled back behind the hills. It was the perfect temperature, the sun warm but not hot. The unhurried rhythm of digging and planting made it easy for Catherine's thoughts to roam.

"Going back to your question," she said at last. "I love working on this garden. It's my way of being an artist, I think." Her trowel had uncovered a worm, which writhed in alarm, and she re-covered it with soil. "It won't make me famous, but it doesn't have to. If I can create something that I love, and that brings joy to people around me, that's enough." She thought of her mother kneeling in the dirt, creating rock flowers long since vanished, just to make her daughter smile again. Those little moments were easy to overlook, but they were the core of a good life, a meaningful life, even if the world as a whole never knew about them.

Reaching for the next sweet william, she surveyed her small bank of flowers. She frowned. "These seem so far apart. Should I be planting them closer together?"

Thomas put down the delphinium he was holding and crossed over to her flower bed. He smiled at her work.

"They're perfect," he said. "Always leave room for a flower to grow."

THIRTY-FIVE

*H*arriet, who had been sorry to bid goodbye to the Laws, was pleased she did not have long to wait before welcoming Martin Madsen. "We have quite a few guests this month, don't we," she said over breakfast the morning of his arrival. "I do like the activity."

"He's not a guest," said William. "He's been hired to paint a portrait."

"Don't be churlish," said Harriet, putting Catherine's thoughts into words. "If he's staying with us, he is a guest."

Catherine wondered what to expect from their visitor. Her image of an artist was shaped by the memories of her father, who wore old hats and cared more about his latest canvas than about wearing a hole in his shoe. But Martin Madsen was a society portrait artist, not a struggling painter; surely there was a difference.

He lived up to his reputation, wearing a suit with a respectable cut. He was in his late thirties and had light-brown hair, a beard, and a handsome, rugged profile. He also had dimples, large vertical arcs that appeared in his cheeks on the rare moments that he smiled. Surprisingly, the dimples gave him a cynical air rather than an innocent one, perhaps because his smiles themselves always seemed to express irony. He was reserved and polite but had a way of looking intently at his listener that made Catherine wonder what he was truly thinking.

"Are you originally from California?" asked Harriet at dinner.

"No," he said. His low voice had the hint of an English accent. "My parents were expatriates, so I grew up in Europe. London and Rome, mostly. I spent a brief time in New York before coming west."

"Miss Ogden is from New York," said Harriet.

He nodded politely. "I remember reading that in the papers."

"I've never sat for a portrait before," said Catherine. "Is it a long process?"

Martin cut precisely into a spear of asparagus. "My sittings are usually two hours at a time. Mornings, typically, when the light is best."

Catherine's heart sank; mornings were a beautiful time in the garden. "Every day?"

"If you'd like me to finish in two weeks' time, then we would have to have a sitting nearly every day."

"I believe that's best," said William to Catherine. "I don't see any point in drawing it out. The wedding is not very far away."

"You are, of course, welcome to stay as long as it takes and longer," said Harriet to Martin. "It's our pleasure to have you."

"Thank you, Mrs. Cartwright," said Martin. "But my own art will call me back to Monterey as soon as I am done with this commission." He took a sip of wine, and Catherine felt a moment's admiration for how neatly and clearly he had asserted his independence.

❧

The following morning, directly after breakfast, Catherine and William took the painter to the ballroom. It had not been used for several weeks. It echoed and felt cooler than the rest of the house.

Martin walked slowly around the room, hands in his pockets, eyes on the ceiling and windows.

"I'd like Miss Ogden to be sitting with the fireplace in the background," said William. The ornate mantel was decorated with carved, exaggerated faces of the Muses; Catherine privately disliked them.

Martin glanced at the fireplace, then turned back to the adjoining wall, where the tall windows looked out onto the courtyard. He crossed over to one and pushed aside the brocade drapes.

"No," he said, "she will be here. I need the light."

"What will be in the background?" asked Catherine.

"Part of the drapery, perhaps the paneling. But the background will be minimal, with just a hint of color and shape."

"I don't want anything modern," said William. "It should be clear that she's in the ballroom."

"This is a portrait, not a landscape, Mr. Brandt," Martin said. "Too much background detail will take the focus off the subject. But I could do a painting of the ballroom instead, if you prefer."

There was nothing but politeness in his tone, but the ironic look in his eyes did not escape Catherine's notice. Nor, it seemed, did it escape William's, for a muscle in his jaw twitched. He doesn't like Martin, she thought, and the feeling is mutual.

"Very well," said William. "I look forward to seeing your progress."

"I only show my work when I'm ready to do so." Martin turned again to the window. "I will let you know when I am."

❦

The first sitting did not take place right away. Martin requested a platform for Catherine to sit on—"You will need to be eye level with me," he told her—and this necessitated an impromptu conference with McNeil, the groundskeeper and estate carpenter. When William left for the city, Catherine went out to the garden.

Thomas was setting out purple heliotrope plants, and Catherine knelt to admire them. "I love how they smell," she said, putting her face close to their small petals. "Like candy. Or jelly."

"When I was a boy, my father found me trying to eat one." Thomas laughed. "I didn't do that again."

She admired the purple. It was dusky but bright, and it reminded her of her childhood, though she could not remember having seen such a flower before.

"Are you going to help plant today?" Thomas asked.

"I am," she said joyfully. "An artist is here to paint me, but we won't be starting until tomorrow."

"I've brought some of my mother's old gloves. She was much shorter than you are, but they just might work." He took them out of his pocket. "I brushed them off as best I could, but they never get entirely clean."

Catherine eagerly slid them over the embroidered cuff of her dress. She was careful to angle away as she did so, for her sleeves just barely covered the now-plum-colored bruise on her wrist, and she did not want to risk revealing it to Thomas. The gloves were brown canvas and tight, but not uncomfortably so.

"I think they will work," she said, flexing her fingers. Compared to her own gloves, they were stiff and coarse. She liked that; she felt like a woman who was doing something useful.

"Good," he said.

She was so absorbed in the feel of the gloves on her hands

that it was a moment before she looked up. He was watching her, and something in his eyes made her catch her breath.

Then he picked up a heliotrope plant and handed it to her. He cleared his throat. "Let's get started."

THIRTY-SIX

*T*he next morning, Catherine put on the red dress and bracelet, then met Martin in the ballroom. He had set up an easel with a sketch pad and there was a table to his right, stocked with tubes of paint, brushes, charcoal pencils, a small clock, and an empty palette.

"I'll start with a sketch," he said. "I won't actually put paint on canvas until tomorrow."

"Is there any particular way I should sit?" she asked.

"Any way you like."

He gave a hand to help her onto the platform. Seated there in the gilt chair, she was at eye level with him. It was an odd feeling, being his height. She noticed a small white scar above one eyebrow.

"How would you normally sit in a chair like this?" he asked. He smiled briefly. "I know this isn't a normal situation. But try to imagine you're sitting and talking to a friend."

Catherine imagined Lavinia sitting across from her and found that it helped. She sat forward, hands resting lightly on her lap.

"If I may," said Martin, taking her shoulders and gently angling them. He stepped back, assessing her. It was an odd look, devoid of the undercurrent of attraction that she saw in the eyes of most men. Perhaps a good artist kept himself at a distance. She remembered William's satisfaction at the obvious interest in

Nathaniel Law's eyes and wondered if this was part of the reason why William disliked the painter. He wants all men to desire me, she realized.

"There," said Martin. "Is that pose comfortable for you?"

"Yes."

"Good." He went back to the easel and, after studying her again, began to sketch.

She thought of her mother sitting for portraits in the garret flat. It was as different a setting from the ballroom as she could imagine. Even without moving her head, she could see the gilt paneling, the marble fireplace with its ugly faces, and the parquet floors gleaming like the surface of a lake in the moonlight. The wedding luncheon would be held here, and after the honeymoon there would be balls and concerts, for years and years to come. When they were not in Washington, of course.

Martin's voice broke into her reverie. "What would you rather be doing right now?"

"I beg your pardon?"

"What would you rather be doing?" His gaze moved from her to the paper and then back, his right arm in constant motion. "If you didn't have to be sitting here."

Her first instinct was to protest politely, but he looked her right in the eye, briefly, with a hint of his ironic smile.

"I'd rather be in the garden," she said. "I'm happier there than anywhere else."

"Why?"

"The color. The sunlight and the fresh air. Have you seen the gardens yet?"

"Most of them, yes. They're lovely."

"I'm designing a new section, back by the orchard," she said.

"All alone?"

"No. With a friend." She was surprised that her instinct was to say "friend" rather than "gardener." She added, "It's just a little project."

"It doesn't sound little."

"No, I suppose it isn't." She recalled her first time seeing the empty garden, the forgotten sketchbook under her arm. So much had changed since then. "I didn't know how involved I would get when I began. It's taken on a life of its own."

He smiled. "That's the nature of art."

For a few minutes, the only sound was the faint scratch of his pencil on the paper. Catherine realized she was far more relaxed than she had been when the sitting began.

"What about you?" she asked. "What would you be doing if you weren't here?"

He must have begun sketching her face, for he was looking directly at her. "I'd be back on the coast," he said. "In my favorite cypress grove. I paint it in all kinds of weather. And then I'd have a glass of burgundy and listen to the waves."

"All alone?"

"No. With a friend." He did not elaborate.

"It's always nicer with a friend." She thought of Thomas handing her the gloves; she imagined him carefully brushing them, remembering his mother as he did so.

"Always," said Martin.

♀

They settled into a comfortable rhythm. At times they would speak, and at other times she would let her thoughts wander. She recalled her mother sitting for portraits, explaining how she used the time to think of happy things, so Catherine did the same. Memories from childhood filled her mind: Mrs. Groat's blue-and-white kitchen; the corner of sky and roof she could see out of her little garret window; the mornings she and her mother would walk to the shore to watch the Italian salt boats unload their cargo; the way her father would quote Shakespeare and the way her mother would laugh, a comfortable laugh she often heard in her drowsy moments on the other side of the painted wall. She remembered other long-forgotten things, too: the time her father had trained a seagull to eat off of their front step; the way her mother had said, "Jesus, Mary, and Joseph!" and run to help when they saw a wagon overturn in the street; and the small pile of books her father had, novels by Thomas Hardy and Emily Brontë, books with handsome leather covers that she loved to touch. It was strange how one little memory led to another.

"My father was an artist," she said to Martin on the third morning. "A painter. He lived in Gloucester."

"What was his name?"

"Arthur Ogden."

Martin shook his head. "I'm sorry. I've never been to Gloucester. Or Massachusetts, for that matter."

Catherine had known it was unlikely he would have heard of her father, but it was disappointing all the same. "He died when I was eight. I lost my mother shortly after."

She thought of the conversation with Thomas in the garden and the prospect of finding out more about her mother's fate. It was an idea she'd returned to often at night as she gazed at the sketch. She wondered what William would say. At one time she would have been sure he'd support her in a search, but now she suspected he was more likely to discourage her. The past was not something one could control. The evening of the dinner party had shown just how intolerable any lack of control was to him.

It was not a pleasing train of thought, so she returned her attention to Martin, watching the small, sure movements he made with the brush.

"What did your father paint?" he asked her.

"Landscapes, mostly. And portraits. Only of my mother, really. He wasn't very successful."

"If he painted what he loved," said Martin, "he was successful. If he loved what he painted, even better."

"Do you enjoy painting portraits?"

"They're a good challenge," he said. "Trying to capture the essence of a person. And they give me the freedom to paint what I choose in my spare time."

"You must have met many interesting people that way."

"You could say that. Some are easier to work with than others."

"I hope I'm in the first category," she said with a smile.

He smiled too, dimples showing. "Don't worry. You are." He checked the small clock he had set up on the table. "Time for a break."

He helped her down from the platform, and she walked around the easel to see the canvas. It was a collection of splotches of color, no details yet. "It's so fascinating. You start with nothing and end up with a likeness."

"That's proof you're easy to work with. Some people would see this and be horrified."

William had not seen the canvas; he would not, said Martin, until it was finished. She felt pleasantly privileged, being able to witness it at every stage of composition.

"Your father," Martin said, cleaning off a brush. "Do you have any of his artwork?"

"Just one sketch." She crossed her hands over her chest, covering her bare upper arms. "Of my mother."

"I'd love to see it."

She thought of the naked back, the intimacy of her mother's smile. "Another time, perhaps," she said.

THIRTY-SEVEN

A letter from Lavinia arrived the next day. It had apparently crossed with Catherine's, which was disappointing; she was eager to hear what her friend thought of her new foray into gardening.

The first two pages were an amusing account of the Perrys' arrival in London, followed by an effusive paragraph praising Clarence's masterful handling of the disappearance of one of their trunks. The last half page was about Catherine's wedding.

How are preparations coming along? I am sure you are sailing through them with your usual grace & style. It won't be long now! You'll be glad to know that I've found a sky-blue gown on Bond Street for my dignified role as bridesmaid. It's heavenly, but not heavenly enough to upstage you. (As if anything could!) And I've just found the perfect wedding gift for you. It will remain a surprise, of course, but I assure you it's not a gargoyle. Aren't you relieved?

Catherine put the letter aside. She would have felt strange admitting it to Lavinia, but the wedding occupied surprisingly little of her time and energy. Most of the planning she had ceded to Harriet, who attributed Catherine's reticence to inexperience and was delighted to take charge.

There were increasingly frequent letters between Harriet and Abigail, discussing travel and the reception. Harriet gave Catherine an account of each one, sparing no details. "We were thinking of nile green bunting on each chair," Harriet would say, "with a posy in the center. Light purple, perhaps." Catherine readily assented to nearly every suggestion, prompting Harriet to comment on what an agreeable bride-to-be she was.

Whenever Catherine received a letter from her aunt, it was a striking reminder of how much had changed. Abigail, once such a dominant daily force in Catherine's life, was now someone who could only influence her at a distance. Still, in her letters back, Catherine carefully avoided any mention of the hours spent working in the garden. She could easily imagine her aunt's horror upon learning that Catherine was regularly sitting in the dirt, digging and planting. "You are forgetting your place," she would write back, disapproval emanating from the page.

In the absence of her aunt, William was the one most likely to object, so Catherine found herself working in the garden only when he was in the city. If she could keep him from knowing how much of her free time was spent there, perhaps she could avoid his intent, speculative look . . . or worse, a confrontation like the one after the dinner party. She did not let herself acknowledge how much that evening had affected her. Though the bruise had faded, the memory occasionally came to mind, and she always pushed it resolutely away. I will focus on the future, she told herself, not relive the past.

But in the garden, she lived entirely in the present. Seeing her design take shape, talking comfortably with Thomas to the chorus of birds and the breeze, it was easy to close her eyes to everything else.

The wedding intruded memorably one day during lunch with Peter and Vivian. As they were finishing dessert, Hayes entered the dining room. "Pardon me, Miss Ogden. Miss Barlowe, the seamstress, has arrived with your wedding dress. She will wait until you are ready to meet her."

"Well," said Vivian. "This makes it all very real, doesn't it?"

"I'm sure you're dying to see it," said Harriet, folding her napkin eagerly.

"Go ahead," said William to Catherine. "Peter and I will entertain ourselves while you show the ladies." He was already reaching for a cigarette, offering one to Peter.

There was nothing for Catherine to do but to go up to her room, the other women in tow, and watch as Miss Barlowe opened the box and removed a princess-line gown in cream silk, with delicate lace oversleeves. Catherine remembered selecting the fabric with her aunt in New York, the idea of the dress still vague and unreal. To see it as a finished gown was a shock.

"If you will try it on, Miss Ogden," said the seamstress, "we can see if we need to make any adjustments."

"What a shame it's Agnes's afternoon off," said Harriet. "She will be so sorry to have missed this."

Catherine slipped modestly behind the screen as Miss Barlowe helped her with the dress. For all its lacework and apparent delicacy, it was heavier than she had expected. "That's because of the train," said the seamstress, and as Catherine moved out from behind the screen she felt the backward drag of the skirt, longer and weightier than any she'd ever worn.

"Oh, my dear." Harriet's smile was radiant. "You look absolutely beautiful. Like an angel."

"Very nice," said Vivian.

"Wait until you see the whole picture," said Miss Barlowe, opening the second box and removing a long veil of lace. She stood on tiptoe to place it gently on Catherine's head, then arranged the folds around her shoulders. "Look."

In the mirror, Catherine saw a tall, dark-haired woman, her head and neck veiled in ivory. Into her inward eye flashed a picture of her mother standing before the mirror with the blue scarf wrapped around her head while she, a small child, clamored for her turn. She felt an unexpected, sudden wave of grief, so visceral that tears came to her eyes. The longing for her mother was so strong she could not speak.

"You are not the first to become emotional," said Miss Barlowe kindly. "Many girls are when they try on their wedding dress."

Vivian handed Catherine a handkerchief. She took it and dabbed at her eyes while Miss Barlowe circled her slowly, carefully avoiding the train, assessing the fit of the dress. Harriet, in her element, kept up a rapturous monologue about the beauties of the dress and about the kind of gown she hoped that her son Howard's unknown bride would one day wear. "Perhaps you will be the one to make it," she said generously, and Miss Barlowe smiled and nodded her recognition of the compliment.

Composed once again, Catherine glanced at the mirror. In the background, Vivian stood by the window, studying the wedding dress, a look in her eyes that Catherine had never seen before.

"The fit seems quite good," said the seamstress. "What do you think, Miss Ogden?"

"It fits well."

"I suggest that you leave it on for a few more minutes. See if you feel the need for any slight alterations."

"While we wait," said Harriet to Miss Barlowe, "may I borrow you to ask about a dress of my own? Last night I caught the edge of a dinner gown on a nail and tore a hole in the chiffon. I'm hoping it can be mended."

"I'll be glad to look at it, Mrs. Cartwright."

"Splendid," said Harriet. She smiled at the girls. "You two stay here and enjoy the dress. Don't take it off before I return, though. I want another look at it." She led the seamstress into the hall, closing the door behind them.

Catherine turned, not an easy feat with the train. "Will it do?" she asked, striving to make her tone light.

"You're a vision," said Vivian. "William will love it."

Catherine pushed the veil back behind her shoulders. "What did your wedding dress look like?"

Vivian sat on the edge of the bed. "Longer train, not as much lace. My mother picked it out. I didn't much care what I wore."

"I suppose not every bride is interested in clothes," Catherine said diplomatically.

"Or in her groom," said Vivian. At Catherine's expression, she cocked an eyebrow. "Don't look shocked. It's obvious that my relationship with Peter is not the stuff of romantic legend."

"Why did you . . ." Catherine was not sure how to finish the sentence in a way that did not sound accusatory.

"Marry him? Fair question." Vivian walked to the window and looked out over the hills, her red hair vivid against the white curtains. It was a long moment before she spoke.

"I loved someone else, but it ended," she said to the window, her voice careful. "The man's decision, not mine. After that, nothing seemed to matter. Peter was lonely after the death of his wife, so my parents thought it would be the perfect match. The sad widower and the fallen woman." She gave a short laugh. "Peter knows I wasn't exactly an angel, but he doesn't know the details. Maybe it wouldn't matter if he did. He's pretty magnanimous, you know, in his own blustery sort of way. It all worked out, I suppose."

"Do you love Peter now?"

Vivian shrugged. "It's affection, I guess. I wouldn't call it love. Not like what I felt before." She pleated the curtain with her fingers. "But life doesn't give us storybook endings, does it? Not all of us, anyhow."

Catherine thought of her father and mother. "You didn't want to fight to be with the man you loved?"

Vivian let go of the curtain. Her gaze was direct and without flippancy, and it occurred to Catherine that she was truly seeing her friend for the first time. "There's no point in fighting for love if you're the only one doing the fighting."

Catherine remembered George Langley standing in the hall, hat in hand. "No," she said slowly. "No, I suppose there isn't."

In the silence the clock ticked audibly. *Who was the man?* Catherine opened her mouth to ask, but something held her back: a sudden wariness in Vivian's eyes, a mute appeal not to continue.

The door swung open, and Harriet entered, followed by the seamstress, her arms full of mauve chiffon.

"It can be fixed!" Harriet said. "What a relief. I'm so fond of that gown." She smiled at Catherine. "Getting used to the dress, are you? It won't be long before you wear it for real."

Catherine reached up to remove the veil. "Please, let me," said Miss Barlowe, putting the evening dress on the bed. "We have to be careful or it will tear."

"Wasn't there some book with a torn wedding veil?" asked Harriet. "A bride gets her veil ripped right before the wedding. Which story am I thinking of?"

"*Jane Eyre*," said Catherine. "Rochester has a secret wife. She comes in and tears it during the night."

The veil floated like a wraith as the seamstress lifted it from her head and moved to set it back in the box. In the depths of the mirror, Vivian moved carefully out of its path.

"Well, you needn't worry about that," said Harriet contentedly. 'You're the only girl my brother has ever wanted to marry."

THIRTY-EIGHT

"It might be helpful," said Thomas the next day, "for you to draw up some plans for the garden in spring." He was removing the spent blooms from a lavender rosebush. "Fall is the time to plant bulbs, like daffodils and tulips."

The thought of spring, normally Catherine's favorite time of year, made her depressed. She gingerly picked up one of the flowers he had tossed in the wheelbarrow. The petals were limp but the thorns were still fierce. "I hate to think of the garden changing, even though I know it has to."

"I'll make sure the new gardener has your designs," said Thomas. "Next summer, you can do a copy of what we've done. Or maybe you'll have new ideas to try."

"Maybe so." The day's planting was done, and she knew she should return to the house, but it was a perfect, still afternoon, with long unwavering shadows extending along the paths. When Thomas had moved into the rose garden, she had followed, not wanting to leave the sunlight or their conversation.

"Have they hired someone to take your place?" she asked.

"Not yet. A position like this draws a lot of interest, but it's good to be particular." He moved to a yellow rosebush. "They'll probably reach out quietly to someone employed at a nearby estate. This is a desirable place to be head gardener. I'm sure many of them would want to make the move."

"I hate to think of stealing a friend's gardener. That doesn't seem very neighborly."

"I know what you mean," he said. "Though many would say it's perfectly fair."

Many like William, she thought. She imagined him in the study with Peter, cigar in hand, pouring his friend a drink. "Nothing personal, Peter," he would say. "Your man wanted to move to a new place; I needed a new gardener. It's merely business." No doubt William would be successful in both acquiring the gardener and keeping the friendship.

Catherine turned back to the rosebush. There was an open bloom in the center, light lavender in color, as perfectly formed as one in a painting. She had just reached out for it when a small dark beetle suddenly moved among the petals. She instinctively pulled back, raking the back of her hand along a thorn, and gave a brief cry of surprise and pain.

"Are you all right?" Thomas quickly put down his shears.

"I'm fine. It was just a beetle." But her hand was stinging, and there was a cut between the thumb and the first finger, an inch-long line, puffy and already beaded with blood. "I've scratched myself."

"May I see?" At her nod, Thomas gently took hold of her hand and tilted it to the sun. For a moment the novelty of his touch overrode the pain.

"It's not deep," he said, "but it does need a bandage." He indicated the brick gardener's cottage, its roof visible over the top of the orchard wall. "We can take care of it in the cottage, if you'd like. It's closer than the house."

As they walked along the path, she realized she would be entering the place where he had been a child, the rooms where he spent his nights and mornings. It was one of the few parts of the estate she'd never seen before.

"So silly of me," she said almost nervously. "It was just a beetle. Nothing sinister."

"Beetles are very sinister," he said with a grin. "Any rose gardener will tell you that."

When they reached the cottage, he opened the front door. "To the right is the living room, and the kitchen is just behind. We can use the basin there."

The living room was small but inviting. There was a rug on the floor, a fireplace with a clock on its mantel, a divan, and a small walnut bookcase. Through the doorway in the back wall was the kitchen, where a drop-leaf table was pushed underneath a window framed by wisteria vines. There were blue calico curtains at the window, and the calendar from a seed company, showing brightly colored zinnias, was tacked on the wall.

Thomas disappeared for a moment and then returned with a cloth, a small jar of ointment, and adhesive plaster. After washing his hands, he folded the cloth and ran it under the faucet, then took her hand and lightly sponged away the blood. His hand was warm, and she was ashamed how much she liked the feel of it. She felt she should make some lighthearted comment, but nothing came to mind. She kept her eyes on what he was doing because she was somehow afraid to look at his face.

He applied the ointment, then the adhesive plaster. "All done," he said, letting her hand go.

"It's lucky that you know so much about medicine," Catherine said. "Thank you."

"I'm happy to help. It should be fine now, but if it becomes red or continues to be painful, talk to a doctor."

"Or you."

"You can always talk to me, yes."

The words were like a bridge, closing the small distance between them. As Catherine looked at him, it seemed the air in the room had changed. She thought, from the swift, almost imperceptible shift of expression on his face, that he felt it, too. But then he abruptly turned toward the table and she moved back a step, and in doing so she saw a black rosary hanging from a nail, right by the doorway.

"You have a rosary," she said in surprise.

"It was my mother's. She was holding it when she died."

"May I touch it?"

"Of course."

She reached out for it, not removing it from the wall but gently letting the beads slide along her fingers. It had been a long time since she had held her own rosary, but the sensation was so immediately familiar that it made her throat ache. She let the beads go, and they swayed as they settled back into place.

"I have one, too," she said. "My mother gave it to me, right before I left for my aunt's house. She said to hold it when I felt lonely."

"There's something comforting about a rosary."

"Do you pray with yours?"

"Not often, no. But most nights I take it down. I like to hold the beads and remember good times my mother and I had." He gently adjusted the rosary on the nail. "Perhaps that is prayer."

She watched the beads sway lightly against the wall. His words had filled her with so much emotion that she did not trust herself to speak.

"Come into the parlor," he said. "I'll show you a picture of my mother."

She followed him into the front room, and he handed her a frame from the bookcase. It was a photograph of Thomas and his parents, standing in front of the cottage; she recognized the windows and vines.

"I was sixteen," he said. "It was just before she became ill."

She was a petite woman, comfortably round, with wavy, dark hair pulled back with combs. She wore a light-colored dress and a large cameo. The sun must have been in her eyes, for she was squinting slightly, but in the line of her mouth Catherine saw humor and strength. "She was lovely. What was her name?"

"Carmel."

Thomas was standing between his parents, a lanky teenager, looking uncomfortable in a suit and tall collar. He, too, was squinting slightly, and, unlike his mother, his expression was serious.

"I wish I'd smiled in that photo," he said. "I was a little moody when I was an adolescent. After my mother died, I wished I hadn't been."

"I am sure she forgave you."

He smiled. "Mothers are good at that."

His father was tall, hatless, and wearing an ill-fitting suit, a man clearly more at home in work clothes. His hair was thick and his face deep with lines, the face of a man who spent his days out of doors. He, like Carmel, was smiling, and in his eyes Catherine could see the same wrinkles she saw in his son's. "He looks like a kind man," she said. "Thomas was his name, wasn't it?"

"Mother called him Thomas and me Tomás. That's how we knew which of us she was calling for."

"Do you think of yourself more as Thomas or Tomás?"

"It depends on who I'm with," he said. "I've learned to think of myself as both."

She gazed at the photo for another moment before placing it back on the bookshelf. "Thank you for showing me," she said, and then she added impulsively, "I think I would have liked your mother. And your father."

Thomas smiled at her. *They would have liked you, too,* she thought she read in his eyes.

In silence they walked back into the small entry hall. Thomas opened the cottage door and a rectangle of trees appeared, drenched in golden afternoon light, beautiful and still. But for the first time in Catherine's memory, entering the garden felt like a loss.

THIRTY-NINE

*W*illiam noticed Catherine's hand within minutes of returning home from the city. "What happened here?"

"I scraped it on a thorn in the garden. It's fine. It doesn't hurt anymore."

He was holding a glass of lemonade, and he took another swallow and put it down. Reaching for her hand, he examined it closely. His fingers were cold from the chilled tumbler.

"It's fine," she said. "Thomas helped me bandage it."

He looked up, and she instantly regretted the words.

"He's studying medicine, you know," she said casually. "He knew what to do." She put both hands behind her back. "It doesn't hurt anymore. Let's go into the music room, and I can play you the new song I'm learning."

"As long as you're more careful in future." William picked up his drink again. "The garden can be a dangerous place."

"I promise to stay away from all serpents and forbidden fruit," she said lightly.

"Good," he said. "In fact, I'd like you to focus less on the garden and more on the portrait, and the wedding. Those are the most important things right now."

She did not respond, merely smiled noncommittally and led the way to the music room.

The next morning, as she took her place in the chair, Martin's gaze was focused on her right wrist. He had not been alarmed by the adhesive plaster—"I won't include it in the portrait, obviously," he had said—but now he studied the diamond-and-ruby bracelet.

"I'm not sure about the bracelet," he said at last. "I think it might be too much."

"Too much?"

"It's beautiful, but beautiful things can still be wrong for a portrait. Would you mind if I left it out?"

"I don't mind. But William might."

He shrugged. "Let's leave it out. If the portrait is too plain, I can always paint it in."

She took it off and Martin carefully set it aside, then went back behind the easel.

As he painted, she let her mind wander over the events of the previous day. A host of images came easily to mind: the lavender rose; the cozy cottage living room; the brightly colored zinnias on the wall calendar; the black rosary and the photo of Thomas's mother, short and smiling, with her cameo. And the moment when Thomas had bandaged her small wound, his hands competent and warm.

His mother had called him Tomás. Catherine repeated it in her mind: *Tomás, Tomás, Tomás.* The accent on the second syllable made it a totally different name. It did not assert itself at the beginning, as Thomas did. Tomás began in an unassuming way, quiet even, with the emphasis coming only at the end. You could ignore it at first but not at the last.

"This is much better without the bracelet," said Martin from behind the easel.

"Good," she said. She looked down at her right hand, liking the fact that the bandage was the only thing there.

℘

That night she unearthed her rosary from the bottom of the jewelry case. In the silence of her room, she sat on the bed and held it by the crucifix, pooling the beads in her cupped palm. She did not return to her old ritual, but it felt good merely to hold the rosary and listen to the gentle clacking of the beads.

She started to put the rosary back in the jewelry case, then stopped. After a moment's thought, she put the beads in the drawer of the small table by her bed, where she kept the folded sketch of her mother.

℘

The next morning, the sitting was shorter than usual. After forty-five minutes, Martin stepped back from the easel, regarded the canvas for a moment, then put down his brush.

"I'm at a good stopping place here," he said. "Let's wait until tomorrow to do your face."

"We're done for the day?"

"Done. Finished. You are free as a bird." He helped her down from the platform. "Enjoy the morning."

William was on the train to the city, and Harriet was spending the morning running errands in San Mateo; there were no claims on Catherine's time. As quickly as she could, she went upstairs and changed out of the red evening gown and into a skirt and shirtwaist.

Thomas, whom she found staking delphiniums by the front fountain, was surprised to see her. "No painting this morning?" he asked, straightening at her approach.

"We're finished already," she said joyfully, adjusting her hat. "Today is the day for the marigolds, isn't it?"

"It is indeed. I'll bring them around."

Twenty minutes later they were both kneeling in the garden. Catherine made neat holes with her trowel, eased in the little orange and yellow plants, and patted the dirt firmly. She could do it efficiently now, knowing exactly how far apart to space them.

She looked up at one point to see Thomas watching her. He smiled. "Look at you. You've become a gardener."

"I think I was always one. I just never knew it."

"And you're far better with design than I could ever be." He nodded toward the beds around them, a patchwork quilt of vivid color. "This is all you."

"My father gave me the idea. And I couldn't have done any of it without you."

"Let yourself take the compliment," he said quietly. "You've earned it."

His words and the tone of his voice caused her pulse to quicken. Striving for equanimity, she reached for another plant. "I love these," she said, holding up the small orange flower. "They look just like sunlight."

"Good for days like today." The sky was still overcast, gray with fog, though she had been in California long enough to know that by noon, it would break up and the sun would shine.

"I remember when I first came here," she said. "I kept thinking these skies meant rain. That's one of the big differences between New York and here."

"Do you ever miss it?"

She thought for a moment, reaching across the dirt to move a stone. Her skirt would be filthy, but a soiled skirt was a witness to a close encounter with the earth, proof she had done something meaningful with her day.

"I miss the rain," she said. "The summer storms we used to have. When they pass, the air is so fresh and everything sparkles, even in the city. You know that something has begun and ended and begun again."

"It's hard to imagine," he said. "Here we live without rain for months on end. It's so welcome when it finally comes back."

"The small rain down can rain," she said, remembering.

"Sorry?"

"It's a poem my father loved. From the medieval times, he said. He would say it every time it rained." Sitting back on her heels, she recited:

Western wind, when wilt thou blow?
The small rain down can rain.
Christ, that my love were in my arms
And I in my bed again.

She had heard the poem countless times when she was a child, but it was the first time she had ever spoken the words aloud. As she did so, she realized that there was an intimacy to the poem that had entirely eluded her as a child. For a moment, she sat still, her cheeks burning at the words she had just said to him.

"I've never said that poem out loud before," she offered by means of explanation.

Across the flower bed, Thomas's eyes met hers. Rather than ashamed, she felt perfectly understood.

"It's a very short poem, isn't it," she said to fill the silence.

"It's beautiful," he said. "It doesn't need to say anything more." And this time he, not she, busied himself with the marigolds.

They planted until long after the clouds scrolled away. At noon, Catherine sent word with Gerald that she would not be returning to the house for lunch. There was no one to object; William and Harriet were gone all day, and Martin never took lunch. He preferred to walk at midday, leaving Oakview and walking the long, dusty road with a sketch pad under his arm.

It was three o'clock when she finally walked back to the house, idly brushing dirt off her sleeves. No wonder pioneer women wore dresses made of calico, not silk. She smiled at the thought of what her aunt would have said if Catherine had requested work clothes as part of her trousseau. Then again, in May she'd had no idea that she would be creating a garden.

As they'd planted, Thomas had taught her some more Spanish words. *Flores*; *agua*; *verde*; *mariposa*. She repeated them to herself as she walked, committing them to memory. And there was the Spanish version of his name, Tomás. She said it over and over in her mind, internalizing it like a heartbeat.

Mounting the terrace steps, she came into the reception room. The house was cool and dark after the garden. She had plenty of time to bathe and change before William and Harriet arrived home.

But Hayes was standing at the entrance to the hall. "Miss Ogden," he said. "Mr. Brandt is looking for you."

"Oh. I didn't realize he was home."

"He's in the study."

The study door was slightly ajar, and Catherine paused. It was just long enough for her to recall the summons from William the morning after the dinner party and the apprehension she'd felt as she waited to enter. Don't be silly, she told herself. She pushed open the door and went in.

William was sitting in the leather club chair, smoking a cigar. He did not stand up when she entered.

"Hello," she said. "I'm sorry. How long have you been back?"

His eyes took in her skirt and the shirtwaist smudged with dirt, then moved to her face. "Since one o'clock."

"I'm sorry. I thought you would be gone all day."

"That's evident."

"I know," she said, indicating her clothes. "I'm a sight, aren't I? Luckily everything can be washed." She took off her hat, put the hatpin into the crown, and set it on a free corner of the desk. "But you should see the garden. Tomás says it's nearly done."

"Who?"

She was instantly aware of two things: first, that she had blundered, and second, that she could not reveal she had. "Thomas," she said evenly, forcing herself to look William in the face. "The gardener. His name is Tomás in Spanish."

He sat with both arms resting loosely on the nail-studded arms of the chair, his right hand holding the cigar. The smoke drifting upward was the only movement in the room.

"I should go change," she said finally.

He tapped some ash into the ashtray, then lifted the cigar to his mouth. "Not yet. Come here."

The back of her neck prickled with apprehension. She stopped three feet away from him in the middle of the carpet.

He blew a smoke ring. "Closer than that."

She moved forward until the fabric of her skirt was almost touching his knees. Remaining seated, he set his cigar down in the ashtray, then put his right hand on her waist. She thought for a moment that he was going to brush the dirt off her skirt, but instead he moved his hand slowly down and up her outer thigh. Then his hand moved to her backside, deliberately tracing the contours of her body, and she wanted to break away, but she was caught between his hand and his knees.

"William," she said helplessly.

Out of the stillness, the study door creaked on its hinges. William's hold relaxed just enough for Catherine to move back a few steps, her heart pounding as the door opened. Harriet came into the room, holding a large parcel.

"There you are," she said to Catherine. "I've had such a successful day in town; just wait until you see." She put the parcel down on a chair, and then she saw Catherine's skirt and her eyes widened. "My dear, what on earth have you been doing?"

"Playing in the dirt," said William as he picked up his cigar.

"I was planting some flowers," Catherine said. "In the garden."

"We do have gardeners for that, you know," said Harriet. "But no matter. Put on something clean and then come down. I'll show you the ribbons I've found for the bouquets."

As she picked up her hat, Catherine ventured a glance at William. He was still watching her, his cigar poised at his lips.

FORTY

"Should I smile?" asked Catherine. "Or should I be serious?"

"It's always best," said Martin, "to do what feels most natural." He lightly tilted her chin toward the left.

"But sometimes I'm happy and sometimes I'm not," she challenged him. "Who's to say which one is more natural?"

He laughed. "The lady is a philosopher." He stepped back a few feet, surveying her, then moved behind the easel. "No one wants to look glum in a portrait, but a smile can look forced. I tell my sitters to think of things they like. If you do that, you'll smile without knowing it." He squeezed a tube of ochre paint onto the palette. "How does that sound?"

"Perfect."

She thought of the garden, surveying it in her mind's eye. She thought of the sugary smell of the heliotrope, the small, crimped edges of the sweet williams, and the sunset color of the snapdragons. She thought of how it felt to pat down the dirt, so dark and rich and fragrant. In the garden, there was the sound of birds and occasionally the chittering or buzz of an insect. There were yellow butterflies, big ones, which moved gracefully through the air like small kites.

There was Thomas, too. She thought of his easy movements, the wavy dark hair that glinted red in the sun, the creases in the corners of his eyes. She thought of the hands that pruned dead limbs and pulled weeds and planted and reached out, thoughtfully, to adjust a rosary on a wall. It was a friendship she had never expected to have.

And one she would not have much longer, for in a few weeks' time, he would go back to his studies, and she would be married. Involuntarily she shifted in her seat, unconscious of the fact that she was breaking her pose.

At breakfast that morning, William had been courteous and attentive. He'd left at nine o'clock for the city, without making any reference to the unsettling incident in his study the previous day. It was as if it had never happened. Like his outburst the night of the dinner party, Catherine thought, perhaps this was something they were both meant to look beyond. Something to stuff away in the back of her mind, to forget if she could.

Martin's voice broke the silence. "Whatever you were thinking of a few minutes ago," he said, "try to think of it again."

⁂

It was a longer sitting than usual, and when she was done, she resolved to eat lunch quickly and then go out to the garden. But Harriet wanted to discuss details of the wedding, and just as they were finishing, Emmeline Platt and her mother dropped in unexpectedly for a call. Catherine greeted them with warm words of delight and a feeling of bitter disappointment.

Mrs. Ida Dent was an older version of her daughter, pink-cheeked and talkative. Visiting from New Hampshire, she seized upon the fact that Catherine was also from the East and was eager to compare impressions of the two coasts, asking Catherine's opinions on everything from the weather to the quality of the drinking water. When Harriet suggested they show Mrs. Dent the gardens, Catherine's feelings were divided between the agony of knowing the visit would be prolonged and eagerness to see Thomas, so she could explain her absence.

On their tour of the garden, moving slowly due to Mrs. Dent's "difficult hip," she didn't see him. Gerald was pulling weeds by the garden house, but in the company of the other women, Catherine could not ask him where Thomas might be.

"You should add something like this to your property," said Mrs. Dent to her daughter, pointing her walking stick toward the reflecting pool with its fringe of lavender and the cypresses standing like sentinels.

"Wouldn't that be nice," sighed Emmeline. "Our own garden is so pedestrian. I admire those who have a vision for landscaping. It must be a talent you're born with, like a good singing voice."

"William is much like our father was," said Harriet. "He isn't happy until the gardens are the best they can be."

"He must spend a great deal of time outdoors," said Mrs. Dent.

"Actually, he doesn't," said Harriet. "I think it's enough for him simply to know that the garden is here."

❧

By the time the ladies left, it was nearly four thirty. Although William would soon be home, Catherine hurried out to the back garden.

It had not changed since they had planted the marigolds the day before. The last remaining spaces, waiting to be filled with pink petunias, were still empty. Thomas must have decided to wait for her before planting them. There would be no time for any work before dinner, but she could at least find him and explain her absence.

But he was not in the rose garden, by the Tree of Knowledge, or in the orchard. He was not watering the large pots in the garden house nor was he weeding the lavender by the reflecting pool. She paused irresolutely on the path by the camellias, now bare of blossoms, showing their glossy green leaves to the late sun.

Gerald passed by, a rake over one shoulder, and she stopped him. "Gerald. Have you seen Thomas?"

"Yes, Miss Ogden. He's in the cottage getting ready."

"Thank you."

She hurried toward the orchard, wondering what Thomas was getting ready to do. Perhaps he was washing up for dinner; she knew he often ate early, then returned to do more work in the cool of the evening.

The door of the cottage was ajar, and she knocked. A moment later, Thomas appeared in the doorway. He was wearing the brown suit he had worn the day of the beach and a dark blue necktie. It was only the second time she had ever seen him out of work clothes.

"Catherine." He had never before called her by her first name, but even more surprising was the audible relief in his voice. "Thank you for coming."

"Is something wrong?"

He hesitated, then said, "Come inside."

She walked through the small entry hall into the parlor. Something was different from the last time she had been in the cottage, and after a moment she realized what it was: a suitcase and a carpetbag, lined up beside the divan.

She turned to him in alarm.

He ran a hand through his hair. "You saw the note I sent you."

"What note?"

"I gave it to Hayes. About eleven o'clock." At her expression he asked, "Didn't you get it?"

"No. What did it say?"

His blue eyes were grave. "I'm leaving today. They've hired someone to take my place. Effective immediately."

It was as if the floor had dropped out from underneath her feet. "Hired someone?"

"That's what Mr. Brandt said this morning. I was told it was time for me to pack and leave. The six o'clock evening train, no later."

She stared at him, trying to absorb the news.

"I'm going north, to my aunt's in Santa Rosa," he said. "I'll stay there until they're ready for me again at my lodgings in the city."

"But you can't go now. You can't pack so quickly," she said absurdly, unable to process the thoughts tumbling through her mind.

"I already have. There isn't much I need to take."

"But I thought you had more time. A few weeks, at least."

"So did I," he said. She saw bitter resignation in his eyes and something else she could not entirely identify. "But the garden isn't mine, and I don't own this cottage. I don't get to choose when to stay or go."

She had to look away, to collect her thoughts and fight against the tears.

"I'm sorry," he said. "I wish I could stay and finish the garden with you. We were so close to being done."

Catherine realized she had not even been thinking of the garden. He stood a few feet away from her in his unfamiliar suit, with the golden light from the afternoon pouring into the windows and the trills of the birds muted by the glass panes. Everything seemed muffled, suspended, as if the rest of the world slept and only the two of them were awake.

"I'll tell Gerald what to do," he said. "He's a good fellow."

She did not trust herself to speak.

"It will be all right in the end," he said gently. "The garden will be just as we'd planned."

She looked up and met his eyes. It was likely the last time she would ever see him, and there was no reason not to say what she was thinking.

"It's not the garden," she said, her voice breaking. "It's you. I'm going to miss you terribly."

The expression on his face changed, a change both swift and surprising. She had just enough time to register that her words had affected him more deeply than she had expected when he suddenly crossed the floor, took her head in his hands, and kissed her.

There was a split second of surprise; then she became aware of a kind of pleasure she had never known before. She kissed him back unreservedly, without fear or self-consciousness, an action that felt as natural and right as breathing. Their hours together in the garden, the weeks of companionship and trust: they had become something electric, friendship turned into fire. She did not remember doing anything with her hands, but when they finally pulled apart her arms were around his lower back, and she could feel the muscle and sinew under his coat. She marveled at the sensation and at his hands framing her face, the intoxicating tenderness in his eyes, the taste of him still on her mouth, the warmth that filled her body like quicksilver.

He smiled and she smiled, inches apart from each other. She loved the feel of his hands now moving in her hair and the look in his eyes that she had never seen before.

"Come with me," he said abruptly.

"What?"

"Come with me." He was smoothing the tendrils of hair that had escaped her combs. "Take the train with me tonight."

She felt cold inside, a dizzying switch to reality. There was a world outside this cottage, this room, and this embrace, and while she had forgotten it for a few glorious minutes, she could not do so any longer. "I can't."

"I love you, Catherine," he said. "Come with me to Santa Rosa. Let's get married there."

"I can't." She pulled her face away, overcome.

He reached for her cheek. "Yes, you can."

"I'm engaged," she said helplessly. "How can I walk away from that?"

"You just walk." He leaned in, resting his forehead against hers. "I'll be with you."

She shut her eyes tightly, not even daring to imagine what he was offering. All she could think of were the faces of her family, the wedding guests with train tickets, the plans Harriet had made: the entire intricate edifice of a decision that had taken on a life of its own and which she did not know how to undo.

"No," she said wretchedly. "I can't."

He pulled his head back and looked at her.

"I'm sorry, for all of this. I didn't mean . . . ," and she could not finish the sentence because she was not entirely sure what she had actually meant when she said the words that made him cross the room and kiss her.

His gaze was different now. She saw something in it that she had not seen since the first few weeks of their acquaintance: the guard, the distance.

"It's too big to stop," she said. "The wedding, everything." *I'm scared to try*, she wanted to say, but she was stopped by the expression on his face and the sickening realization of what he was thinking. She remembered when Vivian had flirtatiously invited him to work in her garden; she recalled Alma's keen interest in his race, as if he were a horse she was breeding. And in his eyes, she saw the fiancée of a rich man, a woman who would willingly kiss the gardener in the shadows of the cottage but who would not acknowledge it in the light. She was suffused with misery and fumbled in her pocket for a handkerchief.

He pulled one from his suit coat and extended it wordlessly just as she found her own. For a moment he stood there, holding out his handkerchief, but she did not take it, and he finally put it back in his pocket.

"I'm sorry," she repeated, wiping her eyes. There had to be something more she could say beyond those totally inadequate words.

Just then there were footsteps in the entry hall. "Thomas?" Gerald came into the parlor, panting as if he had been running. Upon seeing Catherine in tears, his eyes widened.

"What is it?" Thomas's voice was toneless.

"I'm sorry, Miss Ogden," said Gerald, twisting his cap. "Mr. Hayes is looking for you. He's right behind me. And Thomas, Anderson has pulled the car up to take you to the station. I'm to help you with the suitcases."

There was silence.

"I'll just wait outside," said Gerald awkwardly. But as he edged toward the door, they heard more footsteps on the wooden floor, and Hayes entered the room. His formal suit was absurdly incongruous in the modest cottage. His face, as always, was impassive.

"Miss Ogden," he said. "Mr. Brandt wanted me to find you and bring you back to the house. He thinks you may have forgotten that there are guests coming for dinner."

"Thank you," she said automatically. She cast about for something else to say to Thomas, any way to make things better. But Hayes stood waiting and watching, and Gerald in the entry hall stood waiting too, and she realized as she looked at Thomas that any opportunity was irrevocably gone.

"I have to go," she said. She wiped her eyes and straightened her back. "Thank you for all your help in the garden." Her voice, and the words, seemed brittle and wrong.

There was a brief pause; then he spoke.

"It was an honor," he said quietly. His back was to the other men, and they could hear his words, but only she saw the expression in his eyes, the disappointment, and, oh God, the pain. She'd never again see them creased in a smile.

Suddenly, she only wanted to leave. "Goodbye," she said, and she walked as swiftly as she could out of the cottage and toward the house, so fast that Hayes had to run to keep up.

FORTY-ONE

*T*he dinner guests were Peter and Vivian. Although Agnes had done an admirable job of fixing Catherine's tousled hair and powder had evened out the blotches in her complexion, Vivian immediately noticed something was wrong. "Have you been ill?" she asked as the maid helped her off with her evening wrap. "You look so pale."

"I'm fine," said Catherine. She actually felt numb, in a daze.

Vivian's eyes were speculative. William's were confident and unconcerned.

"Too much time in the sun, I think," he said, taking Catherine's elbow. "You should spend more time indoors from now on."

The evening wore on, and though she participated in the conversation, Catherine felt detached from it, her answers automatic and brief. It was like experiencing the evening through the wrong end of opera glasses; everyone seemed smaller, remote, and she was present but not truly there. She rightly recognized it as shock. The significance of the afternoon would sink in later, but she was temporarily insulated from the full force of feeling.

After dinner, as they sat down to play a game of cards, William suggested some music. Peter stood up and went over to the gramophone.

"Any requests?" he asked.

"Whatever you like," William said.

Catherine watched him deal, his large hands in their crisp cuffs moving inexorably around the table. She thought of

Thomas's hands holding her head as if it were the most precious thing he knew.

There was a brief crackle from the gramophone; then the song began. It was "I Wonder Who's Kissing Her Now."

Catherine pushed back her chair, making William stop in his movements and the others look up. "I'm so sorry," she said. "I've got a terrible headache. I have to say goodnight."

She did not wait for the others to respond before leaving the room and hurrying up the stairs.

※

She held herself together while Agnes helped her undress and took down her hair. But the moment the door closed behind her, Catherine threw herself down on the bed and cried huge, jagged sobs. The down pillows and comforter absorbed the sound, and she wished they could swallow up her wretchedness. Her excuse to the others soon became a reality, and she had a headache that throbbed.

After the sobs had subsided, she took the rosary from the drawer by her bed and wound it around her hand, pulling it taut as if it were a lifeline. She stared up at the ceiling with its plaster molding but did not see it. All she could see was the look on Thomas's face. *I was wrong about you*, his eyes had said. *I thought you felt for me what I feel for you.*

She did feel it. For weeks she had denied it to herself, but now it was a truth that could no longer be ignored. And now it was too late.

※

Catherine had finally drifted off to sleep when there was a knock at her door. She sat up, confused. A few moments later she heard it again, discreet but insistent. Harriet must have come to inquire after her headache before going to bed and it would be rude not to answer. She put the rosary on the bedside table, pushed her hair away from her face, and went to the door.

It was not Harriet but William. He had never before come to her bedroom door, and she stood frozen in surprise.

He did not ask if he could enter but came in anyhow, brushing past her and closing the door behind him. He wore a maroon silk dressing gown and the trousers from his evening suit but not, she registered with sudden alarm, a shirt. His chest was bare, dark hair just visible in the V of his neckline.

"Are you feeling better?" he asked.

"Yes," she said automatically.

He looked her over, taking in the white cotton nightgown, the dark curls hanging down her back. She realized he had never seen her with her hair loose before. She wished she had put on her dressing gown before answering the door.

"What do you want?" she asked, even though instinct had already told her what it was.

He had a glass of brandy in one hand, and he took a sip. Perhaps he is drunk, she thought, but he never was.

"I would like," he said, "to be with you. Tonight."

"We're not married yet."

"We will be soon. Only a few more weeks. Why wait?"

She stepped back, wanting to put distance between them. "But we aren't married," she said again. "We can't do this before the wedding."

"That's what you've been told your whole life, isn't it? That a girl should wait. But it's different when the man is her fiancé."

"But I don't want this," she said, fear making her blunt.

He looked at her, not angry but amused. His dark eyes compelled hers. "Ever?"

She was caught and she knew it. He smiled, almost gently. "What difference does a few weeks make?" he asked. "It's inevitable. You have a ring. And I'm not going to abandon you. I've wanted this marriage from the moment we met."

She remembered something he had told her weeks before, in the garden. "In every contest there can only be one winner," he had said by the reflecting pool. And now he was in her room: her room in his house, far from New York and the protective presence of family. She had a moment's awareness of just what her aunt had feared in letting her go for the summer alone. And she knew with a cold certainty that in this particular contest, as in all the others, he would find a way to prevail.

"But what if I . . . ," she began, then stopped.

"Conceive a child?" He walked to the bedside table to put down the tumbler. "There are ways to avoid that. And even if you do, it's close enough to the wedding that no one will possibly object."

She could sweep past him and go wake Harriet for support, but pride and her upbringing made that unthinkable, as he had surely known they would. And he was right; whether it happened tonight or on their wedding day, the encounter was inevitable. It was the path she herself had chosen. For a brief time, there had been another path, one that had opened before her in the gardener's cottage, but she had blundered and missed it and it was forever barred to her now.

He read the defeat in her eyes and smiled. "Good girl," he said. He walked over to the dresser and turned off the light.

Dawn came at last. From the armchair by the window, Catherine watched the sky change, darkness coexisting for a brief moment with light. It was sunny, with no fog and no clouds. A beautiful day to work in the garden, she thought with dull irony. She closed her eyes, exhausted both in body and spirit.

The encounter had been nothing like Lavinia had said. When William had started undoing the buttons of her nightgown, she had pulled back in instinctive resistance and had not known what to say other than the obvious. "I've never done this before."

That had amused him. "Of course not," he said, reaching for the tumbler of brandy. "You wouldn't be here if you had."

She watched him drink. The lights were off, but the moonlight was bright enough to see the muscles in his throat. "Have you?"

He looked at her over the glass. "Yes," he said. Then he put the tumbler down and reached for her again.

The act itself had been both terrifying and ridiculous, two adjectives she would never have thought could be used in tandem. The satisfaction Lavinia had alluded to was obviously felt by William, but she herself had known nothing but the expected pain and the unexpected feeling of no longer belonging to herself. She had not known how much it would feel like being invaded, as if there was no place in her that was still safe and her own. But he could not reach her mind, and she had shut her eyes and imagined the ocean, sun and sea and gulls and sand and rocks, anything to take her away from the present moment.

When he had disengaged from her and reached for his dressing gown, she pulled the sheet over herself. He smiled at her. "You're as beautiful as I thought you'd be," he said, and yet it felt nothing like a compliment. She only wanted him to go.

But as he stood up and reached for the tumbler, he paused. He looked more closely at the end table, then picked something up. She remembered that she had not put the rosary back in the bedside drawer.

He turned to her, holding it between thumb and forefinger as if it were something curious and distasteful. "What's this?"

"A rosary."

"Where did you get it?"

"It was a gift. Long ago." She sat up, holding the sheet to her chest, and reached for it. He continued to hold it, staring at the beads as if perplexed.

"Do you use it?" he asked.

"No."

After a moment, he shrugged and tossed the rosary on the bed. "I suppose it's harmless," he said, cinching the sash on his dressing gown, "as long as you don't turn Catholic. The Brandts don't worship with the staff."

He picked up the glass and his clothes, looked back at her tousled hair and bare shoulders, and smiled. "I'll see you tomorrow," he said. "Or, more accurately, today." And he left.

FORTY-TWO

*C*atherine had no desire to go down to breakfast but realized she would gain nothing by staying away. Her absence might bring William to her door to inquire after her; she could face him far more easily over the neutral normalcy of the breakfast room.

William was the only one at the table. He rose as she entered. "Good morning."

"Good morning," she said with effort. Hayes poured her a cup of coffee and she busied herself with the pitcher of cream.

William folded his newspaper. "You look well today."

It was a lie. She looked as she felt, terrible. William, in contrast, appeared well rested and vibrant. She found it hard to meet his eyes.

He was all solicitude, passing her the toast, commenting on the weather. He hoped it was just as clear in the city. He was going there and planned to stay overnight. "Another meeting," he said, smiling philosophically. "That's business." It meant there was no chance he would come to her room that night, but she felt too flat for anything like gladness.

"Will you work in the garden again today?" he asked.

"I don't think so," she said dully. "I can leave the rest of the planting to Gerald."

"I'm sure Harriet will appreciate having your help with the wedding plans," he said, putting down his napkin and pushing back his chair. "And you can wrap up the portrait. It must be nearly finished by now."

"It is."

"Good." He crossed to her chair and bent down to kiss her. It was a brief, proprietary kiss, and she became consciously aware of what she had already known intuitively. His visit to her room had not just been about desire. It had been about putting his brand on her, about tying her to him with a bond he knew she would not have the courage to break.

⁊

In the ballroom, Martin scanned her face and frowned. "Are you unwell?" he asked as she took her place in the chair.

"Yes," she said. "I mean no. I'm fine."

She adjusted the folds of her skirt. She could not confide in Martin any more than she could in Harriet, for what on earth would she say? *I'm engaged but I love another man, and I've lost him forever. And William came to my bed last night and I hated it, every moment.*

"I see," said Martin. He looked as if he wanted to say more, then went back behind the easel and began to work.

She stared ahead, feeling wretched.

"I'm painting your face again today," he said after a few minutes. He smiled gently. "I don't suppose you could think of what you were thinking of yesterday."

Yesterday seemed like a lifetime ago. "I'll try," she said, but thinking of the garden was painful and thinking of Thomas was even more so. She had to concentrate hard to keep from crying.

The memory of William above and inside her invaded her thoughts, and with it came the painful recognition that it would have been an entirely different experience with a different man.

With someone you loved, as she had learned from Lavinia's letter, it would surely be wonderful. She remembered Thomas holding her face and felt again the exquisite pleasure of his lips on hers. With the thought of what could have been, the ballroom, Martin, and the easel wavered and blurred in front of her.

"I'm sorry," she said, getting up. "I can't do this today."

Martin helped her down from the platform. "Can I get you anything?" His concern was genuine. Even in her misery, she recognized it and was grateful.

"No," she said. She turned to the window and rested her warm forehead on the glass.

He returned to his easel and table, moving things about quietly. A moment later there was a knock on the ballroom door and the voice of Hayes. "A letter just came for you, Mr. Madsen."

She heard the unfolding of paper as she stared at the courtyard, numbly registering the blue sky, the green vines, and a maid opening a second-floor window and shaking out a feather duster before closing it again. A crow cawed and pecked at the gravel walk and then flew off again. One of the gardeners went to the front fountain toting a bucket. After looking up appreciatively at the draped figure of the stone nymph, he took out a net and lightly skimmed small leaves out of the water.

A bird flew into the glass of the window near her, with an alarming thud. It was not an unusual experience—the staff did an excellent job of keeping the panes clean—but it startled her all the same. She turned to Martin, but he was absorbed in the letter, his brow furrowed.

"Is something wrong?" she asked.

He did not react, just kept reading.

"Is something wrong?" she asked again, moving toward him.

He looked up at her then, as if surfacing from another dimension. "No," he said. "No." He frowned and folded the paper.

"It's not bad news, I hope."

"No," he said. "Not bad news, no." He tucked the paper inside the envelope again and then gazed at her intently, as if searching for something in her that he had not thought to find before. He opened his mouth as if to speak, then stopped himself. After a moment, he put the envelope into his coat pocket.

"Let's stop for now and try again tomorrow," he said. "If that's all right with you."

"That's fine."

"Good." He gave her one more odd look, then left the room.

৯৹

The wakeful night caught up with her, and she fell asleep in her room, dozing through lunch. When she woke, it was nearly two o'clock and she wondered what to do with the rest of the afternoon. She had no desire to call Vivian to come for tea or croquet. She could imagine her appraising glance and her quick, relentless curiosity. Any social interaction felt distasteful.

At last she went outside and wandered the garden paths. She hesitated before entering the back walled garden, but she would have to do it sometime, so she summoned her courage and walked through the brick archway. There were still the same bare places Thomas had left. No one had worked in it that morning. It was painful to look at the beds, for every type of flower reminded her of some conversation, some moment with him.

On the way back through the orchard, she saw Gerald. "Is the new head gardener arriving today?" she asked.

He frowned. "New head gardener?"

"I thought one had been hired."

"No, Miss Ogden," he said. "I haven't heard anything about that."

Catherine nodded and moved on. She was not surprised.

The cottage stood before her, cloaked in its vines like a house in a fairy tale. The door was unlocked and, after hesitating, she went in. She wandered through the parlor and into the kitchen, avoiding the spot where she and Thomas had stood.

He had said he did not have much to take, and he was right. The furniture was still there, and the embroidered cushion on the divan, and the calendar in the kitchen with its brightly colored zinnias. But the family photograph was gone from the bookshelf, and the black rosary was no longer hanging from its nail.

She put her hands over her face and, in the silence of the little house, let herself cry.

∾

She dreaded the dinner hour when she would have to make small talk with Harriet, but she was lucky. Harriet had just received a letter from her son, and much of the conversation was dominated by her fond summary of his travels through Switzerland, France, and England. "He and his father will be on the ship by now," she said. "I will be so glad to see them again. And of course, you will get to meet them, at last."

At one point she looked at Catherine, who had eaten very little. "You seem to have no appetite lately, my dear. We'll have to call back the seamstress to adjust your dress."

Martin was also preoccupied. He said very little, responding to Harriet with polite if somewhat delayed responses. When she asked about his day, he said he had taken a long walk along the road.

"Looking for a landscape to paint?" she asked.

"No," he said. "Just walking."

After dinner, they adjourned to the music room, and Catherine played the piano. Doing so was a welcome respite from misery. Her fingers moved by instinct over the keys, and she was grateful that she could pour her feelings into music, with no fear of revealing them to the others.

Harriet stayed through three songs, then said goodnight and went upstairs. Catherine expected Martin to do the same—he had seemed disinclined to conversation and company at dinner—but he stayed on, turning the pages of a book about Renaissance art.

She chose Schumann next, playing intently, soothed by the familiar melody. When she finished, she turned on the piano bench to see Martin standing near the fireplace, smoking and watching her with the same look he'd had in the ballroom. She had never seen him smoke before. His demeanor was keen and nervous, as if he were a coiled spring.

"What is that one called?" he asked.

"'Scenes from Childhood.'"

"Ah," he said. He stubbed his cigarette out on an ashtray.

The warm day had become a perfect evening, with the breath of a soft breeze from the open window. Catherine wondered how the lighted rooms of Oakview would appear to someone standing outside on the terrace. It would seem like a stage set, an elegant one where beautifully dressed people moved about in ease. No one on the outside would begin to suspect the conflict in her heart; no one on the inside did, either. Only the rosary was privy to her true feelings.

She closed the sheet music and set it in the middle of the music rail. She was just about to say goodnight and go upstairs when Martin spoke.

"You said something once." He was holding a goblet of water, moving it in small, quick movements, the water circling in the glass. "You said you would show me the sketch of your mother."

"Yes."

"May I see it now?"

Initially she had hesitated. The nakedness of the picture seemed somehow shameful, not for a stranger's eyes. But after the last day and all she had experienced, it hardly mattered. And Martin was no longer a stranger.

"I'll bring it down," she said.

⁊◦

Descending the staircase, sketch in hand, Catherine thought of the evening her uncle had given it to her. She remembered the cozy intimacy of his study and the affection on his face as he told her the story of her parents and their lives together. He had been envious, he said, of how her mother was willing to fight to be with the man she loved. Again, Catherine felt the sting of her own failure to see and act upon love.

Martin was still holding the glass, but he set it down the moment she entered the room. She handed him the sketch.

"I don't have a date for this," she said. "My father did it sometime before I was born."

She expected a certain expression on Martin's face as he studied the drawing—the academic gaze of the artist, assessing composition and line. She did not expect the swift intensity with which he focused on her mother's face, the quick change in his eyes, or the way he lifted them and looked at her, silently, for a long moment.

"What is it?" she asked.

"What was your mother's name?"

"Anne Ogden."

"You told me your father's name . . . it was . . ."

"Arthur. Arthur Ogden."

He nodded once, rubbing his chin.

"Is something wrong?"

He put the sketch down, reached for a cigarette in the box on the mantel, then changed his mind and closed the lid. The clock ticked as she watched him, waiting for him to speak.

"There's no easy way to say this," he finally said. His eyes met hers. "I . . . knew your mother."

"You knew my mother?"

"Yes. But I did not know you were her daughter until this morning."

"This morning?" Then she remembered. "The letter."

He nodded. "Yes, it was the letter."

She stared at him, wanting him to go on, but he hesitated. In the silence, she had just enough time to process what it meant: that the man standing before her, looking at her with eyes that were kind and yet somehow agonized, could tell her things about her mother that she did not know. It was like a gift dropping right into her lap, out of nowhere, all the more precious for being a surprise.

She impulsively reached for his hand. "You knew her," she said, her heart beating faster. "My mother."

"Yes."

"You met her in New York? Before I was born?"

"No," he said. The words seemed to come with effort. "No. I didn't meet her in New York."

"Where did you meet her?"

Martin put his hand on top of hers, holding it close. His eyes were compassionate but grave.

"I met her in Monterey," he said gently. "Six weeks ago."

FORTY-THREE

*C*atherine stared at him. "You met her," she repeated. "In Monterey."

"Yes."

"Six weeks ago."

"Yes."

"She . . ." The shock was so great Catherine could hardly think of the words, let alone say them. But behind the shock, slowly consuming it, was something else. It was hope, leaping like a flame.

"My mother is alive?"

Martin squeezed her hand. "She is alive."

"But how . . ."

"Let's sit down."

She let him lead her to the divan. "But how can it be?" Her pulse was racing and her thoughts ran in all directions. "I don't understand."

"It seems impossible, I know," he said. "But it is your mother. I recognized the sketch immediately."

"But why . . ." She had no idea which question, of the many tumbling wildly in her mind, to ask him first.

"I don't know the whole story," he said, "but I will tell you what I can."

He picked up his water glass and offered it to her. She shook her head, and he put the glass on the table, reached for her hand again, and began.

"This summer, as you know, I was working at the Hotel Del Monte in Monterey," he said. "I was the resident art tutor for the summer, teaching guests how to sketch and paint. Local residents who could afford the fee were able to attend as well. And that's how I met her. Your mother. She introduced herself as Anne Arthur."

"Arthur. My father's name."

"She was living—still lives—in Pacific Grove, just down the road from the hotel. She's the companion to an elderly woman named Mrs. Goode, Hannah Goode, who has a home there. Anne came for the art classes, and after we finished the first day, she and I got to talking." Affection softened the seriousness of his voice. "You know me well enough to know I don't make friends lightly. But Anne was different. She was kind and entirely without pretense, and our friendship began immediately. In a summer where I was leaning over sketchbooks and having to tell rich debutantes they had more talent than they really did, her company was . . . well, it was like fresh air to me.

"We had tea together a few times after class. She went for morning strolls with me and David, a friend of mine. One evening, she and Mrs. Goode invited me for dinner at Sea Glass Cottage, their home. It was shortly before I came here. They were about to leave to go to San Francisco. Mrs. Goode needed some medical care, and they planned to be there for a month or so.

"Anne asked me what I was going to do when the art course ended. I told her I had just accepted a commission to go to Oakview to paint the portrait of the fiancée of William Brandt. 'He is marrying a girl from New York City,' I told her. 'Her name is Catherine Ogden.'

"Anne instantly went pale. I asked if anything was wrong. She got up from the table and went over to the sideboard, then came and sat back down. 'No,' she said. And that was all.

"For the rest of the evening, though, she seemed far away. I teased her that she was away with the fairies, and she said she was just thinking of packing for San Francisco. She did ask me, later in the evening, if I had ever met you, and I said no.

"And then yesterday I received this letter." He took it out of his coat pocket and handed it to Catherine.

She had not seen Anne's handwriting for more than ten years. She had no conscious memory of what it looked like, but as she unfolded the paper with trembling hands and saw the small, imperfect script, she knew instantly she was holding something her mother had written.

July 18, 1910

Dear Martin,

I hope this letter finds you well at Oakview. I have something to say that will be most surprising to you, and I do not know how to say it. I am not a great writer, so you will forgive me if I just rush headlong into the news.

One thing you did not know about me is my real name. For the past ten years I have called myself Anne Arthur, the first name of my late husband, but my real name is Anne Ogden. The other thing you did not know is that I had a daughter. When she was eight and my husband died, she went to live with my brother- and sister-in-law, who had the money to care for her. I have not seen her since. The story behind that is more than I can tell here. But my daughter's name is Catherine Ogden, and it is she whose portrait you are painting. Now you understand

my reaction when you told me that night at Sea Glass
Cottage. I had thought I would never again be
reunited with her, and to have that sudden
connection to her felt like something from the hands
of fate.

I am enclosing a letter for my daughter. May I
ask that you give it to her?

I can only imagine what you must be thinking.
You are not naive about human nature, and in your
travels around this world you have surely encountered
people who have no shame about deceiving others. As
God is my witness, what I am writing here is the
truth.

If Catherine should wish to contact me, I am at
the Goode residence on California Street.

I have put you in a difficult position and I
apologize. I am however comforted that you are there
with her. Even if I never see her again, I feel that
you are a link that connects my beloved child with
me. For that I am so grateful.

With affection,
Anne Ogden

Catherine looked up at Martin. Wordlessly, he passed her
another letter. She opened it, her heart pounding.

July 18, 1910

Dear Cathy,
I have sat here for half an hour trying to decide

how to begin this letter. I don't know how a mother starts writing to the daughter who did not know she was still alive. And my confusion is nothing compared to yours, I am sure.

If you are reading this, it is because Martin has given it to you. He has surely told you of our friendship and of the letter I sent him. There is much he does not know about my story and of course you do not, either. Let me simply say that there has never been a day or even an hour that I have not thought of you. You have lived in my heart as the little girl with the hair ribbons always untied, and in my memory I have seen you dance along the beach with your little bare legs, so happy and curious about everything. I see you as you slept in the cot next to the garden your father painted, and I hold that little peaceful face to my heart, even though now you are a grown woman and about to marry. Those memories have been painful at times, but they have also been the rock I have held on to.

The story of the past eleven years is not an easy one. It involves many mistakes, especially my own. And yet I want to see you and tell you, if you will let me. If it is too much to ask of you, I understand. Your life has continued on and is about to make a big change, and if you are happy and do not want to bring the past to life I will accept that.

I am in San Francisco with Mrs. Hannah Goode, the kind woman to whom I have been a companion *these past ten years. We will be here for a few more weeks at her home, and after that we will return to Pacific Grove. Martin knows the address there. If you wish to write to me you may do so at either place.*

I will finish by saying that I have always loved you and I always will. If you choose to let the past stay in the past, I will understand. But no matter what happens I will go on sending my silent love and prayers and blessings to my little, now big, Cathy.

With all my love and affection,

Your mother Anne Ogden

There were two small blots on the letter, places where the blue ink had smeared. Catherine's tears added two more. She hastily wiped them with her fingers, trying not to blur the writing in her mother's hand.

Martin pressed a handkerchief in her palm, and she took it gratefully. For a moment there was no sound but her sniffling and the soft sighs of the last of the fire.

Then she looked up at Martin. "My mother is alive," she said in wonder, and then she began to cry again. He put his arm around her and held her to his white shirtfront as all the emotion of the letters and the revelation came out of her in sobs.

When the tears had subsided, she straightened, once more wiping her eyes. The past day had been a storm of change and confusion. But through all of it, there was something she knew for certain, a decision she could make without thinking.

Martin saw it in her eyes and smiled. He gave her hand a squeeze. "Let's go tomorrow," he said.

FORTY-FOUR

A small girl stood on the platform at the Burlingame station. She had a copper-colored bob topped with a huge green bow and held her mother's hand tightly, looking at the train with fearful eyes as if it were a thing she had never seen before and whose movements she could not predict.

Her mother was a young woman with freckles and the same red hair and a well-brushed, if unfashionable, coat. From inside the train, Catherine watched the mother speak to her daughter, her manner calm and reassuring. As the train let out a whistle, the girl huddled against her mother's side, and the woman put a protective arm around her. *You have nothing to fear*, the gesture said, *as long as I am here.*

Catherine looked at Martin, sitting in the seat opposite. He smiled gently. "How are you feeling?"

"Nervous," she said. "And eager. And confused. And other things I can't quite explain."

He nodded. "There's no precedent for this."

She thought of all he had done to get them to the train. He was the one who had found the timetable and arranged for Anderson to drive them to and from the station. He had phoned the Goode residence and left word that they would be arriving in the late morning. He had even told Harriet he would be taking Catherine to the city to meet a friend of his. ("It's entirely the truth, of course," he said to Catherine.) She had barely seen Harriet, who was spending her day helping with a charity auction in Menlo Park. This was fortunate, as Catherine had been certain the news about her mother was not something she could conceal. Surely everything about her—the way she talked, walked, the look in her eyes—would reveal that she had just been privy to a miracle.

"Thank you for everything, Martin," she said. "This would not have happened without you."

He smiled. She knew she had a friend in him and always would.

"And I thought it was just another commission," he said. "I never dreamed I would be witness to a resurrection."

A white-haired man with a gray derby and a newspaper under his arm approached the seat next to Martin. He lifted his hat to Catherine, nodded to Martin, and sat down.

"A lovely morning," he said politely.

"It is," she said.

She wondered how she looked to him and all the other passengers, sitting upright in her ecru coat with the brown trim, gloved hands folded neatly in her lap. To all outward appearances, she was just a young woman going to the city for a day of social calls or perhaps to visit the shops. No one could possibly guess the reason why she was on the train. No one could know how her mind swirled with speculation, avoiding some possible explanations and hoping for others, as she wondered what would keep a woman dead for eleven years and what would make her come back to life.

❧

The taxi stopped at California Street in front of a large, handsome home. It had columns and stairs leading up to a front door flanked by two stone urns planted with begonias. As Martin paid the driver, Catherine adjusted her hat, her heart pounding. Large windows showed gauze curtains looped at the corners, letting in as much light as possible, even though it also meant letting in the gazes of people on the busy city street. Was her mother looking out one of those windows, seeing her daughter approach, waiting in a parlor for the maid to announce her?

She thought about what would happen once she rang the bell. The maid would open the door, bring them in, and take their coats. They would be taken into the parlor or perhaps the conservatory visible on the west side of the house, and her mother would be sitting there, waiting. At their entry she would rise and come toward them—

Martin took her elbow. "Ready?"

Together they climbed the steps, and Catherine heard her own heart beating. This cannot be real, she thought, this cannot be happening. But it was, and she reached out and rang the bell.

There was a brief moment; then the door swung open and Catherine opened her mouth to greet the maid. But it was not a maid. It was her mother.

She was not as tall as Catherine expected, only an inch or two above her in height. Her hair was still black, though with a streak of gray in front, like the marking on the wing of a bird. And there was the sudden, startling impact of her beauty, a beauty that went even beyond what Catherine had expected, beyond what she knew from the sketch and her memories. As the two women stood across the threshold from each other, Catherine saw her mother's eyes fill with tears.

"Cathy," she said.

"Mama." It felt strange to say it, like using a language she had not spoken since childhood. For a moment they stood and looked at each other. Then her mother opened her arms, and the strangeness was gone.

Anne's body was thin but strong, warm, and instantly familiar. She smelled like Pears soap, a remembered scent from child-hood. Catherine could not speak or think; she could only cry, her tears falling freely on her mother's neck and shoulders. It was an overwhelming, almost painful joy to be in her presence, touching her and smelling her, knowing she was not a memory or a sketch but flesh and blood.

Then Anne pulled away and held Catherine at arm's length, taking in every detail of her face. "Cathy," she said. "My little Cathy." There was wonder in her eyes. "You are so like your fa-ther." She reached up to touch Catherine's dark hair. "But like me, too, I think."

She had fine lines in the corners of her eyes, and there was a scar on her lower left cheek, three inches long, running at an angle to her jawbone. It had not been there before.

Her mother turned to Martin, who stood at a discreet dis-tance on the porch. "Martin," she said, reaching out to him. "Thank you for bringing her here."

"Anne." He took her hand in both of his and gave it a kiss. "It was my privilege."

"Come in," Anne said, indicating the open door. There was a quick gracefulness to her gesture, reminding Catherine of Gloucester. She wore a sea-green dress trimmed with silver braid, made of fine cloth but simple, with large sleeves and clean lines. Her hair was arranged in the familiar braids coiled and pinned low behind her ears; with the dress they gave her the look of a Pre-Raphaelite painting.

"I'll go out for a walk, I think," said Martin. "You'll want to visit alone."

Catherine barely heard him, her attention was so focused on her mother. Anne, too, accepted his statement without com-ment. She was gazing at her daughter as if she could not get enough of the sight of her.

Martin turned to Catherine. "I'll come back at three? That will give us time to get back to the station."

"Thank you."

He smiled at them and left.

"He's a dear man," her mother said. Her voice was low, with a tinge of Irish brogue. Catherine had never been able to remember her voice. It had been an elusive thing, lost over the years, but now she realized the memory had merely been dormant. Had the voice come to her without a face or a body, she'd have recognized it instantly.

"Yes, Mama," Catherine said. "He is."

Anne took her hand and squeezed it. Her eyes were shining. "Come in. Come into the parlor."

She led the way through the spacious entrance hall into a pretty room with toile-covered sofas, tall windows, and a chess set laid out on a small table. A portrait over the mantel showed a woman wearing a gray evening gown and a diamond necklace. She had white hair and a benevolent expression.

"That's Mrs. Goode," said her mother. "She's upstairs recovering from an operation. Nothing serious, thankfully, but she won't be able to meet you today. She sends her regards."

A maid appeared in the doorway, taking Catherine's coat and hat. "Frances," said her mother, "this is my daughter, Catherine."

Frances smiled. "It's nice to meet you, miss." She turned to Anne. "I can bring tea whenever you like it."

"We're fine for a time, Frances. But thank you."

The door closed behind the maid and Anne led Catherine to the nearest sofa. They sat side by side, and Catherine could not stop looking at her mother: the dark hair, the scar, the crinkles in her eyes, the remembered freckle on her right earlobe. And Anne could not stop smiling at her daughter, eyes traveling in wonder over her face.

"Cathy," she said. "You are so tall, so grown-up." She squeezed Catherine's hand, then indicated the sapphire engagement ring. "And you are going to be married."

"Yes. In September."

"What is he like?"

For the first time, Catherine could not meet her mother's eyes. "He is very wealthy," she said, pleating the fabric of her skirt. "And he has a beautiful home."

"Do you love him?"

Catherine's first instinct, after years of living in Madison Avenue society, was to say yes. But her mother was not part of Madison Avenue society, nor was she part of Oakview. She was from another world, one where women came back from the dead and the usual rules did not apply. Her gaze was clear and calm, and Catherine realized that she had the freedom to be completely truthful.

"No," she said.

"You are unhappy," her mother said gently.

Catherine shook her head briefly, as if to change the subject. "Tell me about you," she said. "I want to know. I want to know everything. What happened all those years ago?"

A shadow came over Anne's face, swift and unmistakable. But it passed quickly, and she once again looked at her daughter with steady eyes. "I will tell you," she said. "I will tell you everything you want to know."

"You left me in New York," said Catherine. Tears filled her eyes, sharp tears of self-pity. "You never wrote again. We all thought you were dead."

Her mother closed her eyes and bowed her head. It was so silent that Catherine heard the ticking of the grandfather clock. Then Anne let go of her daughter's hand and got up from the divan and walked to the window.

"I will tell you everything," she said. "Though it will not be easy to say and probably not easy to hear." She stood, straight and tall in her green dress, sunlight behind her. "But you deserve to know the truth, Cathy. The whole truth. And here it is."

FORTY-FIVE

"To start, I must go back before you were even born," said Anne. "To things you never knew, Cathy, because I never had a chance to tell you. I came over on the boat when I was nine, with my aunt and uncle and cousins. My mother was ill, and my father stayed back in Ireland with her. I cried and cried to leave them."

She gave a small smile. "How odd it is. Both of us, you and I, raised by an aunt and uncle. In such different places, though. For me it was a tenement on Canal Street, nothing like the green fields of home. I was young, but old enough to know that . . ." She struggled for the right words. "That life could be so much more, should be so much more, than crowded streets and piecing dresses for a few cents an hour.

"So I was glad to go into service as a kitchen maid. It was a new world, living in a grand house by the park, even if I got to see very little of it. I started at fourteen, and when I was sixteen, I was made a parlor maid, which meant better wages. No more raw hands from the sink, either.

"I remember thinking it was a small family for such a big house. There was a son studying at university and two young daughters. They were not unpleasant to work for, all in all. I did not always like how the father looked at me, but he never did anything to cause me grief. Not all girls in service are so lucky, you see." She smiled gently at her daughter. "You may not know, Cathy, how vulnerable such girls can be."

Catherine nodded, thinking of Graciela.

"Then everything changed one summer," said Anne, "the summer I was seventeen. The son of the family came home with a friend. Edward was the friend's name. He stayed there while he found lodgings of his own. He was an artist, and he set up an easel in his room. I'd never seen such a thing before, and it fascinated me.

"One morning as I was making the bed, I saw the canvas he was painting, a picture of the clock and vase on the mantel. I stopped my work to look at it more closely. It was like his painting showed them in a new light, these things I dusted every day. Somehow the painting could make me see them with new eyes.

"I was so lost in looking that when Edward came up behind me, I was embarrassed. I apologized and tried to leave, but he stopped me. 'Don't go,' he said. 'Tell me what you think of my painting.'

"I couldn't believe he was asking me, a maid, what I thought. But there was something about him; I felt safe with him. Then and always, I felt safe. I told him I liked it and why.

"The next day I was polishing the brassware in the library when he came in. He was smiling, like he'd made a great discovery. 'I know who you remind me of.' He opened a book he was holding. He covered part of the page with his hand and showed me the rest. It was the head of a blond woman with her hair in the wind. 'It's *The Birth of Venus*,' he said. 'You have the same eyes.'"

Anne nodded at the recognition on Catherine's face. "So you know the painting. He was right, wasn't he? And seeing myself on the page was like seeing myself in a new way. I felt powerful, almost. It was like I was part of something more than myself.

"Then I did something that surprised him and even me. I moved his hand away to see what he was covering up, and it was her naked body. Oh, I was so bold, touching him and standing there looking at a naked woman with him, but I didn't care. Me, Annie Donovan—I was a part of something new. Part of a world of books and artists." Her eyes were alight, reliving the moment. "I remember it so well, Cathy, the feeling that life suddenly held something I had not expected to find."

Catherine's first view of the garden, its flower beds empty and waiting, tugged at her memory. She leaned forward, not wanting to miss a word.

"So we became friends, Edward and I," her mother continued. "As much as we could, with him a guest in the house where I was a maid. You might think I wanted him for a beau, but no. I never dreamed of kissing him. It was different in a way I couldn't explain.

"He found lodgings later in the summer and invited me to come on my afternoon off. At his studio, he told me I had the perfect face to draw, that he'd love to sketch me. And when he showed me the finished drawing, I couldn't believe it. It showed not just what I looked like, but somehow who I was, in my very soul. Like he really saw me. It's a rare thing, being seen like that.

"I went back every day off that I had. And I realized why I felt so safe with him when one of his friends, a young blond man, came to the studio for the first time. He greeted Edward by kissing him on the mouth, and Edward kissed him back. It may seem strange, Cathy, but this did not shock me. I think I was born with the knowledge that some people are different in that way, and it was not anything I feared.

"So when Edward asked if I would pose for him without any clothes on, I said yes. Oh, if my aunt and uncle had known they would have been horrified and I would have been beaten, even though I was nearly eighteen. It felt strange at first, but I had no shame about it. And when I was naked, I could be anyone. A woman from Five Points or one from Fifth Avenue. I'd never known it before, that sort of—freedom."

She met her daughter's eyes. "It's a shocking thing, perhaps."

"No," said Catherine slowly. "I think I understand."

"I'm glad you do. Most would not. Like the butler at the house where I worked. He found out what I was doing on my afternoons off, and I was turned out on my ear within the hour. Without my wages, even. I couldn't go back to my aunt after that, but Edward let me stay at his studio. He also found me work modeling for a drawing class at the art college. And maybe it was fate."

"Because that's where you met Papa."

"Yes."

"What was it like? Meeting him?"

"Like any other day, at first," said Anne. "I was lying on the divan in front of all the easels and then he came into the room. I noticed him right away, the tall young man with the limp. It was the first thing you noticed about him but not the last." She gazed into the air, as if visualizing the scene. "He saw me there naked, and he looked away. I could tell he'd never drawn from a model before. But he set up his easel and began to work, and something about him appealed to me; he seemed so eager and kind. And— this is strange, Cathy—no one else made me feel shy about being naked, but he did. That was the first sign that we would fall in love.

"After class, when I had dressed and was leaving, he was standing outside. I asked if he was happy with his drawing. 'It's not as lovely as the original,' he said, and he turned red." Anne's eyes crinkled at the corners. "It was so endearing, that blush. He didn't have much practice, you see, giving a girl a compliment. We just stood there, traffic all around us, talking for nearly an hour. It was easy being with him and exciting, too. We both felt it.

"We saw each other whenever we could. We went walking and even out to a restaurant. Our worlds were different, but it was easy to forget that. It's like we were two pieces cut from the same cloth. Like we'd been waiting to meet, somehow.

"And then one day, he asked me to marry him. I was so happy I could hardly say yes. 'But what will your family think?' I asked.

"'That doesn't matter,' he said. 'Only you matter.'

"But it did matter to his father. When Arthur and I went to his home, your grandfather said . . . oh, he said horrible things. He called me an Irish whore and said I was only marrying your father for his money.

"Arthur was furious. The things he said to his father." She shook her head. "I was sure he would regret them one day. I didn't like what his father had said, of course, but I remained calm. You learn how to do that, working in service. And I knew who I was and what I was worth. I told your grandfather that I loved Arthur and would marry him even if he did not have a cent. Your uncle was there, too, Cathy. He said very little, but I think he was ashamed of what his father was saying."

"He was," said Catherine. "He told me so, the night before I came to California."

"He was a good man, I think," said her mother. "Just not a brave one. But we all have moments where our courage fails us.

"So your father and I married and moved to Gloucester. We were so happy there. He could find beauty in places most people wouldn't. A corner of a roof was beautiful to him or a rain puddle. It made him a good artist. It also made him happy with very little." She smiled fondly at her daughter. "And then you came along, our little Cathy. Just what we needed for our family to be complete."

Catherine nodded, emotion making it hard to speak. She had been utterly absorbed in her mother's early life, in the revelation of things she'd never thought she would be able to know. Now the story had come to her own memories, the sweetness and pain of her own past. "We were happy."

"So happy. Your father and I were a good match, you know, alike in some ways but different in others. It's funny that he was so idealistic and I was so practical. Or maybe it isn't. Maybe when you grow up in a tenement, you look at life with clear eyes, and when you grow up in a fine, large house, you can ignore the things that you don't want to see.

"He always held a grudge against his family, you know. Not just for what his father said to me but because of a case they were once involved in. Your father believed they had tormented a man to his death just to win, and he couldn't abide that. Even when he learned that your grandfather had died, he would not write to your uncle." She frowned slightly, adding, "I think sometimes it is idealistic to hold on to such a grudge. It is certainly not practical."

Her voice grew quiet. "You remember your father's death, of course."

"I do."

"When he died, I thought my heart would break. But along with the grief was fear about how we would live. There was no money, as you know. I could only find live-in work as a maid, which meant I could not have you with me."

Anne turned to Catherine, eyes heavy with regret. She still stood by the window, as if it were only at a distance from her daughter that she could speak of the past. "I wish I had asked your uncle for money instead and kept you with me. I've wished that so often, Cathy. But your father had always insisted we would never take a penny of the money his family had made from the law. Blood money, he called it. In my grief I wanted to honor that wish. I knew he did not even want me to tell them about his death, but at last I had no choice. But oh, how it pained me to do it. I took you to church the day before I wrote to them, praying for guidance. For forgiveness, too."

A memory flashed into Catherine's mind: a dark nave, a bank of candles. "I think I remember that day."

"I remember it like it was yesterday. I had to believe, you see. I had to believe that your father would forgive me for writing to his family. But saying goodbye to you on that step was the hardest thing I had ever done. I cried for days after you left. All I wanted was to save enough money to get you back with me."

She moved to a small mahogany table under the window, its polished surface reflecting the light. For a moment she ran her fingers along the edge, back and forth, as if reluctant to continue with the story. Then she raised her head.

"What I have told you until now," she said, "is the part that is easy to tell. What comes next is harder. Much harder. But you must hear it all to understand."

Catherine nodded, a flutter of apprehension in her chest. Her folded hands felt weightless and cold.

"After you left with your aunt and uncle," Anne said quietly, "I went into service. In Boston, for a rich old couple. They were so old they could not see things: that the lady's maid was taking money from the housekeeping, or that she called her mistress terrible names behind her back. I hated the maid for being so dishonest and so cruel. I think she feared I would tell the old woman, for she claimed I had been consorting with the butcher's boy and I was dismissed without a reference.

"That was a disaster, you understand. With no reference I had no way to get another position. I knew no one in Boston, and you seemed so far away in New York. Your aunt and uncle would take in a child, but I knew they would never welcome a sister-in-law who was Irish and had been a maid. I remember wandering through the park, not sure what to do. Then I thought I could find an art school and ask if they needed a model.

"A couple happened to be walking by. I stopped them and asked if they knew where an art school would be. The young woman looked at me as if I were the dust on her feet. The man was a little more polite, but he said he did not know where to find one. I kept walking, searching for someone else to ask. But it was a dark day, threatening rain. Not many people were out. I could see the couple I had spoken with at the edge of the park. The man was seeing the woman into a cab, and she left. I continued on my way, and he caught up with me on the path. He asked if I had found my art college yet.

"I said no. He was well-dressed, with a face that looked at me as if he already knew me. He seemed the kind of man who would live in a fine home, so I asked if he needed a maid. He laughed.

"'You a maid?' he said. 'I thought you were an art student.'

"'No,' I said. 'I need work, and if I cannot find it as a maid, I will work as a model again.'

"He looked at me differently then, and I regretted saying it. I turned to leave, but he stopped me.

"'Perhaps I can help you,' he said. 'But first, let's get out of this weather.'

"I should have listened to my instincts, but I did not. I was heartsick with worry and had nowhere to go. So we had dinner at a restaurant and I told him about my plight, and about you." She paused, and Catherine could tell she had to will herself to talk about him. "His name was Silas.

"After dinner, back in the park, he asked where I was going to stay. I had nowhere to stay. He drew me under a tree and tried to kiss me, but I turned away. He grasped my arms and said that I was beautiful and if I would stay with him the night, just one night, he would give me ten dollars."

Anne looked down at the table. "And this, this is so hard for me to tell you. I said yes. I said yes because it was so much money and because I could not think of anywhere else I could go.

"And it felt like a betrayal of your father. Even more, though, it felt like a betrayal of me."

Catherine watched her mother standing by the table, sunlight touching the top of her dark head. Then Anne raised her eyes to the window and continued, her voice quiet but steady.

"When it was over, he said he did not have the money with him. He said he would pay for me to stay in a hotel and come back the next day. But when he came back, he wanted another night before he would pay me. And so I ended up living in that hotel for six weeks, and he came to me almost every night."

She faced Catherine with anguish in her eyes. "I hated myself, Cathy. I had become what your father's father said I was. And the more I got to know this man, the more I saw the darkness in him. He was very rich and important, engaged to the woman in the park. But he showed another side to me, and he did terrible things to me. I will not tell you what they all were. But it was he who gave me this scar one night when I told him I wanted to leave.

"I lost myself. I had always been strong, able to defend myself and others, but that was gone. He chipped away at me, piece by piece, like you chip at a block of ice. He destroyed my hope to be with you, too. What kind of mother was I, to be selling herself? It was like he took the spirit right out of me.

"Then there was one day, one awful day, when he found the sketch of you. Your father had drawn you when you were asleep, in your little nightgown, just a few months before he died. The way Silas looked at you, my sweet girl, oh, it made my blood run cold. 'We should bring your daughter here,' he said. 'You would like to have her with you, wouldn't you?'

"And that's when I realized that I had not lost all of my spirit."

There was fire in Anne's eyes, a mother's protective instinct roused by the memory. "I had just enough left to make sure that he would never come near you. That, at least, was one thing I could do for you.

"But a few nights later, I was at my lowest. I was ill, with a fever coming on. It was no wonder after his treatment of me. He had left and I sat by the window, feeling wretched because I could see no way out. The memory of him looking at your picture made me feel even more afraid. I burned the sketch so that he would never see it again.

"Then I wrote a letter to your uncle. I told them that they should keep you, that I would not be coming back for you. I did not explain, couldn't explain. How could I put it into words, what I had become? As I walked away from the postbox, I decided to do something I had been thinking about for days. I decided to take my own life."

It was so quiet in the room that Catherine could hear her own breath. It did not occur to her to speak, even to move. She sat on the edge of the divan, her muscles tense, listening.

"But as I walked along the river, something happened that I still wonder at. There was a commotion at the water's edge, several people and a policeman. They were gathered around the body of a young woman, tall, with dark hair like mine, who had been taken from the river. She wore a dress that stuck to her legs like another skin, and she lay in such a horrible way, so limp and still, you could hardly believe she had ever been alive. Her pockets were full of stones, bulging with them. She had made the decision I was about to make.

"It horrified me. I stared at that poor woman and realized I could be seeing myself. It took my breath away. I had nothing left in my life that was good, but in that very moment, seeing her, I knew I did not want to die as she had."

Anne shook her head, as if the experience still mystified her. "Some might call it the hand of God, how it happened. I don't, Cathy, and I never could. A woman died; there was no God in that. But to this day I know that seeing her dead is what kept me alive.

"I did not go back to the hotel, of course. Nothing would make me do that. I thought of finding a church to take me in, but I collapsed in the street and was taken to the hospital. The next few weeks are a blur. I was in and out of a fever; I couldn't even say my own name. That was fortunate, for if Silas tried to find me, he was unsuccessful." She lifted an eyebrow. "I doubt he did, though. For him, there would always be another woman needing help in the park.

"When I was finally able to think clearly, I remembered the letter I had written to your uncle. At first, I thought of writing again, of taking you back. But because of everything that had happened in that hotel, I was not the same woman I had been before. I felt I didn't deserve you. That's what I mean when I say that he took my spirit, Cathy. He took my spirit and gave me shame, shame that was still so strong even with him gone. It was like a dress I could not take off.

"But the sisters at the hospital were so kind, God bless them. Once I was well enough, they offered me a bed in exchange for work. I called myself Anne Arthur, as you may know from Martin. I wanted my past to be the past, and I did not want to be found."

An automobile paused outside, giving a raucous blare of its horn, and another auto answered back. Anne reached for the open window and closed it. Then she turned to her daughter, apology on her face. "I am saying so much, Cathy. If you want to stop for a time, perhaps have tea, we can do that."

"No." Catherine's voice was raspy; she realized she had not spoken for a long time. "No. Please tell me the rest."

"Thankfully, the rest is happier." Her mother smiled, her eyes creasing lightly at the corners. "Full of blessings, for a change. A few months later I was given a new life."

"How?"

"Through chance," said Anne. "As so much of life is, I think. I was in the art museum one afternoon. It was my favorite place to go when I had free time from the hospital. In the sculpture room, there were two women on a bench, talking. Beautifully dressed, they were, one young and one old. I sat down nearby to rest my feet, and the older one saw me and smiled kindly. Just a little moment of kindness, but I was still so vulnerable, and it meant so much. I smiled back.

"They got up and walked out. A few minutes later, I realized the older woman had forgotten her cloth bag on the bench. I ran to return it to her. She was so grateful. I think she could tell from my clothes I had little money, and another woman might have kept it. She invited me to tea at her house, which was actually her daughter-in-law's house, the younger woman. The older woman was Mrs. Hannah Goode, visiting from San Francisco."

Anne looked fondly at the portrait above the fireplace. "She was like Edward, you know, or your father. She came into my life when I did not expect it and changed it completely, for the better. I've been lucky to have three people like that in my life. Four, now, counting Martin.

"So I went there for tea. After all those years of carrying it in on a silver tray, it was strange to sit and drink it. Mrs. Goode had just lost her husband, and she was staying with her son's family in Boston. I told her I was a widow, too, with a daughter living in New York. I said you had been adopted by my husband's family because I could not care for you. That was true, mostly. She was such a good listener, so kind. I was sorry to say good-bye, but I was warmed by the time we had spent.

"The next day she came to find me at the hospital. I was so surprised to see her. Even more surprised by what she said next.

"'I have been thinking about you ever since you left yesterday,' she said. 'With my husband gone, I am in need of a lady's companion. Would you like to be that for me?'

"I could hardly believe it. I told her that I was not educated, nor was I a fine writer, as I thought a companion would have to be. She said it didn't matter.

"I remember standing there, twisting my apron strings and deciding to tell her more. I told her what my real name was, and about the man in the park and what had happened for weeks in that hotel. I told her about the walk by the water and the dead woman who had saved me. I needed her to know all of this, to know who she was hiring. I was afraid to look at her, but when I did, there was no disgust in her face, only sadness.

"'You have suffered things you should not have had to suffer,' she said. 'But it does not change what I am offering you.'

"So I came to live with her. Cathy, her name could not be more fitting. She is a good woman, the best I have ever known. I learned she had founded a home in San Francisco to help girls who have been ill-treated, helping them begin again. I had never before met a rich person who used her wealth to bring others up. She offered me her trust. That made me start to feel worthy again."

Catherine raised her eyes to the portrait, absorbing the elderly woman's calm and gentle expression. "She looks very wise."

"She is. Wise and strong. But even so, Cathy, I didn't tell her the full truth about you. She knew you were being raised by your aunt, but she did not know you had expected me to come back and get you. Even with all of her kindness, I couldn't forgive myself. I had so much shame, still; it was easier to act as if I were dead to you, to close off any chance of seeing you again. That's why shame is so dreadful, Cathy. It clouds the eyes.

"After a few months in Boston, Mrs. Goode was ready to move back to San Francisco. She asked if I would be all right going so far away from you, and I told her yes . . . you had a new family, and I had never been part of it and couldn't begin now. Mrs. Goode didn't press me to explain. But I did tell her there was one thing I wished I could know, before we left. I wished I could know that you were healthy and well, even though I could not write to ask."

Anne cast a grateful look at the portrait. "She did that for me. She made inquiries and found out that her daughter-in-law had friends in New York who knew your aunt and uncle. They had been there for a luncheon party and their niece, an orphan, had come in with a governess. They had seen you playing with a small dog in the hall as they left.

"I held on to that picture of you, on that big staircase I had walked down with your father, playing happily with a little dog. You had always wanted a pet; do you remember how your father used to train seagulls to come to our step? If they had not said that about the dog, I would not have been able to bear going so far away."

She nodded toward the window. "And so we came here. It's been a good place for me, Cathy. I have helped Mrs. Goode with her work, helping women and even girls, some of them, who have sold their bodies and need to start over. That's how I learned to forgive myself. It didn't come easily, that forgiveness. That's a story for another day, I think. But I have a peace about my past now that I never thought I would find.

"The last few years, though, we've been mostly in Pacific Grove. Have you seen it, that part of the coast?" Catherine shook her head. "Oh, it's a magical place. The fog feels gentler than the fog here, and there are pine trees and butterflies. It makes me think of Gloucester, and you and your father walk the beach with me in my memory each day. We are apart from the world there, not even reading the newspaper. It's a little Eden, except for not having you, of course."

"And you met Martin there, at the art class," said Catherine.

Anne smiled. "I took that class wanting to feel closer to your father, and it's as if he sent me a new friend. A soul friend, that's what Martin is. Those are rare, you know, and precious.

"Maybe he told you about the day a few weeks ago, when he came to dinner at Sea Glass Cottage. Mrs. Goode was tired and went upstairs, but Martin and I sat and talked until the moon was high. He told me he had just received a commission to paint the fiancée of Mr. William Brandt. She was a girl from New York, named Catherine Ogden."

Anne's eyes were wide as she relived the moment. "You can imagine what I felt, Cathy. My mind was in a storm for the rest of the evening. I couldn't think of anything else. I couldn't sleep, either. I lay in bed and wondered how you came to be in California, of all places. I thought about how you were nineteen and soon to be married. I wondered, as I had wondered so many times before, if you remembered our life in Gloucester, and if you were happy in the life you had now.

"And for the first time, I began to wonder if I could make myself known to you.

"For almost three weeks, I struggled to decide. If I wrote to you, would it distress you at a time when you should be happy? I also worried about how to explain why I had left you. Could I tell you about what I did, and what had been done to me, those weeks in the hotel? I was afraid it would disgust you, make you turn away. Perhaps it was better not to try.

"But something in me would not let me rest. And so I told

Mrs. Goode the whole story about you. I told her you were here in California and that I could easily write to you if I wished. I didn't know if I should burden you with the truth or stay silent. I asked her to help me decide.

"She sat just where you are sitting now, listening. And then she said something that I will never forget.

"'Imagine,' she said, 'that I am handing you a pair of magic glasses. When you put on these glasses, they will help you see. Something in your life that is now blurry will become perfectly clear to you. What do you see that you didn't see before?'

"I closed my eyes and imagined putting the glasses on my face. And I did not even have to think, because what I saw was clearer than water. I saw that I should make myself known to you.

"So the very next day, I wrote to Martin and to you. I sent it off with a prayer. Then Martin called me this morning, early. The moment he said my name, somehow I knew what he would say. I cried into the telephone."

Her voice broke as she gazed at her daughter. "And here you are. My heart is so full, Cathy. That little girl, the one I never stopped loving: here you are. Right here. I can see you with my own eyes."

She closed her eyes and bowed her head, collecting herself. For a few moments she did not speak. Then she raised her eyes to Catherine, and her face was both vulnerable and brave.

"And that is everything, Cathy," she said. "Everything I did, and everything I failed to do. And now you know the truth."

FORTY-SIX

The grandfather clock chimed, marking half past one. It reminded Catherine that there was such a thing as time; she had lost all sense of everything but her mother's story.

As a young girl, she had accepted the explanation that her mother was dead, and now she knew why she had not questioned it. It wasn't only because her family had assumed it to be true, but also because believing it had spared her the pain of being an abandoned child. She had felt that pain right before her mother started telling her story; once the first flush of wonder at the reunion had passed, it had seemed unthinkable that a woman as vibrant as her mother would not have moved heaven and earth to reclaim her daughter. But as Anne spoke, Catherine's self-pity had vanished as the full picture of the past came into view.

It was the picture of a mother who had never stopped loving her child. But it was also the picture of a girl with a hunger for adventure and of a young woman who had known agonizing suffering and shame. As Catherine wiped her eyes, Anne took a tentative seat on the other end of the divan, looking at her daughter with love and—there was no mistaking it—also a trace of fear. The scar on her cheek was a jagged line, a visible reminder of degradation and pain.

"You have suffered so much, Mama," said Catherine, when she could speak again.

"I have told you things few mothers would tell their daughters, I think," Anne said. "But I hid so much, for eleven years, and now is the time to be open. I knew that I owed you the whole truth, even if it meant you would despise me."

"It did hurt, that you left me with no explanation," said Catherine; she would honor her mother's honesty with her own. "It hurts to think you could have come back, and we could have been together. But I think I understand why you did what you did. Why you did all of it, Mama. And I don't despise you."

"But I took your mother from you," said Anne. "And that's a terrible thing for a child to lose."

"You did," said Catherine frankly. "But you have brought her back again."

Her mother's eyes filled with tears. She reached for Catherine's cheek, cupping it in her palm. A moment passed before she spoke. "How fortunate I am. How blessed." She closed her eyes, as if she could not keep in her feeling, then opened them again. She smiled at her daughter. "Here you are. Still. It has to be a dream."

"No, Mama," said Catherine, through her own tears. "It's not a dream."

❧

They had tea, brought in by the maid, Frances; Anne hurried to hold the door open for her as she came in with the tray. Catherine spoke of her childhood on Madison Avenue, telling her mother about Miss Foster, Hawthorne, and the room with the maroon wallpaper. She skipped over the loneliness she felt as a child, but from Anne's expression, it was clear she knew her daughter was editing the story.

"It pains me," she said, "to think of you in that big cold house, alone."

"But I was not alone for long." She told her mother about

her friendship with Lavinia, Mr. Perrin's lessons, and the music and art she loved. "Aunt Abigail and Uncle Oliver were kind, too, in their own way."

Anne set down her teacup. "Your uncle loved your father very much, I think. I sensed that it hurt him deeply, that separation. And it could not have been easy for your aunt to suddenly have a young child to raise."

"Before I left to come here, Uncle Oliver told me he had made inquiries in Boston," said Catherine. "That woman you saw dead, by the river. I think he believed it was you."

"That does not surprise me. I knew from Mrs. Goode's friend you were believed to be an orphan. That dead woman probably made it easier for your uncle and aunt to believe something they were already telling themselves." Anne smiled sadly. "How strange, Cathy, the way things happen."

Catherine stirred her tea slowly. She gazed at the cup and thought of the sequence of events, both good and bad, that had determined the course of her mother's life. Edward staying as a guest in her employer's home, the couple who happened to be walking in the park, the dead woman in the river, the purse left behind accidentally by Mrs. Goode. And there was the fact that her mother had taken an art class taught by Martin, later hired to paint a portrait at Oakview. Such tiny, thin threads of fate had led her mother to where she was now.

She thought of Thomas. She wondered where he was and where he had gone, and it pained her to realize that she might never know. It was strange to think that the man she loved had come into her life because of the man she did not love, the same man who had come into her room to claim her in a way no engagement ring could do.

She grimaced, and her mother noticed. "Tell me, Cathy," she said quietly. "Tell me about this man you do not love."

So Catherine told her mother about the meeting in New York and William's immediate interest in her. She told her about her own indecision and the splendor of Oakview with its blossoming gardens. She told her about the visit of the Laws and William's isolated but sudden violence, and even about his visit to her bedroom and her acquiescence to his wishes, the thing she had not thought she could tell anyone for the shame of it.

When she finished, Anne was quiet. She looked at her daughter with compassion, and Catherine sensed that somewhere in the telling of the story, their roles had shifted.

"You have suffered, too," her mother said at last. "And you still intend to marry him."

"Yes."

"Why?"

Catherine regarded her in surprise; it could not be a real question. Of course her mother would know she could not extricate herself from such an engagement and from such a man as William, particularly after what had happened in her bedroom.

But as her mother waited for her to speak, Catherine realized the question was not a frivolous one after all. *Only a good reason will do*, said Anne's face, sympathetic and searching.

"Because I'm afraid not to," Catherine said. "Afraid of what people will say. Aunt Abigail, Henry. Even people I don't know. It has gone so far."

"But not as far as the altar."

"No," said Catherine. "But it has gone further, in a way." She fought back the image of William in her bed.

"And?" her mother asked gently.

"And that cannot be undone."

There was silence for a moment; then Anne spoke.

"No, it cannot. But sometimes it is not about undoing.

Sometimes it is about looking beyond." She set her teacup and saucer on the tray, her expression thoughtful.

"I will tell you this, Cathy," she said after a pause. "I have made choices based on shame. I did so because I was in a dark place and did not think I deserved happiness." Her eyes, blue and clear, held her daughter's. "And when I let my shame decide, it always made the wrong choice."

She reached out and smoothed the tendrils of Catherine's hair, a familiar gesture, the way she used to do. "And it's only now, seeing you again, that I truly know how much that shame has cost me."

FORTY-SEVEN

*I*n the train on the way home, Catherine sat wrapped in thought. The city, the bay, and the towns slipped past, but though she stared out the window, she did not see them.

It had been painful to leave her mother. Only the necessity of catching the train could tear her away. "We will see each other again," she promised her mother. "Soon."

Anne held her in a long embrace, her hand on Catherine's head. "I am always here," she said. "If you ever need me." She pulled back and looked into her daughter's eyes. "Don't forget that."

Martin, sitting next to her, did not attempt to draw her into conversation. She had given him a brief explanation of her mother's story, with Anne's permission. ("There was a time when I was terrified of anyone knowing my past," her mother had said. "I don't care anymore, now.") But her mind was too full for talk. She thought of her mother and all that she had endured and survived. She thought of what Anne had said about the choices she had made, and why, and what they had cost her. And when she was not pondering her mother's experiences, she saw things that went beyond conscious thought, that seemed to come from a place of pure feeling. In her mind's eye, she saw the image of a door becoming visible where before there had been only a wall. She saw a tall, dark-haired woman open that door and walk through it, into a garden that stretched all the way to the horizon.

"We're nearly there," Martin said, and she started. The station was just visible off in the distance.

Automatically she sat up and smoothed the creases in her coat. She readied herself to get into William's car for the last leg of her journey to Oakview.

❧

The Pierce-Arrow moved down the long drive, past the oaks with moss-trimmed branches, the paddock, the creek. The yellow grass was bright in the late-afternoon sun. There was the slow, unhurried movement of a deer grazing in the foliage, far enough away from the automobile to feel safe from its presence.

As the house came into view, Catherine thought of the first time she had seen it, back in March. The hills had been green then, and hyacinths had flanked the fountain. She had leaned forward in the car, eagerly, and walked for the first time through room after room, each one more beautiful than the last.

She sat back against the upholstery of the auto as the house came closer. Then she leaned forward to tap the shoulder of the chauffeur.

"Anderson," she said. "I would like to go to the garden first. Could you take the drive leading to the greenhouses?"

"Of course, Miss Ogden."

"I have something to do," she said to Martin, "before I go back to the house."

He smiled. "I will keep your whereabouts to myself. And if you need me, I'll be in the ballroom."

The car slowed as it turned down the side road, bypassing the main drive and running parallel to the exterior wall of the garden. The top of the Tree of Knowledge was visible in the distance, standing out like a crown. She looked at it as the car moved slowly along, eventually reaching the greenhouses.

"I'll get out here, Anderson," she said. "Thank you."

Catherine approached the garden from the orchard, moving slowly past the pear and apple trees, heavy with green fruit. At times, she touched the trunks and branches. As she grew closer, she kept her eyes on the ground. When she came at last to the doorway in the brick wall, she stopped and raised her head.

The garden lay before her, finished; Gerald must have used the morning to plant the last remaining flowers. It was a glorious tapestry, its mix of colors making a vivid but harmonious whole. As she gazed, she knew the thrill felt by her father, Martin, and all artists who create something out of nothing. It was a feeling of satisfaction and of completion that she had never known before.

Moving slowly, she made her way down the paths. Every bit of ground, every bloom and color brought back a memory. The flowers would eventually grow and fill in the spaces between them, Thomas had said on one of their last meetings; "In a few weeks, it will look even more lush than it does now." She reached out to touch the tall stalk of a dark-blue delphinium that swayed lightly under her fingers.

By a heliotrope plant, she paused, stooping to take in its perfume. When she had painted the initial designs, she'd never dreamed she would find a plant so beautiful and fragrant. She'd begun the project as a novice, knowing none of the practical aspects of gardening, simply following a vision. With time and the help of Thomas, that vision had been brought to life.

And more than flowers had taken root in this garden. She could see that now, very clearly, even though she had not been able to see it before.

Once she had viewed the garden from every path and angle, she paused in the brick archway of the northern wall. She surveyed the garden in the quiet light; then she closed her eyes and kept them shut for a moment. She opened them again, took a long and loving look, then turned and walked slowly toward the house.

⁊ↄ

She entered from the terrace, going through the French doors into the reception room. The young parlor maid, Nora, appeared and took her coat and hat; then the door to the hall swung open and William entered. Upon seeing his face, Nora disappeared quickly, closing the door behind her.

"Where the hell have you been?" William asked.

"In San Francisco. With Martin. We left word with Harriet."

"She told me. But she didn't say whom you were visiting."

"That's because she didn't know," said Catherine. She felt curiously calm, a still center in the heat of his anger. She walked past him to the sideboard and poured a glass of water.

"Who was it?"

She drank, then put the glass down, turning to face him. "It was my mother."

First he looked at her as if she were insane; then anger flickered across his face. "Don't lie to me."

"I'm not lying," she said quietly. "Yesterday I learned that my mother is alive. She has been living in California for ten years. She is a companion to a woman named Mrs. Goode."

"Goode," he said, then frowned slightly. "Asa Goode?"

"I don't know who her husband was," she said. "But I went to her house on California Street. They spend most of their time in Pacific Grove." She waited for him to say more, but he merely stared at her. "My mother had a difficult time in Boston when I was a child. I was living with my aunt and uncle, and she thought it was better for me to stay with them. In time, we all thought she had died. But Martin happened to meet her in Monterey, and now we've found each other again."

"What do you mean, 'a difficult time'?"

Remembering what her mother had said about being at peace with her past, Catherine hesitated only a moment before answering. "She had no money and no work. And in those cases women do what they must do in order to survive."

She saw a mix of surprise and disgust on his face.

"It was for a few weeks," she said, "more than ten years ago."

"Well," he said, "at least we can be thankful you had nothing more to do with her." He crossed over to the sideboard and poured a drink of brandy. He was calmer now; it occurred to Catherine that he had thought she was with Thomas.

"I'm sorry you had to learn that," he said. "It would probably have been better if you hadn't seen her again. I'm surprised Martin would put you into a situation that distressing."

"Distressing? Finding my mother again?"

"No. I mean finding out what she is." He drained his drink and put the tumbler down with a thump. "But I'll tell Martin to keep it to himself. We'll forget today ever happened."

"No," she said. "I can't do that."

"You'll have to do that. I will not let my wife acknowledge such a mother."

"You will not have to," she said quietly. "Because I am not going to marry you, William."

She had taken him by surprise. He looked at her for a beat, startled; then his face relaxed into its usual confidence.

"Don't be ridiculous," he said.

"I'm not. I've never been less ridiculous. I am not going to marry you."

"Because I am trying to protect your reputation?"

"Because I don't love you. And I never will."

It seemed harsh, saying it out loud, but he did not flinch. "I don't need love from you," he said. She knew he was telling the truth; the evenness of his tone chilled her.

"I know you don't," she said. "But I need to give love. And I can't give it to you."

"You gave me something else the other night, though." He moved closer, and she instinctively took a step back. "You can't have forgotten."

She was filled with revulsion, and that, its own way, was emboldening. She raised herself to her full height. "No, I haven't forgotten. But I still will not marry you."

"You don't mean this," he said. "It's the confusion of seeing your mother again. You'd never undo all the wedding plans and disappoint your family, just for a whim."

"It's not a whim," she said. "I will feel the same way tomorrow and next week and next year. I am not going to marry you."

She slid the sapphire off her finger and held it out to him. He stood still, hands in his pockets, fixing her in his dark gaze. While that gaze always used to affect her, she realized without surprise that it had lost its power to do so. She moved to the mantel and set down the ring.

"I'm sorry," she said, turning back to him. "Sorry that I said yes when I knew deep inside I should have said no. That wasn't fair to either one of us. And Harriet has been so kind. I regret hurting her."

"I will not let you do this," he said. "We will get married in September. As planned."

She thought of Martin in the ballroom. It was a comfort to know he was there, but there was no need to call him to her aid. She would not marry William, no matter what he said or did; of that she was certain, and it gave her a strength and purpose that left no room for fear.

"You think that if we were married, I would pretend to be happy." She looked him right in the eye. "I would not. I will no longer hide what I truly feel. And a miserable wife would do nothing to advance your ambitions."

He was silent. She could tell that her words had cut to the heart of what he valued most. And there was no sadness in his eyes, only a cold weighing of the alternatives, a calculating hardness.

"I could make things very difficult for you," he said at last. "You would never be accepted by society again."

The image of Anne came to mind: tall, graceful, resilient. "That would have frightened me once," Catherine said. "It doesn't anymore." And this, she realized with sudden clarity, this is freedom.

His expression changed perceptibly. She saw surprise, then the slow readjustment of his understanding of her. He had not expected those words from her, any more than she had expected the exhilaration of saying them and knowing them to be true. Sometime in the last twenty-four hours, his most potent weapon had been rendered powerless; they both knew it. And for the first time in her experience of him, he did not know what to say.

"I will go pack my things," she said finally. "Martin can take me where I need to go."

He had not moved, just stood like stone. If he showed any sign of pain, she might have pitied him, but she knew that even if he felt pain, he would find a way to make another emotion stronger. "In every contest, you want to come out the winner," he had said. As she walked to the door, she knew that even in her departure, a decision that he was powerless to stop, he would not rest until he had found a way to feel like the victor.

It did not take long. She had just reached for the doorknob when he spoke.

"So," he said, "this is the kind of woman you are. You let me come into your bed, and, two days later, you break our engagement."

"Yes," she said steadily.

"If I had known that, I never would have proposed. And I hope you don't come to regret this. No man wants to go where another man has already been." He looked her down and up, then met her eyes. "Not when it comes to a wife, that is. Not even a gardener will tolerate that."

This came closest to touching a wound, but she controlled herself and did not react. The conversation was almost over, and she had done it, the thing that a day before she had thought she could never do. Nothing he could say to her, no effort to shame her, would change that.

He crossed to the mantel and reached for a cigarette. "You will go live with your mother, I assume?"

"Yes."

"The woman with the past."

She said nothing.

"Well," he said pointedly, "perhaps with all her experience she has some useful things to teach you."

Catherine lifted her head and met his eyes without flinching. It was clear that he meant her to be diminished by his words, but, instead, she felt taller than she ever had before.

"Yes," she said, putting her hand on the knob and opening the door. "She already has."

PART
THREE

FORTY-EIGHT

*T*he garden at Sea Glass Cottage was larger than most in Pacific Grove. It stretched all the way around the two-story white house in colorful, sprawling beauty, with a cypress tree in the back garden and two pine trees in the front. It was bordered by a low fence separating it from the street, and through the slats orange and yellow nasturtiums grew in unself-conscious abundance, framed by blue salvia and red and pink penstemon.

Hearing Mrs. Goode's home called a "cottage" had made Catherine expect a compact house of stone and timbers. When she had arrived in Pacific Grove, she was surprised to find it was a spacious residence with gabled roofs and a large, wide porch. Inside, though, there was no hint of luxury. It was decorated simply, with Shaker-style furniture, chintz cushions, and faded rugs. There was art on nearly every wall, but no Canalettos or Van Dycks. They were mostly local artists, and their subjects were varied—a gull at water's edge, a vaquero reining in a horse, a bouquet of blue hydrangeas in a jug, and a nymph with long blond hair and a wreath of flowers.

Mrs. Goode, Catherine thought, was like her home. At first glance, she appeared formal, but there was a comfortable warmth to her that belied the initial impression. She had a smooth face and a head of snow-white hair under vivid black eyebrows. Her eyes were the color of coffee, and she had the slow, queenly movements of a woman who had long ago attended finishing school and decided its lessons on posture were worth retaining. She was the first elderly woman whom Catherine had ever seen go barefoot in the house, rarely wearing shoes except to go outside.

Sketching was her hobby, and she kept a collection of small drawing pads around the house. Little things would happen—a hummingbird poised in midair, a conversation between the postman and a passerby at the front gate—and she would draw the scene quickly, in sure, easy movements. "It's how I remember," she said to Catherine. "These sketch pads are my diary."

Sitting on the front porch the first day, she told Catherine how Sea Glass Cottage came to be. "We built it nearly twenty-five years ago. My boys had grown up and moved east, and my husband was retiring from the business and no longer needed me to play hostess quite so often." She settled back in the porch swing, which gave a gentle creak. "I was competent as a hostess, good even, but always felt restless in the city. I told Asa I would love nothing more than a home by the sea to escape to." She looked fondly at the white-painted ceiling of the porch. "It has served me well."

"It's a beautiful place," said Catherine.

"It is," said Mrs. Goode. "I always thought of it as my place, isn't that funny. Asa came here too, of course, but there are times when a woman needs a little space to herself."

"I hope it's not an imposition, having me here," said Catherine, after a moment.

"My dear, not in the least. I am blessed to be in a position to help others. And your mother is like the daughter I never had. It gives me such joy to see her so happy."

A yellow butterfly landed on the pink hollyhock just beyond the porch and rested there, opening and closing its wings. Both women noticed it, and Mrs. Goode slowly reached for the sketch pad on the bench beside her, but before she could make the first line it fluttered away. Catherine felt bereft, but Mrs. Goode merely smiled.

"There will be others," she said. "There always are."

✺

They had stayed in San Francisco for nearly two weeks after the broken engagement. "We will go to Pacific Grove as soon as we can," Anne said to Catherine the night that she and Martin left Oakview and returned to California Street. "Mrs. Goode is longing to get back, but she's not quite strong enough to travel yet." She squeezed her daughter's hand. "Will you be all right, being so near to Oakview?"

"I will," said Catherine. And she was.

Not once had she wavered in her decision to leave William. Even knowing the estate was only a short train ride away, she felt no temptation to return. She did feel a pang every time she thought of Harriet; Catherine's sudden announcement that she was leaving Oakview had shocked her, and there had been no opportunity for an explanation or even a true goodbye. The second night on California Street, Catherine sat down and wrote a letter, thanking Harriet for her kindness and for all her work on a wedding that would never take place.

An envelope from Oakview arrived two days later. "I will not pretend to understand what happened between you and William," Harriet wrote, "but I do know that I miss your company very much. I regret that I will not have the pleasure of having you as a sister-in-law, but be assured that I wish you every happiness in the future." Catherine read it and was moved; Harriet was generous to the last. She wanted to send a similar thank-you to Mrs. Callahan, Agnes, Gerald, and all the estate workers who had been a part of her life that summer, so she wrote a letter to Hayes and asked him to share it with the staff.

There had been no communication from William since the night she and Martin left Oakview. She did not expect any. The broken engagement was reported in the San Francisco papers, briefly, with no explanation as to why it had ended. She had no doubt William had given some reason for her departure to Peter, Vivian, the Eatons, and the other members of his social circle, but what it was she did not know; Mrs. Goode had little contact anymore with the San Francisco elite, and there were no channels for gossip to enter the house. William had hinted that he would say things to shame her, but, upon reflection, she doubted that he would. With an eye to the Senate, any hint of scandal about her would be associated with him. He was too careful to risk that.

Ironically, for all the distance, she knew much more about the reaction of New York society. The morning after leaving Oakview, she had sent a telegram to her uncle, telling him of the end of the engagement and the reunion with her mother. The next day, he sent a telegram to say he was coming to San Francisco. Six days later, he arrived.

"I am not here to convince you to go back to Mr. Brandt," he had said after the maid showed him into the parlor. "I am simply here to see you and to understand. And—" he grimaced, "to report back to your aunt and cousin."

"They did not want to come with you?"

He shook his head. "Your aunt is . . . well, very upset. This is much talked of, as you can imagine. Henry wanted to come, but I would not let him." He smiled wryly. "Apparently I do have some sway over him."

He looked so different, sitting in Mrs. Goode's parlor instead of his own brownstone in New York. She realized how much had changed since she had last seen him.

"I'm sorry for all the trouble I've caused," she said.

"Don't apologize, my dear." He crossed to the end table, fingering a piece of the chess set. "Your aunt and I didn't give you much choice about your own future, did we? You should have had the opportunity to travel or go to college, maybe. We'd have sent you without a second thought if you had been a boy. Times have changed, but we did not."

At the sound of the door opening, he put down the chess piece. Anne stood on the threshold in a violet afternoon dress, the doorway making a white frame around her. There was silence for a moment, and then Oliver spoke.

"Good afternoon." He crossed to her and formally took her hand.

"It's been so long," she said.

"It has."

She was silent, gazing at him, and then she turned away. "I'm sorry," she said, her voice catching. "I see Arthur in you."

Oliver offered her a handkerchief from his breast pocket. When she sat down on the divan, he sat down beside her, carefully, as if afraid she would break.

"I'm glad you are alive," he said awkwardly.

"So am I." Anne blew her nose and then gave a laugh. "This is an extraordinary conversation, isn't it?"

"It certainly is," he said. There was nostalgia in his eyes, just as Catherine had seen in the study when he had shared memories of her father. It occurred to her that both of the people sitting on the sofa, different as they were from each other, had loved her father deeply and missed him still. And she realized that her uncle, too, was recovering something he had thought was forever lost.

꙳

"If only," said her uncle over the remains of lunch, "I had done more to look for you all those years ago." Anne had told him her story, and he had reacted with visible shock and pain upon hearing what she had suffered. "Perhaps it might have made a difference."

"Perhaps," said Anne. "But the past is the past. We can only accept it, not change it."

"But I should have done more," he said, anguish in his voice. "I could have prevented so much pain. For you, for Catherine."

Anne's eyes were gentle. "You looked after my daughter for me," she said. "I will always be grateful for that. I am grateful to your wife, too."

He smiled wryly. "Abigail has never been one to shy away from duty." He turned to Catherine, his face apologetic. "That sounds harsher than I mean, my dear. Your aunt truly does care for you, even though she does not show it easily."

"And now I have put her in the middle of a scandal," Catherine said. She thought of the conversation and gossip that happened over tea tables, in dining rooms, and strolling down Fifth Avenue after church.

"She will recover," said her uncle firmly. "I leave here day after next, and no doubt I'll find her much better than she was when I left. Time is a good healer."

"Do you . . . do you know what is being said about why the engagement ended?"

"There's much speculation, naturally. I've told your aunt you did not feel the love for Mr. Brandt that you should feel, and you realized the marriage would not make you happy. I believe she finds that rather indelicate to share. But from what you've said, it's the truth."

"It is." She thought of Thomas.

"And it does you credit," said Oliver. "That you were able to see that clearly, in the end."

In the end, she thought. If only she had seen it in the beginning.

❧

She had been sorry to say goodbye to her uncle when he left, but she was eager to leave the city and move down to Pacific Grove. It was indeed a magical place, with its lighthouse, rocky shoreline, and groves of pine trees that she soon loved almost as much as she loved the beach. Each day she took at least one walk, sometimes down to the water, other times along the streets dotted with small, neat homes surrounded by low white fences. In the kitchen at the back of Sea Glass Cottage, she learned how to cook and bake bread, things she had never before had a reason to do. Preparing meals reminded her of gardening: a physical activity that brought direct, tangible results.

On the long sill of the kitchen window were the pieces of beach glass that had given the cottage its name. Some were blue, some green, others white or brown. All had smooth edges and were satisfying to hold. On Catherine's second day there, she moved along the window, picking up each piece in turn before putting it back down.

"Did you collect all of this?" she asked Mrs. Goode. The older woman was arranging flowers in a vase while Anne kneaded bread on the table at the far end of the room.

"Much of it," she said, "though my boys have added to the collection over the years. My grandchildren, too."

"They're so beautiful. Like art."

"Art that has been on a journey." Mrs. Goode reached over and picked up a piece of light-green glass. It was curved and had a slight cleft in the center, like an imperfectly drawn heart. "Look at this. This little bit of bottle has traveled who knows how many miles. It's been broken and bumped about, yet out of all that has come something precious." She handed the glass to Catherine. "It's rather a good metaphor for life, don't you think?"

Catherine followed the older woman's gaze to Anne as she worked the bread, the morning sunlight touching the gray in her hair.

"It is," Catherine said. She held the glass between her forefinger and thumb like a rosary bead before setting it gently back in place.

FORTY-NINE

*K*nowing about Catherine's love of flowers, Mrs. Goode invited her to make any changes to the garden that she liked. It was a coastal cottage garden with an easy, rambling feel, so different from the formal grounds of Oakview. Catherine decided to start with the area around the bench in the back corner, and she began clearing away the blackberry bushes with the help of Vincenzo, a local man who did repairs at the cottage. It was difficult work, and she wore long gloves to protect herself from the thorns, but it was deeply satisfying to be back in the soil.

At times, she missed the grounds of Oakview, missed them with an intensity that took her by surprise. She would walk the paths again in her memory and review the back garden as she had last left it, glowing with color. One day she named to herself all the ways the garden had made her feel. Free. Active. Inspired. Creative. Alive. They were all things, she realized, that she felt every day she spent in Pacific Grove. I have lost something, she thought, but I have gained more. And she put on her hat and went out to walk by the sea.

Lavinia, unsurprisingly, proved to be an unwavering source of support. She and Clarence had been crossing the Atlantic when the engagement ended. After they arrived in New York and heard the news, she immediately sent a telegram, which Catherine opened on the front porch of Sea Glass Cottage. It had more punctuation than any telegram Catherine had ever seen. "I CAN HARDLY BELIEVE IT! YOUR MOTHER! WILLIAM! WRITE SOON!"

Catherine wrote a detailed response, describing the reunion with her mother and her awareness that she could never love William. She finished by describing her plans for the future. "I'll be staying on in California with Mama and Mrs. Goode," she wrote. "The only part of that which I dislike is being so far away from you. Maybe you could come visit me? Next spring, maybe? If you can face the disapproval of the ladies of New York, that is."

A long letter came in response. The first few lines made Catherine laugh and cry at the same time.

> Dear Catherine the Brave,
>   Let the old biddies say whatever they want. You did the right thing, my friend. Marriage is _much_ too nice to waste on a man you don't love.

℘

Martin was a frequent visitor at Sea Glass Cottage. He dropped by for meals, at other times to invite Catherine or her mother for a walk along the coast or down the main avenue. Sometimes he was accompanied by his friend David, an architect with whom he shared a stone house in Monterey. They invited the three women to their home for dinner, where Catherine saw Martin's art, the kind he did on his own terms: pine trees in the sunlight, the lighthouse at dawn, sketches of an elderly Chinese fisherman in his boat. She wondered briefly what had happened to the almost-finished portrait at Oakview.

As if reading her mind, Martin said, "That portrait of you was very good, you know."

"I wonder what will happen to it now," she said. "Perhaps William will use it for archery practice."

Martin gave his ironic smile. "I doubt it. For all his faults, he did appreciate beauty when he saw it. I rather suspect he'll keep it."

He looked at Anne, who sat at the end of the table turning the pages of an atlas David had brought her. There was fondness in Martin's eyes as he watched her, and Catherine felt again how miraculous it was that such slim moments of chance had led to this deep and true friendship in Pacific Grove. Or perhaps it was not chance, after all.

"Someday," he said, "I'll do a portrait of you and your mother together. If you can tolerate sitting for me again, that is."

She threaded her arm through his. "I would love to."

❧

Mrs. Goode had called Pacific Grove her escape from society, but she was an active member of the community. Every Sunday morning, she walked to First Methodist Church for services, and twice a week the Ladies' Guild, a group of women of varying ages, met at the cottage. They welcomed Catherine warmly and asked questions about life in New York City but nothing about her experiences at Oakview, for which she was grateful. Most of their time was spent planning activities for the congregation and works of service for the town. Mrs. Goode had a gift for identifying and reaching out to those who were most in need.

And through it all, Catherine had the sense of going back in time. Her life seemed to have returned to its earliest chapters, with the presence of her mother, a house by the sea, and the freedom of a life lived out of society. There was the smell of bread from the kitchen and the sketch pads and pencils around the house, along with the opportunity to go barefoot and to wear her hair down if she did not feel like putting it up. There was even a tabby cat who stalked through the garden, purring loudly when it rubbed against her legs as she sat and read or dreamed on the stone bench under the cypress.

In her room upstairs, with its brass bed, rocking chair, and writing desk, she once again began the rosary ritual she had started as a child. Every night she worked her way around the beads, reviewing the impressions of the day, fixing them into her mind and memory. The sunlight on the sea. The kitchen curtains breathing gently in the breeze. The darkly rich scent of coffee percolating on the stove. The infant son of one of the Methodist ladies, who grasped her index finger in an endearingly tight grip. The comforting tread of Mrs. Goode's bare feet on the floor. Visiting Martin's favorite cypress grove and drinking a tumbler of wine with him under the trees. The warmth of a place where she was free to be herself, even to figure out who that self was in the moments when she was not entirely sure.

Memories of Thomas came back often, particularly when she worked in the garden. She would straighten from pulling weeds or deadheading the lavender and find herself expecting to see him standing there, his blue eyes creased at the corners, his wavy hair with the reddish highlights, his hands with dirt around the fingernails. Fragments of their conversations would come to mind, and she would remember the ease of their time together, how their friendship had grown along with the garden, blossoming into something she now recognized as love.

She had not spoken of him to her mother or to anyone. To do so seemed like opening a carefully corked bottle, letting loose a sorrow she could bear only if it stayed contained. She busied herself with the house, the garden, and her new acquaintances, but as the days passed and she settled into life by the sea, the memories came more frequently than they had before.

Most of all, she recalled their last meeting in the cottage. It had seemed like a dream when it was happening, the feel of his hands on her face and his lips on hers, but if she closed her eyes she could remember it all: the overwhelming pleasure and delight, the way her senses had leapt to life, the look in his eyes that warmed her to her very core. And she felt a longing for him that was almost physically painful.

Then she thought of the last moment she had seen him, standing in the small parlor of the cottage, pain in his eyes as she answered the summons to return to the house. He had not seen the tears in her room later that night as she realized what she had lost.

Did he ever think of her? she wondered. Had he heard the news of her broken engagement? And if so, what did he think?

FIFTY

*I*t was a beautiful Friday afternoon, calm and clear. Catherine waved goodbye to the last of the Methodist ladies while her mother collected the teacups from the dining room table.

"No," said Inge, the only live-in maid at Sea Glass Cottage. "So nice a day." She took the tray out of Anne's hands. "You go outside, you. Both of you. Enjoy the sun while you can."

"I know better than to argue with you, Inge," said her mother. She smiled at Catherine. "Shall we?"

As they walked along the rocky shoreline toward the beach, Catherine's attention was drawn to a young couple strolling several yards ahead, holding hands. Twice the young woman paused to point something out, perhaps a boat on the water or a child frolicking on the sands below. She could not hear what the couple was saying, but it was clear from the way he clasped her hand and the way they leaned toward each other that they took mutual delight in what they saw and in each other. She felt an ache in her chest.

Her mother spoke. "All these years I walked here, and you were with me, in my memory. I still cannot believe that you are here in truth." She tilted her face to the sky and said, "*Go raibh maith agat.*"

The words were like the striking of a bell. Catherine's mind rang with memories. "That's Irish, isn't it?"

"It means 'thank you.'"

"You used to say it in Gloucester. I had forgotten until now."

"Sometimes, when I feel it most, I say it in Irish."

The young couple was strolling along, hands swinging companionably, when the man suddenly stopped and pulled the woman to him for a kiss. As they moved apart, they both glanced about, embarrassed but happy, before continuing onward. In the moment that followed, silent but for the rush of the waves and the occasional cry of a gull, Catherine had an overwhelming desire to tell her mother about Thomas.

"Mama," she said, "there is something I want to tell you. About my life at Oakview."

Her mother did not break her stride. "This is a good place for telling."

As they walked along the rocks and down to the sand, Catherine told her about meeting Thomas, their growing friendship, and the night he left Oakview. Her mother merely walked and listened.

"And I still think of him, even though I've tried to forget," said Catherine. "Even here, as happy as I am. I think of him, and it hurts."

"Of course it does. Love is not forgotten so easily."

A wave crashed, and Catherine skirted its quickly advancing edge. It receded, leaving a ridge of sea-foam in its wake.

"I didn't see my own feelings until it was too late," she said. "But once I saw them, I couldn't stop seeing or feeling them. And I fear I've lost him forever."

"He is where, now?"

"Back in his medical college, I think," Catherine said. "He was going to take a few weeks to visit family before going back."

"You could find out the address of the college, I'm sure."

"Are you saying I should write to him?"

"What would be gained by staying silent?"

Catherine paused near a tangled bed of kelp, spread out on the sand like reddish-brown hair. She stirred it with the toe of her shoe.

"He must surely have heard of your broken engagement," said Anne. "And if he has not, perhaps you could tell him."

"But . . ."

"But what?"

"Nothing."

Anne's blue eyes were knowing. "I think I see," she said at last. "You are thinking of William and the night he came to your room. And you don't feel worthy of Thomas now."

It was hard to hear it said out loud, but Catherine nodded. "It was the very night Thomas kissed me," she said. "It was Thomas, and hours later, it was William. Even after I knew I loved Thomas. It seems like a betrayal of what I felt for him."

"You are ashamed. Ashamed of something that you didn't even choose to happen to you."

Catherine nodded again. Anne reached up and put her hands on either side of her daughter's face.

"Remember what I said weeks ago," she told Catherine, looking right into her eyes. "Remember what I said about shame. You are letting your shame make your decisions. As I once did. And if I had continued to do that, you would not be here with me now."

A tear slipped down Catherine's face. Anne wiped it away with her thumb.

"You are my daughter," she said. "I was out of your life for so many years that I could not teach you things a mother should teach her child. But here, now, this is something I can teach you. A decision like this, you cannot make it from a place of shame or fear. You have to make it from a place of strength."

"But how do I find that place?"

"You become quiet and listen. You listen to the voices that have proved worthy of trust, and you ignore the rest. You look at the patterns in your life and see what brings you real happiness, and peace, even the little things. You love those things and do them as often as you can. And when you do that, you find your true self again."

A wave rushed toward them, spreading nearly to their feet before receding. They resumed walking, slowly, arm in arm.

"But if I write to him," Catherine said after a moment, "he may never answer. Or he may no longer feel the same."

"Or," said Anne, "he may still feel exactly the same."

"But it's easier to stay silent. Because I have the memories. And if he were to reject me, I would lose even those."

They were nearing the end of the beach, coming upon the natural barrier of rocks. The young couple were walking in their direction now, their faces radiant with happiness.

"Let me say to you what Mrs. Goode told me, just a few weeks ago." Anne stopped and faced her daughter. "Imagine I am giving you a pair of magic glasses. When you put them on, you will see one thing clearly that you cannot see clearly now. Put them on. What do you see?"

In front of Catherine was the water, dazzling and sparkling, the speck of a boat off on the distant horizon. But it was not what she saw. What she saw was an answer, swift and definite, as clear as the path made by the sun on the sea.

She turned back to her mother. Anne was watching her, waiting, strands of her black hair dancing in the breeze.

"Thank you," Catherine said. After a moment she added, "*Go raibh maith agat.*"

Anne smiled and gave her daughter a kiss on the forehead. She slipped her arm through Catherine's, and they walked back down the sand.

In her room the following night, a crocheted afghan draped over her nightgown, Catherine sat at the desk by the open window. She sat for a long time, gazing at the lights of the house across the street. When she craned her neck, she could see the moon. Then she began to write.

September 10, 1910

Dear Thomas,

I hope this letter finds you and finds you well. I am writing this from Pacific Grove, where I am now living. It will sound fantastic to say this, but I am living here with my mother. She did not die all those years ago but has been living for the past ten years here in California. We reunited a few weeks ago, and it still feels like I am living a miracle.

The day after I discovered she was alive, I broke my engagement with William. I could not marry someone I did not love. My mother helped me see that. She has helped me see a great deal. I regret that I ever accepted his proposal. Had I been more trusting of my own feelings, I would never have done so.

She listened to the silence of the night. Then she once again took up the pen.

But I do not regret meeting you. I see now what I could not see that evening we said goodbye. I was not strong enough then to look at my feelings squarely. I was too afraid to recognize them and act on them. But I am not afraid now. And I hope, more than anything, that I can once again see you, and tell you this in person.

If your feelings have changed, I will understand. But I have learned the value of honesty now . . . honesty with myself, as well as with others. And the most honest thing I can write is that I love you and miss you.

Catherine Ogden

She read it over once and held the paper in her hands a moment longer. Then she folded it, put it into an envelope, and wrote the address she had found at the library.

And she took out her rosary and held it, her eyes on the sky.

FIFTY-ONE

*T*he next morning, Sunday, was bright and warm. "I love September," said Mrs. Goode. "The nicest time of year, really."

She left after breakfast for church. Anne had already taken the streetcar to Monterey to attend Mass and have lunch with Martin and David. When invited to go along, Catherine had declined. "I have a letter to post," she said, and her mother smiled gently. She did not pry or ask for details, but Catherine knew that whatever happened, her mother would support her. How freeing it was, she reflected as she washed the breakfast dishes, to be unconditionally loved.

After putting on her hat and a light coat, she strolled out through the front gate. Sundays were a curious kind of day in Pacific Grove. Local families went to church while many weekend visitors came by train on the one-day excursion fares to the coast. But she did not go to the beach, instead walking the few blocks downtown to the nearest mailbox.

There she paused, the envelope in her hands. She thought of her mother posting the letter to Martin, a letter whose outcome Anne could not predict. It was tempting to give in to fear and stay silent, but her mother had been courageous, and so would she. I am choosing this from the best that is in me, she thought, and she dropped the letter through the opening in the mailbox, into the darkness where she could not see it land.

She had done what she could. It was out of her hands.

Walking back, her spirits rose. She passed the hotel, Tuttle's Pharmacy, and tidy homes, neat and trim on their small lots. An old, bearded man rocked on a porch, lifting a hand in greeting as she walked by. In another garden, a young girl played jump rope, her blond braids bouncing in regular rhythm. Whatever happened, she had a home in this lovely place.

Catherine walked through the front gate of the cottage, which closed with its usual definitive click. The blue flags of the salvia were brilliant in the sunlight, and she touched them lightly. She would change her clothes, she decided, and do some weeding along the back fence.

The house was empty, for Inge had left to visit her daughter's family. Catherine took off her hat and hung her coat on a hook, then went through the hall to the kitchen for a glass of water. The sea glass glowed along the window ledges, like bits of green, blue, and white flame. As she drank, she admired its beauty. It was a little thing, sunlight on glass, but it was dazzling. Once you saw it, you could not stop seeing it. She felt that every time she looked at the glass, she would remember the morning of the letter and the vivid beauty of the light.

Just as she was heading to the stairs, the doorbell rang. She wondered idly who it could be; the Methodist ladies would all be at church, and it could not be Martin. The wooden floors creaked companionably as she went into the entrance hall and opened the door.

Thomas was on the porch. He wore his brown suit and held his hat in his hands.

"Good morning," he said.

For a moment she thought her letter had brought him; then she realized that it could not possibly have done so. She stood there dumbly, her hand on the knob, as he waited in his brown suit, with the white porch post and the colorful flowers behind him.

"Good morning," she said at last. "Come in."

As he walked past her into the entry hall, she was acutely conscious of his physical presence. She closed the door and turned around irresolutely as he stood, still holding his hat. She could hardly find the words to speak.

"I'm sorry," she said finally. "My mother and Mrs. Goode are both gone. I'm the only one here." It was not what she meant to say or wanted to say. She made a vague gesture and gave a little laugh.

He smiled, his eyes crinkling in the corners in the way she knew so well. She had thought she would never see his smile again. After the initial shock, the miraculous fact of his presence was, at last, starting to become real to her. She smiled back, wanting to cry.

"It's a beautiful day," he said. "Shall we go for a walk?"

She found the hat she had just taken off and put it on. He held the coat as she slipped her arms into it. The nearness of him made her heart beat faster.

They walked through the front garden and down the street. Catherine led the way toward the ocean.

"How did you come here?" she asked. "On the train?"

"Yes. I took the one-day excursion from the city."

"And how did you know where to find me?"

He smiled. "Let's find a place to sit on the beach, and I'll tell you."

$\wp$

The beach was full of people, with children running squealing into the water and two boys valiantly attempting to fly a red kite. Catherine and Thomas found a quiet space back by the rocks, and she thought of their picnic at Half Moon Bay. Here they were, under the same sun and by the same sea, and yet so much had changed.

He sat with his hands around his knees and looked at her. She smiled and he smiled. She felt suddenly shy, as if she were not yet ready to acknowledge the full significance of the moment.

"It's good to see you," he said softly.

"And you."

"So I'll begin at the beginning," he said without preamble. "The night I left Oakview."

She nodded, moving a fraction closer to him on the sand.

"When I left that evening"—he said it quietly, as if aware the memory would be painful for her—"I took the train to the city. Then I took the ferry and went to my aunt and uncle's farm up near Santa Rosa. I spent a few weeks there, until I could go back to school. After . . . well, after the way we said goodbye, I was in a bad place. I just wanted to forget that day. And you.

"I did a lot of work on the farm, helping them build the new barn, and when night came, I was so exhausted I could usually fall asleep. And I managed to tell myself I was getting over you."

She sat perfectly still, absorbing the miracle of his presence.

"Then it was time to return to the city and my studies. And for some reason, Catherine, that was so much harder. Perhaps because it was closer to Oakview, it was harder to tell myself that I no longer cared for you. I would wake up at night and not be able to fall asleep again. I kept seeing you, your face, the look in your eyes as we stood in the cottage."

"I'm sorry," she said, pained by the memory.

He shook his head. "No, I'm the one who should apologize. I wanted too much, too quickly. It wasn't fair to put you on the spot like that.

"Then last week, I heard from someone at school that the engagement was off. I was . . . well, stunned. I asked question after question, but the fellow had only read it in the paper and didn't know the details." He laughed. "I think he was wondering why I cared so much.

"I found myself daring to hope, for the first time in weeks. And I wondered what made you break the engagement."

"How did you know I was the one who broke it?"

"I didn't, for certain," he said. "But I've known William for most of my life. I know that he doesn't give up easily. And perhaps it was wishful thinking. I wanted it to be you who had ended it." He looked at the kite, then back at her. "And I wanted it to be because of me."

It was, she started to say, but she choked up and could not continue. Her eyes must have revealed her thoughts, for he reached out and grasped her hand. His was warm and solid.

"For a while, I didn't know what to do or how to find you. And then I had the idea to write to Mrs. Callahan. I knew you must have given her some way to reach you if she found a glove you had left behind or something." He smiled. "I've known her since I was a child. I think that's why she told me what she knew."

"What did she say?"

"She said that from what the staff could tell, you had been the one to break the engagement. She said there had been rumors that your mother was alive and living in San Francisco, and that you were living with her there."

"Yes," said Catherine. "It's true."

"I'm glad. I hoped it was true. I can only imagine how joyful it was for you to find her again.

"Mrs. Callahan gave me the address of the house in San Francisco, and I wrote to you there. The housekeeper told me you were in Pacific Grove and that you could be reached at Sea Glass Cottage. So I sat down to write to you, but something inside me said to go." He traced her hand gently, back and forth, with his thumb. "Maybe it was because I was thinking about you finding your mother again, but I could almost hear my mother's voice. 'You go in person, Tomás. Don't do this with a letter.'"

"Don't do what with a letter?" Catherine asked, her heart pounding.

He looked up at her. "Tell you that I love you, still. And ask if . . . if there is any chance you feel the same."

The boys below shouted with excitement as the kite rose into the sky, then dipped and bobbed, straining against the line, as if it wanted to sail off to the horizon.

"Yes," she said. "I do." Her eyes filled with tears. "I actually wrote to you, myself, to say so. I mailed it just this morning and when I saw you on the porch I thought . . . somehow, that it was why you were here. But you came even without the letter."

She had never seen such a look on a man's face: joy, gratefulness, humility, and desire, all at once. She had the sudden awareness that she was seeing love. And she wanted to lean in and kiss him, but there was a family now, several feet behind them, settling in with a blanket and basket.

"I did break the engagement," she said, moving closer so she could lower her voice. "I never loved him. And my mother helped me see that I could do it."

"Then God bless your mother." Thomas lowered his voice as well. "For everything."

He took her other hand, clasping both of them tightly. In his eyes she saw the kiss he wanted to give her. And as full as her heart was, there was something she still wanted to say.

"Thomas," she said, looking at his hands as she held them. "There is something I want to tell you. The same night you left, after you left, William came to my bedroom. He said he wanted to be with me that night, not wait for the wedding. I wish it hadn't happened, but it did."

He took one hand away and tilted her chin. She felt there was nothing more beautiful than the expression in his eyes.

"If it caused you pain," he said quietly, "even a moment of pain, then I wish it hadn't happened, too." He let go of her other hand and took her face in both of his. "But if you were afraid it would change how I feel about you, Catherine, then I guess there's still a lot for you to learn about me." His thumb moved to the tear on her left cheek, brushing it away.

"I don't need to be the first, Catherine. But please . . ." His eyes were as blue as the sea behind him. "Please let me be the last."

Through her tears, she caught a glimpse of the kite darting up to the sky. "I will," she said. "Oh, yes, Thomas. Yes." And his face broke into a smile, and she leaned in and he leaned in and the touch of his mouth on hers made the kite and beach and sun and everything else recede, beautifully and perfectly.

When they finally pulled apart, she gradually came back to her other senses. She heard the waves and the boys calling joyfully to each other and felt the sun and breeze on her face. And she saw Thomas smiling into her eyes, and she knew what the future held for her.

Because once you have seen love like this, she thought in wonder as she reached out to touch his face, you can never stop seeing it.

EPILOGUE

1932

*I*t was mid-March, and California was glorious. The green hills glowed in the sunlight, and trees blossomed against a sky of robin's-egg blue.

At Oakview, the last of the hyacinths were in bloom. In pots lining the terrace, the curls of white and violet blue released their musky sweetness into the air. Catherine bent to smell them and then straightened, taking a long look at the garden she had not seen in over twenty years.

She walked slowly toward the wall by the garden house, where camellias drooped on their stalks. With every step, she felt the light weight of the rosary she'd slipped into the pocket of her spring coat. Out of habit, she took it out and wound it round her hand.

As she passed the windows of the garden house, she saw her own reflection: a tall woman with dark hair pinned in a knot at the back of her neck, wearing a dove-gray coat, a navy hat, and a blue dress that left her stockinged legs visible. She thought of how much fashion had changed over the years, smiling at the memory of the long skirts and shirtwaists she had worn the last time she had walked the paths.

The letter inviting her back to Oakview had arrived in the mail the week before. It was utterly unexpected and yet from the moment she read it she knew what her answer would be. When Thomas had finally returned home from delivering a baby at the other end of town, she handed him the envelope before he had even taken off his coat. Tired as he was, he sat down on the chair in the hallway and read the letter while she waited, watching his bent head, the hair now graying at the temples.

Then he looked up at her. He smiled.

"Let's go," he said.

⁊⃝

She walked slowly about the reflecting pool, rosary in her hand. There were so many things to see, to regard with wonder. Some were the same as they had been twenty years before; others were new. Her fingers moved around the rosary as she named the sights and impressions, one for each bead.

> *For blue hyacinths.*
> *The smell of fresh damp earth.*
> *A robin on the path.*
> *The light filtering through the trees.*

The memories of Oakview had never left her, nor had they been absent from her marriage. Sometimes, lying in bed or walking together along the beach, she and Thomas recalled their first meeting in the garden, the early days planning the flower beds, and the companionable hours planting side by side. As the seasons shifted, her thoughts would return to the garden, last seen in the full ripeness of summer. "I wonder what it looks like now," she would say out of nowhere, and Thomas would glance up from paying bills or polishing his glasses and catch her eye and smile.

For the bright blue sky.
The red of the tulips.
The whistle of a gardener in the distance.
The soft newness of the grass.

They had married on September 28, 1910, just weeks after Thomas arrived on the doorstep of Sea Glass Cottage. Almost immediately they had moved into a flat not far from the medical college in San Francisco. It was small and required a walk up three flights of stairs, its windows giving only the barest peek at the trees of Golden Gate Park. But even so, Catherine recalled, those early days as Mr. and Mrs. O'Shea had been precious. The discoveries of sharing a home, a bed, and a life together: she had never before felt so alive.

Her thoughts shifted back to the present as she walked through the archway in the nearby garden wall. The Tree of Knowledge still stood in majesty, as imposing as she remembered. After the winter, it had not yet fully regained its leaves, but she could still see the intricate beauty of each individual branch. They still reminded her of arms, stretching for something just out of reach.

The marble bench was still there, the same bench where she had said yes to William's proposal. She sat down, leaning her back against the trunk, and looked up at the underside of the branches.

Two decades later, she could think back to that evening with compassion for her young self. She had said yes to William's proposal thinking it would bring her the freedom for which she had longed. He had thought marriage would give him what he wanted: a wife to open the one door he felt was closed to him. But they had not been right, either one of them. And with the help of others, she had seen that in time.

For moss on the oak tree.
The smoothness of marble.
The power of memory.
The wisdom of time.

Her path and William's had never crossed again. During that first year in San Francisco, she had steeled herself for the chance encounter with him on a street or in a park, but it never came; their social worlds were too different. And she and Thomas spent much of their free time in Pacific Grove, where a room was always waiting for them at Sea Glass Cottage.

For family.
Friends.
For relationships that endure and change.

Lavinia remained a faithful friend. Twenty years later, they still wrote each other weekly. And though her aunt Abigail had been appalled by Catherine's sudden marriage to Thomas, the passage of time and, Catherine suspected, the influence of Uncle Oliver had gradually led her to a grudging acceptance. "Seeing you so happy will break down the last of her resistance," Thomas had said when Catherine finally went back to New York for a visit, and he had been right.

Catherine got up from the bench and moved slowly west, her fingers still moving from bead to bead as she savored the beauty before her. Rounding a border of pansies, she walked through an archway and saw that a swimming pool had been added to the large back lawn. Attractive outbuildings, probably changing rooms, had been built just beyond the covered terrace. She gazed off in the direction of the stables, remembering the heat of the July day when they had all walked there for lunch. A swim in the pool would have been the perfect close to such an afternoon.

For the warmth of a spring day.
The promise of summer.
The beauty of the hills.

Thinking of the stables made her remember Peter walking beside her, puffing with the exertion. And she recalled the morning in February of 1911, just a few months after her marriage, when she had been idly turning the pages of the newspaper and had been startled to find his obituary. He had died at home the previous day, the paper said, of a massive heart attack. Putting the paper down, she gazed out the window at the rooftops of San Francisco, remembering his red face and bluff manner and the role he had played in her life for the space of a few months. She had not had any conversation with Vivian since leaving Oakview, but she wrote a condolence letter all the same and sent it to Madrone Hill. She did not expect an answer, and she did not receive one.

But eight months later, she was sitting at the kitchen table painting a new design for the garden of Martin's house when Thomas came home. He had a newspaper in hand and a strange expression on his face.

"You have to see this," he said after kissing her. He handed her the folded newspaper, pointing to a boxed item on the society page. It announced that William and Vivian had been married the previous day in New York City, prior to embarking on an extended tour of the continent. "William and Vivian, married," said Thomas. "Can you believe it?"

"Yes," said Catherine slowly, little memories settling into place. "I can."

And four days later, a letter from Vivian herself appeared in the mailbox. Before even removing her hat, Catherine sat down in the foyer of the apartment building and opened the envelope. Reading the scrawled, bold writing was like hearing Vivian's voice again.

October 29, 1911

Dear Catherine,

Thank you for your kind words all those months ago, after Peter's death. It was not unexpected given his general state of health, but it was not what he deserved, poor fellow. I hope I made him happy in some small way in the years we were together.

By the time you get this, you will surely have read the news that William and I are now married. I don't know why I feel the need to write you with an explanation. You did not want him, and it seems clear that you are happy as you are with your handsome gardener/doctor.

I have always wondered if you suspected the truth: that William was the past love affair I told you about the day you tried on the wedding dress. I was forbidden to tell you or anyone that he and I had ever been together. Long before you appeared on the scene, William made his wishes on that score abundantly clear to me. I swear on all I hold sacred (admittedly not much) that it ended years ago and didn't start again until after Peter died. I would have begun it again at any time, shameless woman that I am, but William wouldn't. He had a reputation to keep and a Senate seat to win someday. So there you have it.

He used to think he wanted one kind of wife: not me. But you throwing him over has made him see that perhaps a wife like me isn't the worst thing in the world. I won't be the gracious Senate hostess you would have been, but maybe the Capitol dining rooms need a little bit of my California savagery. And I am happier than I have been in a very long time. Actually, I am <u>happy</u>; I haven't been that at all for a very long time. And William, if you care to know, is happy too.

My best wishes for you and your husband.

Vivian Brandt

Catherine walked into the rose garden. They were not yet in bloom, but some of the bushes had tiny buds among the leaves. She remembered the day she had tried to sketch the roses and failed. She remembered the time she had hurt her hand on the thorn and Thomas had taken her to the cottage, the same cottage visible over the wall, where she had seen the rosary and the picture of his mother. Her fingers moved to the next bead.

For roses.
Rosaries.
Mothers who teach us what they know.
Women who are like mothers to us.

Mrs. Goode had died on the last day of 1911, her heart stopping in her sleep, a quiet and peaceful death. Upon hearing the news, Catherine immediately took the train to Pacific Grove. She was there when Mrs. Goode's oldest son, an elegant and kind man with his mother's deep brown eyes, shared the unexpected news that his mother had left Sea Glass Cottage to Anne.

The legacy made her mother weep. "She has given me so much. She gave me a new life, all those years ago. Even dead she is giving to me still."

Catherine held her mother's hand. Through her own tears she saw the sea glass on the ledge of the kitchen window. It glowed in the sun, as vividly as it had always done, and she felt comforted.

For the sea.
Our home.
Our children.

There were twins, Lucy and Theodore, born in April 1912. They arrived three days after the sinking of the *Titanic*, and the joy of their birth was mingled with Catherine's horror at the thought of so many people sinking below the icy water. "Life comes into the world and life goes out," her mother said. She gave her new granddaughter a kiss on the forehead while Catherine, recovering in bed, nursed Theo. "In the face of such tragedy, all we can do is love the people we are with and be kind to those who suffer. And pour a little goodness into the world, that way."

When Thomas had finished his studies in San Francisco, Anne invited them to live with her at Sea Glass Cottage. Thomas set up a practice in Pacific Grove, and the twins grew up running along the beach, building sandcastles, and finding new bits of sea glass to add to the collection. Catherine kept the garden blooming in all seasons. "Every problem is helped by digging and planting," she would tell the twins. It was a philosophy that had guided her through the dark days of the war, through the uncertainty of the stock market crash, and through all the little challenges of marriage, motherhood, and daily life.

For the shifting of the seasons.
The healing power of a garden.
Planting and harvesting.

She was nearing the orchard now. It was awash with blossoms, white and pink, and a few late daffodils trumpeted their yellow beauty in the grassy space along the edges. The orchard would provide fruit for the estate come summer and fall. Catherine wondered how much of it would be needed by the family.

For in 1920, William had been elected to the Senate. He and Vivian and their son spent much of their time in Washington, returning to California only for occasional visits. Some of the staff still lived at Oakview, keeping it ready for the Brandts whenever they chose to return. Among them was Mrs. Callahan, now in her seventies, who was the reason for the letter inviting Catherine and Thomas back to Oakview.

"She's having trouble with her hearing, poor old girl," Vivian had written, "and though she has a local doctor we do think a second opinion is warranted. It was Mrs. C., actually, who suggested your husband. If it's not too strange for him to return to Oakview, she would be delighted to see him after all this time. And you, of course, are welcome to come and see the old place again. No danger of running into me or William," she wrote with her usual candor. "We'll be in Washington for another month at least."

But running into William would be all right, Catherine realized. Time had passed. Someday, if their paths did cross again, she would be able to greet him with equanimity.

For doctors.
Forgiveness.
Thomas.

She was nearly there, at the garden she and Thomas had created. Before going in, she paused for a moment, rosary in hand, listening for the sound of skipping feet that she had been hearing off in the distance as she strolled alone.

"Marisol?" she called.

There was no answer, only the staccato chirp of a bird from a blossoming pear tree.

"Marisol O'Shea," she called again.

"I'm in here," came her daughter's voice from the other side of the garden wall. "Mama, come find me."

It was a distinctive voice, musical and direct. Ever since she had learned to speak, Marisol had been clear as a bell.

"I'm coming," Catherine called. She smiled to herself as she walked toward her youngest child.

After the twins, there had been one miscarriage and one stillbirth: two losses, both heartbreaking. Just when Catherine was ready to give up hope of another child, she had become pregnant with Marisol, born on a sunlit August day after a quiet walk by the sea. And now, with both twins off at college, ten-year-old Marisol was the only child at Sea Glass Cottage.

For new life.
For second chances.

"Mama," came her daughter's voice again. "Come and see. It's so pretty."

"I'm almost there," Catherine said.

A few more steps, and she had reached the archway in the brick wall. She stopped and lifted her head.

It was not the garden in summer, as she had last seen it. It was the garden in spring, with entirely different plantings. But though the flowers were new, the mix of color was as vibrant as the design she had made with Thomas. Red, yellow, pink, and orange tulips shared the beds. Large urns of blue and purple hyacinths balanced the warmth with coolness. It still looked like an artist's paint box, she thought with delight.

Marisol sat on a small iron bench near the archway, her green plaid dress smudged with dirt from her explorations of the garden. Her dark hair was braided and looped under her ears, the ribbons starting to come untied, but her face glowed.

"Mama," she said. "It's like being inside a kaleidoscope. Or a stained glass window."

"It is. It's just like that."

Marisol swung her legs rapturously. "I've been to every part of this garden. It's so big. You used to live here?"

"For a little while, yes. Long ago."

Marisol's eyes widened. "Why did you ever leave?"

Catherine reached out to smooth her daughter's hair ribbon. "I will tell you someday," she said, "when you're older." And I will tell her, she promised herself. I will tell her everything.

Marisol jumped up from the bench and ran down the path, arms outstretched. "I'm a fairy," she said, twirling. "A fairy of the flowers and I have the power to grant wishes. So close your eyes and think of something you want. And when you know, tell me."

"All right," said Catherine. "I will."

For imagination.
For vision.
For everything that has brought me here.

Catherine savored the sun's warmth on her face. She closed her eyes, listening to the birdsong. And then she opened them and saw the garden, the green figure of her youngest child dancing against a backdrop of color, the tulips nodding their heads. And she heard footsteps on the gravel walk and turned to see Thomas, his black bag in hand and his face alight, coming toward her through the orchard.

"I knew I'd find you here," he said.

She smiled and waited for him to join her in the garden. There were just three beads left on the rosary. And she finished the way she always did, every single night:

Gracias a Dios.
Go raibh maith agat.
Thank you.

Author's Note

I grew up in the heart of Silicon Valley, in a 1960s tract home where an orchard used to be. In that landscape of suburban malls and tech start-ups, I had no idea that just up the road there had once been an entirely different world.

In the late nineteenth and early twentieth centuries, wealthy San Franciscans who wanted country homes looked south to the Peninsula, which had both good train access to the city and better (code for "less foggy") weather. From present-day Millbrae down to Menlo Park and beyond, they built lavish estates with grand houses, formal grounds, and occasionally very individual features, such as a rocky pond resembling a Swiss mountain pass at the Borel Estate in San Mateo. Many of these homes are long gone, bulldozed to make room for offices or housing developments. Some remain privately owned, while others have been transformed into country clubs or schools.

The most accessible of the remaining properties is the Filoli Estate in Woodside, California, completed in 1917 for the Bourn family. Now owned by the National Trust for Historic Preservation, it is open to visitors who can explore its house and gardens. It was an outing to Filoli in my twenties that first fired my imagination—readers who have been there will recognize some of its features in Oakview—but it was only when I began to research this book years later that I learned how many equally grand neighbors it once had.

I am indebted to David C. Streatfield for his extensive two-part series "The San Francisco Peninsula's Great Estates: Mansions, Landscapes, and Gardens in the Late 19th and Early 20th

Centuries" in the Winter and Spring 2012 issues of *Eden*, the journal of the California Garden & Landscape History Society. The books *San Mateo: A Centennial History* by Mitchell P. Postel and *From Frontier to Suburb: The Story of the San Mateo Peninsula* by Alan Hynding proved invaluable, as did Kevin Starr's *Americans and the California Dream, 1850–1915*. The San Mateo County History Museum offers an excellent exhibit on Peninsula estate life, and I am grateful for the resources of its research library.

For visuals of the period, I highly recommend *Gabriel Moulin's San Francisco Peninsula: Town & Country Homes 1910–1930*, compiled by Donald DeNevi and Thomas Moulin. Gabriel Moulin was a society photographer whose images—in some cases showing even the bedrooms of these grand houses—offer an intimate glimpse into the lifestyles of the real Brandts and Powells of the time.

Lastly, the 1915 book *Stately Homes of California* by Porter Garnett provided a fascinating contemporaneous look at these houses and grounds. Garnett's descriptions of the architecture, interior decoration, and landscaping of these estates were integral in helping me design Oakview, both inside and out.

Acknowledgments

First, I want to express my thanks to all who research, preserve, and cherish the history of the San Francisco Bay Area. In a region that is famous for looking to the future, I am grateful to those who record its past.

I can't begin to express my gratitude to Tarn Wilson, but I'll try anyhow! I am so blessed by your enthusiasm, your keen writer's eye, and—most of all—your friendship. Big thanks to Angela Dellaporta and Erin Niumata for key questions and thoughtful suggestions that made this a much stronger book. I'm grateful to Margaret Silf for her wise writings about discernment, which helped me find the heart of this story. Gratitude to my English department colleagues, past and present—your passion and love of the written word always inspire me.

I'd like to express my heartfelt thanks to Brooke Warner and Shannon Green of She Writes Press for their vision and guidance throughout this project. Huge thanks to Lorraine White and Barrett Briske for their editorial assistance and to Julie Metz for the evocative cover design. I am also grateful for the expertise and dedication of publicist Caitlin Hamilton Summie.

Mom and Dad: You gave me a safe and supportive place from which to grow as a reader and writer. I'm so grateful for that, and for the Filoli memories we share. Amy: thanks for being my best friend and for knowing exactly how to make me laugh. Matthew and Luke: thank you for helping me keep this project (and everything else) in its proper perspective. I love being your mom.

Mary Donovan-Kansora: You taught me so much about creativity, beauty, and heart. It seems fitting that the last time I saw you alive, it was in a garden. I know that you always have my back, even from the world beyond this one.

And thank you to my husband, Scott. Once again, you helped make a dream come true.

About the Author

GINNY KUBITZ MOYER is a California native with a love of local history. A graduate of Pomona College and Stanford University, her nonfiction books include *Taste and See: Experiencing the Goodness of God with Our Five Senses*. An English instructor and avid weekend gardener, she lives in the San Francisco Bay Area with her husband, two sons, and one adorable rescue dog. *The Seeing Garden* is her first novel. Her website is ginnymoyer.org.

SELECTED TITLES FROM SHE WRITES PRESS

She Writes Press is an independent publishing company
founded to serve women writers everywhere.
Visit us at www.shewritespress.com.

The Vintner's Daughter by Kristen Harnisch. $16.95,
978-1-63152-929-0. Set against the sweeping canvas of French and
California vineyard life in the late 1890s, this is the compelling tale
of one woman's struggle to reclaim her family's Loire Valley vineyard—and her life.

The California Wife by Kristen Harnisch. $17.95, 978-1-63152-087-
7. The sequel to *The Vintner's Daughter*, this is a rich, romantic tale
of wine, love, new beginnings, and a family's determination to fight
for what really matters.

Among the Beautiful Beasts: A Novel by Lori McMullen. $16.95,
978-1-64742-106-9. The untold story of the early life of Marjory
Stoneman Douglas, a tireless activist for the Florida Everglades in
the early 1900s—and a woman ultimately forced to decide whether
to commit to a life of subjugation or leap into the wild unknown.

Guesthouse for Ganesha by Judith Teitelman. $16.95, 978-1-63152-
521-6. In 1923, seventeen-year-old Esther Grünspan arrives in Köln
with a hardened heart as her sole luggage. Thus she begins a twenty-
two-year journey, woven against the backdrops of the European
Holocaust and the Hindu Kali Yuga (the "Age of Darkness" when
human civilization degenerates spiritually), in search of a place of
sanctuary.

Swearing off Stars by Danielle Wong. $16.95, 978-1-63152-284-0.
When Lia Cole travels from New York to Oxford University to study
abroad in the 1920s, she quickly falls for another female student—
sparking a love story that spans decades and continents.

Stitching a Life: An Immigration Story by Mary Helen Fein. $16.95,
978-1-63152-677-0. After sixteen-year-old Helen, a Jewish girl
from Russia, comes alone across the Atlantic to the Lower East Side
of New York in the year 1900, she devotes herself to bringing the
rest of her family to safety and opportunity in the new world—and
finds love along the way.